THE LONGEST YEAR

THE LONGEST YEAR

DANIEL GRENIER

TRANSLATED BY PABLO STRAUSS

ARACHNIDE

First published as *L'année la plus longue* in 2015 by Le Quartanier
First published in English in 2017 by House of Anansi Press Inc.
www.houseofanansi.com

This is a work of fiction. The events and characters in this book are fictitious,
and where real historical figures and events are depicted liberties have been
taken for the benefit of the story.

House of Anansi Press is committed to protecting our natural environment. As part
of our efforts, the interior of this book is printed on paper that contains 100% post-
consumer recycled fibres, is acid-free, and is processed chlorine-free.

21 20 19 18 17   1 2 3 4 5

Library and Archives Canada Cataloguing in Publication

Grenier, Daniel, 1980-
[Année la plus longue. English]
The longest year / Daniel Grenier ; translated by Pablo Strauss.

Translation of: L'année la plus longue.
Issued in print and electronic formats.
ISBN 978-1-4870-0153-7 (paperback).—ISBN 978-1-4870-0154-4 (html)

I. Strauss, Pablo, illustrator II. Title. III Title: Année la plus longue. English

PS8613.R4486A6613 2017   C843'.6   C2016-901573-4
C2016-901574-2

Book design: Alysia Shewchuk

*We acknowledge for their financial support of our publishing program the Canada Council for
the Arts, the Ontario Arts Council, and the Government of Canada through the Canada Book
Fund. We acknowledge the financial support of the Government of Canada, through the National
Translation Program for Book Publishing, an initiative of the Roadmap for Canada's Official
Languages 2013–2018: Education, Immigration, Communities, for our translation activities.*

Printed and bound in Canada

Alma wanted to go to sleep right there, in the heap of blood and shit. But they got back on the road. Wading through the creek, they'd dye the water red. They'd steal fruit to fill their mouths with the living taste of sugar, reach camp after nightfall, lay down on the bare ground, and when Alma looked up at the stars her head would fill with the strains of an old, unrhymed song.

Catherine Leroux, La marche en forêt

The clanking arms of the column near him made him soar on the red wings of war. For a few moments he was sublime.

Stephen Crane, The Red Badge of Courage

Of course I don't think I'm going to die. That would be un-American.

Pierre Yergeau, L'écrivain public

THE LONGEST YEAR

NU NA DA UL TSUN YI

JULY 1838
RED CLAY, TN—OHIO RIVER, IL

WHAT WE COULD see, from behind, was a silhouette. He sat down on a rock a little off the road to pick a stone out of his left boot. The boot came up almost to his knee, fit a bit tight, wasn't his size. How, he wondered, had a stone clambered up high enough to slip inside? He massaged his toes and the sole of his foot. Open carts, coaches, covered wagons laden with furniture and men and women ambled by in front of him. Horseshoes kicked up dust. On the horizon a troubled sky loomed, and soon the dust would turn to the kind of silty mud liable to swallow up an unwatched child. At the edge of the boundless flatlands, a screen of rain was advancing and lightning was spreading its fingers across the sky from cloud to cloud. In the distance a violent storm pounded down on the prairie. You couldn't yet hear the rain, crashing down like still waterfalls, but it was on its way, there would be no escaping it. He knew it and so did the others, marching forward, faces drawn. The accumulated experience of each rain shower and every thunderstorm, on the plains and in the woods, sat heavy on this ragtag group of wrinkled elders and pregnant women and long-haired boys, sat with the weight of several thousand years. They weren't all Cherokee. Some old Seminole warriors had joined them, and a handful of Choctaw, the ones who hadn't followed their people years before. The Seminole were easy to pick out with their European dress and dark, almost black skin.

He wearily shook his boot out onto the ground in front of him. The rifle he had leaned against a rock started silently sliding to the right, and he caught it by the leather strap with his free hand at the last second. He heard the rhythmic sounds of human and animal footsteps. You couldn't make out head or tail of this long march. The convoy must have been a good half mile long, and when he turned his head it was people and animals as far as the eye could see. The women carried children and wore blankets to shelter them from squalls. As days went by a living line had formed, roughly along the path of the trade road. Here and there along the way, men had broken off to light fires, have a drink and a chat. Some stood behind jury-rigged counters selling old tools and provisions, expensive but poorly stitched moccasins, dented cookpots, rotting furs.

THEY'D LEFT RED CLAY at the Tennessee border in late May, over six thousand strong, after first militia and then regular corps men appeared in their villages, practically right in their homes, making it abundantly clear that this business had gone on long enough. Eight years they'd been given to leave of their own free will. Now, five weeks later, they were closing in on the Ohio River. They'd have to cross with several hundred head of livestock and wagons packed with keepsakes, chests, and mattresses. Even in defeat they were proud Indians, warriors and tribal chiefs, and still spoke with their heads held high. They'd left their dead behind, stripped naked, but were weighed down by what few possessions they'd managed to salvage. They'd been warned the ferry-man would jack up the fares at the crossing. They weren't pioneers joining the gold rush or settlers looking for farm-land. They were savages.

A couple hours earlier he'd had a short discussion with a few young Cherokee about the danger of talking back or questioning the fares. In a tone that was respectful, though not perhaps as firm as he would have liked, he'd tried to warn them that any stunt they pulled was sure to back-fire. There would be wounded; there would be a massacre. Weapons had been confiscated long before they set off. There were just too many soldiers. The nostrils of one of the Indians flared while he talked and a red violence flushed over his whole face, free of makeup and Warpaint. He knew the young man had to hold back to refrain from killing him then and there, could see the muscles tensing all along his arm and his wrist, fingers clenched tight around a walking stick he'd fashioned from a branch. The wood was polished smooth, worn down at the end, ready to break in several spots. See, there's nothing to do but agree to the ferryman's terms. They all understood that this was one more trial to test their will and courage, measure their determination not to disappear, fade away, and cede everything to this European civilization with its myths of new beginnings. It was but the latest in a long series of trials and tribulations that would go on for generations, in the elongated time of mountains, and it was up to them, honourable members of an ancient people, to rise to them. That's what he told them. He almost believed it. In the meantime, like the other Whites paid handsomely by the State of Georgia and the State of Tennessee, he walked alongside them, kept them safe, made sure the convoy kept moving.

Five hundred miles further out lay the fertile lands granted by presidential decree in 1830. They would remain Indian Territories for all time, according to the most plausible scenario and the treaties ratified by Congress and the Senate. Everyone knew the United States would never reach that far west of the Mississippi.

As he put his boot back on he heard high-pitched shrieking. Out behind the convoy, on the edge of a stand of trees, a group had formed. Raised voices, women's voices, shrill cries in a dialect unrecognizable to him, a thousand miles away from his native French and adopted English and his smattering of Innu. He went to look, rifle drawn. Fifty people were crammed into a tightly packed circle around two men fighting. He broke through the crowd, giving onlookers a nudge in the ribs with his gun barrel or his shoulders and clearing a path toward the commotion of raised fists.

A roof of dust clouds hung over those gathered around a massive bare-chested Cherokee warrior who was kicking a young Choctaw in the gut. His long black braid swung like a metronome behind his back, brushing his shoulder blades with every blow. The young man put up no resistance, just kept tucking further into himself. Blood flowed freely from his nose and only by its red colour could you tell him apart from the dried earth. He could barely move to defend or protect himself. Close to his outstretched arm lay a piece of black bread. After a short break to catch his breath, the Cherokee swung back around and lifted his leg. Shod in wood-soled boots, he bent his knee and pounded his foot down on the other man's jaw, unjointing it in a single blow and leaving his rival dead in a picture of grotesque asymmetry.

"Stop it!" he yelled. "Now!" But no one heard. His hands were wet on the rifle butt. The storm was approaching. No one took any heed, the cries grew louder, the circle closed around the fighters: one standing upright as the other came to pieces. Behind this scene the convoy marched on, breathing as one in their shared fatigue.

When he turned around we saw a face of uncertain age, at once boy and old man, an old knotty soul still capable of unselfconscious laughter or descanting at length on his ancestors' past. We saw him close his eyes, wondered what he was doing there, alone with his history and memories in the middle of this blood-drunk crowd, people on the march and in tears and ready to beat their neighbour to death over a hunk of bread.

He turned around and asked himself what he was doing there, and we can't help but second the notion, share in his doubts, his ghosts, his nightmares.

Because there's no way he could have been there. At that time, that exact moment in July 1838, under that troubled sky on the American grasslands where the Cherokee were on the march, he was somewhere else. Almost all the sources confirm it.

PART ONE

GREAT SMOKIES

CHAPTER ONE

FEBRUARY 1987
HIGHLAND PARK, CHATTANOOGA, TS

THREE YEARS OUT of four, Thomas Langlois didn't exist. He became transparent, a miscalculation only later corrected, a clause hotly disputed behind closed doors at Royal Society meetings centuries earlier. He was barely tall enough to look at the calendar when the very course of his existence was inexplicably called into question by the teachings of astronomers and scientists in powdered wigs. Every February, Thomas held his breath, and at the end of the month he stopped breathing altogether. He learned that an annual celebration to mark his coming into the world would sooner or later upset the equilibrium of the planets and the stars. It would be disastrous. His education instilled humility and good manners. Young man, it asked of him: What's more important? Your birthday or the earth's stability? So he turned transparent. He stopped living in time and dedicated himself to space.

The Appalachian Mountains were without end, their majesty affected neither by the short years nor the long ones, technological progress nor the names they shared with Indian princes. Around Chattanooga, Tennessee, these mountains formed a logical, solid chain at once circular and linear; they were Thomas Langlois's wellspring and his homeland and they stood in contrast to the friability of his own existence. For Thomas Langlois, mountains were reassuring, almost divine. They gave him purchase in the story that denied him the right to age normally.

Thomas leaned against a mountain that met up with another mountain, his back to yet another. He contemplated it like someone puzzling out a problem. By considering the way geological strata were layered one upon another in space, and not in time, Thomas could reconcile the contradiction of his birth. He meditated on these mountains when he was young, at first because he was younger than everyone else and later because he was older. It was absurd, he got it. In 1984, Thomas's first birthday was celebrated with very little fuss.

We're talking about the Appalachians because they are the first thing connecting him to us, us readers: the bedrock of our connection, far deeper than themes and impressions. As this chain of mountains runs northward they meet us here, inside our homes where the great seaway narrows into a river like any other.

THOMAS LANGLOIS SAT on the steel track, thinking about fate and destiny and the many ghosts in the closet of an

American family as long and old as the Mason–Dixon Line, but much more full of twists and turns. When the rail began vibrating he got up slowly and stood further back, closer to the station, a blade of grass between his teeth. He looked at once ten and seventy years old, his palm laid on the station's exterior wall, daydreaming like any other kid, or some old wandering soul. A tad melancholic, sort of peaceful. The train didn't much pass or stop in Chattanooga, Tennessee.

He lay his hand on the station wall to hold on to the vibration rising to meet him, climbing from the earth up the wall; to hold on to that early morning several months back when his father came into his room and told him he was heading back up North. Where? Thomas asked. *Dans le nord*, he replied, up North. That's where my funny English comes from. That's where I'm from. Why? Thomas asked, and his father said, Because. Leaving no room for more. And now he had his hand on the wall and was watching the train go by and telling himself that this strange vibration rising through the wooden planks of the building, making the ground move, connected him to his father riding the train to this inconceivably distant North, over the mountains, across the Appalachians; the bond was stronger than the similar cast of their eyes and mouths. Very early on that morning several months before his father had closed the door to his room and, as the rectangle of light contracted, Thomas thought he saw the old army duffle on his father's shoulder. Like the train, the vibrating ground in the afternoon was much more concrete to Thomas than any facial features he and his father shared.

Of course, this chain of thought possessed a broken link. Thomas had a hard time separating his ideas from other information, took it all and knitted it together into strange stitches of meaning; he could fathom the symbolism's depths but could not comprehend its span. It was all mixed up in his mind, thrown in together with the rest of what his father had said. Like how he knew a fishing line dropped in a lake might reach the bottom, but had never surmised that the same bottom reached all the way across the lake. Or how he knew his feet could get permanently stuck on the lake bottom, but didn't understand that sand and silt were one and the same substance. He also knew his father wasn't coming back. He knew the language full of dry, cracking sounds his father and mother spoke in secret sometimes, a tongue he didn't understand and would never learn, was the language of the plank his palm rested on now.

Ten feet to his right there was a wild animal. He was good with distances.

ONE FACT OF Thomas Langlois's life we need to know from the outset is this: he was born in a leap year. We mentioned it earlier, in more abstract terms. It may not mean a thing to us, but throughout Thomas's childhood it meant a great deal to him. It's important for us to consider this fact now, not to assimilate or be inspired by it, but because it weighed on Thomas's life and shaped his worldview. We're not saying he was obsessed by stars, planetary movements, the moon's pull on Lake Chickamauga and Lake Nickajack, though he was; we're saying his birthdate made him feel separate from the others, at once younger and older than everyone else, whiter than the white prairie trash, blacker than the wor-shippers at the Union Avenue Baptist Church, redder than the first Cherokee to settle the valley.

Another reason he felt separate from everyone else was the foreign way his name was pronounced in his own home. *To-ma*: that's how his father said it. He understood, his father didn't speak the same language as him and everyone around him, and this was unusual, wonderful. At home his name was *To-ma* and outside it was *Taw-mass*, with a crisply ren-dered final "s." That "s" disappeared when he crossed the threshold of his home. Even his mother, who spoke the same language he did, and whose every word he understood per-fectly, called him *To-ma*, and it sounded even stranger com-ing from her, as if she'd found a laborious method of cleaving the word "tomahawk" in two. Somehow Thomas's name sounded undecided, not quite finished, when his mother said it.

After his father went up North for good, his mother started saying the final "s" in Thomas's name. She also started telling him about her family and Thomas's family tree.

From our standpoint this arborescence is intriguing. We can look at it, ponder the branches and the roots and connect them to our own existence on the other side of the moun-tains. One of the first details we have to remember about this family tree, about Thomas's ancestry and family story, is that the characters' roots and histories connect with ours, up here, up North. These people cover sentimental and geo-graphical terrain that eventually reaches and touches us. Though these are stories of the South we have no choice but to tell them here. They'll traverse the Appalachian Range and Canadian Shield; it's important to discuss them here, even up North where it gets so much colder and we don't see colour quite the same.

THOMAS'S FATHER WAS a man of principle. Sometimes he'd hold his son by the shoulder, kneeling, his big hands exerting pressure, while he explained the complex movements of the planets and the stars, which were responsible for magnificent natural phenomena like the Northern Lights, and for injustice as well. Injustice, Thomas's father explained, was almost as old as the mountain ranges, and sometimes concealed great opportunities. The man of principle would lean down in front of Thomas, three years out of four, and squeeze him on the shoulder and tell him, again and again, Don't worry, you just have to wait, be patient, the sun will come out before you know it. Patience was a virtue, something you could learn, along the lines of generosity and honesty. If only he could have known how long his father had had to wait in this life, how long history's great men had had to wait, Thomas wouldn't cry, he'd find a way to turn his anxiousness into patience. Sometimes he stopped listening and focused instead on the difference between the shape of his father's words and those he heard outside his home. How could they be the same yet sound so different? When his father spoke, it was hard to force himself to stop thinking about the sound and instead locate the meaning, what they were meant to express.

This was a rather old form of education, learning

through trial and error, deductive and empirical logic, a far
cry from the Board of Education's books of lies. Can't you
see it's March 1 today? Sorry, you're still not two. Maybe
next year. His father cultivated patience the hard way, and
it took. Now he sat Thomas on his lap, on the rocking chair.
Aren't you proud to be part of a group of special people?
And he showed it to him one more time, the famous letter addressed to Thomas, mailed all the way from Kansas.
There aren't many kids who know how to read at one, don't
you think that makes you special? Do you know where
Kansas is? On the other side of the Missouri, on the other
side of the big river, over the state line. It's real far away.
There's a Pittsburg there too. There's Pittsburghs all over.
And they read the letter together one more time. It had
been mailed to Thomas when he was born, from other
people just like him, on the other side of the river that
crossed the country, the river that had borne the famous
adventurers who had first met the Indians and founded
the nation. A fly was patiently, noiselessly, eating away at
the screen near the bottom of the door. From the corner of
his eye, as he read along with his father, he tried to guess
whether it was inside or out.

Perhaps one day he'd talk it over with other people.
They'd explain that it was nothing more than a joke, a
bad joke to play on a kid, but no big deal. They might say
Thomas was unlucky, that his father had acted badly, cruelly
even—had he really done that, all those years? Where was
the mother? What did she say? But for Thomas there would
be no sudden illumination, no revelation of his father's personality. Nothing would be added to his understanding of

the man who had left without looking back one day near the end of November.

As far as Thomas knew his dad had never killed a fly. But then Thomas also knew that flies never bothered him. They didn't even come close, mosquitoes neither, as if they had an understanding. His father had almost gotten up to kill the fly on that day, as he insisted that Thomas read the words from the conclave of well-intentioned strangers who gathered in a circle with their hands joined. Thomas had felt the muscles in his father's thighs tense, felt him begin to turn ever so slightly. It was enough to scare the fly away.

Dear new Leaper,

It is our pleasure to welcome you to Chapter No. 1, Order of Twentyniners, one of the world's most exclusive organizations.

You are hereby enrolled in the elite fraternity whose membership is limited to those who have birthdays only every four years. There are no initiation fees, no membership dues, and no meetings, other than the "grand conclave" each February twenty-ninth (29), when members from all over the world gather "in spirit."

An attractive membership scroll is enclosed. I am sure you will want to keep it in order to identify yourself with pride as a member of World Chapter No. 1. The scroll is designed to permit the member to put his name at the bottom, and is suitable for framing.

The charge for this scroll is $1 to cover costs of

engraving and mailing. Please send $1 so your organ-
ization can continue operations on behalf of the Order
of Twentyniners—those persons born on February 29.

Fraternally yours,

Kenneth B. Simons
Executive Secretary, Order of Twentyniners
Editor-in-Chief, *Headlight Sun*
Pittsburg, KS 66872

Then they closed their eyes and shared one of their final
moments together as father and son, imagining a faraway
Pittsburg that may not have a baseball team but still had
a newspaper with an editor-in-chief. His father breathed
through his nose and held the letter in his hand on the rocking chair armrest. A vein was throbbing in his forearm.
Thomas wondered whether his father had actually mailed
the dollar bill, but was afraid to ask. That would have been
insulting. Of course he had.

A little later, climbing off his father's lap, he felt the wood
creak and the knots on the old floorboards shift, but no anger
was forthcoming. His father simply opened his eyes, like
someone waking from a short nap. He folded the letter and
slowly repositioned himself, shifting to the back of the chair.
With a neutral facial expression, his sentence was delivered
in what he called his "accent." Mixed with words in another
language. It was a warning, a reminder for Thomas: You
aren't to wake your mother, she's had a long day. She's busier
than us. Her shifts are long, her work is hard, let her sleep,

don't ever disturb her. He said this patiently, while looking at the wall, as if he'd forgotten that Thomas already knew, that he was probably the least disruptive person in the world.

The house had thin walls. There was a fist-sized hole in one. Thomas almost never made a sound.

AFTER THE FREIGHT train had come and gone, carrying many different things but surely not his father, Thomas walked home through the tree-lined backstreets of the north side of town. It was cold that year, they had been talking about it on TV, and a thin layer of snow blanketed the lawns and certain cars and trucks that hadn't been started for a while. Though he was far from home he walked in the middle of the road, as if he owned the place. He walked along the yellow line until he heard a car, then got out of the way.

His mother was waiting for him. She wasn't on the doorstep, but it felt as if she were. Somewhere he'd picked up an image of a mother that stuck with him: In a long dress and matching scarf she waited for her kid on the doorstep, wiping flour off her hands with her apron. Maybe she'd called out his name, Thomas, all over town: Thomas, come home, your father's gone for good, come home, come eat, come back.

His mother was waiting for him with a meal laid out on a table set for two. She watched him eat, her chin resting in her hand, and then suddenly got up, disappeared behind the open fridge door, and came back with a white box tied with a golden ribbon. She held out a pair of scissors, handle first, as she sat down at the table. Without getting his hopes too high, and with a certain trepidation, he cut the ribbon and opened the box to find his name in cursive chocolate script on the vanilla icing of a cake. A birthday cake. His hands were sweaty and he set the carton down so he wouldn't dirty it.

He looked up at his mother, a pretty woman with circles under her eyes, younger than most of the mothers he knew and saw around Chattanooga or at the public library. She wore jeans, she had black friends. Or at least she had one black friend, Mary, who lived in Avondale where he had never set foot alone. Often when he got back from school, especially since his father left, she would play some music on the living room stereo, as if to welcome him home with The Beach Boys or R.E.M. She smiled at Thomas and gestured to show him how to pull the box apart, take the cake out, lay it on the table.

She got up again to find a sparkler in a kitchen drawer. Lit her lighter and smiled, and Thomas admired her profile. He thought about his cake, and his mother, and how without his mother there would be no cake, and the ways they were connected, and he had a strange feeling in his chest, his heartbeat sped up as she approached with the burning, hissing sparkler. Something important was happening. A new alliance had been forged between them in the absence of his father, who wasn't coming back, who might never come back.

Thomas looked at his mother and she started singing. Happy birthday to you. Happy birthday to you. Happy birthday, dear Thomas. Happy birthday to you. Birthday. Birth day. The day of his birth. He didn't understand. His birthday was tomorrow. But it wasn't tomorrow, there was no tomorrow. He wanted to contradict her, with all the powers of reason he possessed, everything he had been painstakingly taught. Tomorrow was March 1, his father had explained it hundreds of times. His heart beat fast. He felt like crying and smiling and letting go of his fear, all at once. His mother winked at him as she sang. She was smiling, and her voice was sweet, almost quiet as a whisper. He didn't understand. It wasn't his birthday, his birthday wasn't until next year: February 29, 1988. And the one after that would be February 29, 1992, and so on until he would be at once eighteen and seventy-two, twenty-nine and one hundred and sixteen.

She waited until the sparkler went out to say it again: Happy birthday, sweetie. Before she cut the cake she stuck her finger in the icing and tasted it. "Mmmmmm." That brought a smile to his face. He couldn't stop looking at her, admiring this woman unafraid to question the calendar and the consecrated teachings of the popes and the scientists in Rome and London. She cut a slice, nearly a quarter of the cake, and slid it onto a saucer. It was so big it hung over the edges. She laughed, and then he was laughing with her. She licked her fingers one more time, held out the saucer overflowing with cake and looked at him with eyes full of love and said it one last time:

"Happy birthday, sweetie. We're done with this nonsense. From now on your birthday is February 28."

CHAPTER TWO

MARCH 1994
HIGHLAND PARK—WOODMORE, CHATTANOOGA, TS

THOMAS LOST AN entire family pantheon in one fell swoop the day his mother died. She'd talked so much about her family and had given such detailed descriptions of people and characters, he felt he knew them personally. Not long after his father slung his bag over his shoulder and packed his funny accent up for good to head North, she'd started telling Thomas stories, dramatizing her memories, bringing them to life for his amusement and edification. She was a good storyteller. Especially in the kitchen, after work, when she would sigh and rub her tired eyes at length, palms over their lids, then serve Thomas and herself each a tall glass of milk, which they would take into the living room where she sank into the couch, legs folded under her. From age seven to fourteen Thomas listened to his mother's stories so carefully it chased away all absence and loneliness. Sometimes they made a fire and the story of her grandparents—Confederate sons and daughters of worthy Methodist pastors and preachers—crackled like the logs over the bed of grey ash seamed with red.

Overnight he found himself totally alone, his father across the ancestral mountains, his mother crushed under debris, burned up and lying somewhere at the bottom of the ocean. Much later he received his mother's passport in the mail with other U.S. government documents and official letters from the airline. The passport had been drifting amid millions of shards of metal and plastic, and had been sent to him as proof and testament. In Thomas's adolescent mind, which was eternally occupied with constructing worlds through objects and placing them in context, he pictured an aseptic white table in a sterile white room with fluorescent lighting, where his mother's passport had been laid out to dry. Men in rubber gloves and masks would have handled it, if not with respect, at least with professional care. The corners of the passport photo were turned up and warped, but you could still make out a young woman's face looking candidly into the camera, back when smiles were still permitted. His mother was present in this photo and nowhere else, it contained all that had come with her and all that had left with her as well.

Thomas got it. No matter how many times he turned it around in his head it was over and done with. From the day his mother ceased to exist, all interest in the story of her family had been lost, lost with her vanished body, abstract and unreachable as if separated from him by an abyss. He almost felt it physically, this break she had described and her estrangement from a family she may have loved telling stories about but had not actually seen since she married a penniless foreigner who barely spoke English. A man who bucked convention, a zealot proud to admit that he didn't believe in anything, let alone angels. Who said that? What kind of man said such a thing while eating and sleeping under a stranger's roof? He had barely suppressed his laughter on their second visit and left the table without properly excusing himself, still clutching a napkin in his hand. He would never set foot in her parent's home again. After that incident it was clear that he was no longer welcome.

Thomas's mother cut ties with her family a few weeks later. They got married, but at City Hall, not the Methodist church. Nothing was asked of them beyond consent and proof of identity. No one had talked to them since, though money had changed hands across enemy lines. The arrangement suited everyone. A photo had been passed on when Thomas was born, nothing more. Living in the same town complicated movements somewhat but, as Thomas's father liked to say, Chattanooga was big enough for everyone.

FROM NOW ON we'll use their first names, for clarity's sake and also to attenuate the distance Thomas's perceptions put between us and them. Even after they were gone Thomas heard "Mom" and "Dad" in his head when he thought of his parents, but we'd rather give them their own personalities. This story belongs to them as well. They're rooted in it, like their son, and are motive forces as well as dead ends. Their similar experiences provide depth of field. It's the kind of thing that gets passed down.

Like when Thomas's mother Laura Howells climbed Mount Lookout as a teenager and reached the top not far from the state line, and she thought about where the mountain range began, in another country several thousand miles north. And in these thoughts she projected a fairly detailed image — a young man crossing an ageless mountain range, over hiking trail and mining road and tourist track, water in his bottle, walking stick in hand. He'd have started in the Chic-Chocs. She'd heard that range they had up there was as eroded as the mountains around Chattanooga. Then Laura put her pack and canteen down and took a seat on the summit of Mount Lookout. As she gazed north, the sunbeams piercing the clouds made her believe in something and sense the foolishness of believing in anything at all. She imagined leaving Tennessee with some water and a sturdy pair of shoes, setting out and crossing right through the middle of this world bursting with fall colours, walking until, after a hundred days of walking, she would cross paths with him, a young man with a beard and plans as lofty as her own.

Laura hadn't understood that meeting this ambitious young man from up North, the one she'd dreamed of, would mean turning around and following him back to where she had begun, so that he might answer his own calling, what he referred to (always under his breath) as his "destiny." She didn't foresee that this man's contagious enthusiasm would turn her around.

On May 17, 1979, Albert Langlois got off the train in Chattanooga, Tennessee, and started looking for a cheap place to stay. He asked around while he had a cup of coffee in the diner where Laura worked. Though he hadn't shaved in two weeks he had managed to find a shower almost every night. He smelled good, a fragrant mix of pine, spruce, and lavender, and so did his clothes and the big Canadian army duffle he set down next to the swivelling stool at the counter. His entrance hadn't gone unnoticed. It was past noon, when the place was always slow, and Albert had stumbled, despite the giant sign that read "Watch Your Step," black letters on yellow, and said *"Câlisse!"* and then sorry. It was straight out of a French movie, or something similar that the people in Chattanooga couldn't quite put a finger on.

With her thumb in her mouth, about to turn the page in her pad to note the order of a couple regulars in the corner booth, Laura looked up.

He came up to the counter, pretending to limp a few more steps. He must have stubbed his toe, mouthed the word "ouch" as he looked toward the back of the restaurant, and his gaze came to rest just beside Laura's head on a framed print of the Statue of Liberty proudly standing guard over Manhattan. Her reflex was to back up an inch, and for the first six years of their marriage she thought she had done the right thing. As her son grew up she often thought she had done well to take the initiative that fateful day. By standing in front of the photo of Manhattan, with the Flame of Liberty seeming to rise from her head, she had given him the chance to notice her before he sat down on the stool.

Laura was wearing new glasses. She didn't especially like them, but felt blessed to see without squinting and scrunching up her nose, everyone said she wasn't pretty when she did that. Her stockings were free of runs and she felt confident, sure-footed in her white Nikes, ready to go behind the counter and show him her smile, in profile, nose in the order pad. She tore out the page and placed it next to the others on the metal rack for Richard the cook, and stood in front of him with cup, saucer, paper placemat, and coffee pot. She poured him a burning hot cup of coffee and told him to hold on, she'd be back in a jiffy, to give her time to bring a warmup to the couple at the rear of the restaurant. She was hopping in her runners, ponytail bobbing behind her. Though no one in the restaurant noticed she was, in fact, hopping.

When she came back and stopped in front of him there were six empty sugar packets next to his cup. He was stirring the black liquid with his teaspoon and didn't seem overwhelmed by her presence. He didn't wear glasses, could probably see as far as he wanted, every detail and shade and colour, without even trying. She lay her palms on the counter and rested her waist on it, her head almost directly over the coffee cup.

"Now, that's a lot of sugar."

"Hmm? Oh. Yes. I like it, very...*sucré*, like that."

His accent was so strong she had to smile and pretend to understand until, by analyzing sounds, grappling with them like the poorly translated fortunes in cookies, she managed to decipher what he'd said a few seconds later. His English would get better in time. So would her French. She'd learn enough to string together a few sentences, savour a few expressions that were so close and yet so far away, grammatically and phonetically. The first time she brought Albert to her parents' house the conversation turned almost entirely around language, accent, and cultural differences, conveniently papering over questions of values and beliefs that would wreck everything a few months later.

"Can I get you anything else? Besides that coffee syrup?"

He was looking her in the eye now, his lips moving in the centre of his pretty blond beard. He got the joke, she could tell, and stopped stirring for a while, blushed, asked if it was too late for breakfast. She answered no, it wasn't, they served breakfast any time. He'd have three eggs with ham, bacon, and sausage. He had to use gestures to show her how he wanted his eggs because he didn't know the word.

"You know, uhh, cooked on one side and then, *hop*, you turn it with the, the thing . . ."

Richard was listening from a distance, spatula in hand, interested. He yelled out a little too loudly:

"Over easy, Laura. He wants them over easy."

And Albert pointed at Richard with his index finger, a smile on his face, looking Laura square in the eye.

"*C'est ça.* Over easy! Thank you. To remember, this is *not* so easy."

"No, it's like an expression. How do you say it in French?"

"We say '*tourné*.'"

"*Tur-nay.*"

"Like, uh, turned."

"Oh, okay. That is easier, you're right."

And he laughed and she told herself there was no way that he could be just passing through, waiting for the next Greyhound out of town. It couldn't be. She wanted to ask him right away how he liked Chattanooga, and where he was planning to stay, and whether he had seen how pretty the mountains around the town were, but she went and took a few orders instead, heart racing, feet suddenly heavier. Richard started whistling "Hot Stuff," the Donna Summer tune with a melody you could whistle even while doing four things at once. He was prancing around in front of the griddle, dancing in the smoke rising from the sizzling meat, and whenever Laura passed in front of him he winked. When Laura came out with Albert's plate and gently set it on the mat in front of him, she asked:

"Do you know how to say the other kinds of eggs?"

"No. We say '*miroir*.' Like a mirror."

"Huh. *Mir-wahr*. That's nice. We say 'sunny side up.'"

"Sunny side up."

"Yup. Sunny side up."

ALBERT CAME BACK to the restaurant the next day, and again the day after. He had rented a room nearby, on Broad and 6th. He always came early and he always ordered the same thing. After a couple days it got to be a bit of a joke between Richard and him: Over easy? Over easy. Over and out. He always chose the same stool, where the counter formed an elbow. He had shaved the beard and underneath Laura discovered a much younger man than she'd expected, no older than she was, or not much at any rate. Even with his new face, Albert had retained the bearded man's habit of rubbing his chin and cheeks. His hair was almost red in spots, and getting lighter by the day under the Tennessee sun. He liked to push it to the side and run his fingers through his bangs. Watching him felt to Laura like observing someone who had stepped out of a time machine and plonked down at her counter, a marine on shore leave with a toothpick in his mouth. Her father must have looked something like that when he came back from Europe: adrift in his hometown, embarrassed to be back in his country somehow, a touch aloof, with proper manners and upright posture. She asked her boss Margaret if the Galaxy was already open in '46. Sure was, it was open long before that, you'd be surprised.

She would bring him coffee the moment he came in and immediately feel like she'd had one too many cups herself, with six or seven sugars. On his second visit he asked her name, though it was written on the little metal tag she wore pinned to her uniform, and he'd blushed when she said "Laura," pointing to her chest, gently poking fun. Her smile revealed a girl who would never tire of making fun of him, head slightly cocked, ponytail bouncing, a mischievous expression waiting in the wings. "Me, I'm Albert." Yeah, I know, she said, it's written in black marker on the army bag you were carrying when you got to Chattanooga.

Between two orders she'd stop to chat with him, put the dishes away, dry the clean cups as they came out of the dishwasher. One morning, while a late spring rain fell over the city, he started explaining what he was doing there, where he was from. When he said the word "Quebec," a little louder the second time because she hadn't heard the first, everyone in the restaurant turned around to look at him. Again he said, "*Excusez*, sorry," sweeping the room with his metallic grey eyes. Laura imagined Quebec. She saw a boundless stretch of ice and snow, though part of her felt bad she couldn't do a little better. She knew there was something ridiculous about her image of a vast white windswept plain, with mountain ranges in the distance. The men she pictured were all good looking and bearded, like Albert, descendants of Vikings who only shaved when their travels were over and they reached their destination.

She loved talking to him, taking the time to let him find his words, it made her feel like he was going to great lengths to please her. When Albert hesitated, stammered, or made an error, she took the liberty of gently sidling up and proffering the word he was looking for like a small gift. She would slowly lean over the counter while Albert snapped his fingers, trying to find the right word or correct expression, or when he made that frustrated "tsk" sound, or swore in French: *Voyons, câlisse*. What was it again? How do you say it? At times like these he'd look her in the eyes without a trace of bashfulness. Lost in his thoughts, his shyness abated. Laura, ever the good sport, would bring him the answer he was looking for. One day she caught a sudden change coming over his face and realized he had smelled her new perfume.

Albert ate at the Galaxy every morning during his first three weeks in Chattanooga, except Laura's days off. After a month the whole staff would start whistling "Hot Stuff" the moment he came in the door. Regulars shot him knowing smiles. Even when Laura was slammed, none of the other servers even thought about taking Albert's order. He'd wait patiently on his stool, spinning around, feet in the air.

IN THE MIDDLE of June he finally made up his mind and asked if she was free.

"You mean generally, or tonight in particular?"

"Well, both."

"Both."

"Would you come with me to, I don't know, a movie? We could eat too. But it seems all I do is eat when I'm with you."

"Do you like bowling?"

"Bowling, *mets-en*! I love bowling. Good *id-ee*."

She felt comfortable with him, in front of him. It was easy to talk to someone who may have randomly showed up in her life but whose soothing, peaceful presence needed no justification. On his side of the counter Albert may have been nervous, but everything he said and did felt natural, and she sensed that the nervousness which had won her over in the early days was giving way to something even more attractive, a particular clumsiness that only came out in her presence. When he talked to others, like Richard or Margaret, his tone flattened and grew more confident. Laura even started pronouncing his name the French way, just like him: *Al-bear*.

She deftly redid her ponytail, her elastic held between her teeth. Albert picked up his nearly empty cup and drank the last syrupy sips. He wiped his hands on his jeans. She pushed her glasses up. They looked at each other, and we can all understand what they were feeling, though they're far away from us and we have never met them. Albert asked if he should stop by to pick her up and she said no, it would be better to meet there, at the bowling alley. There was one on Brainerd, on the edge of town, not far from the bus station. She turned his placemat over and pulled a pen from her apron pocket to draw a quick map and write the numbers of the buses he'd need to take. It wouldn't make sense to pick her up, she lived on the north side, in Woodmore, it was residential, he was sure to get lost. Albert nodded in agreement, then folded the placemat in four and slid it into his shirt pocket. After paying for his coffee and breakfast he set off with a clear sense of purpose, a man on a mission. When he looked at her one last time before heading out into the street she understood exactly what it meant.

That afternoon Laura's mother came to see her in her second-floor bedroom. Her questions were pointed enough for Laura to put two and two together. Someone had been talking about Albert. Laura's mother began the conversation standing in the doorframe. As Laura gave answers that were both evasive and enthusiastic she came all the way into the room and sat down on the bed. Laura was holding the closet doors wide open, enthralled by the options before her, unable to make a decision.

"What's his name?" asked Laura's mother.

"Albert."

"Is he French?"

"French Canadian. From the Gaspé Peninsula."

Laura held a dress against her body with the hanger under her chin, and spun around in front of the standing mirror.

"The Gaspé Peninsula. Sounds far away. What's he doing here?"

"Research."

"Research on what?"

"The Civil War, I think."

"What do you mean, you think? Is he a student?"

"I don't think so. It's personal research."

"He didn't tell you what he's hoping to find?"

"Yeah, yeah, he explained it to me."

"And I reckon he's Catholic."

"Mom, I don't know. How would I know that?"

"All French Canadians are Catholics. Everyone's Catholic over there."

"What difference does it make?"

"Well, everyone knows Catholics are . . ."

"Mom, can you just let me get dressed please?"

"Okay, okay, I'll leave you alone. I just wanted to know a little something about him."

"Maybe you'll meet him soon. If things go well tonight. Maybe you'll get to meet him."

"I'd love to meet him, dear."

And she closed the door behind herself, blowing her daughter a kiss, her open hand under her chin like a launch pad. Laura was looking for a pair of faded jeans she'd bought to look like Debbie Harry. She noticed her prom dress at the back of her closet, all ruffles and cream-coloured satin. That was probably what her mother would have wanted her to wear.

THE DAY LAURA Howells died somewhere over the Atlantic, on an American Airlines flight from New York to Paris, she hadn't seen her mother in nearly fifteen years. When Thomas's grandmother came to pick up her orphaned grandson, he didn't know how to react.

Thomas knew her name and reputation. He had heard

her spoken of. And he often thought he saw her around town as he left school or the park. Any shadow could be enough to trigger this sense, like something crawling under his skin, as if someone was watching him. This woman was an invisible but abiding presence for Thomas, an invisible figure always lurking in the background, at the periphery of Thomas's and his parents' lives, though he likely knew more about her story than his own parents' pasts. He knew baby photos had travelled through obscure, convoluted back channels to change hands in secret and against his father's wishes. But even after Albert left for good and the divorce went through, no matter how much resentment had built up, Laura never changed her tune about her parents. When Thomas was alone with her on weeknights, lights dimmed to keep from taxing her tired eyes, he would listen as she told family stories that illustrated concepts like stubbornness, stupidity, and bigotry. Mrs. Howells featured prominently.

Laura described her mother as a hysterical, withdrawn woman who had ruined everything without noticing. Watch out for do-gooders, she liked reminding Thomas, they can be the very worst of all. Watch out for the pious ones, she told him, standing in front of you with folded hands and nodding their heads with condescending empathy. This was Laura's mother in a nutshell: she was pious. Laura never forgot her mother's reaction when her father ordered her to immediately stop seeing that young Canadian, that atheist who held nothing precious, that abortionist, nigger-lover (here he realized he'd gone too far and apologized: I shouldn't have said that, my tongue got away from me). But the damage was done. It was July 1979. Laura was already pregnant. No one knew, not even her. The three of them were standing in the hall beneath a crystal chandelier that cast long shadows. She had just returned from a hike in the mountains. Her key was barely out of the lock. She hadn't even seen Albert that day. It was the morning after the dinner when he had revealed his true nature. Her parents were waiting in their robes, despite the heat, standing apart in their usual postures, each on a different step, hands in their robes' capacious pockets, slippers on their feet. Her father's speech didn't take long. In a series of short, performative utterances he painted his colours on the wall. It's him or us. She tried to catch the eye of her mother, who held onto her husband's arm, gave Laura a searching, pitiful look, and said a silent prayer for Albert's salvation. It didn't matter what exactly Laura had been asking that day; she had her answer.

She left home a few days later and married the unbeliever who spoke broken English at City Hall. She never told her parents. That, at least, was the story Thomas had heard a thousand times. He'd always taken it to be true until the doorbell rang, after Laura's death.

It had come the day before, on a Wednesday evening: the call that would change Thomas Langlois's life, leaving him orphaned, whatever that might mean. Now a carefully made-up, sixty-year-old woman, thin lipped and quite pretty, was in front of him, standing straight and unsupported. Thomas's bum was sore from hours sitting almost perfectly still on the living room couch, slowly ingesting the news like a boa constrictor swallowing an ostrich egg. He sat, still and silent, in the empty house. With the cordless phone on his knee he sat long enough to start believing nothing was going to happen. It wasn't just that nothing would change; nothing would even happen. No one would come, no one would do anything at all. Not one tear had been shed yet, as if every one of them were occupied elsewhere, somewhere behind his eyes, lubricating his confusion. As he got up to answer the door the words of the responsible, empathetic woman who had kept calling him "sweetie" were running through his mind in a loop. Are you alone, is your dad home? There's something I have to tell you. There's been an accident.

His grandmother was standing in front of him. He knew it was her immediately. A woman from social services stood behind her, she looked Latin American and she also called him "sweetie" and Thomas felt sick. Then she said his name. It was his mother's voice, recreated, emanating from a face that looked at once identical to hers and nothing like it. Without warning she grasped onto a balcony post and started crying.

WHILE THOMAS SAT still on the living room couch a mechanism had sprung into action, arrangements had been made, authorities consulted. He'd fallen asleep in a sitting position and his fate had been decided. He asked his grandmother whether she had spoken to his father. No, honey, no, they haven't spoken to your father. No one had spoken to his father. They might have tried to contact him, but no one knew where he was. They knew he was out of the country. That complicated the search even more. The search? In a manner of speaking. No one was exactly searching for Albert, they just wanted to let him know what had happened, he deserved to know. They weren't expecting anything from him. They just wanted him to know.

She drove like his mother, with two hands firmly planted on the wheel at ten and two o'clock. She glanced at him from the corner of her eye, from time to time, without taking her eyes off the road. He could tell she didn't like driving and was trying to look confident, chattering away as she performed every regulation shoulder check. She explained that they, his grandfather and herself, would look after Thomas from now on. Their house, the one where Laura had grown up, was a welcoming home; they were hospitable, loving people. They would have liked to get to know him earlier and under better circumstances, but life was hard to understand sometimes. In Albert's absence his maternal grandparents had been appointed guardians, ideally until he reached adulthood. There were words she said exactly like his mother. They had the same pitch, the same nervous laugh that burst out at the wrong time, delighting Thomas and catching him by surprise without fail. His grandmother was an older version of his mother. In the features of her face, sharpened by wrinkles and redrawn by age, he could discern the ones that disappeared the day before and were now before him again, like a disconcerting optical illusion. The closeness of her voice to Laura's confirmed that his mother was no more. Thomas listened, politely and attentively.

"We have a room all ready for you. It was Laura's room, your mother's room, where she slept the whole time she lived with us. You'll see, it's not too girly, your mom was a bit of a tomboy, she loved sports, football and basketball. In fact, she wanted to be a professional basketball player. Your mother played all kinds of sports when she was a girl, and had a lot of friends. She wasn't the type to sit around twiddling her thumbs. She started working for pocket money when she was sixteen. She was always ready to lend a hand. You know when Laura met your father, back in 1979, Margaret at the Galaxy was going to make her manager? You knew your mother worked at the Galaxy, right? If she hadn't left at that point to be with your father she would probably have been manager a month later. Who knows, she might even have taken over from Margaret one day. Don't get me wrong, your grandfather and I were proud when she went back to school after you were born. It wasn't that. We've always done everything we could to support her. Anyway, you'll see, you'll be happy in that room. It's full of good memories. Team pennants on the wall. We didn't change a thing. It's just the way she left it. I even kept all her stuffed animals, but we can take them away if you'd prefer, we could put them somewhere else. Laura loved stuffed animals, she talked to them like real people, loved petting them and rocking them like babies. If you want we'll box them up, you're fourteen after all, you're a big boy. Won't be long now, we're almost there. Do you know your mother's old neighbourhood? It's hard to believe that all these years we've been living so close and never once saw each other. It's all a misunderstanding, a horrible misunderstanding. It's a shame, that's all. A crying shame."

And she started weeping silently again, no sobs, only tears running down her cheeks. She didn't know if Laura had talked to him much about God, but they would pray together for her anyway. Will you pray with me, sweetie? At the next traffic light we'll say a short prayer, okay? Thomas stared straight ahead, the road went on as far as the eye could see: Tennessee spring all red and gold, low rundown buildings and sidewalks on either side of McCallie Avenue, and living people everywhere, in cars and behind windows and standing next to rusted metal fences. He was polite with this woman he didn't know personally but had heard so much about. He still felt sick, it wasn't going away, he could feel it faintly in his lungs, it was something he'd been trying to get under control for a while but his nose was still kind of plugged. He silently prayed they wouldn't hit a red light.

IT WAS STRANGE for Thomas, at fourteen, to see someone for the first time and know she'd been a secret smoker for decades, going everywhere with a bottle of perfume and moist towlettes to hide the smell. Just knowing she was the kind of person who would do that was strange, even as pure information, free of connotation, and then, out of nowhere, to find yourself sitting beside her. He imagined the blend of nicotine and eau de toilette, it was a smell with no associated mental image because he couldn't imagine himself smelling it.

They were heading out of town, getting further away from the house on 17th Avenue. It felt like they were on a tightly regulated schedule, yet at the same time floating aimlessly through space, as if their cold, calculated plan were melting in the new warmth of spring. Having no control over where they were going made Thomas nervous, but their route seemed precise, its inevitability embodied in this old woman's firm grip on the steering wheel, leaving Thomas no option but to go with it. Beside him she was focused on the road, occasionally fixing a loose strand of her hair, it was grey and her nails were red and she wore a jumble of bracelets that clacked on her wrist. He knew she was coquettish (his mother said "vain"; his father, with open scorn, "materialistic"), and he also knew she had wanted to pass on this plastic, superficial femininity to her daughter. She was smug, phony, a hypocrite. That's what Thomas knew, what he'd always known. He also knew that, though she wasn't doing it now, she often made little burping sounds from gastric reflux.

The feeling of being held hostage was hard for Thomas to adjust to. It was making him sick to his stomach, a feeling that would soon be joined by a silent fear as they approached the end of their drive, when he would meet his grandfather. He didn't speak during the entire trip, his moist hands resting on his knees, back very straight against the seat, sinking deep into the sweet-smelling worn leather.

They emerged from the highway tunnel into jarring bright light, "Dear God," his grandmother exclaimed as she lowered the sunshade with a jerky movement. Thomas didn't recognize the neighbourhoods they were driving through. There were lots of trees, old, massive ones of a kind that was rare downtown, trees whose broad trunks were overrun by green moss, covered with a layer of damp, planted generations ago. Hilly streets meandered, up and down and left and right, instead of stretching out in unbroken straight lines. He wanted to roll down his window but she made it known that he shouldn't, the air conditioning was running.

It was the first time they touched, her hand exerting delicate but firm pressure, No, sweetie, she said with a bossy smile, the A/C is on. To comfort him she turned a dial next to the radio and angled one of her vents toward him. He wanted to close his mouth and breathe in through his nose, like an adult, but his left nostril was totally plugged, and it made an unpleasant, asthmatic sound.

She drove slowly and with an almost dangerous caution. At stop signs she counted, One, two, three, you could practically see her lips moving. Other cars passed them, engines revving. She didn't seem to care. He wondered if she was thinking about Laura. Or maybe about airplanes more generally, air traffic, the expanse of the ocean and her daughter in it somewhere only experts could determine with certainty. He wondered if she was thinking about the same things he was, or about nothing at all, if the emptiness worked its way into her head when she didn't express her grief openly, didn't put it into words.

She put on her blinker and took a small street called Evergreen. The trees were tall, Thomas couldn't see their tops, even with his cheek pressed up against the glass. At the end of the winding road, on this March afternoon, after crossing the town from west to east, they came to a Victorian two-storey house whose bland colour contrasted with the green of the young leaves springing up all around them. She pointed vaguely toward an upstairs window, set at the same slope as the roof, and turned toward the garage: That's your room, that was your mother's room. The car came to a halt. She told him to get out, as if that were the obvious course of action. He opened his door. The paint on the walls of his new house seemed to be crackling with static, but then it could have been something in nature, or the wind in the high branches.

WHEN LAURA WOULD get home from her shift at the public library her shoulders slumped the moment she came through the door. She loved having Thomas there to greet her and spending their evenings together. The tradition had taken root soon after Albert left, and she often had a hard time squaring her joy that her son was almost always home with her concern that he didn't seem to have any friends. In his room he kept a collection of minerals, quartz, and igneous rock. He enjoyed saying their names and listing their characteristics. When they saw *Jurassic Park* together he shared his opinion that, according to his research, the theory that DNA could be preserved in amber was preposterous. It was a good movie anyway, sure, but he wasn't buying this prehistoric amber business. She asked why and he answered with a long sentence about the difference between geology and DNA, or something like that. She'd never thought about dinosaurs except as mythical giants conjured up to entertain kids and make work for special effects teams.

When she got home from work, often late because the library was in another part of town, she liked to sit with Thomas on the living room sofa and tell him about her parents, a family tree full of pastors and judges. Sometimes her words grew heated and a certain animosity crept in that she regretted only later, alone in bed. With lights dimmed and a glass of milk in hand she'd describe the atmosphere of her family home. One night in particular, a year before she died, she'd attempted a physical description of her father. She was adamant; this was the best way to understand him. You had to start from a distance and then zoom in for a close-up, take in his features, the cut of his jib, it was the only way to get an accurate sense of who he was. This man's appearance and his personality were all of a piece. She told Thomas that she had learned this late, well into adolescence. No matter what she said, or what he thought, everything you needed to know about this man was visible in the shape of his eyes, nose, and lips, the cast of his shoulders and his posture. Without being especially tall, or for that matter strong, he managed to be so imposing that his shadow sometimes seemed to wrap around his body, as if the light couldn't figure out how to approach him. She was certain he would not have changed. She took another sip of milk, observing Thomas, and said again that she was sure he hadn't changed a bit. Fifteen years may have passed, but he was the kind of man who wouldn't have aged. When she thought of her mother, she pictured a woman somewhat different than the one she'd known, maybe paler and a little more stooped—but not her father, he would be identical. He had unquestionably retained his bearing and his stature, there was no doubt about it. Maybe one day Thomas would meet him. For his sake she hoped not.

She finished her glass of milk and turned on the TV. Thomas, beside her, noticed his own glass was untouched. Albert's rocking chair sat still in the corner of the room, no one had used it for a long time. He took his glass back to the kitchen and poured the milk into a cereal bowl so it wouldn't go to waste. Plus he was always hungry after listening to his mother, as if a corresponding space emptied out in his stomach while his head was filled with blurry yet vivid images.

One of them was the image of a timeless man who seemed to be preserved in amber or cryogenic ice, refusing to age or weaken, an image Thomas associated with his own father, Albert, who had disappeared years ago. It was ridiculous, but he couldn't help it. He didn't dare talk to Laura about it, worried she would be disappointed in him for some strange reason. No, you don't understand, your father and my father have nothing in common, far from it; they're opposites. Yes, Thomas would answer, I get it, but in my head it's their *absence* that ties them together and mixes them up. Those may not have been the exact words but that was the gist of the thoughts roiling in his mind, the magma of hazy impressions with sharp edges: his grandfather, as described in Laura's stories, must resemble Albert, because Albert possessed the very same authority in his memories. He didn't dare talk to Laura about it because he knew how much both men had hurt her. At the end of his mother's stories he would never have dared ask to see a photo to compare impressions, to use these prints and souvenirs to recast the double face that appeared in his mind: Albert's eyes with brows like ash pointing every which way. Albert ageing, or just plain old. Albert wasting away. If Thomas concentrated on a way to make him younger he would only grow weaker more quickly. That's what happened when Thomas tried to stop the turning or change the direction of the wheel spinning in his mind. He lost control and scrunched up his closed eyes a little harder, but nothing changed, the wheel just kept spinning faster, there was no way to slow it down, as his face, like a sea sponge eroded by time or an old film played in fast-forward, would show all its wrinkles and cracks. His father and grandfather resolved as a single concave image, still in the vivid blackness of the movie theatre in his mind, and he understood that his father was all he ever thought about, almost all the time, almost at all times.

Thomas slurped his bowl of cereal, celebrating the departure of this man who had left them six years earlier one last time with a giant final sip of milk that almost made him choke. In the living room his mother muted the TV.

"You okay, honey?"

"Yeah, there were just some chunks at the bottom of the bowl. I drank it too fast. I'm okay."

SO HE GOT out of the car. Closed the door with a two-handed push and looked at himself in the window, an image superimposed over the leather seats and the big trees behind and around them. Huge trees with trunks eaten away by green moss, taller than he was, trees older than all the actors in this story put together. He was postponing the moment when he'd have to look in the right direction, but his grandmother was coming closer, no doubt to firmly and solemnly direct him. There was no point putting it off any longer. The asphalt in the driveway was cracked in several places. The garage door was new, the windows too. The first- and second-floor shutters had been repainted, but the rest of the exterior walls seemed to be peeling badly. The trees were tall and powerful, rooted deep under the asphalt, probably all the way under the house, wrapped around the pipes so they groaned in the night. There was no point.

When he saw the man waiting for them, standing on firmly planted feet under the unlit lamp at the front door of the large hundred-year-old home, Thomas remembered the image his mother had used to describe his grandfather. He was surrounded by a halo of shadow that both attracted and repelled the light. He looked like a calm, solitary patriarch who hadn't yet heard the news of his only son's demise in the trenches. And he looked like an old, slumped man who had just learned of his only daughter's death over the Atlantic. His hands were stuffed in his jacket pockets, his collar was turned up, and a pipe hung over his chin, he was the kind of man who could convince a crowd of the Maker's intelligent design by appealing to their reason and emotions.

Thomas was drawn forward, not by his own force, but under the sway of some independent gravity. His grandmother, like some minor moon, was buzzing next to him, just outside his field of vision. The car engine had been turned off, you could hear the insects swarming, talking amongst themselves, alert to the collision of forces. The man didn't move, and the smoke expelled from his mouth and nostrils travelled along the contours of his hollowed-out face before fading away. He was waiting for Thomas to move forward, a bit further. He was waiting for Thomas to take a few more steps toward him, understand that he was now on his grandfather's turf, and feel the solidity of the ground he would walk on, before formally welcoming him with firm words that sounded like a summons: This is your home now. Your home is my home.

Beside him, Thomas's grandmother had lit a cigarette. Thomas failed to understand how that could be. She was a secret smoker, Laura had told him the story dozens of times. Her mother hid her smoking from her father. This trait expressed her personality, epitomized her, shed light on who she was and helped explain the kind of relationship her parents had, full of dirty secrets and hypocrisy. Thomas didn't see how this woman could light a cigarette in front of this man, how she dared to do out in the open what she had concealed her whole life behind a screen of mouthwash and eau de toilette. This was one of the details that came up more than any other in Laura's memories of her mother: she smoked a secret cigarette between the parking spot and the shopping centre door, a ritual that had remained etched in her daughter's memory. She had never said that it was their little secret. Laura knew without being told.

That was how Thomas ended up between two smokers, between a pipe and a cigarette, with curls of smoke that didn't reach his nose but coloured the air. His grandmother exhaled vigorously; his grandfather let the smoke slip languorously out of his mouth and nose in opaque curlicues. He was between the two of them. No one said a thing. Nature was full of sounds, or maybe it was a plane high overhead, invisible to Thomas through the foliage of the great elms.

CHAPTER THREE

APRIL 1998
WOODMORE—AVONDALE, CHATTANOOGA, TS

ALMOST ALL THE facts of Thomas Langlois's life are ordinary, believable, everyday occurrences despite the shape they take here, seen through the prism of our faraway, speculative imagination. It's not hard to see ourselves in Thomas. The fears and emotions that brought him here are our own, the very same, just like a thousand others: the feeling of emerging from childhood and adolescence, the fear of growing up without the support of parents we've rejected or otherwise lost. We may have chosen to tell the stories of his father's departure and his mother's death, out of our desire to dig all the way down to the very heart of an experience, but it doesn't change one simple fact: for the eighteen years described above, his was largely a monotonous existence.

We could also have talked about the thousand other days when nothing much happened in Chattanooga, as Thomas grew up, increasingly alone and self-absorbed. Entire days that, piled one upon another, eventually turned into one single thing. The same day over and over again. The same sky that cleared up in late afternoon to let the sun break through. The same walk home through the side streets along the railroad track. We could have talked about Thomas's attempts to collect various objects, maybe find the missing link connecting them all. Or the changing colours of the leaves, or the giant rock in a neighbour's yard split clean in half that he walked by for years on his way home from school or for a hike in the woods south of the river. This massive stone had been cloven by mechanical or natural forces, a bolt of lightning or the blade of a giant saw. Thomas had never asked anyone: what could cut a stone like that, so straight and neat, split clean in half? It was displayed in a carefully chosen spot in the yard where it looked good and added a decorative touch that set a scene. He had passed by it almost every day for fourteen years before he moved to a new neighbourhood; had passed by, lost in his thoughts, thinking things over. Sometimes he noticed it and stopped for what almost turned into a moment, but more often he didn't. It had been part of his life and it helps us understand him, even more perhaps than certain dramatic events that neatly separate one episode from the next. For years he also captured living insects, like everyone used to, and placed them in jars and observed their behaviour; he wanted to see certain things for himself, like how they suffered as their feet raced ever faster on the transparent glass surface, unable to gain a foothold, antennae sprawling everywhere. Eventually he freed the insects and set the jar back down on the counter. One day he realized he no longer saw it from the same point of view. The day before, it seemed, he had looked up at the counter from below; today he looked down from above. It was an observation of facts: he had grown, time had passed unnoticed, and as the days slipped by they all began to look the same, like two sentences spoken at the same time so their meanings blur together. He tried to articulate what he was feeling but had to content himself with touching the counter and nodding his head, convinced of something, not quite certain what.

The two tragic and unusual events we've described hold a place in Thomas Langlois's life like unexplained phenomena, the kind that occur only when no witness is present, the kind we later try unsuccessfully to explain to incredulous friends. With no one there to notice their importance or assay their true worth we keep them to ourselves, to prevent them from sticking with or coming to define us. Thomas would tell himself his grandparents were there, somewhere outside his field of vision. That they had taken him into their home but he was still alone in his efforts to understand and draw conclusions—about absence, death, lack, and those memories becoming less distinct, tiny sparks like jellyfish in deep water.

The process of growing up alone began for Thomas when his father left. With increasing frequency he retreated into his igneous imagination, holding onto Laura like a buoy, but instinctively understanding that she had no desire to be reduced to this. He never saw anyone, barely had any friends, but his mother was changing. She'd started wearing tight jeans and contact lenses. She was pretty, why not? He couldn't blame her. Albert's leaving wouldn't change a thing for Thomas, wouldn't alter his personality one iota. There would be, starting now, one fewer thing in his life, something whose importance he recognized, and whose absence he felt often, but which had not "taken a weight off his shoulders," as he heard his mother say on the phone to her friend Mary.

Laura started wearing her old clothes again. They had been sitting at the back of her closet for years, and if Thomas had seen them before he had no memory of it. There were jeans torn at the knees, blouses with golden spangles. He went to bed early so he would be in good shape the next day, he didn't want to fall asleep at his desk, and just before falling asleep, feeling uneasy and unconsciously listening to the sound of his breathing in his nose, he'd hear his mother leaving through the kitchen door. There was the sound of the rusty screen door followed by the clacking of high heels on the porch, and then she'd be outside and the car would start. During that period, the last years of Laura's life, she started going out at night more often. But she never once missed having breakfast with her son. These breakfasts were like silent extensions of their evenings, as if they had spent the night together waiting for the sun to come up and were a little hoarser but just going about their routine. Laura felt no need to justify herself.

Evenings with his mom were spent in one-way conversation on the living room couch, whole evenings when she would go right on talking, as if he had answered. She'd say, Yeah, you're right, I know, it's crazy but . . . She'd say, What was it you wanted to know again? I've lost the thread. Okay, wait here and I'll explain it. She would speak for them both and Thomas never complained, why would he? They spent whole afternoons together and he enjoyed the feeling of their shared weight flattening the sofa cushions, Laura with her legs folded under her, Thomas sitting cross-legged facing her, a big glass of milk in hand. He got back from school at quarter to five and she'd come home from work exhausted, always exhausted, at six thirty, and heat up their dinner in the microwave and give Mary a call to let her know she'd gotten home okay, sighing with a mixture of comfort and fatigue whose exact meaning he could never pin down. They'd drink their milk under the dim lights and talk about another family that had erupted into conflict one day before he was born, but on account of him, in a sense, or rather of the idea they held at the time of who he would be.

WHEN HE MOVED to his grandparents', Thomas took control of his solitude. It was so normal, in a sense: he was balanced, grounded, and happy to go with the flow as he grew into a highly confident young man with no serious complexes. He didn't feel much affinity with his guardians but did have a vague sense of respect for this couple whose posture showed signs of age yet who remained imposing in so many ways. Grampa Wright and Grandma Josephine weren't the monstrous cretins Laura had made them out to be. Thomas could see what his father had tried to warn him against, but also came to appreciate certain qualities below the surface: Wright's discretion, his seriousness, and a rectitude that reassured him and meshed with his own personality. These qualities reminded him of his own father.

Their faces looked nothing alike, of course, but there was something about his grandfather, the way he had of sitting in the rocking chair staring out the window, into the distance, in which Albert lived on despite himself. For the first few days Thomas had feared his grandfather, but force of habit eventually prevailed. By eighteen he barely spoke to his grandparents, who were little more to him than twin pillars holding up the house. Were they to leave, it would likely fall down. He respected them, in a sense. Their paths crossed on the landing of the stairs or, often, in the dining room, and Thomas would watch them going about their lives, supporting each other; he admired them, in a way. It was something like admiration. Whenever he thought of his mother he felt bad, but he couldn't help it. There were things he couldn't help admiring about them.

Like the way Wright walked with his back so straight the top of his head nearly touched the hall chandelier, despite his seventy-two years and the dozen other reasons it might have found to bend. Watching his grandfather from the corner of his eye reminded Thomas that seventy-two wasn't that old, though the pure-white hair and carefully trimmed moustache told another story. Wright walked around his home with confidence and composure. He neither slid nor shuffled. He may have stepped down as head pastor of the Methodist congregation a decade ago, but he still attended worship every Wednesday, Saturday, and Sunday, in a massive Buick with plush seats and a woman's voice that reminded him to fasten his seatbelt. Very early in the dark September morning, before dawn even, long before Thomas left for high school, Wright would wake up, shave, and comb his hair with the black plastic comb he carried on his person at all times. Thomas, half asleep, would hear the drawn-out rasping of him clearing his throat a single time in the bath-room. He heard Wright descend the main staircase, leave the house without breakfast, and start his car. At times like these Thomas imagined how his adolescent mother would have felt, in the presence of this upright man who wrote articles for the church newsletter, a man she wasn't yet old enough to truly understand. There were articles on abor-tion and on the use of contraception by young girls such as herself. Wright's output had earned him a certain renown, you could see black-and-white photos of his face in print, it made her proud at first, and later ashamed. Thomas listened to him leaving, the car's mechanical voice alerting him that the door was ajar, until it finally shut with a dry muffled clack, and he had a hard time, a great deal of difficulty, rec-onciling the feeling of shame that had been passed down to him, at being the grandchild of this devout, intolerant racist, with the affection he felt for this man who was so stable and firmly grounded, with such an unyielding spine.

Nor did Josephine quite match Thomas's image of her. It might have been how much she looked like his mother, a resemblance so striking he was always slightly sad in her presence, as she must have been when she looked in the mir-ror, Thomas imagined. She dressed elegantly in dark cloth-ing that was always perfectly accessorized, and there was no brusqueness in her manners. She spoke in a composed tone of voice and there was a hint of worry in her eyes that never quite left, even when she smiled. Thomas liked talk-ing to her, it reminded him of the one-sided conversational style favoured by his mother. With Jo it was different: she let him talk, but anticipated what he would say. Hers was an unpleasant habit and a fascinating gift, one he found endlessly intriguing and never tired of putting to the test. They would sit down together for lunch, when Wright was out, eating and talking about everything and nothing, about school and the people they met and the encyclopedic knowledge they shared, and sometimes Jo would say the words he was about to use before they were out of his mouth. Sometimes she got the intonation wrong, or put the stress on the wrong syllable, said "I" when she meant "you," let him be the one who had come up with the idea. It made no difference. She would say what he was about to, before he got to it, and then agree with him: Oh yes, you're right, I know. Thomas would sit open-mouthed at the vapid obviousness of what she said, trying to remember whether his mother had done the same thing. He was sure it was different. When she wasn't doing that, Jo would let him explain himself, but the way she nodded signalled something beyond mere approval or understanding; her nod confirmed that he had indeed said what he should, he hadn't committed an error. They'd sit at the counter on backless wicker stools and stare at the wall above the stove like two sages who had uncovered some profound, long-lost meaning. Normally Jo was very, very calm, and Thomas liked watching her chin resting in the palm of her hand, elbows on the counter, an elegant, self-possessed woman whose age was hard to guess and who called him "sweetheart" without a second thought. How could he resent her? She wasn't hysterical, and when she held his gaze he saw no hypocrisy in her eyes.

Thomas had slept in Laura's old room since moving in with his grandparents. It was decorated with the blue and grey pennants of the Boyd Buchanan Buccaneers. His mother had attended Boyd Buchanan until graduation, but he didn't go to private school like her, he went to Brainerd High, a few blocks east. He walked to school. He never talked about Laura, or Albert, with his grandparents, or about the childhood he had spent with them. On that day four years earlier, after he'd gotten out of the car and Josephine explained the sleeping arrangements, he had shaken hands with his grandfather, who was standing waiting for them on the porch. "Shake" maybe isn't quite right, he had held out his hand like an automaton in response to his grandfather's gesture, and it had moved forward of its own volition, as if drawn by gravitational pull, and Laura Howells was never spoken of again, despite her presence in the room where he would spend most of his time, and the way her absence could be felt in the silence that hung over the house. No one cried. His grandparents went to pick up her personal effects, but they never breathed a word of it to him. If he hadn't one day stumbled on his mother's waterlogged passport he would never have known. He grieved her loss in the order and tranquility of a house so firmly planted in the ground, a house with stable walls. Thomas couldn't fail to respect that.

He may have hated everything religious in his grandparents' lives, but the subject was never broached. It wasn't a bone of contention. Wright and Jo understood instinctively that their daughter had instilled Albert Langlois's values, the foreign values of a French Catholic atheist who'd repeatedly failed to show the respect they were due, at their own table, by questioning truths plain for all to see. Despite Thomas's fears on arriving at the house, compounded by Josephine's prayers in the car, Wright never made Thomas go to church with them, or kneel down to pray at the foot of his bed before going to sleep. When he said grace, Wright closed his eyes, so he wouldn't see that Thomas hadn't closed his own and wasn't saying the blessing along with him or clasping his hands. Wright rarely said anything to Thomas. Josephine talked to him more, but never asked him to pray. She'd done so once and once only.

AT FOURTEEN THOMAS had dreamed of being a paleontologist, or maybe some other "ologist" who got to work with fossils or ancient artifacts dug out of the layers of wet mud. He spent hours looking up the etymology of the suffix "ologist": -*logist, logos, logic*; he suspected that maybe deep down what he really wanted to be when he grew up was a philologist, but as he went into it further he realized that there was no such thing any more, the term was reserved for those men with powder on their faces who had managed, so many years ago, to convince his father that leap years cancelled birthdays. At eighteen he didn't have a clearly defined dream, but that didn't worry him. His marks were good, he was confident he could get into whatever university he wanted, his future was wide open. He liked words as much as numbers, could estimate distances in the blink of an eye, was one of the select group for whom a cosine was more than a strange word to be memorized and forgotten once class was over.

Nearly everyone thought he was a nice guy, though he

often wore a serious, absorbed expression. He was comfortable talking to people of all walks of life, especially adults. When you saw him walking off into the horizon, in the light of the setting sun, that was your feeling: He'll go far, that one. For a young man abandoned by his father, a kid who lost his mother tragically, he seemed to be doing very well indeed. You figured he wouldn't let himself be beaten. That he had grown into a fine young man, that he seemed happy. His hair was always clean and neatly combed, he dressed plainly and ate healthily. You never heard anyone say a bad word about him. You could count his friends on one hand, sure, but who really has more than that? He actually had only one true friend, a single person in whose presence he could clearly see his strengths and weaknesses, successes and failures, what the future held for him.

One thing we need to know about Thomas's life at that time is that, from Laura's death until the day he ran off into the mountains, he never lost contact with his mother's best friend and colleague, Mary. Just weeks after finding out Laura had died, Mary showed up at Thomas's new school. She was there when the bell rang, leaning against her Volkswagen Cabriolet in the cool afternoon. The heat didn't work, she warned him. She told him how sad she was, and it came out so blunt and so honest that Thomas started crying with her, in front of the other students leaving the schoolyard and boarding the school bus. She took him in her arms and he felt that this was exactly what he'd been missing since the accident: a hand in his hair; this hand not another. When he was younger, Mary would come over sometimes, so he was intimately familiar with her voice and her laugh, and he liked her a lot because she never took his spot on the couch, had always preferred to hang out in the kitchen. He'd never felt any competition between them, they weren't fighting for his mother's affection. Each lived out their relationship with Laura in a different room.

He got in Mary's car and she took him out to eat in her neighbourhood, Avondale. They had fried chicken and French fries and he was the only white person in the restaurant. Then they went to her place, where he met her sister Michelle and brother Byron. As they drove toward Mary's the faces got blacker and blacker, hundreds of faces, each one darker than the last. It was as if the city had been divided into colour-coded zones, precise quadrilaterals: between Cleveland and Walker was reserved for mixed-race folks, while Windsor to Ruby was for those so black they looked African, their Nigerian and Angolan ancestry written on their faces. Mary had introduced him to her sister and brother, and a few teenagers sitting on the front steps braiding their hair or rolling cigarettes, kids whose names he could never keep straight. They went inside. In a room at the back of the house they sat together on the bed and Mary showed him a photo. She insisted on giving him a silver brooch his mother had left there. Thomas tried to refuse. Mary wouldn't take no for an answer.

"You should keep it," he said. "She would have wanted you to keep it, don't you think?"

"No. She would have wanted me to give it to you, you to come here so I could give it to you. So I'd have an excuse to bring you here. And we could talk about her. Together."

"You think so?"

"I know so. Anyway, don't worry, it's not like I'm leaving you the most important thing I have of hers."

She smiled and the room lit up. Thomas had never looked at anyone that way. She got up one more time, to move toward the back of the room to the dresser with a boom box on it. She pressed a button and then came back to sit down close to him, holding a tape.

"See, your mom also left me something else, and this one I'm keeping for myself. So we'll both have our own souvenir of her. This tape has all the songs we used to listen to together, we'd sing them together in the car, or when we were getting ready to go out. There's all kinds of stuff, The Supremes, The Doors, A Tribe Called Quest, all kinds of stuff. Do you like music?"

Mary had worked at the library from the beginning, and helped set up programs for the public, storytelling evenings, stuff like that. They were popular. There'd been a time, after Albert left, when she and Laura had grown very close. Thomas liked it a lot when she came by the house. They'd order pizza and the girls would help him with his homework, reciting the answers in affected voices like lines in a play. But his mother had never brought him here.

As he climbed the stairs of the little one-storey house on Roanoke Avenue, following close on Mary's heels, he didn't catch a hint of animosity in the eyes of the boys and girls hanging out on the stoop in the setting sun. He would raise a hand in greeting, and was relieved when it was returned, without ever really understanding why. On the way home in Mary's Cabriolet he thought of his grandfather and his cheeks grew red. History wasn't one of Thomas's favourite subjects. He was more partial to rocks, mountains, and the winding paths of rivers. But history was sitting heavy on his shoulders at that moment, and he was having a hard time figuring out exactly why. It had something to do with his grandfather's white hair and the Confederate flags flying in front of certain neighbours' houses. Something in his grandfather's unvarnished pride in his white hair, how people talked about the past and history with fire in their eyes, forgetting to swallow their spit. No, history wasn't his best subject because he was convinced that, unlike geology and rock strata, history's sole purpose is to erase as it progresses, leaving us free to move on to other things. Flags and borders may disappear, but plateaus and valleys leave traces. He clasped his mother's brooch tight. Mary drove fast.

After that first trip to Avondale he had gone to see Mary often, and in the last few years he'd made his own way there. He took the bus and walked the streets alone, even late at night. The neighbourhood kids recognized him, he'd even been nicknamed "Thomas Jefferson" by one of the most outgoing of the bunch, who could be found sitting on the steps or leaning on the metal fence between the yards. Thomas took his time coming up with an answer, and settled on "Frederick Douglass," though he had no idea what his real name was. The kid just laughed. He got the reference, that's what mattered. After that, Thomas felt this thing they shared whenever he walked by, a sneaky erudition, something known to them alone. When he came into Mary's house she'd say, "Hey big man," though he was only fifteen, then sixteen, then seventeen. The door and even the screen door were always wide open, Thomas would go right in, taking care not to step on the rickety threshold, and he'd follow the light to find Mary's smile in one of the rooms. Sometimes she'd say, "Hey, honey." She was at least fifteen years older than him.

His grandparents didn't know about his relationship with his mother's old friend. Why would they? He had never talked about his first trip to Avondale, or the ones that followed. Wright and Jo didn't care what he got up to after school, and the summer holidays were his to do what he wanted. Often when Thomas left the house after a silent breakfast his grandmother would light a cigarette outside and watch him walk into the distance. She'd say to herself: This one is going far.

There had never been physical contact between Mary and him, other than the accidental, friendly kind, what she might have called innocent, friendly touching. Thomas had never hoped for more. But he also didn't look at anyone in the world the way he looked at her, or listen to anyone the way he listened to her. He didn't pay attention to much, but when she opened her mouth to speak or beckoned him over, Thomas was immediately present, attentive, and considerate. She was his one true friend, the only one he could share his thoughts with. She was interested in what he had to say, the information he tried to convey. When he talked about asteroids, or described the Perseids, the experience of meteor showers lighting up the late-August night sky, she closed her eyes and he could hear her sighing at his side, not out of boredom but rather pure happiness, deep contentment. He knew this instinctively, the proof was that he never had to ask why she was sighing.

Over the years they had fallen into a routine, a way of being together that was amenable to both of them. She wasn't his lover, nor was she his babysitter. Thomas filled out his college applications at Mary's house. She helped him choose from the schools offering scholarships. Sometimes he would spend the whole day in Avondale, or further west on Martin Luther King, not too far from his old house, chatting with Mary or with all the other people who, as far as Thomas could tell, accepted him without a second thought, though he came from the other side of town where massive trees made it feel like the residents had occupied their homes for a thousand years. No one here looked at him sideways, with mistrust or disdain. His presence here was justified, understood, integrated, normal.

WHAT HAPPENED ON the morning of April 4, 1998, is so far out of the ordinary that we have to take a moment to underscore the fact that it all really happened. Because the events in question occurred decisively and instantaneously, our telling will give the impression of a rupture in the narrative of Thomas's life. There was a before, there was an after. In the warmth of our own homes, here along the great river where winter is digging in its heels and we can see the smoke from the factories, thick and opaque against the steel blue sky, it's hard to make out the contours of that day that changed the course of Thomas's life. There is the distance and there are social mores and there is a whole other culture with tensions of its own, which we may be familiar with from history books and documentaries. We can try to plunge right in to what happened there, on that hot April day in Tennessee, but we know it won't be easily believed.

Yet there's no denying that it happened, it was in the papers the next day and on the evening news as well. His grandparents learned about it at the same time they learned how he'd been spending his days. Thomas found himself alone between two worlds, each unable to forgive what he had done, acts he was unable to find fault with, but whose impact and magnitude were undeniable. Of course, he felt bad about scaring the little girl, the consequences were dire and she would bear the scars her whole life, but people's reactions on both sides were so far out of all proportion that he chose the one remaining option and slipped off to the hills.

That morning Thomas was euphoric. For the first time he and Mary had spent the night together in the big bed in the back room. They hadn't touched, but for the first time he had felt a slight unease on her part when she realized her offer would be taken up: It's late, if you want to sleep here that's fine, there's lots of room, it's a big bed. He had looked up from his math book and pushed his glasses back on his nose and simply said yes, with a slight widening of his eyes, before turning his thoughts back to logarithms and prime numbers. Mary was standing up next to the microwave holding a mug of Cup-a-Soup. A half hour later, when she got back from the bathroom where she had changed into pyjama bottoms and a plain blue tank top, she had sat down on the bed where he was already pretending to sleep, under the sheets, on his back, arms at his sides, lying still like a recently deceased corpse intent on causing minimal disturbance. The house was silent. Outside you could hear the occasional squeal of a tire or burst of laughter. He hadn't phoned to tell his grandparents he wasn't coming home.

Thomas stared at the white label sticking out from Mary's tank top, against her black skin. It was the last thing he saw before she reached to turn off the bedside-table lamp, and their first night together began. It would be a long one spent in half-states of slumber and brimming with mysterious questions whose origin he held suspicions about and whose source he wasn't eager to determine. In his head, vague notions of applied mathematics blurred together with concrete images of kinky hair and dark lips. Several times during those long hours he thought a glass of water might be his salvation, but he had never fully woken up. Nor had he fallen totally asleep. The sheets absorbed his sweat.

They ate breakfast in silence and Thomas was euphoric without showing it, and when he left Mary's house fairly early, they passed several groups of children walking down Wilcox Boulevard on their way to school, carefree like him, with a bowl of cereal in their stomachs and a fantastic day ahead of them, only just beginning. He felt a lightness, like someone who had just done a good deed, helped an old woman cross the street or lug a heavy grocery trolley up a staircase. On the sidewalk hopscotch squares were drawn in chalk and the word HEAVEN had no spelling mistakes.

It came out of nowhere and it was preposterous, over the top. On the corner of North Orchard Knob and Wilcox, a few minutes after leaving Mary's with his backpack slung over his shoulder, Thomas came across a group of kids. One of the young girls was talking excitedly to her friends. She was waving her arms wildly and kept adjusting the straps of her outsized backpack and when Thomas saw her he understood she was telling a scary, emotionally charged story. It was going well, she seemed fully invested in her words; she put her arms and hands over her head, as if to imitate a monster or a ghost. As he drew nearer he began to understand her story and his smile widened. She walked backwards confidently, without once looking where she put her feet. The sidewalk seemed to echo her movements. She was small but her voice was commanding. We have no idea what went through his mind at that moment, but Thomas listened to the instinct telling him to join in the story, to become its protagonist. In our view he believed he could join in the story of the young girl marching backwards toward him at the head of a gaggle of enraptured friends. We believe he suddenly had the first wholly positive impulse of his life, at the age of eighteen, that morning, after a long night with Mary, a night that may have been the start of something new in his life, something akin to becoming a man, finding himself, but it's hard to figure out because everything changed afterwards, and even those who liked Thomas started staring at the ground when he came near.

The little girl was backing toward him, telling her story, and the others saw him approaching but didn't say anything, held rapt by their leader's every word and gesture. Thomas, a few steps away from making his entrance, placed his index finger in front of his mouth to signal to the others to keep quiet. They immediately came on board as accomplices. Two or three jaws dropped in surprise, but they were the only open mouths. The kids all wore the same blue and white uniform, as if they were on their way to private school, though they were in fact heading toward the public school further east. According to the account published in the paper, the children were between seven and eleven. She was eight. Thomas's signal was meant to show the children that his presence was a secret, and you could feel a sort of electrical charge in the air, like before a joke that is going to connect, just before everyone starts laughing, at someone in particular perhaps but all together nonetheless. He let her back up a few more steps, and as she raised her arms one more time to imitate the monster she was imagining, Thomas also raised his arms and roared like a giant blond lion, right there on Wilcox Boulevard, under the scrawny neighbourhood trees, in the Chattanooga sun, but he didn't get the chance to break into laughter along with the six or eight stunned kids in front of him because the little girl leaped into the air, started yelling, and, in some kind of nonsensical, over-the-top, unforeseeable, and completely unbridled move, she jumped into the street, to the left of the group, where, despite the nearby primary school, the posted speed limit was forty miles per hour.

A deformed, disagreeable sound came from her mouth a fraction of a second later when she was struck by the car. Ten feet further up, on the roadside, she was nearly killed instantly. The impact was brutal, she was thrown backwards and rolled over onto her backpack. We won't describe it in detail but the vivid Technicolor images of that day have been lodged in our minds ever since.

CHAPTER FOUR

JUNE–JULY 1998
AVONDALE—WOODMORE, CHATTANOOGA, TS

HERE'S WHAT HAPPENED next. Time started slowing down and speeding up in the same breath. Up and down the boulevard, front doors opened in unison, hundreds of front doors, it seemed to Thomas, and also one car door, driver's side. A woman got out. She broke her high heel on the road, and ran over to the little girl lying a ways away, on the ground, not moving at all. The children's cries were mixed in with the squealing of tires and other vehicles stopping to help or to look. Someone pulled out a cell phone, 911 was flooded with calls, and a few seconds later an ambulance showed up, followed by several police cars. People stayed put on their porches, or walked down the handful of steps to the sidewalk; most were still wearing pyjamas and were covering their mouths. The woman from the car was yelling in the face of a policeman who was holding her upright with a firm hand, so she wouldn't collapse. It felt like nighttime, it was raining, the cruiser's flashing lights shone bright as they revolved, but in fact it was day, the start of a brand-new day.

Thomas hadn't moved. He couldn't move a muscle. In a matter of seconds his life had taken an unexpected turn. A woman came over to ask whether he had seen what happened, while she tried to round up the other children and get them to go home to their parents, and he told her it had been his fault. He whispered it. She turned around and said "What?"—arms wrapped around the two young girls who were having trouble walking. He looked at the horrific scene, the tragic event he had caused, and his eyes lost focus and distances lost their definition and everything turned into a mass of disparate colours thrown thinly and haphazardly onto canvas. He never lost consciousness but felt like he was about to, it was close to happening, he felt something like a warmth in his ankles and his head at the same time. He said it again—"It's my fault"—as a way to find focus by voicing these incriminating, honest words, the only ones possible. The woman, helped by neighbours, pushed the last of the children inside, the door was just yards from the scene, and she came up to Thomas and put a hand on his shoulder. He swallowed his saliva in his dry mouth and said it again.

"It's my fault. I snuck up behind and scared her."

"Ssssh. Of course not. It was an accident."

"No, I wanted to startle her. On purpose. I wanted to startle her by sneaking up and yelling."

"What?"

"She was backing up and telling a story and I made a sign to the other kids not to give it away, that I was there, and I yelled to scare her, and make her laugh."

"Oh my God."

Just like the others she covered her mouth with her hand, the same one that had been on his shoulder. As Thomas explained she slowly took it off and brought it to her mouth. She had brown skin like Mary's and dark eyes. One of the policemen unfurling a long yellow roll of tape came over to them, he was black, he asked Thomas who he was, what he was doing there, what he had seen. Thomas told the same story one more time, in the same words, with the same neutral expression on his blank face and his heart pressed up against his throat and his mouth, somehow pushing simultaneously on his diaphragm and his uvula. The policeman's expression changed. He turned to his colleague and yelled for him. The other cop came over, he had black skin and bloodshot eyes, as if he hadn't slept all night, as if he had spent the night dreaming of this young girl who would be hit by a car a few hours later. He came over and the two of them talked privately, Thomas couldn't hear what they were saying, or maybe didn't want to. The neighbours kept going into their houses and coming out again, coming out to see and going back in to call up someone or turn on the TV to get a better sense of what was happening, because the journalists were arriving and unpacking their equipment. Everyone was black, from the paramedics pushing the stretcher the girl lay on to the drivers who had stopped and were talking on cell phones to the neighbours being told to back up by the police to the journalists and cameramen and sound men. The kids were all black and the little girl had her hair in braids held in place by silk ribbons, a yellow one and a pink one, and Thomas thought she had glasses too, but over there, where the black men were putting her on a stretcher, she wasn't wearing them anymore. He wasn't sure of anything anymore. He hadn't really seen her face, she hadn't had time to turn around, had barely pulled off half a turn. Her terrified arabesque was brought to an abrupt halt by the car. In the days that followed no one would ask him what she was wearing that day, it wasn't part of the investigation, but it was what he would have liked to talk about because he remembered. Her face was blurry in his mind but he remembered her clothing, its colour and fabric.

Just before the little girl's mother came running over, screaming and crying, overtaken by hysteria and demanding to know exactly what had happened, looking for the woman who had run over her daughter, the two policemen asked Thomas if he would please follow them, they had a few questions for him, would appreciate his co-operation. When Thomas didn't move they repeated their request, and one asked whether he'd understood, and Thomas nodded, without looking in the right direction. They took him to the local station in a blue and white cruiser, to question him and get to the bottom of this whole story.

IT WAS IN the morning papers. Interviews with witnesses brought certain details to light, but most people in Chattanooga already knew what had happened because the TV news stations had been on the scene minutes after the incident. The little girl had been rushed to hospital and was in stable condition. Her name was Keysha-Ann. There was talk of contusions, lacerations, commotion, impact absorbed

by schoolbooks, low speeds, careful driving. They used shop-
worn phrases: it was a horrible accident, it was no one's fault,
there was nothing the driver could have done. The poor
young man who'd tried to make a bad joke was being pun-
ished with a disproportionate sense of guilt that must be
haunting him as we speak. He'd been taken to the station,
then to the hospital, they were worried about nervous shock.
The other kids were fine; the girl would be okay. All the
experts kept saying she would be okay, and then, the next
day, during prime time, another kind of expert came forward to tell a different story, a reverend of impressive stature, who guested first on one show and then on another,
asking the question that was on everyone's mind but that
no one in a town like Chattanooga, which sat shamefully
atop the per-capita crime rates, in a state like Tennessee, in
a supposedly free and equal country like the United States
of America, dared ask: Why had this happened in that particular neighbourhood, I want you to ask yourself, why was
the victim black, as usual, and what exactly was that young
white man doing so far from his affluent neighbourhood, far
from his private school, why are we dealing with another
young black victim, one more, in a city with more than
1,400 violent crimes every year, a staggering 84 percent of
them committed by black people, ask yourselves, look me in
the eyes and answer this question — what business did this
young white man have coming around making faces behind
the back of an innocent young black girl? The host nodded
her head as she listened to this expert, who pointed his index
finger skyward and then rapped on the table with it, a gesture he repeated soon thereafter, endowing his words with

great authority. People listened in silence in front of their televisions, and later that evening the same phrases were heard again on the call-in shows. Thomas had been released from hospital after a few tests. The journalists wanted to talk to him. He'd gone home in his grandmother's car and the journalists were waiting in their little tree-lined street. They wanted to know what he was doing in a predominantly African-American neighbourhood that day, what he was doing on Wilcox Boulevard before school. They wanted to know what was going through his head, if there wasn't a touch of cruelty or, yes, racism behind his actions, and he took a roundabout route into his house, without saying a word, stunned by the force of so many questions all aimed at him. The next day it was clear: he was no longer welcome in Avondale.

WRIGHT WAS THE first to bring up the idea of a lawyer. He knew good people. The girl was going to be okay, she was just injured, but it was better to be safe than sorry, best to lay their options on the table as early as possible. Wright had welcomed Thomas, nearly hugged him, Thomas felt his grandfather had almost made a move to hug him. He saw Josephine heading to the backyard to smoke a cigarette: the first time she'd done that, she was avoiding the journalists in front of the house. Thomas had barely come into the hallway when Wright started talking to him about a friend of his, a lawyer who could surely counsel them, especially about this issue of the so-called underlying racism, the idea was completely absurd and, worse, it was snowballing on account of all this political-correctness nonsense taking over the air-waves. It felt like the story was spiralling out of control. No one was taking a moment to stop and think. Thomas had nothing to fear, Wright knew a good lawyer who could give them sensible advice and good counsel, the key was to lay low until people calmed down and the tension dissipated. He said much of this with his back to Thomas, peering out the window, like any elderly retiree wondering what the neighbourhood was coming to.

THE LITTLE GIRL was discharged from hospital. The journalists had new and more pressing concerns. They'd spent a few days camped out in front of Thomas's grandparents' house, filmed a story about his mother's death in the 1994 plane crash, it was still fresh in people's minds, the plane sunk in the ocean somewhere between JFK and Charles de Gaulle: hundreds dead, including Thomas Langlois's mother, Laura Howells—librarian, city employee—who'd been on her way to an international conference on the changing image of the book. The young man must have been distraught, he must have been rudderless, he'd lost his mother at a tender age and under tragic circumstances. Now he was living with his grandparents and, despite what people were saying, he didn't go to private school. Thomas was a public school kid, he went to the same high school as everyone else. The whole thing lasted no more than a few days. The talking heads and sociologists each got a turn to talk, the journalists described the little girl like an angel who had touched down on earth to visit, a slow zoom over the photo of her smiling face was in heavy rotation. No one talked about the driver. Less than a week after the story broke, the newspapers lost interest. The girl hadn't died, she'd get off with some scars, her name was Keysha-Ann Johnston and she lived a few hundred yards from the site of the accident. No one talked about the driver because Keysha-Ann and Thomas were the story. And then no one talked about it at all.

OVER THE PHONE, Thomas told Mary that he understood it was a bad idea, of course it was, he saw her point, but he was seriously considering going to see Keysha-Ann at home, at her house. The dust had settled, she was getting better, surrounded by loved ones. There were things he had to say to her, things he wanted clear up, it was so important, Mary got it, didn't she? Mary got it, of course she did, but she said it again, it was a really bad idea all the same; she said it many times, a really, really, *really* bad idea. People around here are mad, see what I mean? Yes, of course, of course Thomas understood, he would be mad too, he could put himself in their shoes, but if he knew them, and if they got to know him, they would understand, they would understand in the end. Thomas had to try, he had to tell the girl he was sorry, ask the community for forgiveness, her mother too, he wanted to show her he wasn't a coward, he understood the gravity of what he'd done, he was the kind of person who understood that actions had serious consequences. Mary interrupted him:

"Thomas, it's not about whether you're a coward."

"I know. But still, that doesn't change anything, I have

to go. Know what I mean? I have no choice."

"Yeah, I see that. But, Thomas, you're the one who's got to understand, they're not going to welcome you with open arms. And you've also got to understand why. There isn't going to be any forgiveness, or, I don't know, redemption. No one is going to take you in their arms. Do you get that?"

"Yeah, I get it, I totally get it. I don't expect anything like that. That's not what I'm picturing, Mary. Not at all. It's between me and Keysha. I have to do it for me. Do you get that?"

"Yeah, I get it."

HE KNOCKED ON the door of the little bungalow a few days later. It was a hot, late-June afternoon and Thomas was empty-handed, his arms at his side, wearing a white T-shirt. His glasses were spotless, his hair neatly combed. He knocked and heard voices inside, a woman's and a man's, they were coming nearer. The door opened a little and Keysha-Ann's mother looked him in the eyes for a fraction of a second and then started crying and, unable to do anything else, backed up a little with her hand still on the doorknob. At the end of the hallway he heard a man's voice yelling out "Who is it?" or maybe "What is it?" — he wasn't quite sure which — and Keysha-Ann's mother didn't seem to understand what Thomas was doing standing there on her front porch. She'd only ever seen him on TV, this person who had almost killed her daughter, scared her and sent her jumping backwards. His palms were instantly sweaty and he wanted to wipe them on his jeans. She was still looking at him with tears in her eyes. She asked him what he wanted and he didn't have time to answer, the man's voice was back, louder, like a wave of menacing sound in Thomas's ears, like a wave cresting and breaking at the same time and making the plaster on the walls shake. Mom! What is it? She turned around, the door opened wide and Thomas saw that she was carrying a baby in her arms, in one of her arms. The baby had lighter skin than its mother's, almost pink, and black, curly hair. She answered the voice from the back of the house:

"Nothing, baby. It's nothing. Just him, the guy. That guy. Him."

"Who?"

Thomas spoke quietly so as not to wake the baby:

"I came to see Keysha-Ann. Do you think I could . . ."

She said it again, louder:

"The guy. Thomas."

A powerful groundswell shook the walls and the roof of the house, and Thomas saw a black shape appear in the hallway in front of him. He wasn't wearing a shirt, not even a T-shirt, and his upper body was dark brown and shiny. He came forward and Thomas instinctively backed up and stumbled on the step leading down to the little concrete landing. The young man pushed his mother. She started yelling at him to calm down. He was Thomas's age, you could tell, and his arms and torso were muscular. There was a great violence in his movements, you could see the muscles tensing up in his neck and above his shoulder blades. Thomas tumbled backwards and tripped and landed on the sidewalk, holding onto the metal fence. He was barely back on his feet, in a defensive position, bent double in a stance meant to be non-confrontational, when the young man started pushing his chest and yelling, cursing. He was yelling so loud while pushing him toward the street that Thomas feared for his eardrums before he feared for his life. When he fell down on the sidewalk the young man checked himself. That's when the neighbours started coming out, drawn by the noise. He pointed his index finger in Thomas's face, nearly touching his forehead, and told him to never come back here. To never try to contact his sister. That if he ever saw him in the neighbourhood again he'd kill him.

THE FOLLOWING WEEK Wright Howells wrote an article for a small-circulation Methodist newsletter. After not publishing anything in more than a decade he had found his voice again. His outings in the old Buick lasted longer and longer, he would set off to meet people, plan events, and come home with legal documents and statistics. Thomas found himself unable even to open his mouth in Wright's presence. The old man was increasingly intimidating. He felt uncomfortable, had a hard time accepting this improbable alliance his grandfather seemed to hold so dear, as if Thomas's nearly killing a young girl and now dealing with the fallout were supposed to bring them together. Wright talked non-stop about the hot-blooded people who lived downtown, about self-ghettoization, how the suburbs were held hostage by a "black belt" of violence and drug abuse. With Thomas he used sociology terms and scrupulously avoided religious rhetoric, but beneath the surface of his words lurked a deep-seated anger, the exasperation of a fair man who believed he had given his all to the community, only to watch it go to pot before his very eyes. They had assaulted his grandson. At first Wright had spoken of lawyers; now he was talking about getting out in the streets, holding public meetings, bringing different parishes together to take a united stand against the wild accusations certain reactionaries had brought against Thomas, making him out to be something he wasn't. Wright railed against the way opinion leaders spat venom, had no idea what they were talking about. Josephine wasn't sure how to react. She hadn't seen Wright like this for years. Thomas was trying to get closer to her, slowly, unconsciously, but she just seemed to be moving further away, lost in thoughts and memories that belonged to her alone and which she felt no inclination to share, content to signal her approval with a nod whenever Wright asked her a direct question or demanded, straight out, Am I right? One day, very early in the morning, Wright came into Thomas's bedroom, something he never did, in the half light of dawn, and said, Those niggers ain't going to get us, boy. And to Thomas's ear, coming from his grandfather, that uncompromising man of martial bearing who loomed so large in his mother's stories and descriptions, it wasn't the word "nigger" that was most shocking or incongruous, no, he had been expecting that. It was the incorrect, common, downright ungrammatical "ain't."

THE BUS TOOK Wilcox Boulevard all the way from Thomas's neighbourhood to Mary's. It was still Wilcox Boulevard in

Avondale but there were no massive elms and when Thomas got off the bus he thought he noticed something strange about three young men leaning against the wall of the 7-Eleven smoking a joint. They were staring at him. And he sensed that they kept on staring at him, staring at his tingling spine, as he set off toward Mary's. He was afraid they would follow him. There was something unnatural about his walk, and this awareness only made it worse. His spine was tingling, the fibres of his shirt chafing against pools of sweat gathering in the hollows of his back. It was hot, a real Tennessee scorcher, the kind of day that ends in evening windstorms, or even thunderstorms, or maybe the first tornado in over a decade. They never got twisters around here, no one had seen one in years. Tornadoes rarely developed between the mountains, or in the cordillera between Mount Lookout and Mount Signal.

When Thomas reached Mary's, his shoulders were bent under the weight of a thousand stares. She welcomed him with a smile but he couldn't help feeling she was watching the street after she let him in and shut the front door. After a long conversation, during which Mary cried profusely, as she served him coffee and lay her hands on his, she showed him a letter she had gotten that day: a letter from Albert Langlois to his son, addressed to Mary, with a short introduction explaining that he preferred to make contact through her, though he didn't want it to burden her. He'd always trusted and respected her, he wrote in his strange English, which even he called "rusty." On a separate piece of paper Albert told Thomas where he was, what part of the world, what he was doing there. When he read that information, tucked away in the middle of a short sentence about his sadness at having learned of Laura's death, long after the event, Thomas felt no surprise, every line was a confirmation, one detail at a time, of what he had always known without actually knowing: his father had gone back to Quebec, to a town called Sainte-Anne-des-Monts, where he was born and had grown up, between the Chic-Chocs and the St. Lawrence River, not far from us at all if you stop and think about it. His father had left Chattanooga because he thought he had finally found what he had been searching for without respite for more than thirteen years. He had found information about his ancestor, a certain Aimé Bolduc, and thought it was the answer to the riddle that brought him to Tennessee in the first place, where he had met Laura and he had married her and they had had a son.

He read the words of his father, Albert Langlois, who had abandoned his family and felt guilty about it. This was the first time since he'd left that he communicated with Thomas, and he would wait for an answer from him before reaching out again. If Thomas agreed, they could try to mend the fences that had fallen into disrepair and collapsed in the years of silence.

He looked up and Mary looked back at him, with love almost, with what looked to him like love in the process of cracking and breaking apart under the stress of multiple emotions, like so many juggling balls she couldn't quite keep in the air. She looked at him with her big brown eyes and asked if this letter was what he had been waiting for. Was he happy it had finally come? He said he didn't know exactly what this would mean to him, but he was happy to learn his father was doing well, or was still alive at any rate, up there. Mary rested her hand on his and said to Thomas: I don't think it's a good idea for you to come back here, not for a while at least.

She offered to walk him to the bus stop, to keep him safe, hold his hand and protect him from the people who wanted to hurt him, those who might believe he was trying to provoke them by coming back around here. She held his hand until the bus stopped and Thomas got on, but it didn't change a thing because on the bus ride home he was beaten up by a bunch of guys who wore black coats and work boots even in the suffocating heat. There was nothing the driver could do to stop it.

Before he passed out Thomas thought about waves breaking on the rocks, the salty breeze and drafts of seaweed, but it might have been an illusion caused by the smell of blood and dust in his nostrils and the corner of his mouth.

PART TWO

ALLEGHENIES

CHAPTER FIVE

DECEMBER 1864
NEWPORT, VT

AS FAR AS anyone can tell, Aimé left Montreal in November and crossed the border a couple weeks later, somewhere around Stanstead, likely in the middle of some field or on the fringes of an uncleared forest, almost certainly under cover of darkness. Perhaps he sailed the frigid waters of Lake Memphremagog on some junky skiff with a pair of young Abenaki men he knew and trusted. He could also have travelled by stagecoach, hurtling over the landscape to the clopping of horseshoes and snorting of horses, but that seems unlikely since his aim by that point was to go unnoticed and be forgotten.

The scattered documents and testimonies Albert Langlois had gathered in over a decade of research mostly place Aimé in Newport, Vermont, starting in December 1864. It was there he came in contact with the Van Ness family and entered their social circle. But the paper trail is rife with contradictions. It's hard to ascertain anything with certainty. To retrace his story and give it even a modicum of linearity we will, at times, have to choose one tack over another, bearing in mind the possibility that errors of fact have slipped in. The strictures of intellectual honesty and our respect for our sources demand that we keep a watchful eye out for discrepancies between the teller's horizon of expectation and the rigour of his investigation. We feel this is how Albert would have wanted it, though it's too late to ask him now.

In early December, Newport was in an uproar. A company of green recruits had just left for Washington, sent off with speeches and choked-back tears on the front steps of City Hall. It didn't help that the cavalry had returned bearing news of a rebel attack at St. Albans, on the banks of Lake Champlain, some sixty miles west. The hostilities were drawing dangerously close. Twenty armed men led by Bennett Young had come in by the northern highway and taken over Main Street. They proclaimed St. Albans part of the Confederacy, claimed victory in the name of President Jefferson Davis. Barns were burned and all three banks robbed, even the City Bank, despite the soldiers posted at the door. The skirmish lasted several days and took one life before the perpetrators made off with a hefty sum. People said they were hiding out in Quebec City or Montreal, where the Royalist government would never extradite them to the Union. People said they'd planned to kill the governor and burn his house down, but settled for emptying the bank vaults and firing their rifles in the air, accompanied by credible imitations of Sioux and Apache war cries.

Word was they'd left town three days later, on October 21, at dawn. News was trickling into Newport now, too late as always, with the urgency of cavalry soldiers dismounting their steeds. The townsfolk were barricading themselves in their homes. In some families, every son had enlisted, leaving the old men to clean the family rifle and practise shouldering and reloading as they'd done in the War of 1812. There were lineups at the blacksmith, people waiting to melt down jewellery for shot, and poring over maps to mark strategic locations to post men.

Aimé had come to a town where this atmosphere coloured even the nights, when torches burned bright and shots rang out more frequently. He took a room at Frederick Van Ness's hotel, where he was at first suspected of spying, a common fate of travellers in dark times, though nothing came of it. There were plenty of strangers in town, especially Canadians come to work or write articles, and Aimé stood out only for his slight accent that people found hard to place. Preparations were taking a great deal of time and energy. Envoys had been dispatched to the surrounding territories, to summon the few men who were still on their land and so raise a militia. Norwich Military College had sent a division, they were expected by train at any moment. Days were spent casting bullets and ramming cannon, nights gathered in the hotel lobby or on the church steps, in silence or in noisy preparation, awaiting the enemy reprisal.

The first time he talked to Aimé, Frederick Van Ness took him for a Dutchman, an intuition he chose not to corroborate. Van Ness asked his guests as few questions as possible. How long was he planning to stay? How would he paying?

We don't take foreign currency anymore, it's the inflation. Aimé approached the hotel front desk and Van Ness was struck by how much he resembled his own son William. They exchanged a few words, standard niceties, and Aimé went off up the main staircase to his room, with all the vigour and weariness of a man aged at once twenty-six and one hundred and four. On the streets outside, people were running around with torches. Sometimes you could hear the faraway cries of a patrol convinced it had seen horses off in the distance at the river bend. Evacuation plans had been drawn up for the dignitaries: they would flee by boat to Quebec's Eastern Townships, where their allies would be waiting for them. Twice during these days of constant panic the alarm sounded, and a fight broke out after heated words in a tavern that stayed open too late.

But nothing happened. No enemy raid broke through the lines of defence, and only the grey snow that fell at the end of every year coloured the hastily constructed barricades. Around a week later the townspeople finally unclenched their teeth, calm of a sort returned, the militia disbanded, and the students went back to military college. By Christmas no one talked about it anymore. The army recruiters came back to convince people of the importance of enlisting. They had reached the north shore of the Potomac, up at the Shenandoah Valley; it was now every man's duty to halt the Confederate advance.

The day after the town council's quiet celebrations, a recruiting station was set up near the post office and the population summoned. The soldiers described the latest fighting, answered families' questions. All wore hats and

dark blue frock coats with gold braid. Their boots were polished to a shine, that martial shine that calls out to every
farmer's son, and the sight of these men, ramrod straight
and in full feather, inspired respect and fear.

One man read out the names of soldiers who had fallen
bravely in combat, killed by the band of traitors under
Robert E. Lee, Jefferson Davies, and their ilk, men who lay
dead in muddy battlefields in far-flung locales like Tupelo,
Peachtree Creek, Chickamauga, Spotsylvania, Chattanooga,
and Smithfield Crossing. In these farmers' minds it may as
well have been California or Mexico. The man held a long
unrolled parchment in front of his face as he listed them off:
Osborne. Macpherson. Woods. Thorngood. O'Reilly. Keller.
Langston. Murray. Aimé hung back.

They were all Johns, or so it seemed: every one of these
dead men shared a single Christian name. Another man
stepped forward and said that today, until the end of the
afternoon, the families concerned by this announcement
were called to come forward and claim the relevant documents. They would be in town one week, he said, till New
Year's Eve, and intended to set off with at least thirty volunteers. The time for shilly-shallying and excuses was behind
them. The good American women would look after the children and the harvest. They were prepared to do their part.
They fully expected to leave with no fewer than thirty brave
volunteers, and not only farm boys: this War was the concern of one and all, from hired drudge to rich man's son. The
time for pretexts and excuses was past; the time for Bravery
was upon them. There would be new uniforms. If men failed
to step forward of their own free will they would have no

choice but to enforce the Enrollment Act passed by Congress last March. There was nothing to be gained from hiding.

As he spoke these words an immaculate Union Flag fluttered, planted in the ground by the strong hands of the federal war machine, its fabric interwoven with golden threads.

PERHAPS BECAUSE THEY looked alike, which in the eyes of many created a strange and unavoidable doubling effect, and though they shared few interests or acquaintances, Aimé and William developed a natural understanding and quickly grew close. The moment they crossed paths in the hotel lobby was one of mutual recognition. William was embarking on a legal career. He was a creature of logic and reason, a young man who knew Latin and loved physics and whose protracted education had taught him to formulate simple solutions to complex problems. Aimé, on the other hand, had long felt he had nothing to lose. He'd landed here after fleeing Saint-Henri, but Newport was no destination, just a place where a man such as himself (there weren't many) might find a new path. They ran into each other in the morning, when William came to say hello to his father and inquire about an urgent matter, a formality to do with army recruiters. He spoke nervously and jumped when he heard another man approach. After a moment of uncomfortable silence, with Aimé stopped on the landing, staring straight at William's bushy sideburns and full lips and sallow skin that bore traces of a childhood fever, Frederick introduced them. They looked alike in a way that wasn't quite alarming but still turned heads most of the time, if you saw them

huddled in close for a chat on Main Street, or through a carriage door, or in the shadow of an alley. They were up to
something, those two, in front of the Van Ness Hotel or out
by the lake, walking along the docks, the biting December
winds ruffling their long coats. William held his hat in his
left hand. Aimé spoke with a light French-Canadian accent,
it was barely perceptible when he spoke quickly, you might
mistake it for a stutter. His mastery of English was beyond
reproach. It was as if he enjoyed pretending not to speak
perfect English. He knew a lot about birds and spoke affectionately about Audubon and his drawings, as if he were a
personal acquaintance.

Within weeks they had become what you could call
friends, why not, though neither knew the first thing about
the other. Aimé told William he'd left Montreal strictly for
adventure, despite or maybe because of the war down south,
adventure being clearly something that started here, he said,
pointing an index finger at the ground, walking assuredly,
tracing a line toward the mountains and the South with his
hand. William didn't ask questions, he was looking for a way
out, putting out feelers. Aimé was looking for adventure?
Had he considered a military career? He seemed to have no
responsibilities, no family, no mouths to feed. Was he in need
of money? Was he aware of the great opportunities offered
by the army? He may not be a U.S. citizen, it may not be his
war, his cause, but they had slaves in Canada as well, didn't
they? Were there slaves in Canada? Of course, it wasn't his
war, but didn't war itself have an irresistible grandeur, when
you stopped to think about it? A noble tradition? He wasn't
the first to say so.

William sketched out his idea, frequently repeating that he was a man of means, generous with his friends, a man who knew how to show appreciation. He was working up to a proposition that was already fully formed in his mind, arrangements that might be struck between two men whose interests diverged but who could clearly find common ground, men who had, after all, found each other in a town full of strangers. William looked over his shoulder frequently and held his hat when strong winds rose up off Lake Memphremagog, from over the border, and his friend who had arrived in town less than a month ago turned his back to the squall rising on the horizon which would mark the arrival of the new year, 1865. When they looked off into the distance it was clear. The clouds were moving quickly, the clouds didn't lie. Old dry snow cracked under their footsteps.

At twenty-five William was recently engaged to Margaret Tarrant. Her father was Cornelius Tarrant, the tycoon from Montpelier, Vermont who had built the Vermont–New Hampshire railway and linked it to the rest of New England. William was only twenty-five, had his whole life ahead of him, if only this vile war would finally end, and this vile conscription law be repealed. He tried to look more outraged than scared at the prospect of dying in combat, or coming back a cripple. He'd seen men, mere youths, return from battle missing legs, missing arms, with no pension or means of support for themselves or their families and no hope for the future. He'd seen kids come back so wrecked no one would talk to them out of the fear of catching what they had.

When Aimé offered to take his place he looked genuinely surprised but accepted immediately. One evening in the hotel, in the private parlour where the lights were low and warm and the leather armchairs smelled like fire and ash, Aimé floated the idea as if it were his own, as if he'd been thinking it over a long while, weighing the pros and cons. They looked so alike, it seemed almost meant to be. It wasn't a favour, exactly, nor was it explicitly illegal. All that remained was to set a price. Aimé wasn't asking much, just enough to be sure he would never want for sustenance, new boots when he needed them, a pair of not-too-thread-bare breeches. He didn't want to be reduced to stripping corpses to survive. It was fairly simple, when you got right down to it. William merely had to hole up for a few weeks, long enough for the dust kicked up by the horseshoes to settle and the snow to melt, and then it would be back to business as usual. There were rumours of cases like theirs, in other counties. William's father and future father-in-law were of a like mind, they approved in principle. Neither was a Republican in his soul, though both had come out in support of the war effort, time and again. Van Ness had never hidden his misgivings about the outcome of Lincoln's campaign. He thought it too great a wager for any man, let alone one with a dangerous penchant for populist propa-ganda; it was Lincoln's fault this war would never end, nei-ther side would ever win, the country would lose a whole generation of young men, and why, he said in private, for whom? For these fundamentally inferior beings who may not deserve to live in chains, but certainly didn't warrant the sacrifice of a son? Tarrant, for his part, had always voted Democrat, and had supported the pacifist faction in the elec-tion, though the bitter internecine squabbling ultimately cost them victory. He was an ardent pacifist who always said that if only Lincoln had sat down with Davis over a bottle of whiskey and a couple good cigars, this whole mess could have been avoided. So when Aimé suggested he take William's place, when he said he would report to the recruiting station the very next morning, the two honourable men concluded the arrangement without hesitation. They got the question of money out of the way quickly, struck a bargain that was profitable for all concerned. Aimé was told he would never be forgotten. Margaret, who was sleeping on the top floor, was informed.

Aimé had nothing to lose. His life had drawn on so long he no longer remembered the meaning of childhood, ignorance, or fear, not even fear of dying on a battlefield far from home, though he'd once known feelings of this kind. He was in the process of forgetting and had, probably for that very reason, stopped fighting the possibility of placing himself in harm's way and facing the death that seemed perfectly indifferent to his existence. In every previous brush with death he'd managed to slip by unseen. He didn't know what to think anymore. Sometimes he understood his immortality almost literally; he'd look at himself in the mirror and the word would rise to his lips but get stuck in his throat. He might entertain the thought but refused to countenance it, figured it was an impossible, absurd exaggeration. Surely he would die one day, like everyone else. It made him laugh that, after so much time had gone by, and now that time seemed to have almost stopped, with no apparent hold over him, he should want something so commonplace.

So it is under the name William Van Ness — infantry

sergeant, standard-bearer, drummer, cavalry soldier, or humble private – that Aimé makes occasional appearances in the scattered, unreliable registers of the American Civil War, where he fought first in Virginia and then in Georgia, and where a few months later he took part in certain illicit actions led by little-known militias in Alabama and Tennessee, long after the surrender of the Confederate States and the dismantling of General Lee's army. No death registry bears his name.

CHAPTER SIX

FEBRUARY 1760
QUEBEC, QC

UNDER CONDITIONS DIFFICULT for us to describe or imagine, here in the comfort of our armchairs, it was undoubtedly in fear and in suffering that Aimé came into the world, on a bed of hay or in a pool of dung water, under the protection and yoke of an occupying army, behind a door that creaked and didn't close properly, a Union Jack snapping in every gust of wind atop the highest tower of the fort.

The world he came into was one where soldiers marched right into people's homes to ferret out militiamen hidden under beds and in wardrobes, insurgents already being called traitors as if the order they were rebelling against were immutable. They burst into houses and warned the occupants in both tongues, addressed those in hiding first in French and then in English. They wore heavy uniforms of red and white felt that weighed down their shoulders, and carried beautifully crafted rifles of English manufacture, straight from George II's private magazines, where the British arsenal lay alongside gold and jewels. These weapons never caught fire or blew up in the soldiers' faces, unlike the volatile old gunpowder used by the *habitants*. On Chemin Sainte-Foy, the King's Road that ran north from the city, far from the fortifications, just before the cliff overlooking the countryside and farms, sounds of the latest skirmishes could be heard coming from the remaining pockets of resistance. The city was abustle with vice and British soldiery, the streets overtaken by puddles of melted snow on warm days, petrified by piercing cold on others. The locals hid from the redcoats with their ruddy faces and perfect elocution and frostbitten lips.

People had gotten so thin you could scarcely tell the men from the women. That was nothing next to what they'd look like a few months later. Spring came; the promised staples didn't. Fall would bring no bounty that year. There were no arms for the harvest anyway.

The woman who gave birth to Aimé, late on the night of February 29, was as thin as the others. No one had noticed she was pregnant, and neither had she. Her nausea was slight, but then she hadn't known a day without nausea since her tenth birthday. Acid from daily vomiting had stained her teeth. She wore brown, beige, and off-white rags like a dirty, sickly second skin, torn in the most sensitive areas. Her gaze was furtive as a hummingbird's wings.

The cramps began on her way to army camp, to visit an officer who'd insisted on seeing her one last time before being posted back to Montreal. As she walked down the street, alone in the dark, she suddenly found herself doubled over, you could hear her cries echoing in the seeping stone hallways of the Hôtel-Dieu, where hundreds of cripples from both camps lay, months after the battle, bodies riddled with metal shards, legs sawed off to halt infection.

Mother Juchereau de Saint-Ambroise, who had set out with a fur coat on her shoulders and an oil lamp that she held away from her body, found her lying in the snow where she had fainted, moaning and panting through her spells of consciousness. She was young, as was the nun who turned around and called for help. Other lights appeared. Between the woman's legs, covered with coagulating blood, you could see a baby's head. They laid a wool blanket on the ground and tried to produce as much heat as they could. Some of the sisters weren't yet fourteen.

Seeing that the woman was already stiff, but the baby was breathing and crying heartily, they carried mother and son into the hospital through different doors. The nuns took her to join the bodies of those who had frozen to death that day or that week. The cold was glacial and it would be months before anyone managed to dig a hole. Her body was placed next to a young man who, even with a missing eye, seemed to watch her with interest. He lay on his side, one arm hanging into the void, as if intent on cuddling up and enjoying what little warmth remained in her flesh. Mother Juchereau gave her a cursory wash, then discarded the rags. Meanwhile they took the tiny, blood-covered Aimé to another room one floor above to be baptized immediately. There was no guarantee he would live through the night.

She was never identified. No one asked after the corpse, or came forward to claim the child. They never knew who she was or who had impregnated her, but there were signs of violence on her face, swollen patches that weren't caused by cold or fever. The sides of her nose and eyebrows were scarred with burn marks and she'd been bitten repeatedly, on the left forearm, by a dog or wolf.

THE SISTERS OF the congregation had Aimé baptized, someone with authority chose a name to their liking, and at dawn, safe in a Moses basket, he was taken to a room deep in the west wing of the seminary where Father Clovis ran an orphanage of sorts.

On the road, in the indefatigable arms of a young Augustinian sister, he passed uniformed soldiers with barrel and snare drums, drilling for one more parade in front of an officer and the King's Colours planted in the frozen ground. They were preparing to attack on the position at Saint-Augustin with the few hundred healthy men remaining. Discussions drew on as they awaited the British Navy vessels whose arrival would confirm their victory and rightful dominion over this land. There was always a good crowd on the ramparts, eyes trained on the horizon, waiting to relay the joyous news.

Fewer *habitants* were dying of scurvy, and the officers reminded the troops to treat the locals well. Without the people's support they were as good as dead. Stop kicking in doors. Stop insulting the women. Hands off private stores. Fingers were too frozen to point, but the impulse to warm them over a flame was in fact the worst possible idea; instead you had to act against your better instincts, rub hands in the cold snow and patiently wait for the heat to return to the knuckles. Regiments had been sent out four miles west with makeshift carts in search of wood.

In the room at the end of the hall, nursemaids were busy with the newborns. No one wanted to see them die before they'd had a chance to live. In exchange for a few hunks of bread and fresh water to take home, the women lined up to help Father Clovis with his good works. The authorities didn't have to know. A seamless understanding obtained between women and priest. They came to help out and kept it quiet, even the babies, good children all, the fallen sons and daughters of *habitants* or the poorly armed French forced to retreat to Montreal. Since September's end they had gathered thirty babies and mourned the thirty mothers who'd frozen to death or succumbed to malnutrition or died for no better reason than failure to recognize the symptoms of pregnancy. Some had been abandoned, by people who may not have meant badly.

Of all these babies only Aimé survived the winter. When the warmth returned, as if brought back by the British ships, to the garrison's shouts of joy, he had gained a lot of weight. He was sure on his feet and chattered away in three or four unknown languages. He had the look of a child who would age prematurely, grow up fast, and die young out of sheer impatience to get out into the world.

CHAPTER SEVEN

AUGUST 1863
MONTREAL, QC

THE FIRST TIME Aimé saw Jeanne Beaudry she was getting off a two-horse streetcar on Saint-Laurent. He was leaning, with an apple in his hand, against a rotten wooden post outside a shop. The heat was choking the city. Buildings trembled in the mirages of freshly paved streets, and the blue sky stretched out like an opaque dome over the thoroughfare. Everyone was yelling, yet their surprisingly heavy voices petered out after a few yards.

Aimé had stolen fruit stashed in his satchel and wore a loosely knotted scarf. His shoulder leaned against the post, gently testing its strength, and he liked the feel and sound of the creaking wood over and above the tumult of hollers and cries. There were raised voices all around but none addressed him. Passersby pushed and cursed with a zeal that quickened the pace of human interaction. Along the boulevard, people came and went and carts zigzagged in every direction, missing pedestrians by a hair.

On a stand beside Aimé, huge keen-eyed fish were laid out on crushed ice. The fishmonger called out prices and made propositions, paying Aimé no mind as he crunched his apple while, across the street, she alighted from the tram and stepped delicately onto the road's dirty shoulder. In her wake came a gaggle of children, some very young and some not far from her in age. Aimé numbered them at five, not counting her; she was already in a class of her own.

She placed first one foot on the ground, and then the other, with a firm grip on the metal bar of the tram, which had stopped on the corner of Sainte-Catherine. The colourful troupe of kids encircled her, holding hands. She adjusted her hat, crossed the street to the store, and walked in without looking Aimé in the eye, where she might have discerned something of importance, something they could share for a fraction of a second and cherish to the end of their days. Caught in the middle of this din, Aimé dropped his apple and hurried over to the front window to observe her reflection.

Even from behind, and in spite of her modest dress, she was resplendent in the dusty store. Aimé had never seen anything so beautiful. Her brown dress reached the floor, hiding the elegant shoes with visible stitching he'd glimpsed earlier. He even saw a sliver of petticoat when she approached the counter, and one of the kids, a small girl, leaned over to fix a fold. Aimé figured it must be her sister, and the four boys her brothers. From what little he had seen of her face, mostly in profile as she walked toward him, he believed they were related. The oldest, who seemed almost her same age, looked impatient. He hung back. Maybe deep down he longed to take the reins of this family outing, address the merchants as the family patriarch. But Aimé could tell she was the eldest and in charge of the group. After giving the shopkeeper her order, without a backward glance, she placed a gloved, authoritative hand on the wrist of her brother, whose breathing slowed as he stared at the ground..

At a glance Aimé guessed sixteen. He wasn't wrong: she was born in 1846, the first in a family whose children would number ten when the last one came into the world. The little girl turned around and almost caught Aimé spying on them, but he hid behind a protruding wall. Aimé dried his moist hands on his pants and wondered what her name could be. From there, he would have guessed Marie or Angéline. He pictured names in a baptistery, pretty as slowly polished pearls or expertly blown glass beads. The excitement in the street was palpable, and it was rubbing off on him, he could feel it in his chest and down into his boots. He walked at a steady, natural pace past the window and glanced inside, as if it were nothing, as if he were ambling down the Main from store to store, on his way to buy (or steal) a round of pastrami from the Jew at the bottom of the hill. For a second, after stopping on the other side, he wondered whether he shouldn't simply have followed her in, waited for her to finish, and then placed an order of his own, for anything or nothing, just to hear the sound of her voice, listen to her tell her brother off and maybe see her turn around to face him when the doorbell rang. She would turn and, at the exact same moment, they would both understand one and the same thing. And for the rest of their lives they would tell themselves the story of this moment, though when she died he would still look like a man in his prime, only just beginning to age and to stoop. He'd long been aware of his unnaturally slow metabolism. No one had ever explained it to him, and he never talked about it, not even to himself, not much at any rate, though it defined and explained his incongruous presence wherever he went. It was as much a part of him as everything else, his tastes and his memory, his frustrations and his transitory anger. He was a nice man, an agreeable man, people liked him. He had had an incredibly long time to develop his charm. His last job had been loading barrels and crates onto Europe-bound ships. He stole gleefully and without compunction. No prison had found a way to keep him more than a day or two; no one ever remembered him once he was gone.

Aimé observed the inside of the store, the shopkeeper behind the counter with a large slab of salt pork and other provisions in a basket, and for the first time in his life thought of heading to Europe himself. With her, why not? He had no particular interest in crossing the ocean, there was so much to discover on this continent, to the north and south, but if she were to ask he wouldn't think twice.

In his head he was busy hatching a plan to lay hands on tickets to England or France, on a sumptuous liner with dazzling chandeliers hanging from the ceiling, cut with precious gemstones, when out she came with the children in tow. The smallest, who had turned around, looked Aimé in the eye and he smiled at her, gratefully, as if she were already his accomplice, as if their exchange of glances contained the love story of Aimé and this beautiful young woman, ripe for the picking, ready to begin.

HE LEARNED HER name a few seconds later when the five children cried out as one, at the top of their lungs, to save her life: *"Jeanne!"* A split second longer and the four-horse milk wagon would have run her over. Aimé was mentally rehearsing how he might fleece the Royal Steamships' purser when he felt a visceral reflex to run toward her. He raised his arm and only stayed it at the last minute. The temperature somehow rose a few degrees; sweat ran down frightened faces. The driver didn't stop or even slow down. The clatter of sixteen horseshoes was lost in the ambient hubbub, and each child picked an item from their order off the ground. The youngest, barely old enough to walk, took the loaf of bread and gave it a quick wipe with spittle-wet hands. Jeanne's pulse slowed. Her brow was still furrowed, anxious and stupefied, but her heart rate dropped at the same time as Aimé's, and they agreed on a shared rhythm.

A hundred yards south of the store, the small troupe took its place to wait for the tram. It soon appeared, full as ever, announcing its arrival with the ringing of a bell. The kids cleared a path through the crowd, still holding hands, while Jeanne carried the basket. Aimé followed them, unnoticed by the busybodies and the merchants, who went right on touting the freshness of their produce. In a single fluid motion he climbed onto the back of the tram and grasped the metal pole. Half his body was left hanging over the emptiness, his leg suspended in the air.

Aimé was wearing patchwork trousers with suspenders criss-crossed behind his back and a puffy shirt that had once been white. The artificial breeze from the tram's motion wafted in through his open collar, whipping his scarf. Other men wore jackets and hats they would be loath to remove for anything in the world, even on a day as hot as this. They sat sweating it out with dignity, pressed up against each other, shoulders curled in, and several stood to offer Jeanne and her sister their seats. To the south you could begin to see the river poking through, glints of sun on the mirror-like surface of the water. The street sloped steeply, the tram gathered speed. As they approached the port, the soundscape changed. A powerful smell of flour and molasses colonized the air, along with a huge cloud of grey smoke that immediately turned to vapour.

At Rue Notre-Dame they got off the tram and waited for a westbound car. Jeanne and the others watched the crowds bound for Champ-de-Mars. Women and men travelled together in small, chatty groups. Some were using parasols they'd brought along. It made the kids laugh, from a distance, especially the youngest. You could also use umbrellas to make shade, Jeanne explained. You could bring your own shade, in a sense, it kept things cooler, and they came to see her point, it was a good idea, they supposed. The smallest one smiled at Aimé, she had a sparkle in her eyes, as if this repurposing of a familiar object made her so happy she could burst. Her big sister held her hand as she squirmed and smiled, full of wonder. Aimé was hidden but longed to go see them and pay for their trip, no big deal, no reason to make them uncomfortable. He wanted to go with them.

With Jeanne, really, but he could live with the others as chap-
erones. He was still far away from them, in position at the
back of the scene, but he was good with distances, knew the
tram would pull up soon, like a second chance.

Without hesitation he walked a few yards over past them
and hailed the conductor with an upraised hand, a hand
raised up so high you couldn't miss it. With his other hand
he placed his fingers on his tongue, pressed his lips together,
and whistled. The horses stopped right in front of them,
showing discipline, and the conductor winked, in on the
story taking shape here, and turned to them with a polite
bow, inviting them to board, and Aimé knew Jeanne was
finally looking at him. It only lasted a moment, he felt her
eyes on him, on his scalp, on his blushing cheeks, lending
him ballast and sudden purpose, but also asking him to do
no more for the time being, to take care not to wreck this.

Standing face to face like that they seemed to be the same
age, and to have shared the same experiences in the same
places: two young people coming of age in a big city, slowly
growing into independence, casting aside old-fashioned
conventions to find ways to live more happily than their
forbears. Jeanne's tight braids bespoke a sense of discipline
and respectable upbringing, but that didn't stop Aimé from
seeing in them a suggestion of curves and winding roads,
the ones that lead to fortuitous events. He hadn't paid their
fares, had understood that it was time to fade into the background again, but he had paid his own, for the first time
ever, five cents. He took a seat at the rear, already forgotten, already invisible. For the entire ride, as banks gave way
to factories and then to farmers' fields, he continued the

work of inventing this young woman in his imagination, of making this meeting the beginning of the story they would share. In a few weeks, once they'd formally met, he would find that his intuitions had been accurate: it *was* as if they already knew each other. Everything made sense. In a few weeks, once they had started spending time together, meeting up in secret places chosen by her or by him and written on little scraps of paper clandestinely exchanged, he would learn all he needed to know to love her. Her way of pointing her finger at sounds, as if they consisted in a specific place, just beside them, right next to their ears. Her fears about her and her family's immediate future. The sometimes-morbid anger of her younger brother, who constantly undermined her authority, and who she feared might finally decide to wrest control of the family and ship her off to a convent. Her way of shielding the oil lamp's flame, even once they were in the barn, where no wind could penetrate the walls, to make sure no spark leaped out and set fire to the hay bales where Aimé lay waiting. How she managed to forget her troubles, for a while, in his arms.

He could see it already: it was going to happen a certain way, and he would never cease to be amazed at how prescient his fantasies would prove to be. Here on the tram he was experiencing it as he dreamed it, and later he would dream it as he experienced it. In his head, immersed in their love, they were silent; Jeanne didn't say a thing, neither did he, the hours slipped gently by as, all around, the world violently churned or languorously crumbled.

He was too excited. He closed his eyes, had to take a moment; for the first time in his long and often boring and at times eccentric existence, it felt good to remember that he was in no hurry.

The tram stopped. People got off. Aimé leaned back in his seat. Jeanne wasn't thinking about him, not yet. For the hundredth time she stopped to do a head count of her brothers and sisters, making sure she hadn't lost one. The conductor yelled, a whip cracked, and the horses clopped off toward the Village des Tanneries.

CHAPTER EIGHT

JULY 1893
PHILADELPHIA, PA

AIMÉ HAD REPLIED by pneumatic post to a discreet ad in the back of the *Ledger* and he found himself at the door of a second-floor studio in the heart of Southwark, with his collection of still-vivid memories in the garish colours of anachronistic paintings. At the building's entrance an open-mouthed, wild-eyed child sat starving on the steps. He didn't ask for anything, seemed to be waiting for someone to show up and cart him off to greener pastures where he would meet exotic animals and savour a bouquet of spices. Aimé didn't take in every detail, as we did, just brushed by without paying the young urchin any mind. He'd seen others who had it worse, especially in the border towns and mountains west of Piedmont, kids with soot from the mines' dynamite smudged all over their faces, chiselling out wrinkles and clogging their airways. He'd seen a nine-year-old hack up his lungs and then hawk a black loogie while looking him square in the eye: What, got something to say about it? This kid on the stairs had a clean face and trembling hands. A little brown dog slumbered at his side, but its ears pricked up at the slightest sound and the boy's every sniffle.

He didn't ask the boy his name or age, didn't toss him a coin, just climbed the front stairs two at a time, holding his coattails. You could see the chain of a watch fob and a certain refinement in his every move and the cut of his suit, even as he rushed, even in this heat. There was something contagious in the rectitude of his bearing. His presence seemed to somehow make the dark orange brick of the walls lie straighter. Through a suite of windows you could glimpse the life inside, hear the laughter, see the clothes and bed sheets hanging on lines above the street.

Just before his meeting Aimé had visited Independence Hall. For decades he'd felt like an American, and there he worked his way through the crowd of pilgrims, upstanding citizens, and young pickpockets to the glass case displaying an original copy of the Constitution of the United States of America. He gathered his thoughts, which he kept to himself; he scrutinized each signature, the ink that had seeped into the warp and woof of the old parchment. It was his first time in Philadelphia. He had an appointment with a reporter, a poet who had come from New York to do research in the City of Brotherly Love.

CALLING ALL VETERANS – WANTED: True information
and eye-witness accounts of fighting in Tennessee,
West Virginia, and Georgia; Grant, Hancock, and
Hooker campaigns; 1863–1865. Preference to privates,
infantrymen, lieutenants, and standard-bearers. First-
hand combat experience a must. For the purpose of
a written narrative in the form of a True Historical
Account. NOT A NOVEL. Homage to nobility and bravery of the men who fought. Friendly encounter; con-
fidentiality guaranteed. All persons answering above
criteria contact STEPHEN J. CRANE c/o the *Public Ledger*,
6 Chestnut Street.

He was almost thirty-four, with only a few patches of
grey, a prominent jawbone, and a strongly arched brow.
The young man who opened the door was sceptical. Aimé
smiled into the peephole and spoke politely.

"I know what you're thinking, but I just look young. I'm
actually much older than you think."

The other man visibly continued to doubt him. There
was just no way this man could have fought in the Civil War.
He'd expected dozens of replies, especially in Philadelphia
where, if a spate of recent articles were to be believed, veterans had retired in great numbers. Only one man had
come forward. Here he stood, a dandy, scarcely older than
himself. A slender, carefully trimmed moustache. No visible signs of age, save perhaps a certain depth in the pupils,
and what exactly did that mean anyway? The door was
half open, half closed; he wasn't sure he wanted to let this
man into his apartment, didn't feel like wasting his time

on some crackpot. Two weeks earlier, getting off the train, he'd been accosted on the platform by a bearded man with a wooden leg who'd held him captive by the sleeve while he went on a rant. The government was denying him his pension, the government had never recognized his service. He was considering taking revenge, taking control. But when the young man asked whether he'd fought on the Union or Confederate side the old man looked offended and puffed up his chest. Don't you recognize me? I'm Stonewall Jackson. Thomas Jonathan Stonewall Jackson, they shot at me at Chancellorsville, the sons of bitches. That man had slipped off without taking leave. Crane was in no mood for more of that rigmarole today.

"How old did you say you were?"

"Forty-seven."

"You're forty-seven? And how old were you when you enrolled?"

"Sixteen. May I come in?"

"And your name is William Van Ness, correct?"

"That's right. I know what you're thinking, it's not what you think. Don't worry. I'm, well, you might say I'm well preserved. I've been lucky."

"It's just that —"

"I'm not here to waste your time. If you want to know about the war, I'm your man. I was there. I saw it all. I pretty much saw it all."

The young man inside the doorway was scarcely twenty, you could see it by the colour of his cheeks and his fair hair as fine as cornsilk in the mid-July sun. A few hairs floated in the air, which was alive with static electricity. He wore a moustache which he liked to stroke, it was an affectation and a nervous habit. Aimé remained friendly, stood straight as the walls around him in the grim hallway, waiting for Stephen J. Crane to formally invite him inside. Crane was sizing him up, trying to square this fellow's incongruous appearance with the claim that he had seen it all. Giving in to curiosity, he backed into the room and opened the door wide, beckoning Aimé inside.

Mr. Van Ness was welcome. Have a seat, just a moment, Crane would be back in a second. He had bourbon, would fetch glasses, there was cocaine powder on the table if Van Ness wanted. Don't worry about the state of the apartment, Crane was borrowing it, from a good friend, for the length of his sojourn. He lived in New York but had grown up on the other side of the Hudson, in Newark and Hoboken. Crane liked Philadelphia, liked that the idea he had formed of Philadelphia matched the reality of Philadelphia, if Van Ness took his meaning. His talk was casual like that. He went to get the glasses.

The leather couch Aimé sat on clashed with the rest of the furniture and the walls. Canvases were everywhere, hanging or strewn over the floor alongside battered, paint-stained easels. Crane made some noise in the cupboards, in the kitchen, a puny room at the back of the studio, and when he came back all trace of unease had vanished, his face told only of his eagerness and excitement to finally speak to a man who had seen, up close, what he was preparing to put into words: the thrill of combat, imminent danger, the whistle of flying bullets and the deafening report of cannon, inspiring hope of victory while wreaking havoc with ear drums. He undid the buttons of his navy blue blazer and sat down on the sofa across from Aimé, crossed his legs, took a deep breath, then uncrossed them to lean in toward the bottle. He poured liquor into the glasses and handed one to Aimé, who kept his hands in the air, ready to toast. Crane served himself and clinked Aimé's glass with his own. Each man smiled and stroked his respective moustache, sculpting it to an upturned tip. Crane reclined comfortably deep in the sofa and crossed his legs. He shot Aimé an ironic look.

"You're old for your age."

Aimé didn't say anything to that, but started to open his mouth. Crane continued:

"Or maybe the opposite. It's hard to say."

"I know. It's hard to believe. I've always been healthy. But I feel old at the same time, it's weird. Sometimes, in my head, I feel two hundred years old, know what I mean? I *feel* old, when I think about it, but my body can still do whatever I ask it to: my legs never get tired, my arms move smoothly, there's no particular pain in my muscles."

"They say war makes men age faster. Yet here you are. What do you figure happened?"

Crane took a sip. When you stopped to think about it, took a closer look at the interest he seemed to attract wherever he went and whatever he did, he also seemed to be, deep down, a stranger to his age. His was the attitude of a much older man, who'd lived a thousand lives before making a brief stopover in this one. He moved and talked with a wisdom that was hard to place, a mental acuity quite distinct from mere vigour.

"It's as if nature had overlooked you."

"Too kind."

Aimé took a sip of bourbon. It was bad. Evidence of economic depression was all around. Only the rich could afford good whiskey now. Aimé had laid aside a stash over the years, bottles of Dickel and Old Bushmills. He held the liquid in his mouth for a long time, rolled it around on his tongue and the roof of his mouth as if it were a venerable Irish. It tasted like backwoods Kansas rotgut.

"I'm not sure it's a compliment. I mean, it's as if you'd been abandoned, forsaken by nature, left to your own devices."

"That's the impression I give you?"

"As if it were up to you to decide what happens, if you take my meaning."

"Yes."

"As if it were up to you alone. A heavy weight for any man."

He came forward one more time, to open the little metal box on the table. Inside was a small mound of very fine white powder.

"Or not. I don't know. Maybe you'll grow old in the blink of an eye, then drop dead, like a man flattened by an explosion. A bolt of lightning, the blow of a hammer. Who knows? A falling piano. A black cat."

"For now, everything seems normal. It's a matter of appearances, when you get down to it. Consider it a matter of appearances. As everyone knows, they aren't to be trusted."

Crane took a snort off a little iron key he dipped in the powder, and offered the box to Aimé, who picked it up carefully. Crane shot him a look signalling that he was welcome to it, all he had to do was help himself. The tiny key was shedding powder. He inhaled vigorously, then pinched the side of his nose. At his house, somewhere in Oregon or maybe New Mexico, in a sealed, humidity-controlled cellar, that's where they were, the bottles of whiskey he'd been saving for a long time. As dust gathered, the flavours were growing in complexity. He was saving them for a special occasion.

A ray of light came through the window, slicing the room in two. Between noon and one, if the weather was fine, the sun shone down on the buildings nestled against each other up and down the street, you had to enjoy it while it lasted. When the ray came into sight, Crane stood up and went over to the large curtain. Then he walked back and sat down, and they started in on serious matters. Aimé had expected him to take notes, scribble on a pad as he talked. But he didn't. Crane listened, occasionally smiling with pleasure at a detail, reshaping his moustache with his fingertips. When Aimé began to veer off he would nudge him back on track with specific questions about, say, the types of weapons he'd used, or the number of cannon at Morrisville in April '65, one of the final battles of the long war, one of the very last co-ordinated cavalry movements.

When Aimé turned to more personal matters the story grew more interesting. Crane's expression changed. Gone was the ironic smile. He wasn't quite sitting on his artist friend's sofa anymore, you couldn't really call what he was doing "sitting" anymore. He was listening to Aimé, and the people in the paintings strewn around the studio without apparent rhyme or reason seemed to do the same.

AIMÉ DESCRIBED HOW the sun poking through the long grey rainclouds had made him feel like it was all over and everyone would head home, marked forever but still alive, and this had given him a misguided idea that the horror was coming to an end. It had happened many times, more than he could count. But it was inevitable, he couldn't stop believing it. He explained how he'd thought of his mother, the mother he'd never known but liked to imagine, bidding him goodbye as he cried silently, saying farewell by the fence they would have built to keep the hens safe from foxes and coyotes. He didn't think about his wife, or the woman he'd been in love with, or the fleeting paramours he'd left behind, but about a mother who might have let him head off for the war, alone with his illusions of heroism and courage, shedding silent tears from stoic eyes.

He liked to imagine this mother of his, see her again in his mind when the enemy artillery fire fell on his position and the whole area for miles around. That way, he carried his mother with him, her image imprinted on his mind, and thought of her, in the midst of the cannon and gunfire, surrounded by men spitting and coughing in fits and the shouts of an officer whose dismount was cut short by a bullet to the face. It landed on a mouth that, right before being blown off his face, had given an order, arm gesturing toward the heart of the battle, where they must head to truly join the fighting. No matter what they may have thought, despite the unarguable violence of the explosions and the broken pieces of bark and stone flying in every direction, they weren't there yet. They were far from the battlefield. The officers never stopped barking orders, ordering them to get moving, individually and collectively, like a giant rearing up to crush the enemy.

One thing Crane had to wrap his head around was that there was no way to describe a battle from a single point of view, unless it was that of an eagle, or a general examining a map, or a historian after the fact. Aimé liked to tell how, once battle was underway, it took on its own living shape, had its own life, its own ecology and geology and breathing pattern, panting followed by shortness of breath and then moments of otherworldly repose. Whichever way a soldier looked there was always an outcropping of violence around the edges, often miles from the supposed epicentre of the battle where the fate of the war and the country were to be decided.

Aimé talked about how, to feel the power of combat, it was vital to understand its counterweight, the crushing boredom that was the lot of the soldier and his entire regiment, boredom dragging on so long you could almost believe victory or defeat might be achieved without you and your contribution. Out of this boredom grew the potential for heroism, mirages, hallucinations in the cold night, agitated dreams that transformed even the most humble of men into conquering emperors. Nothing would happen for so long that, when something actually began to occur, it was unreal, almost inconceivable. The regiment marched, and marched, and marched some more, over whole states, it seemed, across entire mountain ranges, only to arrive, after weeks and weeks, in a nameless clearing where everything was blowing up, where the entire universe was strangely concentrated in the colours and the sounds and the visceral fear that took hold in such cacophony that nothing made sense anymore. A few leagues from the clearing there would be an abandoned farm, its frame a collection of cracks, its roof on the brink of collapse. It was built of salvaged lumber, so they must have been far indeed from Washington or Savannah or Richmond or wherever decisions were being made and troop movements co-ordinated.

Also, as he snorted more cocaine and agreed to another glass of bourbon, he explained to Crane, trying to make him understand without belabouring the point, that the true meaning of war, of any war, lay in the apparent contradiction between our cowardice and thirst for heroism. He described how he had run off in the opposite direction with no clear idea why. Aimé, who had volunteered, convinced in the ill-advised wisdom of youth that he wasn't afraid of anything, had run far from the field of battle, guided by the artillery fire that seemed to come from ever further away. He told Crane that was the precise moment he'd lost control of his body in general and his legs in particular. The battle was unfolding up the mountain and he had run down, down toward the clearing, toward a creek they'd crossed days earlier. He'd told himself he was looking for water for the others, that they would need water. He wasn't deserting, was merely thirsty, and the others must be too, the lieutenant was terribly thirsty, you could hear it in his voice when he yelled, a discernable lack of saliva, his mouth was so dry it made his voice husky and muffled, and spittle was whitening the corners of his mouth.

As he snorted he made it clear to Crane, looking him in the eyes, without trying to convince him, that it was perhaps this he should try to find the words for, in the book he was preparing to write: this involuntary movement of the legs that had made Aimé run, far from the gunfire and cannonballs, as far as his legs would carry him. Maybe Crane's words would help him explain, no, not exactly explain, that wasn't the right word, he had no idea what the right word was, but somehow put words to why he had run away, and what it meant in the life of a soldier and the overall economy of war; somehow explain the meanings assigned to war by various classes of men. Was Aimé the kind of man who ran away? Is that how you would describe him—him in particular—or was he rather a type of something much larger than himself? Crane bit his upper lip and ran his finger through his moustache, visibly holding back from asking a question. Aimé stopped talking and waited.

Had he been injured?

Yes, he'd been hit. A rifle butt to the head that nearly killed him, at the hands of a Union soldier. He'd asked where the battle was. When he finally decided to rejoin his regiment, after running around the edge of the fighting for hours, wild-eyed, tripping over dead men, he'd asked a group of soldiers who looked to be halfway through a successful desertion where the battle was, and one of the men had given him a shove, followed by a blow to the head with his rifle. Aimé was knocked unconscious and later, when he joined the others, he was treated by a military doctor convinced he'd been grazed by a bullet. The shape of the wound suggested a bullet scraping his skull as it whistled by. He didn't say a thing. He couldn't tell a full-fledged lie, nor could he tell the truth. They called him a hero.

Aimé leaned over and tilted his head to show his old scar
to Crane, who hadn't asked to see it. In the spot on his hair
where strands of grey were mixed in, Aimé made an opening with his hands, where a line of swollen skin formed a
zigzag. His gesture partook of understated, dignified pride,
as if he were defying Crane to locate the cowardice in this
scar, in this wound sustained in the heat of battle, in the
heart of personal and collective defeat.

They'd been drinking a while and the cocaine was taking
effect. Aimé constructed labyrinthine sentences in his rich
and often antiquated English. He described a sudden fear
that would take hold of his torso, his chest, his Eustachian
tubes, and was slipping into a quasi-scientific register whose
anatomical terms kept him from falling into over-the-top
lyricism. Increasingly, what he was saying grew less focused
and less clear, it spun in circles around different nodes of his
own private story. He talked a lot about the colours of the
landscape, the shades of grey, pink, and dark blue stretching
out on the horizon, which he admired but which had nothing do with what was going on in Five Forks, Fort Bragg, and
Selma, Alabama. Wherever the troops went they were surrounded by the same eternal, ancestral mountains, as if these
mountains would up and run when the skirmishes reached
a pitch of violence that presaged the imminent apocalypse.
You were waiting for the sun to go down, the mountainsides
to crumble, and the giant trunks of the great elms and oaks
to start cracking all around, breaking into pieces that would
rain down on the armies. Aimé wondered where these grim,
somehow pellucid impressions came from. Were they born
of fear, or courage? It all happened in your guts, between the

rising diaphragm and twisting colon. You couldn't name this sensation that made you run in one direction or the other, point your gun and shoot at the fuzzy grey shapes on the edge of your field of vision or run away into the safety of the forest and the calm, impassive mountain peaks, the Blue Ridge stretching as far as the eye could see and up into the clouds; run off and disappear into the Alleghenies.

A FEW HOURS later, when the empty bottle lay on its side on the table, knocked over by a wayward gesture of Crane's, Aimé said he had to go. Crane cracked his back and then his fingers, first toward and then away from himself. They got up at the same time and walked a relatively straight line to the door, which Crane opened for Aimé. They shook hands and Crane started thanking him. His temples throbbed visibly and he was concentrating, his attention focused completely on a spot between his guest's eyebrows. He said it again: You look so young, man.

Aimé smiled and chortled through his nose; a humourless, rational, empathetic laugh. He winked in agreement and freed his hand from Crane's grip. As he left the apartment he stumbled over the railing, and on his way down he could hear the young journalist explaining how to get back downtown. His voice faded in the hallway, then on the steps of the spiral staircase, in the building's distant reaches. The dirty air and absolute blackness enveloping Aimé dispersed once he emerged onto the front steps.

In this neighbourhood without streetlights, people walked around with oil lamps, their dancing flames hypnotic as pendulums. On his way down the steps separating him from the dirt road, Aimé heard a series of high-pitched yelps and lifted his head to walk toward the sound. At one of the building's windows, on the seventh floor or maybe the eighth, a man was bent over. He held a little brown dog he was tossing in the air, laughing. Behind him, mixed in with the animal's wheezing and barking, you could also hear a child's cries. The man turned around and yelled "Shut up!" into the apartment. In an elegant, true, unhesitating movement he hurled the dog into the void. It started spinning very quickly, suddenly silent. The little dog sailed through the space over Aimé's head, crashed into the wall of the building next door, and came to rest in the middle of the road, with a muffled thud absorbed by the dust and rocks kicked up into the dry air. The man turned away from the window, still laughing, and closed the blinds. Some of the lanterns were pointed toward the dog, others toward the window through which you could no longer hear crying or any other sound. A woman pulling sheets off the clothesline had a full smile of clothespins in her mouth. She seemed to be in shock, standing still and upright on the balcony. Aimé looked unsuccessfully for Crane in the interstices of the walls, between the blinding rays of the lanterns.

CHAPTER NINE

SEPTEMBER 1837
NEW ECHOTA, GA

THE WEAPONS CONFISCATED from the men and youths of
the Cherokee Nation were stockpiled in a house belonging
to Major Ridge, who hadn't been consulted. After a hasty
inventory they were left there, long guns on one side, pistols on the other, ready for the militia that would back the
army in the mass relocation ahead. This movement was for
the protection of all, Indian and settler, farmer and soldier.
No one, not even the shamans, doubted the march would
proceed in an orderly manner.

The guns lay waiting to be handed out in a house a few
miles south of New Echota, the capital of the Cherokee
Nation. Someone was standing guard, to protect them in
case of an Indian rising, but everyone knew they could
count on the co-operation of Major Ridge, whose signature
appeared on the recent treaty. Nobody was afraid of the
Indians. They'd kill each other off if any one among them

jeopardized the safety of the families. The week before, three men had spoken out against the Treaty of New Echota that set this westward march in motion. They were found dead, throats slit in the night by persons unknown.

Major Ridge had already moved his family onto land allotted to the Cherokee, oblivious of the plans being made in his name. At the end of the day, that wouldn't change a thing. He still believed in the good faith of all parties involved, was still writing letters urging the holdouts to join their ranks, across the mountains, where they would find a good land and large, a land of milk and honey where the weather was fine, the farming was easy, and the cattle and buffalo roamed free. Over there the Americans would at long last leave the Cherokee to live in peace. The United States would never stretch that far. There was simply no way. The Great Father, as they still called Jackson, had shown time and again that he was a man of his word. He'd promised the Cherokee would be free over there, across the Mississippi, out past the Arkansas River; this land they'd been granted in good faith by the Americans would never be taken from them, never overrun by the White Man. There was plenty of room for everyone, the landscape and the future stretched out in a straight line as far as the eye could see.

A lone armed guard had been posted in the Ridge house. He could summon the aid of the leader's thirty African slaves, should some fool or pair of fools take it upon themselves to revolt. The night was calm, the last cows had been slaughtered that afternoon to feed the convoy dispatched by West Point and expected any day. The Indians had been given over eight years to leave of their own free will. Now the army was preparing to remove them. Word was getting around. There was talk of a long forced march, in February or the month after. In New Echota, the meeting of the Cherokee General Council had grown heated, bitterness and rancour boiled over, clans formed but the dissension was ultimately quelled. One chief may have raised his voice and shouted over the others, but he'd apologized. In the end everyone had swallowed their anger and gone home. Appearances had to be kept up, to show the Americans the Cherokee could get along. Out here, on the massive farm abandoned by Ridge months earlier, not much was left: some animals, a few dozen guns. A handful of farmhand's shacks had been cobbled together in the fields. Their occupants ran stills and had built fences to keep the coyotes out; you could see their tiny lights, flickering in the night.

Three years earlier a prospector had unearthed a gold nugget, on the mountainside or in a riverbed. He brought it to town to be assayed and bought a round at the bar, and then another, and made it known that the time had come for the Redskins to clear out, the White Man was coming. There was gold in these Appalachian hills. Pans and shovels sold out the very next day.

IN ONE OF Albert's notebooks, between two lists of scribbled dates that correspond with the phases of the moon, but are at odds with each other, we learn that Aimé was probably the final link in a complex chain of operators that stretched from the south shore of the St. Lawrence River, somewhere around Saint-Jean, all the way down to Georgia and Alabama. More or less all he knew, and he knew scarcely more than we do, was that Aimé had been hired by one Arthur Pothier, M.D., Esq. He knew his job was to deliver the guns to a Jesuit somewhere outside Chattanooga; the rest was none of his concern. He'd never met Pothier, they'd been put in contact through secret missives, back when Aimé was living around Boston, looking for kicks. Intuition told him the weapons would help lay the ground for the imminent uprising in Lower Canada, but he'd never met a man willing to admit to membership in the company of the Sons of Freedom. We believe his name was known in certain circles. He was trustworthy, fearless, an experienced man who didn't ask questions. According to available sources, which will never be entirely adequate, Aimé was little more than a link, perhaps the last, or maybe the first, in a long chain of influence and contacts working to arm the rebels by any and all possible means. While Louis-Joseph Papineau was trying to convince president Van Buren to back the Patriotes if talks with the Crown soured, other networks were taking shape. Aimé's name was getting around. He was a young man you could count on, a man of honour, available for hire. He knew the States well, had travelled the length and breadth of the Appalachians, was acquainted with persons of interest, and it was said he wasn't scared of anything.

That at least is a version of Aimé's story, one of many that have come down to us. Take it with a grain of salt. The oral and written sources that diverge and converge in the records tell us he was there, hidden under a larch tree, waiting for the right moment to steal the Indians' confiscated guns and deliver them to a Jesuit whose name has not come down to us. The Jesuit transported them across the country and finally to the border, via the same underground byways used twenty years later by runaway slaves on their way to the abolitionist states up North. As far as we know no one ever asked where the guns came from, or revealed the answer to this unasked question, even under torture.

Emerging from his hiding spot under the tree, Aimé snuck onto the grounds, unnoticed, his path lit from behind by the flickering, milky moonlight. Surveillance was more or less non-existent. Clouds floated around in the sky, masking some stars before others and accentuating the curve of the horizon, as if the earth were round. Aimé quickly crossed the mowed grass, then took a dirt path between two small hills. The house appeared in his field of vision. Aimé had a knife strapped to his thigh, ready to use if need be. He touched it with his fingers as he approached the windows of the grand Virginian veranda that ran around Major Ridge's house. He peered through a ground-floor window into a sort of boudoir, fully furnished, dimly lit, where a young soldier in a dirty uniform slept outstretched on a *récamier*. The gleam from the candles on a nearby table flickered in time with his breathing. Aimé walked around the house to check if he was alone, and to verify the accuracy of the information he'd received. In the distance, to the east of the elegant two-storey home, were the slaves' quarters. There was no light over there but Aimé knew where they were, just as he knew that all comings and goings ceased after nightfall. He reached the front door and crept inside, without a sound or moment's hesitation. The screen door didn't creak, his movements were smooth and precise. It was as if he'd been doing this a long time, and did it often, under different circumstances that always required a heightened level of control over his limbs and his entire body.

He went down a hallway to the room where the guns were stored, along a rug that was unrolled for several yards in front of him. The hallway was narrow, with whitewashed walls and ornamental woodwork on the ceiling joists. There was no trace of Cherokee culture in the candleholders, or the bowls of fresh water set out along the shelf built into the wall. As he looked in on the boudoir, through the door on the left, Aimé saw a deer's head on the back wall. He couldn't have seen the bear's head directly across from it, looking the deer square in the eye. The soldier was sleeping. It was nearly four in the morning. On his way out Aimé would help himself to the sleeper's gun, and maybe keep it for himself.

The weapons that had been confiscated from the men of the Cherokee Nation were stockpiled in a back room, a sort of redoubt more crudely finished than the rest of the house. Long guns leaned against a rough plank wall, pistols lay on the floor. The darkness was near total, he used his hands to find his way, slowly but confidently. You could have sworn he'd been here before. His hands made contact with the walls, like rhythmic, confident pulses. His load would soon grow heavy, but he'd promised to deliver an exact number of weapons, and didn't have far to carry them. Above all, the leather strap that held them must not break. Aimé figured he wouldn't think twice about slitting the young soldier's throat if he snuck up on him, or raised the alarm, or cried out for help. He'd never killed a man before. It was something outside his ken, an unfamiliar feeling. It was possible to live as long as he had and never kill another person. He'd never killed a living soul, but knew he would do so without giving it a second thought: it would be just one move amid so many others, a decisive act in the middle of a long series of such acts, a new and unfamiliar one perhaps, but one he carried deep inside him, on his person, strapped to his thigh, somewhere in the hunting knife in its upside-down leather sheath.

He worked quickly, undisturbed by fear, and didn't stop when the house gently creaked, confident he could differentiate the sound of a man waking up, somehow pick up on a deliberate, human languor in the vibrations. His bag full, he pulled the rope to draw it tight and slung it over his shoulder. It weighed over fifty pounds and Aimé slumped a little under its weight, could feel a piece of metal poking him in the back, between two vertebrae. He came out of the cold, dark room and headed for the front door, then turned around and furtively crossed the hallway in the opposite direction to go up to the next floor. The door to the master bedroom was slightly ajar, it hadn't been fully closed since the Ridge family left. In the as yet uncivilized night, faraway lights shone through the large window. An animal skin lay on the floor in front of the bed. The room was redolent of human presence, as if emptied of its inhabitants not five minutes earlier. The canopy on the four-poster bed swayed in the door's gentle draft. Aimé had an eerie feeling that lasted a few seconds, as if a fluorescent ghost were slipping out through the closed window, not breaking the pane but passing right through it. He opened the big mahogany chest of drawers and helped himself to the valuables, a few bibelots and jewels, a dreamcatcher he could sell in town.

He walked by the young soldier one more time, not feeling contemptuous because he was asleep and had failed to resist. As planned, he stole the pistol. Aimé felt no contempt. He realized that, in fact, he had a lot in common with this man. They shared certain facial features and a way of enjoying a moment of peace before hostilities broke out. He knew that, because of him, this young man would probably lose his posting and his pittance. Superior officers would charge him with dereliction of duty. He'd wash up in some Savannah back alley, a forgotten man in a pool of his own piss, pushed over the edge by one swig too many. Looking at him, Aimé wondered what it meant to be a good soldier. What was the difference between wearing the colours of a nation, or a nation in the making, and acting for yourself, under cover of darkness, unnoticed by one and all? This private one-way conversation between Aimé and the sleeping soldier was over in a fraction of a second.

He left Major Ridge's house and ran off into the night. The guns rattling around and the clacking of metal and wood made Aimé nervous. He ran in a straight line, and down below in the darkness he could just make out the slaves' quarters, where the lights had been snuffed out hours ago and would not be lit again until hours later. He crossed the abandoned cotton field and had almost reached the hills slightly further off in the woods when he heard the cracking of a broken branch echoing over the empty, abandoned property. Aimé stopped. A big black man stood before him, just a few steps away. He wore torn dark clothing and carried a saddlebag and a leaky canteen. A nearly invisible presence in the darkness; all Aimé could see, or almost make

out, was the pink of the inside of his lips, and the greyish white around his irises. They looked each other up and
down in silence. Aimé slowly moved his right hand toward
the handle of his hunting knife, and flexed the muscles of
his upper body. The other man watched him do it, breathing out of his open mouth, with a neutral expression on his
face somewhere between a yawn, repressed suffering, and
indifference, like the belaboured beginning of a sneeze that
will never arrive. He seemed to be considering what to do
next. Slowly, he got out of Aimé's way, his bare feet dragging
on the ground, scraping the dry earth, picking up invisible
grains of sand. The moonlight hit him. Aimé took his hand
off his knife, lifted his palms in a gesture of good faith, and
walked past the black man, who had no shackle on his ankle
or neck, but a thick, bumpy scar running down his cheek.
No words were exchanged. Why would there be? Aimé had
no idea what to say to a slave, not even thank you, it was
inconceivable; he wouldn't have known what to say even if
he'd tried. He noticed the swollen scar, it made an indelible
mark on his imagination, and set off running again, toward
the treetops in front of him, which blocked the view of the
stars, and the moon disappearing behind him.

Aimé had left his horse and little cart in a dense patch of
forest by the banks of the Oostanaula River. He took care
not to leave by the same path. He threw his bag in, grabbed
the reins, and jumped on the seat. Chattanooga was just
over the state line, a few dozen miles to the north, along the
river. He knew the Cherokee Indians would have no difficulty tracking him, he'd left plenty of traces. He also knew
no one would ask them to.

A FEW WEEKS later, in a field on the edge of the Richelieu River, in the shadow of Mont Saint-Hilaire, a group of four *habitants* hand-picked for their discretion by Arthur Pothier, M.D., Esq., found a trunk containing eleven Springfield muskets from the War of 1812, twenty-two beat-up Phildelphia Deringer .50 calibre pistols, and a collection of metal jewellery that had belonged to Major Ridge's mixed-blood wife, Susanna Wickett, who'd left all such accoutrements behind. She wouldn't need them where she was going, where she could look forward to growing old in peace and prosperity. Here, up North, in preparation for the battle that might take place at Saint-Denis, or maybe elsewhere, they could be melted down for shot.

CHAPTER TEN

MARCH 1776
QUEBEC, QC

THAT WINTER, LIVING on his own and begging scraps of food, he noticed that the growing pains that had dogged him since birth were gone. Like a silent partner in his life, he'd grown accustomed to the pain running up and down his legs as he walked, and especially when he stopped, in some borrowed corner to sleep for the night or back alley to stretch his muscles. It had become so normal he didn't immediately know how to react. Aimé had been in constant pain for years, a nagging but manageable pain that lingered patiently on the threshold of the bearable, yet gave him tics that reared up the moment he sat still too long. He'd tried to quell the pain by massaging himself, as the sisters had when he was small. It only gave him spasms.

It was most acute in his legs but he felt pretty much the same thing in his arms, around the elbows, coursing through the veins of his forearms to the wrist, and around the joint next to his shoulder blades as well; an internal, untouchable pain that wasn't exacerbated by applying pressure on his skin with his finger; a fully independent pain flowing into his muscles and cartilage like a fluid, like a strong, steady river. People with the knowing look of experts told him he was growing too fast, his body seemed bent on ageing at an improbable rate. Months after his birth, they said, he already weighed more than twenty pounds and had a stretched-out look, as if evil forces were elongating his legs and neck at the same time, like bread dough first kneaded and then rolled out and handled at length. It looked like he might die young with the wizened body of an old man.

It happened just after Aimé turned sixteen, though he wasn't aware of it, absorbed as he was with thoughts of day-to-day survival, like the rest of the legion of ghosts you passed on those streets, people no one wanted anything to do with. There was no one left to take him in, it wasn't anyone's job to look after him once he'd left the seminary. All around him Quebec was like a massive closed door, and he sought out nooks and crannies, deep and dry, where he might be forgotten and safe for a while. He knew all the passages and the vaults and the back alleys where the stench of curling smoke gave a misleading impression of heat.

It hit him a few days after the pain dissipated without warning, in the middle of a snowstorm. He'd taken refuge under a porch in Golden Dog Lane, with a stolen loaf and a box of matches to warm his fingers from time to time without attracting too much attention. He was starting to feel the frostbite on his calves and shins in a way he never had before. His whole body was contracting against the cold, the rags covering his back were full of holes, like the toes of the boots he had pulled off the feet of a dead American patriot left behind by the nurses. He moved his legs and began running on the spot to warm himself, as it dawned on him that he was totally unfettered, his thighs and the backs of his knees suddenly freed of a formerly unshakable weight. He cracked one or two joints on his right ankle, and silently prayed while moving his lips slightly, to make it last. For the first time since his birth he felt good, despite the harsh cold; he was at one with his body, it seemed to be granting him a second chance.

Two hundred years later he would recall this moment in such an idealized light it was hard to refrain from mentioning it to the people he encountered all over the continent. But he didn't say a word. It would have been hard for others to understand how it felt, the precise moment when he stopped growing, a moment that would take on an increasing importance throughout his long life, but that he'd never discuss out loud or describe in writing in any volume of memoirs or document of any other kind. Though this moment left no trace it may well be the very heart of his secret, the epicentre of his personal mystery.

THE SQUALLS ROSE off the St. Lawrence and blew hard inland, effortlessly ascending the cliff under their own momentum and then blowing back down the other side, over field and farm, after whirling around the fortifications and observation posts where sentries' eyes were trained on the south that grew more volatile by the day. The Continental

Army stationed at Montreal had attacked Quebec in the dying days of the previous summer. It was a disaster. You could still stumble over frozen bodies in the woods around the city walls. The inmates packed into the prison's oldest wing were loud and unruly; their shouts for freedom rang out over and beyond the Plains of Abraham. Some hurled insults at the redcoats, while others plied the local *habitants* with conciliatory words. You could hear these prisoners crying out in a dozen different accents, English whose pitch and yaw were unknown in these parts. You could hear them imploring the citizens to set them free, to join them in their revolution—that word that cropped up again and again, full of rage, echoing in the night as if imbued with the power of an incantation.

Aimé devoured his loaf of bread, paying no attention to the cries of prisoners carried by the river wind. The skin on his face was chapping and the patchy beginnings of a beard were sprouting on his cheeks. He kept a low profile. There were more and more soldiers, so they took a hard line with indigents and paupers. It manifested as a suspicion of the masses who lived outside the walls and ventured into the Citadel to buy provisions or sell wilted produce in Place Royale. The red and blue uniforms travelled in packs and in lockstep, suddenly halting their forward march in front of a passerby to ask questions: Where were they from? Where were they going? What were they doing outside at this hour? Often, satisfied with the answers but still not entirely at ease, they'd accompany people toward their homes, even as far as Saint John's Gate, then watch them head down the dirt road to the village of Saint-Roch by the river.

Soldiers were thicker on the ground every day, civilians fewer and further between. As long as the unrest in the southern colonies did not abate, or succumb to British military might, the curfew would remain in effect and sentries keep watching the horizon and the Lévis woods, from where Arnold and Montgomery had once launched missiles over the river at Quebec. Some days a line of fire could be seen in the low sky, further out, as Boston, New York, Philadelphia, and Baltimore made ready to rise up as one.

After swallowing a final mouthful of bread, Aimé struck a match and ran it down his palms and fingertips. He held it to his lips and nostrils, and repeated the process with another when it went out. The little flame was almost immediately snuffed out by a gust of wind that crept under the porch where he had taken shelter. His legs no longer hurt as before. It made him euphoric in a way he couldn't wrap his head around. What he felt was akin to joy, but he lacked the words to articulate it. He was terribly cold but, at the same time, didn't know what else to do, beyond praying and thanking the Lord for this respite from pain. He wore a little cross on his neck and considered giving it a kiss, but quickly abandoned this idea when an icy gust of wind, or maybe blowing snow, forced him to shut his eyes.

A chunk of ice broke loose from the roof above him as a brigade went by on Côte de la Montagne hill. The soldiers halted. Aimé remained still, and even stopped breathing. In the dark he could stay invisible, blend into the shadows, and slip into the openings between the bricks, but if they came into the passage to find the source of the noise he'd have nowhere to hide. One of the men pointed a bayonet into the darkness and, under his officer's orders, was slowly advancing. Aimé understood that he was out of options. He considered the relative warmth of the prison cell where there would be straw on the floor. He raised his arms in surrender and to let the soldiers know where he was, speaking clearly to avoid startling them.

They asked him to come out and step forward into the light of the lantern. No false moves. What was that in his hands? What did he have in his pockets? What was he doing there? This was private property. A few seconds later, the officer making the inspection noticed, and pointed at, Aimé's hole-riddled boots. He spat as he spoke, in the English Aimé associated with the wealthy merchants down at the Port and Customs House.

"Where did you get those boots?"

Aimé hesitated a moment. Fear had stepped in and obstructed the words that should have slipped out right away. The lie that could have saved him wasn't forthcoming, only silence, in the middle of the road, cold, immobilized by the soldiers' guns. The officer repeated himself, in French mostly, and louder:

"*Où avez-vous trouvé ces boots?* Answer me!"

Surrounded by five soldiers with no means of escape, Aimé couldn't fathom a way out. One soldier held his hat down on his head in the nick of time before the wind and blowing snow made off with it. Aimé quickly thought it over. He made a mental list of all possible answers but none seemed to work, all led straight to the gaol. The holes in his toes didn't change a thing, the boots were army property, from the leather to the gilded buttons to the worn-out soles.

When he'd found them Aimé had discarded the removable
spats to avoid attracting notice. But the officer immediately
and effortlessly recognized these pieces of enemy kit. Aimé
felt his nerves, and then impatience. Everyone knew prisoners of war had managed to escape, the prison was poorly
guarded, hard to secure with the threat of attack ever-loom-
ing. There was talk of a full-fledged insurrection, led by a militia under Ethan Allen backed by the Canadiens. American
propaganda continued to reach Montreal and spread around
the city, they were powerless to stop it. Pamphlets were slipping over the border along with printed letters signed by
Franklin and Adams.

The officer looked Aimé in the eye. His pupils were
strangely empty, as if the endless winter he had suffered
through since getting off the ship had robbed him of his
eyesight. What little remained of his teeth seemed to be
disintegrating before their eyes, as he bellowed at Aimé,
Explain yourself, tell me who you are. The Ursuline Sisters'
bell rang eight times in its tower and the officer issued a
peremptory order. The men seized Aimé by his shoulders
and arms, the shoulders and arms that had finally stopped
causing him pain, and started walking again. They took him
to join the three hundred and fifty survivors of Benedict
Arnold's march on Quebec, crammed into the seeping stone
cells of the military prison.

THE WIND SLIPPED in through the loopholes but it was hot
inside, the men's bodies touched as they paced their cell, only
to end up back where they'd started. Aimé tried to settle into

a corner and enjoy the warmth a little, at least until his nose and fingertips had time to thaw. They'd pulled off his boots and pushed him into the cell without further explanation. He didn't know when he'd be sentenced, maybe later that day, maybe not for weeks. Though this worried him, the absence of pain in his limbs was cause to rejoice, something he wanted to experience in silence, simply moving his lips a little. A euphoric feeling was coursing through his body, and he was gradually assimilating it. He touched the cross on his neck, took it out of his shirt as a man came up to welcome him. Deep cracks in his hands told Aimé he'd spent too long outdoors, laying siege to the city last December, and would have scars for the rest of his life. He spoke English and his greasy hair stood out every which way, as if someone had yanked off his wig. Aimé answered in halting English but addressed him respectfully. Clearly he was a man of rank: the others got out of his way when he walked, like tropical insects boring an opening in the swarm.

This man and Aimé spoke at length, while day began to break and the other inmates slept where they could, or yelled out through the arrow slits, wind in their faces. Sometimes a guard came to demand silence. The prisoners answered with insults, mocked his accent. Whenever the man stopped talking to Aimé, to put one of his subordinates in his place or massage his temples with two filthy middle fingers, Aimé drifted off into his thoughts and plotted his escape. It was far from his first time in prison. He observed the walls and composition of the stone, ran his fingers along the iron bars, while the man, in great detail and with an honour none would ever take away from him, told his impassioned story.

His legs had grown thin, the hair had fallen out on his calves. Despite his rank he was not allowed to smoke.

His name was Daniel Morgan. A captain in the Continental Army, he'd fought alongside Benedict Arnold in the attack on Quebec from the north, through the *faubourgs* of the lower town along the St. Charles River. With the regiment of men rotting away in this dank cell, he'd sought to take the British by surprise, waiting for General Montgomery's cannonade to cover them from the south shore. In the blizzard, nothing went according to plan. He'd thumbed his nose at the English by surrendering his sword to a Catholic priest before Governor Carleton arrived. For that he'd been denied a private cell. Which was perfect; he would have been much colder without his men, shut up alone, whiling away the hours penning incoherent missives.

Aimé listened respectfully and politely. Morgan's beard was growing long and matted. He also introduced himself, with profound humility: Aimé Bolduc, after one of the nuns who had cared for him. He had no baptistery certificate to prove it, but knew that when she'd taken to him, the others started calling him by the maiden name she'd renounced when she took her vows. Aimé had been arrested for stealing a dead man's boots, a dead soldier's boots, a pair of boots that had gotten him through the winters up to now. It was an offence sure to land him in this prison for a long time, but then Aimé had never stayed anywhere long; he was restless, knew the city's hidden corners and the many ways to slip through cracks and disappear. While he spoke he fingered the stone of the walls, quarried by men undernourished and broken by fatigue. It stuck to your fingers, the rock powder and sweat of the thousand prisoners who had found themselves here, leaned against this very wall, waiting for their sentences to be executed.

Intrigued and fascinated, Morgan listened to Aimé's tale and tried to properly parse the syllables that piled one upon the other, rough consonants and diphthongs swelling up out of nowhere mid-word. They talked until the sun came up, until they were so tired their eyes tingled, especially Morgan, who hadn't slept in three days. He listened to Aimé talk, French phrases mixed in as if he were reluctant to be fully understood. He recounted a litany of misfortunes in a backhanded way, refusing to dignify them with the seriousness others might. Unlike Morgan, he had no undue attachment to the idea of an independent state. He'd settle for freeing his own body. He didn't put it in exactly those terms, but that's what his new friend took away, after so much time awake. As hours went by, his trust in Aimé grew while he began to doubt this man's existence, his material presence. The soldiers had stopped yelling. It must have been five in the morning. Everyone was listening to Aimé and Morgan chatting away like old chums, friends who'd get together and share serious thoughts. Morgan quietly insisted that it wasn't true, he'd lied, in fact he'd written a few letters, including an especially important one to Wooster, who had been spotted in Montreal. Morgan finally fell asleep after handing a sheet of paper over to Aimé, who secreted it away in an inside fold in his torn-up shirt. For the first time since the rebel troops arrived in the colony, the cell was totally silent. Aimé's eyes didn't close and he wasn't blinking much either, his eyes were too dry from thinking about the end of an era in his veins and under his skin, dreaming about being outside these walls, dreaming hard enough to get there.

He imagined Montreal and everything became possible: journeys down paths through the still-virgin woods, mountains at once faraway and near, in perpetual motion over infinite, immortal ground. He pictured himself elsewhere and in more eventful circumstances, his abnormally long legs, boy's legs, transformed into those of an exotic, mythical animal, at once hind and hunter, his slender arms as strong as the trunks of maple trees. He pictured Montreal, Ville-Marie, a big city where big things were going to happen.

Deep in his dreams of combat in the undulating Connecticut woods, Daniel Morgan was aware that, when he opened his eyes, Aimé Bolduc would be gone.

CHAPTER ELEVEN

OCTOBER 1925
PALM SPRINGS, CA

HE HAD BECOME a handsome man. The twentieth century had been kind to him so far, you could see as much in his appearance and bearing, complexion and deportment. Each new day brought revolutionary new products rolling off the assembly lines of sprawling factories. They were redrawing the horizon with towering chimneys whose dramatic plumes of smoke were indistinguishable from the clouds. He bought pomades for his hair and scalp and dieted to maintain his figure, ordered life-changing emulsions and astringents from the pages of the Sears, Roebuck & Co. catalogue. People were going crazy for radium, walking around with radioactive watches. Aimé had quietly invested in the Pedoscope, an invention that let shoe salesmen take X-rays of their clients' feet on the spot. It was an elegant machine with ornate flourishes, built by master craftsmen out of wood varnished to a shine.

When he applied anti-ageing cream to his wrinkles, Aimé wasn't unaware of the cosmic irony of his action and his wish, the one we all share, even at an advanced age, to live forever. Like the rest of us he acted in a perfectly normal manner most of the time. He was forgetting things. That year, in New York or San Diego or wherever he was, Aimé looked like a man of forty-one. He'd been alive for more than a century and a half.

Aimé believed the promises of the factory-builders and entrepreneurs, men who had dreams and weren't afraid to lay everything on the line for the good of their fellow man. How could he not believe in them? His teeth, a source of shame for nearly the entire second half of the nineteenth century, while life expectancy soared and hygiene was on everyone's lips, those teeth were white today, and why? Radium toothpaste. He could smile without embarrassment, as if the rotten teeth and bad breath that had plagued him for so long, until it became a part of him, had evaporated. X-rays were the greatest discovery in the history of mankind, and Aimé was working hard to keep abreast of the latest developments. He'd tried to get in touch with the Curies, learn more about the science of radiation, but after a few unsuccessful attempts he had shifted his focus to the technology's commercial potential.

Every night and every morning he brushed his teeth with *Doramad Radioaktive Zahncreme*, a privately imported German product that glowed in the dark. He kept the silver tube on his person at all times. His nails were always carefully clipped, with no cuticles. He combed his shiny hair after applying a special mousse developed by retired soldiers who'd made the move to R&D.

In Houston, Seattle, or Great Falls, Aimé always looked good and stood tall, though he liked to keep to the background. People at receptions and charity balls were always wondering who he was. There would be whispers: He might be William Van Ness, heard of him? The name sounded familiar, but no one knew why. Was he one of the Vermont Van Nesses? Probably, but hadn't the Van Nesses gone bankrupt after the governor's political misadventures, not long after the Civil War? That man in his tailored suits sure didn't look like the scion of a ruined family. He dressed in the finest fabrics, always stuck to the periphery of activities and conversations. You could talk to the man, sure, but he always answered curtly, with a half-formed, distant smile. He was polite, like a man who had something to hide, people would say as they stepped away. They'd think about it for a few seconds, then forget all about him as they snatched a flute of champagne from a passing tray. There were dozens of other interesting, influential people to meet and fraternize with. Bursts of laughter could be heard all around, erupting at the slightest provocation.

The truth was simple: Aimé brought the booze. That was his role and he excelled at it. He walked around the immense ballroom making sure everyone had everything they needed. Not many people knew who he really was, but that took nothing away from his efficiency and expertise. In the middle of Prohibition you could call on Aimé and rest easy knowing your function would be well supplied with European wines and quality spirits, for a soiree that never disappointed. It came in by the caseload, through secret back alleys behind reputed establishments. With Aimé you never got anything doctored, that was his trademark. Unlike the other bootleggers in Chicago and elsewhere, who plied their trade over the Canadian border, men like Gursky and Capone, Aimé's catalogue listed only controlled-origin products. No matter where he did business, he always delivered and oversaw distribution personally, to make certain everything ran smoothly, from start to finish. Aimé was a high-class caterer like no other, with discretion and strict standards to match. He arrived early, rang the doorbell, and settled payment terms with his host, while the cases and barrels came in through the municipal gutters and storm drains.

No matter where he found himself in those years of prosperity when federal legislation made him rich, he always stayed modest, discreet, and anonymous. People talked about him, in the sophisticated circles that sprung up and mutated and disappeared in a puff of smoke, but this man with gleaming hair and a slender moustache remained unfailingly impossible to size up. He wasn't a servant, that much was clear at a glance, and everyone wanted to know who his family was. He'd smile politely but never engage. Or almost never. People would wonder about him for a few seconds and eventually forget all about his presence, as evanescent as that of the chandeliers and other touches of opulence — they created an ambiance, but everyone got used to it and stopped noticing after a while. He became part of the furniture. People stopped asking questions and kept right on drinking. That night, in Palm Springs in the California desert, they were mostly drinking Dupeyron Armagnac and a fine Saint-Émilion of the fabled 1900 vintage.

NO INFORMATION ABOUT this period of Aimé's life would
have come down to us through Albert's notebooks, no matter how comprehensive they have proven on other, often
much older episodes, were it not for a man of uncertain age
who sat down next to him that day, on the bench of a grand
piano. He sipped a martini; Aimé, as was his custom, drank
nothing. The man put his glass down on the instrument
and lay his hands on the keyboard, as if readying to play a
polonaise, but then stopped himself just in time. He was
young, barely thirty, but Aimé could discern something in
his movements and his eyes, which stared straight ahead,
an ancient wisdom he was not unfamiliar with himself, the
one you see in trees and giant tortoises, living creatures that
grow old according to another rhythm and bear witness to
entire eons in the blink of an eye. If it almost looked like he
was wearing makeup, it was just his features receding into
the overall melancholy of his face. In the shoulders of this
young man sitting next to him, their gentle slope, Aimé
could read the passage of long stretches of time. This other
man wore the years differently, but Aimé could easily see
them nonetheless.

The two men barely looked at each other. Conversation
took time to get going but soon gathered steam, Aimé listening with interest to his companion's scattered, darting
gambits, before weighing in himself, taking the floor and
making it his own, opening up for the first time in ages.
The man began by asking Aimé if he was also obsessed with
films, the new possibilities opening up with moving pictures.
Aimé said he didn't really know much about it, he preferred
real life, and sometimes books. The other man was watching

the spectacle in front of him, couples dancing to the band, men smoking cigars.

"As far as I'm concerned, there *is* no difference. Life, movies. There's no difference anymore! It's the same images, superimposed. Sound crazy? Just wait, you'll see I'm not a nut."

Aimé flagged down a waiter, who came to replace the empty martini glass with a full champagne flute.

"Soon they'll make the actors talk. Then there'll really be no difference, none at all. No more music, the actors will talk, and their voices will be recorded right on the film. Synchronized with the images. After that the sky's the limit, you'll see. One day it'll all be in colour. And then there'll really be no difference between the movies and life."

The man wasn't drunk. He was waving his hands in front of his face, miming a spinning reel, at one with the phenomenon he was describing. Aimé just listened. He pointed out that reality was three-dimensional. But there was no way to experience three-dimensionality, the man countered, with your eyes or your mind. Aimé talked to him about touch, and this gave him pause. They weren't looking at each other, they were watching the celebration unfold.

Exotic meats imported from Brazil, a hemisphere away, were served impaled on large metal skewers. The waiters walked from table to table, leaning low to send the odours wafting, transporting the guests. Pastry chefs had been brought in all the way from New York City. People were eating, sitting and standing, drinking too, you could hear laughter of every sort.

A man in a tuxedo appeared from under a white tablecloth

and grabbed the ankle of a young woman, who yelled for help, but everyone just laughed. The man picked up his monocle, which had fallen, and pretended to dry off his knees as he stood. The circle of guests gathered around, and the conversation grew lively. At the back of the room, on a stair, a colonel of the Merchant Marine began a speech that attracted few listeners. People were moving quickly, touching each other affectionately with their fingertips, as if they'd known each other forever.

Rumour had it William Randolph Hearst had been invited and was actually in attendance, over there, or maybe at the back of the room. They said he'd rolled up in a convertible Packard with chrome running boards, a model no one had ever seen before. A squealing trumpet occasionally made itself heard over the clicking of pearls, jewellery, and crystal glassware.

The two men watched this opulent evening unfold, admiring the guests' elegance without really partaking of it. Aimé stood while the man sat on the piano bench with legs crossed and a champagne flute in his hand. Sometimes, when it seemed he was about to play something, he would suddenly snap to attention and realize the band was there for that.

"But the movies aren't there to replace our sense of touch—just our sense of sight. And our imagination—by turning those two into one and the same thing. That's what the movies are for: to take the place of all the images we see while our eyes are open, and the ones that haunt us once our eyes are closed as well. Movies work better than dreams, because they follow an order, despite their... artificiality. Is that even a word?"

"Artificiality? Sure, I think so. Why not?"

"Me, I'm obsessed with the movies. I've been making movies forever, as long as I can remember, in my mind that is, even if I didn't actually lay my hands on a camera until ten years ago or so. When I was ten I used to act in plays with my parents, but I was already thinking about movies, about film. I didn't know it yet, but I was organizing space for a take, not for a scene. I always used to tell myself: That far, no further, otherwise you'll be out of the frame, it won't look good. Like if there were more than five paces between my father and me, it wouldn't look good. I was framing the shot, see. I was constantly on the set. So I could always see things from the audience's point of view. I've always been obsessed, so when Fatty put me behind a camera, it all clicked. Can I tell you a story?"

"Sure."

"You really interested?"

"Absolutely."

"Don't let me bore you, now."

"You don't bore me. I don't agree with what you were saying about movies and the imagination, at least I don't think so. But you aren't boring, not by a long shot."

"I don't want to *importune* you either. The last thing I want is to bother you. I just want to make myself understood. What I'm saying is that movies and imagination have the same job: to give us a sense of wonder, entertain us. If you think the human imagination is there for any other reason, well, you're missing the point."

It was Aimé's turn to think. He thought about how his mind worked, how he would get lost in the meandering paths of far-off memories, like flashes, which he had a different name for, the way they rose up behind his eyes and mixed in with the reality before his eyes at a given moment. He thought about his mind and his imagination and his nearly unfathomable memory. He saw soldiers and priests in dozens of different uniforms all blurred together, blue here, grey there, dark green too, blending into the landscape. And the priests spoke different languages: Latin, French, English, Italian, even German in some of the parishes he could or could not remember passing through.

"We'd planned everything down to the last second, down to a sixteenth of an inch, there was no room to take chances. We have to make people think everything is happening naturally, but also make them unconsciously understand that it's a choreography, it's orchestrated like a symphony. You have to take risks, too. I understood that early — that's what makes us laugh, and what moves us too. We'd planned a scene on one of the drawing tables, and we rehearsed it without water, and without a camera. I was supposed to be running on train cars that were moving a little faster in the opposite direction, and then, at the last minute, grab onto the rope hanging from the cistern, to get back down to the ground. Right then I set off the valve by accidentally turning on the pump. You know the scene? A lot of people saw it. A lot of people talk to me about it, happens all the time."

Ideas were changing. What everyone believed yesterday wouldn't mean a thing tomorrow. Like medicine: we used to think bleeding was the only cure, we made deep incisions as we watched the blood flow into a basin or a vial, and then decades later we stopped believing in it, laughed at what our fathers and grandfathers had done. Aimé thought about the first time he washed his hands with a bar of soap, how he'd grown used to it in a couple years. How could the movies explain that? Superimposition, as this man claimed? He thought about black slaves, fields teeming with them, something he'd seen without ever thinking twice. Or the black men in costumes and makeup in the movies, decades later, chased by knights in robes and pointed hats with eye-holes cut out.

"We only shot one take, it was now or never. The plan was so perfect no one noticed when I broke my neck, not even me, that's the story I wanted to tell you. So when I hanged myself with the rope the water came gushing out of the giant tank, gushing so hard I almost passed out. The water came crashing down and my neck twisted and I could feel my ear touching my shoulder, and it felt like I was yelling, but the crashing sound—you can't hear it in the movie—it was so loud I thought I was hallucinating. I still remember that it didn't hurt, I remember the adrenaline, the powerful rush right after I let go of the rope and was shaken. You can see that feeling in the film. When I watch myself in the movie I can see it. I stayed there in front of the pump for four or five seconds, swaying back and forth, before the other people started running toward me. My spinal cord had snapped, at the third cervical vertebrae, and I had a severe concussion. I've had a high-pitched ringing in my ears ever since."

Aimé thought about all the former slaves who'd been made up and dressed as soldiers. Someone had imagined that, without experiencing it, someone had decided on a camera angle and imagined everything, to entertain and create a sense of wonder, to shape reality and give it larger meaning. The camera steered toward painted men, dressed in rags torn in the most revealing of possible places, play-acting the horror, playing at being assassinated, pretending to be lynched. Aimé had seen it in a dark, smoky theatre, sitting in a comfortable chair surrounded by handsome men and pretty women. When the light came back on they applauded, talked about how realistic it all was, about realism, how real it felt. But no one could remember those days, the heat and the cold, the certainty that they'd never make it out alive, those long days more than two generations earlier, now represented by actors with music and recorded on film. The slightly artificial speed of the images unfurling was the one remaining connection with how things actually were.

Was it the same for this man he was talking to now? Were his memories and his imaginings confused, after so many years behind a camera? Did he have a hard time making the distinction? Was it the same thing, when you got down to it? Aimé might only have one memory, might lack imagination or be unable to summon this sense of wonder, as the other man put it. At another time, during his first youth, he had created a life for himself in his dreams, and acted accordingly. He vaguely believed he remembered it. But after a certain point, around his fiftieth year on earth, when his body was finally as hairy as other men's, he was no more than a collection of memories, his memories, a past on the march toward an uncertain future, an ever more powerful past chipping away at his ability to reinvent himself.

"But, see—I know it's strange, but I only realized last

month. My doctor finally figured it out. I always had this sharp pain, around the carotid artery, right here. It kept me from turning my head to the left. It's still very sensitive, see? I can barely turn toward you. I actually have to turn my whole torso, or else it hurts. There are mornings I literally can't move. And others when I'm perfectly fine."

Aimé wanted to hear more without necessarily trying to understand where all this was going. He was almost tempted to have a drink himself, for the first time in twenty years. He trusted this young man, his capacity for introspection, though he was a filmmaker and had never experienced anything significant, anything tragic. But how could he know? Maybe he grew up in a vomit-stained hovel in a squalid corner of Manhattan. Maybe he'd crossed the Atlantic with his parents in the hold of a freighter. What did Aimé know about it?

"I broke my ankle once," Aimé said. "And I just kept walking, didn't realize it was broken, through the forest, in the middle of nowhere. It took sixteen hours, I could tell from the sun's movement in my memory, trying to get somewhere. My shin bone broke to pieces when I fell, it was totally crushed, as if it had been put through a gristmill."

The other man tipped back his champagne, barely tasting it, unable to appreciate what was undoubtedly a *grand cru*. He was concentrating on Aimé's words, while observing the guests. No one came close enough to talk to them, they were offstage, as if abandoned to their fate. Aimé continued:

"I know someone, an old man who fought on the Confederate side. Third Tennessee Regiment. He also told me a story about a train. He's ancient now. He told me the same story lots of times, as if that way he could somehow save something of that time, a vivid picture. He came out unscathed, not so much as a broken fingernail. But there was always the fear that never quite left him. He liked to tell me about the one true act of bravery he witnessed, a guy who wasn't even a soldier. He said normal folks were much braver than the army, in those years."

"What was it, this act of bravery?"

"An entire Confederate Army train was stolen by Union spies. They'd blended in with the civilians at the station. And what'd the conductor do? He ran right after them, without a moment's hesitation. He ran down the rails, then jumped on a handcar and set off in pursuit. Unarmed, mind you."

"Did he make it back?"

"No, he never came back. And no one ever saw the train again. Not in Memphis or Jackson, anyway."

"So it was more foolhardy than brave."

"That's not how the old man put it. For him, it was about moving forward, with no hesitation. The sight of this man running along the railway, to defend something dear to him, something he was determined to get back—well, that was a shining example of courage. There's always a touch of fool-hardiness in courage, I'll give you that."

"And vice versa, I guess. But why didn't the soldiers run with him, to get the train back?"

"As far as the old man was concerned, this was the very opposite of war. The flipside of the coin, if you will. Chasing after the train was pointless. He was adamant on that point."

"Hmmm."

"Yeah. He told me the regiment fired at the locomotive,

which was disappearing fast. The troops assumed the position and fired, under the captain's orders. But by the time they figured out the train had been stolen it had already built up speed and was disappearing around a curve, pulling out of downtown."

In the crowd, Aimé had noticed a few old men in pincenez and extravagant bow ties, men light on their feet, with little time to spare. They probably had the first-hand knowledge of the war he and his new acquaintance were talking about over the piano. Other, younger men were dancing too, without a care in the world it seemed, many had come back from another battlefield, a mere seven years ago, in Europe, a continent Aimé had never set foot on, not even to visit castles older than himself. One of the ones who'd caught Aimé's eye while he was chatting with the young man had what was clearly an artificial right leg, and wore a medal pinned to his jacket. His limp was apparent when he moved, and added a doubtful shimmy to his dance steps. A steady flow of people would come up and congratulate him with a pat on the shoulder or a squeeze of the forearm. The women who spoke to him would bow slightly and hold their wineglasses in both hands. There was no trickery to this man's elegance.

The filmmaker said, without a hint of cynicism:

"What about that guy there. Was he really brave? Can we know for sure, just 'cause he's wearing a medal?"

"Hard to say. But he definitely looks happy. He wears it with pride."

"I hated my uniform. I felt ridiculous in it, and I looked ridiculous too. The commissary general clearly never planned for a man under five-foot-five in the U.S. Army."

For the first time Aimé felt a need to look directly at the man. His last sentence added a layer of complexity to the image he had drawn in his head, and he felt bad for a sort of petty naivety he'd thought he'd grown out of.

"You served?"

"Just seven months, in France. Fortieth Infantry Division. My pants were too long and my coat looked like a potato sack, and I could never properly wrap the puttees the army gave us to protect our legs. Oh, and the shoes? Way too big. Eights. I'm a six-and-a-half. In our division, the old-timers had long given up hope of getting uniforms that actually fit. They'd have them altered by civilian tailors. And they'd buy proper workman's boots too, rig 'em up to pass inspection."

Aimé threw in a lie, to keep the conversation going:

"I wasn't sent to the front. I was already married."

"No need to justify yourself."

"No, it's not that. Just mentioning it."

"I wasn't at the front either. Didn't see much beyond the mud in the trenches before they called me home. I almost died—from an ear infection. They treated me back home, in Virginia actually, in a veteran's hospital, same as all the others. Never saw that guy over there, though."

"Makes sense, there were thousands of you."

"I know. Thousands upon thousands."

"There's no way you could have seen all the others."

"Nope."

At one point, as evening was turning to night, they understood that something rare was going on between them, and were quiet for a few seconds, long enough to gauge what was happening and savour it. Then they kept going a little further, beginning a few phrases and a few ideas, but with a sense of lost innocence, as if genuine communication depended on not knowing you were in the thick of it. After snapping up a final glass of fine champagne, the young man shook Aimé's hand, without ever looking him in the eye, and disappeared behind the draperies on the ballroom wall. A taxi was waiting on the esplanade. He'd be back in Hollywood the next day, reviewing his script, shifting emphases here and there.

On the way, he'd surely think of Aimé, the worldly man he'd met, who talked about war as if he'd been there, with words anyone could understand, fearful words that sent a chill down your spine, anguished words that could make you feverish, a man who'd spoken of those rare moments where something came into play, something you could call courage, for lack of a better word, a rare thing that was almost never self-aware. While he took a quick stop by the side of the road, to admire the massive mountain range that ran all the way up to the Yukon, where the gold was getting scarce, he decided that his hero, who he would play himself, without a single smile, would be assigned the rank of lieutenant, and live in the midst of the absurd actions of his fellow men. And the only general in the entire movie would be the train, that would be its name, the runaway train, crossing back and forth over the line of fire, screaming on the spark-filled rails. The camera in his head was already rolling.

CHAPTER TWELVE

SEPTEMBER 1863
SAINT-HENRI-DES-TANNERIES, QC

THE SMELL OF leather and burnt fur impregnated the air in every street, and along the canal where the heat brought together swarms of insects and smoke from the factories down at the port. Morning, noon, and night, there was no escaping the racket. Sewers were being dug and built and tons of bricks and stone were piling up in front of houses, sometimes higher than the rooftops. A man could show up with nothing but a shovel, with nothing but a few plugs of chew and a pair of willing hands, and work he would find.

Aimé knew the area well. He'd been spending whole days poking around here and there, waiting for evening when he could meet up with Jeanne, talk to her, set her at ease, and wordlessly convince her to let him slip his fingers under her clothing and caress the back of her neck. He never stopped thinking about her, and he knew she never stopped thinking about him either. He ate rarely, whenever he was hungry, with no desire for the company of others or concern for the honest people whose fruit and vegetables he spirited away. He hadn't showed up for work in weeks. They'd most likely forgotten all about him, as if he had never existed. His name wasn't written in any register.

Jeanne and he had developed a system of codes for their rendezvous. Often they'd meet in the barn next to Brody's farm. It was more or less abandoned, no one had bothered to fix the broken window. During one of their first nights together he'd pulled out the last few triangles of glass cling-ing to the frame, to make sure she wouldn't hurt herself, though they never came in through the window, why would they when they could walk right in through the barn door. No one ever came to the barn, it was practically abandoned since the Brodys stopped raising milk cows and the rail-road laid track behind it, on the Brody property. The train went by, a few paces from the barn wall, which would start vibrating, and Aimé often chose the moment of the train's approach to say something important, something Jeanne would listen to intently as the noise grew ever louder. When it exploded right behind them, as the locomotive passed in a symphony of metal and steam, they felt no fear, just drew closer together. No one was scared of trains anymore, least of all lovers.

Aimé walked freely and attracted no attention on Rue Saint-Jacques and Saint-Antoine and Notre-Dame, the long thoroughfares of Saint-Henri that linked the village to downtown. He was an anonymous face among the scores of labourers working on the canal and in the factories open-ing all along the shoreline. It was crawling with people, they were pouring in from far and wide, Montreal and Dublin and Rome, labourers who spoke twenty different languages at once and carried toolboxes and sacks of potatoes. They had muscular arms and the weight of the sacks made their veins pop out. These were men who could carry two fifty-pound sacks at once, one on each shoulder, no problem, with enough strength left in their voices to tell any man to get the hell out of the way.

Jeanne lived in a little two-storey wood house on the north shore of the canal, a house built for a foreman, prettily painted but smeared with soot from passing boats and nearby chimneys. The family's home was in the heart of the worker's quarter, but they did their shopping with the bourgeois citizens along Rue Saint-Antoine. She had four brothers and five sisters, the youngest born at the end of August. Their father had died under nebulous circumstances. Had he been deliberately killed? Jeanne had doubts; her brother, Jean Junior, was convinced. His talk turned constantly to retribution and punishment and it was causing tension in the home.

Usually Jeanne dressed plainly, in grey or brown, but when she was meeting Aimé she'd slip brightly coloured fabrics between layers. On the rare occasions when she found herself home alone, she'd rub her neck and armpits with borage and with bergamot, a hard-to-find product in a dazzling silver box she'd found in her grandmother's things. The first time Aimé saw her, on that scorching day the month before, when she stepped off the tram in front of him, he'd found something irresistible in her austere, dutiful bearing. She'd struck him as a studious young woman, assiduously fulfilling her responsibilities as the eldest child, unconsciously torn between being so pretty, for herself, and so important, for the others. Now, in the evening, in the dim light of the Brody's barn, he was discovering her coquettish side. She smelled sweet, of perfume, and was quick to flash a mischievous smile when his advances grew too brazen. She said his name exactly how he'd always wanted it to be pronounced.

After he'd taken those natural, unhurried first steps toward her, he went from being a strangely reassuring presence in the shadows, discernible but never visible, to a sweet, charming face that appeared when she was out doing errands. He made going from place to place more pleasant by adding an element of surprise and the tender beginnings of secrecy. Aimé soon realized that to get to know her he'd have to catch her on her own, which didn't happen often. The gaggle of children was never far behind her, tugging on her skirts and arms, needy and dependent, as if Jeanne were standing in for both their father and their mother. And to a point that's just what had happened. The role had been thrust upon her, as if it were only natural. Her mother was still alive but Jeanne was taking her place none the less, with a mixture of resignation and empathy, to give her space to fully embrace her grief in a manner befitting an ageing widow, while sinking into the onset of an apathetic madness, a listlessness that had reared its head after her last pregnancy and never really gone away. Jeanne hadn't seen her mother out of bed in weeks. She'd taken over all the daily work. The children were now, for all intents and purposes, hers. As he observed her from a distance, gradually honing in on her with the subtlest of advances, Aimé felt this weight on his shoulders as well. It was one he would happily have been rid of.

So he patiently waited his turn. Sooner or later it always arrived. Whenever Jeanne left home, there he was. At first he was content to say hello in silence by doffing an imaginary cap. As days went by, he noticed that her smile when he passed was increasingly candid, as if she'd been waiting to see him right there, like a familiar, inviting image urging her to come see what the world had to offer, and he knew that somewhere in her memories she'd saved a spot for the young man who'd hailed the tram for her and her brothers and sisters a few weeks, or years, or decades earlier.

One morning he confidently approached to help her step over a puddle of urine and dirty water, and she held out her hand, without a second thought. She hadn't planned this gesture, which was both out of character and perfectly natural, an offering that felt like part of some larger plan, as serene and coherent as the work of a master painter in which every inch of space is so much more than mere detail. Jeanne had looked Aimé in the eyes and caught a glimpse of his century-old soul. And, she might have said to herself, how could I not trust someone with so much experience, someone so tried and tested? Or maybe not. When they parted ways on a street corner, they would make polite small talk and Jeanne, who never believed she might come to understand this type of thing, had grasped it in all its intricacies and unspoken subtexts. She blushed and he came back the next day, as she'd trusted he would. It had rained; the puddle was even bigger.

BECAUSE HE LIED at all times and to everyone, to protect himself, though he didn't know from what, and since his relationship with Jeanne, sincere though it may have been, was no exception to this general rule, he'd told her he worked at the Redpath refinery. By day he conveyed sacks of raw or refined sugar, he laboured in the tank room and sometimes in the massive warehouse where they stacked cane shipped in directly from the tropics. He was a smooth talker, had had time to learn to express all kinds of notions in just the right tone, supported here and there by memorable images that had etched themselves in Jeanne's mind, as she listened with closed eyes, ready to hear everything he had to say and hold it in her memory. Aimé spoke like a worldly man who'd had hundreds of adventures, but was only now discovering a woman's body for the first time. She was a melody, a theme of a thousand variations that would transport him to unknown lands where he would feel at home. Without being too clear on his own role in them, Aimé told her stories of crossing mountains and surprising encounters with legendary figures. He had, he said, met musicians who held their fiddles between their thighs and their bows between their teeth, like this. He'd broken bread with a thousand men in bearskins, men who lived in caves like savages, but read the Bible by the light of gas lamps bought in town. Laid out on a hay bale with Jeanne tucked under his armpit, he talked with his hands interlaced behind his neck, stories unfurling in a monologue unchecked by premeditation. It was hard to know whether he was an eyewitness to the events he described, or had simply heard the stories and collected them to offer Jeanne, these stories like gifts to be unwrapped slowly and peeled of their layers on her own and at her leisure. She tried to keep up but wasn't always able. Aimé clearly enjoyed talking to her like that, to her and no one else, and she agreed to share this intimacy with him.

He'd told her that he spent his days hauling sacks of sugar on giant trade ships bound for the four corners of the earth, from Chile to Sweden to New York. No, he'd never been to New York but he'd take her there one day, cross his heart. He promised to take her with him, away from her crazy family, away from the crazy revenge-fantasies of her brother Jean, who was convinced her father had been deliberately drowned in a mixture of beer and methylene blue. He promised to take her away from there, to a little place no one knew except him, on the Maryland–Pennsylvania border, in coal country where he'd once found a little golden nugget the size of a fingernail. And he gently squeezed her finger up to the nail, to impress on her the size of the nugget, and the wealth it represented.

BY THE END of September, Jeanne was ready to give up everything and follow Aimé wherever he might take her, without a care for the responsibilities that had been thrust on her. She thought long and hard on it, in silence, in front of the mirror of the room she shared with four children who were not her own and who slept all around her, the youngest on beds, the oldest on the floor. These children weren't hers. She owed them nothing, neither her body nor her time. Such was the conclusion she came to when she opened her grandmother's silver box and sunk the hem of her handkerchief into the perfumed powder. Jeanne left quickly and without a sound, carefully stepping around every creaky floorboard.

She went down Saint-Ambroise, where the first gas lamps had now been installed, to help people get their bearings and feel safe, avoiding their little halos of light. Soon she crossed Beaudoin, a narrow and scarcely inhabited packed-dirt alley leading north to Brody's fallow fields, in the middle of which, next to a few great maples that had not moved since before Aimé was born, stood a lone barn where she felt beautiful, young, and desired.

That night Aimé promised to protect her forever, and never abandon her. He promised he'd be there for her until death did they part, in this way asking for her hand, and she put her index finger to her lips, whispering to him not to make any promises, but it was too late.

CHAPTER THIRTEEN

JUNE 1980
PITTSBURG, KS—MOUNT SPRINGER, GA

PERUSING ALBERT LANGLOIS's notebooks, most of which were filled after the birth of his son Thomas, we cannot fail to be impressed by the wealth of obscure references and sources and the arduous labour that went into deciphering archival material and collating disparate elements. The few photographs buttressing the thousands of sentences and paragraphs Albert Langlois wrote over a period of many years are of such poor quality as to be barely usable. Certain particularly dog-eared, beat-up pages seem to be more important than others, but we must not judge too hastily, appearances are deceptive, who's to say that, hidden somewhere in the folds of an unimportant sentence, we may not lay a finger on a grain of truth. That, at any rate, is what Albert would tell himself as he pored over his notes by the floor lamp's soft light.

These notebooks are not Albert's personal journals,

though his enthusiasm or his disappointment as he finds or loses a trace of his ancestor is physically tangible at times, as it is when he struggles to make connections between vague clues and precise locations. At the end of 1985, for example, Albert wrote that he was practically certain that Aimé had, in fact, crossed the Tennessee–North Carolina border one year after his own arrival in Chattanooga. This "practically" is what remains of Albert's honesty, which, in order to keep his reason intact, he could never totally abandon. Still, his mind was made up. Aimé had come close but then slipped through his fingers, he'd missed him. He'd missed him, that was all.

Where had he been that day? At the public library, rifling like a madman through late-nineteenth-century newspapers, with the help of a colleague of his wife, who had only recently given birth to his son. Was he beside this newborn child, his child, who had miraculously arrived on the anticipated date, his own tiny little leaper, born on the last day of an extraordinary February? Could it be that he was in the process of wondering at this gift from Providence — a notion he couldn't accept — in the company of his son, who would live several hundred years as Aimé had? No, Albert didn't believe in divine Providence; he felt everyone was responsible for shaping their future. Nor did he believe in the Fountain of Youth. But that didn't stop him from searching for clues in the stories and careers of this other leaper whose trace seemed ever to elude him. He didn't believe in much, but he believed in himself and this story that never stopped growing more prodigious and convoluted, with multiple ramifications that he painstakingly reconstructed in his notebooks and in his roiling mind. Had he felt Aimé coming into view before fading into the distance, only to drop him another signal, or avoid him, again and forever? Weren't these two things one and the same?

Where had he been on that day, while his ancestor walked the trails of Clingman's Dome, the state's highest point, equipped only with a canteen and waterproof boots? Was he poring over an anonymous sepia-toned photograph that showed a boy of barely sixteen, in uniform, with drumsticks in hand and a Union Army drum strapped to his shoulder? The image had been eaten away by the years to the point where it had little left to tell him, save the suggestion of possible immortality. Was he trying to convince Laura that their child was special, more than all the other kids, and that she must understand why? That she had to give him a few years for this experiment and she'd understand when the time was right? Was he trying to convince her of a possible miracle at the precise moment when Aimé, a concrete example of what he was trying to explain and express and make tangible, was so close at hand? It was 1980 and his son had just been born, on the twenty-ninth day of the second month of the longest year.

A few years later, in 1985, torn between joy at knowing a little more and anger at being led astray, he had written that there was no longer a doubt in his mind: the evidence he had gathered—he had reams of it—was conclusive.

For example, when he crossed the Appalachian Range along the interminable path that ran from Georgia all the way to Maine, Aimé had signed registers in the name of B. Van Ness. Albert had seen them with his own eyes. No one had seen him and no one cared. It came down to the same thing, he had torn out the pages where Aimé's signature appeared, faded, worn, so real and yet false. When he closed his eyes he saw Aimé walking.

HE'D BEEN THINKING about it for ages, it was one of those grandiose projects he'd fallen into the habit of putting off by unconsciously telling himself there was no need to rush. He had celebrated his fifty-fifth birthday earlier that year, alone as always. There was no rush. It sometimes seemed the world was just getting started, a new day dawning. He spoke five languages and read seven. He had been a vegetarian for the last twenty-three years. He invented mechanical objects that were of great utility both at home and in the woods, inventions he'd never patented that had become household staples. Of the many people he'd met in the course of his life, of the hundreds of people he'd spent time with and liked and even loved, sometimes over long periods of time, no one knew his secret. There were times when the desire to tell all and get everything off his chest was strong, but he knew people wouldn't take him seriously. They'd think he was crazy. He said it over and over in his head, the first sentence of a dialogue that led absolutely nowhere, ever, and was destined to derail and come apart under the weight of its contradictions.

I was born in 1760 by the Plains of Abraham.

Increasingly these words made him blush, as the wrinkles appeared on his face and around his nose, and he would say it aloud for his ears only. It made him blush and he felt a pang of shame. His reflection was less and less forgiving. He was getting older. Who would believe him? He'd seen Benjamin Franklin early one morning not long after he moved to Montreal. The great statesman was leaving the Château Ramezay with a four-soldier escort, well dressed and armed with rifles, and Aimé caught a glimpse of him. People had gathered, there were rumours he would address the crowd. It was the year his body started slowing down, as if his biological clock had suddenly stopped, perhaps crushed by a powerful, angry fist. Who would believe him when he was starting to doubt himself? Had he actually seen Franklin? He was a prisoner of mysterious images that forced him to put words to things he couldn't understand, an endless parade of images and metaphors, improbable and inappropriate, one after another, perpetually spinning around internal works that were broken somehow, out of tune. He recalled a brief acquaintance with a man who said that he would never be near- or far-sighted, it had been confirmed by leading doctors, there was no specific word for this phenomenon. They called it a "handicap," that was the only way to accurately describe it. He was the handicapped one, not the others with bifocals or contact lenses for their ageing, tired eyes; the mechanism of his eyesight was off somehow, the damage had been done in his mother's womb, or maybe after. Aimé thought about this man and imagined he might have been able to understand him. But it was too late for that now. The man had died in the sixties. Which sixties? The nineteenth or twentieth century? So many questions, it was so hard to say. And, anyway, Aimé had never been close to the man. As he looked at himself in the mirror and saw new crow's feet, he realized he was going through his worst existential crisis in two centuries.

Everywhere you looked, new inventions of every description were popping up. Life was getting easier. In a small, secret way, he'd played a part in these developments. In his spare time he'd invented sophisticated machines, spent years developing solutions to specific functional problems. It was all a game to Aimé. He never patented anything, just kept improving processes and observing his inventions out in the world from a distance. When he wasn't thinking about the tools used to accomplish everyday tasks, he studied Latin languages and read linguistics and anthropology treatises that explained how Germanic dialects had transformed into Old English and Swedish ten centuries ago. He had a passion for things older than himself: igneous rocks, fossils, trees, languages.

He lived in a large house with columns and a balustrade porch on three of four sides, a house built for cotton traders, surrounded by farmland, outside Pittsburg, Kansas. There were nights out there when the wind blew fiercely and he missed the mountains. That year, the need to walk had grown impossible to ignore and, despite his accumulated wealth and the growing circulation of his weekly newspaper, nothing could stand in the way of his desire to prove he was still capable of accomplishing something great. Who cared if it was something everyone else would file under superfluous?

He'd crossed America more times than he could count, from north to south and east to west, by car and plane and train and carriage, on horseback and on homemade rafts, but he'd never walked from coast to coast. His enthusiasm for new technology and advances in transportation made him lose sight of the joy to be had in something as simple as walking for pleasure. He remembered he'd taken a keen interest in the building of the Appalachian Trail, a saga that spanned close to forty years. The newspapers reported on fights and squabbling among partners, competition and conflicts of interest. Best friends would suddenly find themselves embroiled in hatred. People started talking when Myron Avery and Arthur Perkins took over the project from Benton MacKaye, an eccentric visionary who essentially invented hiking during the Great Depression. Mountains were on everyone's lips, from Buffalo to Atlanta. People were learning of the existence of that long, ancient mountain range which had lost pride of place in a modern world that had seemingly sprouted up overnight. Breathless editorials by radical ecologists argued for the protection of hundreds of thousands of hectares of forest. They wanted to block mining development for generations, protect the flora and fauna and trees and the mushrooms, for the sole purpose of giving Americans a place to walk through the forest.

The idea may have been counterintuitive — build a two-thousand-mile trail through the mountains that belonged to no one, were marked yet wild, alive with bears and magnificent birds — but it caught on. And Aimé got swept up in the movement: one day, why not, he'd retrace his steps and take possession of the land of his continental memory, behold it stretching out into breathtaking landscapes, never-ending mountains that would come into view in a new light, unclouded by fears of freezing to death or outrunning a gang of bootleggers he'd relieved of a cask of brandy.

For Aimé, heading out on the Appalachian Trail was a chance to rediscover places that had been important to him throughout his long life. Some of these memories were fading and disappearing. He'd spent so many years hiding out in the Alleghenies, or concealing things like his fear of being discovered, or having unimaginable adventures. For years he'd worked in coal mines, an invisible witness to industrialization, seeing and hearing men and children making up songs and telling tall tales to get through cold nights in drafty bunkhouses with no heat except for their own bodies packed in like sardines. Some of these storytellers were living legends, and when they got started even the wind fell silent, to better take in their stories. You'd encounter tame grizzlies, fish as long as farms and strong as millwheels, men who could break through seven prison walls and travel ten leagues in a single bound. He remembered long nights in cabins in the woods with men whose mouths never opened by day, they were too busy carving out the mine walls with picks and shovels. Men who might at first seem to be mutes but who, once they got going, seemed congenitally unable to shut up. Had he really been one of them? He had turned fifty-five this year, and his joints were starting to hurt as if the cartilage had finally woken up. He was often taciturn and was thinking about setting off with nothing but a backpack, canteen, and walking stick. Had he really once been that chatterbox, capable of holding an audience spellbound? In his mind's eye he could still see a storyteller whose cup ran over with beer and fanciful tales.

Late one night at a Christmas party near the very end of the last century he'd tried, to the accompaniment of a glum-faced fiddler, to tell the true story, his story, the story of a man who couldn't grow old. He had a reputation for never speaking, so when he did, people turned to listen. It was, he remembered, a pretty night, a long, grand night like a never-ending story with a thousand and one digressions. Aimé had talked about the stars and the planets, the powdered-wig scientists of the Royal Academy; he'd explained the adoption of the Gregorian calendar; the life of Isaac Newton with his dilemmas and famous apple. He'd touched on the importance of the moon and the tides, of precise calculations that prevented the world from crumbling under the weight of accumulated mathematical errors. February 29 was the most important date in the universe. Why? Because it was the date that let us live forever. He implored them to never forget this date, his El Dorado and his Fountain of Youth and Philosopher's Stone rolled into one, the point where everything converged, where lead could be transmuted into gold and coal compressed into diamonds. They were in a leap year, mind you. If pregnant women wanted their children to experience eternal life, they knew what to do. He had just explained it to them. There was no such thing as Providence, we were all responsible for shaping the future. Not a single sound upset the balance his voice found. Even the violin had fallen silent. Aimé had never spoken so eloquently before. He was developing a taste for it.

Yes, he'd developed a taste, he remembered it now. He scared himself, that night; he'd believed himself. On the chair they set out for him, he'd seemed to grow, to take on gigantic proportions, like a wise man or a sorcerer, and the four legs of the chair had started cracking under his weight. Every eye was watching him carefully and he suddenly stopped and ran out of the room, leaving a wide-open door behind him. No one ever saw him again.

SO IT WAS that one day, in another age and a world otherwise more rational, he started walking. Because he felt like it. He hit the trail with the joy of a new man. To provoke his body and remember what had happened in the past, enjoy himself in silence instead of simply growing bitter, because it was starting to drag on too long and his memories were making him sick to his stomach. Who would have believed him? Who would have believed he had watched the Brooklyn Bridge being built and walked across before its two halves met? More and more often he wondered whether his joints, the backs of his knees and his Achilles tendons would make him suffer another hundred years. His heart was far from atrophied, but he felt little sharp pains, more and more often, like electric shocks, as if a doctor were trying to rouse him with a defibrillator.

It was time to get going. He outfitted himself as best he knew how, bought everything he'd need to make sure he didn't freeze or starve to death, and a few books explaining the risks of long hikes. He might meet certain trees he'd known before, perhaps the great elms of his youth. In his new waterproof cleated boots, he might once again step in his old footsteps. In early June 1980 he reached the foot of Mount Springer, with a little smile on his face, looking like a young retiree who knows how to live, eager to make the most of his last good days. He had the best equipment money

could buy, in sweet-smelling natural and synthetic materi-
als. His walking stick alone cost more than all the clothes
he wore in the first third of his life.

In the right-hand pocket of his jacket he carried a sort
of compass of his own invention, a round object of golden
metal and crystal. It was a precise instrument, an alethiom-
eter he'd designed at the beginning of the century, and that
he would have liked to give to someone, had the opportunity ever presented itself.

As he walked into the forest, alone, he thought of her,
as he had before her death, when he decided to go see her
one last time. It must have been the massive trees waiting
to engulf him, working their magic. He just started walking and let his memory guide him. The dark green dome of
pines and beeches soon concealed the mountains awaiting
his return.

CHAPTER FOURTEEN

DECEMBER 1900
PHOENIX, AZ—MONTREAL, QC

WHEN HE THOUGHT of her he pictured an ageless face through a curtain of fog. It was a young woman's face, she was barely an adolescent when they'd first met and she would now be over fifty, if his count was right. Fifty years with all that entailed, the loosening and slackening skin, and wisdom lodged deep in her eyes, and beauty built up over time. He had seen so many people grow old and fade away without ever really knowing them, without ever being touched by their fate. How many men and women had he survived? As the number of years apart from each other grew, Jeanne continued to appear in his mind from time to time. He saw her more often, like a negative image at once blurry and focused, troubling him in the middle of whatever he was doing, a diversion and digression from his daily routine.

He thought of her at strange and unexpected times:

coming out of an important meeting with a businessman who'd hired him through obscure middlemen and had unwittingly found himself in Aimé's presence; when he suddenly noticed daylight slipping in between the slats of a poorly built or abandoned house; in the middle of a field he was crossing for the first time, up to his shoulders in wheat; in the night, between two blows of a pickaxe as he dug a grave for an old dog, the only living being who'd kept him company for a long time, and the only one who had succeeded in gaining his trust.

Without ever actually seeing for himself, either up close or at a distance, the new life she'd begun after his brief, meteoric passage, he'd learned that she was married and had managed to give birth under safe and respectable circumstances, through her brother's influence. The child had been born a Langlois, and recognized as such by the Rue Saint-Antoine merchant who'd generously agreed to take Jeanne's hand in marriage. That's what Aimé had heard and what he believed, barring credible proof to the contrary. He'd never checked, had tried everything to forget and start again, with a new name and a rifle, a bayonet and an increasingly deep-rooted hatred of the men in grey approaching from across the battlefield. The war had almost been enough to make him completely forget Jeanne and the thing he had left in her stomach. The truth was that Aimé had no idea what had happened to Jeanne in the days and months since their love-making. He hadn't set foot in Canada since the night he fled after they were surprised, limbs entwined in the hay, two young lovers guilty of a long list of crimes and unforgivable sins. He could still clearly see Jeanne's brother's face at that moment, a silhouette with razor-sharp edges. In the light of the lantern, his left hand hoisting a large brick, held high, he stood ready to strike, with three other dark, menacing silhouettes behind him.

AIMÉ SET OFF with very little: a change of clothing, a well-thumbed volume of natural science, and a not yet functional prototype of the four-needle compass he'd worked on day and night. His intuition told him it would be a short stay. He waited at the train station with a growing crowd of passengers, imagining that every one of them was on their way to visit loved ones. In their faces he could read a form of melancholy he associated with filial love and nostalgia. On that warm December day, the people waiting with him on the platform missed their parents, their hometowns, the particular countryside they'd left behind in order to seek their fortunes in the city, toil at the textile mills, or drill for oil. Some had indeed made a fortune. They wore watches on fobs and elegant clothing and were travelling great distances, north or east, to visit ageing parents before they passed away irrevocably, as if they had never existed.

Aimé exchanged polite smiles with a visibly pregnant woman sitting on one of platform's few benches. She was pretty, confident, and never stopped rubbing her stomach. Aimé figured she must have been born into poverty, somewhere in North Carolina maybe, and prospered in these territories that stretched on forever beyond the last great rivers, land the government was giving away to anyone who'd take it. She would have prospered in the company of a young, ambitious man, a man free of complexes who knew how to farm dry land and play the market. It was her first pregnancy and she was feeling good.

At the appointed time, with a whistle of steam, the train stopped at the station and the steward came down onto the platform with a cry: Hurry up, the train departs in fifteen minutes. Passengers for Amarillo, Oklahoma City, Fayetteville, Little Rock, Jackson, Nashville, Lexington, Columbus. All aboard! Railroad men hopped to and helped passengers load their baggage. With a polite apology, Aimé slipped between the members of a family that seemed to hesitate between two cars, and climbed the metal steps. His reserved compartment had a couchette and private wash-room. The sliding doors locked from the inside without a squeak and the dining car was a few steps away. He sat in the padded seat, and unbuttoned his jacket with a sigh of relief. He took in the unabated excitement of the crowd on the platform. At the edge of his field of vision, the station-master stood erect, watch in hand and whistle in mouth. He wore a moustache waxed smooth, like Aimé. This man was not taken lightly; only once he blew his whistle was the ingeniously designed and meticulously crafted mech-anism set in motion. Jets of steam emerged from the axles, brakes disengaged, and dozens of wheels started spinning, very slowly at first, so the latecomers holding onto the bars of the doors could be pulled aboard by uniformed railway-men at the last second.

The train gathered speed, quickly drawn by motive and centrifugal forces and the efficiency of a furnace fed by stok-ers. The racket all around intensified to clearly signal the train's departure, and Aimé saw a child who looked about ten, alone on the platform, so overcome with sadness he couldn't bring himself to wave goodbye.

THE DAYS PASSED and so did the nights, and landscapes that kept changing yet were always alike in colour and contour. Aimé thought about Jeanne and the state he might find her in, slightly faded but still alive and well. Her undefined face was imprinted on his retina, he was unable to properly focus on the features he had so often contemplated in the light of a gas lamp, in their secret hiding spots, or in the middle of the afternoon on the bank of the Lachine Canal, while further out on the St. Lawrence River, great ships were being fitted. Time had passed and Aimé was trying to reconcile two conflicting faces. Jeanne was in his head, there was no doubt about it, she was the reason he had left, but he had no idea what was waiting for him when he got there.

He slept well, ate well, smoked fine cigars offered by men who leaned over to light them. The seats were comfortable, the restaurant tastefully decorated. The other travellers gathered around card games and rarely spoke to him. He gave off the scent of a man who wanted to preserve his anonymity and be left alone. Nor did he speak to anyone, beyond politely thanking the waiters who brought him highballs on ice. People watched him from a distance, with a mix of admiration and envy. Perhaps he was a magnate, one of the new self-made men who were in on the bank trusts. Maybe he lived in New York City, and was on his way back with cases stuffed with treasury bonds and deeds of title. There was speculation surrounding the little metal object he frequently pulled from his pants pocket and rubbed gently as he watched the landscape unfurl. People figured he must live in one of those grand hotels that had gone up along Central Park, west of the reservoir.

The meals were good, the meat was always fresh, even after Columbus where he changed trains and was seated in a much older car. This venerable north-south line smelled different, more leathery somehow, and smoke clung to the curtains, but Aimé enjoyed his quiet, comfortable couchette. Suddenly, a little after he crossed the Pennsylvania border, the mountains appeared in the distance.

It had been years since he gained weight, he could still boast a slender waist and the ropy hands of a young man. He ran his finger over his collarbone, and felt the way it stuck out, an oft-repeated gesture that was almost a nervous tic. When he met Jeanne, people figured he'd been alive less than a quarter century. No one suspected how much older he was. But the next time he saw her she would be older than him. An explanation would be required. Or not. He already felt presumptuous in assuming she'd see him, or that he'd even manage to make contact. He might have to settle for observing her from afar. Every time the train pulled into a station, in a small town or major city, Aimé thought about getting off and turning his back on this whim of his that wouldn't make anything different or new. In those few seconds of complete hesitation, he redefined what closure meant to him. And, if he stood up, he'd sit down. Take a breath, fight off his boyish nervousness. High-flying cottony clouds formed complex patterns in the sky, a forewarning of hard rain. The train hurtled along fast. You'd need a lot of imagination to read anything in the white shapes colouring the sky, as far as the eye could see.

Aimé had abandoned her to her fate thirty-six years ago. He wondered whether she'd even remember him. How many people had he forgotten? But the child, the oldest child, who'd been named Langlois like the others who must surely have come after—wouldn't he be a constant reminder to Jeanne? Had he even survived? If remembering Jeanne's face with any degree of precision had become a challenge, picturing the child was an outright impossibility. While the train approached Albany, Aimé cleared his mind, tormented by this fiction of a child growing up in the bosom of a happy, healthy family in Montreal, striding into the twentieth century. One thing was certain: he wasn't coming back for him; he was coming back for her.

He hadn't been a coward often in his long life. The exception was that one time he'd run away, without looking back, in the middle of what was left of the night. Thanks to his network of contacts and intimate knowledge of back roads, he'd made it to the border by dawn. It was as if the consequences of his actions had been too heavy to bear, in the hours and months that followed, so he'd fled without looking back. Jeanne had been taken in by an honest man. He was sure to hate Aimé without ever having laid eyes on him. It had to be admitted, he was also her saviour.

Now that decades had passed, it was easy to say: perhaps he should have come back for her instead of joining the army in place of that shirker who was disinclined to squander his birthright. It was easy to say, but Aimé felt it bore repeating. He judged himself harshly, his heart beat quickly and unsteadily. His skin grew pale as the outside temperature fell, as the North drew closer and snowflakes took the place of raindrops. He took out his compass and noted that the mechanism was off-kilter again: the needles were vibrating constantly but not pointing at any one symbol, not indicating anything definite, except a magnetic agitation in the air, as if parallel worlds were colliding.

AIMÉ GOT OFF the train, which had been like a home for the past week of his life. Last Tuesday he'd left Phoenix, where the temperature was 37 degrees Celsius, and here he was in Montreal, in the middle of a snowstorm. When he got off at Windsor Station, the Neo-Romanesque palace of columns and arched ceilings that hadn't been there forty years earlier, a gust of wind blew down narrow Rue de la Gauchetière and Aimé caught his hat at the last second. You couldn't even see the spire of St. George's church. The passersby seemed to be walking on magic carpets, and the horses pulling the carriages of the bourgeois citizens snorted noisily in the icy wind.

The city had changed. On the streets adjacent to the station the buildings stood closer together. The lamps were electric now, and their wan yellow gleam was the only colour in the sea of white and grey of the snowy late afternoon. Canadian Pacific employees were hard at work clearing the station entrance with enormous shovels, the fringes of their coats heavy with snow, their moustaches frozen. Hundreds of people were in the street, as in any other city, on foot and on omnibuses and even in automobiles. The blizzard had slowed all traffic to a crawl. Power lines for the tramway criss-crossed the street overhead, forming spiderwebs and mosaics between the facades.

After confidently striding to the small hotel on Rue Saint-Jacques, the staff was waiting for him with a blanket and a steaming hot grog. There was a fire crackling in his room, and Aimé immediately set to work. While his clothes dried on the hearth, he summoned one of the hotelier's sons and sent him on an errand downtown, thanking him in advance with American coins stamped with the face of a great president. The Canadian stared at them in his palm, not knowing what to say. Aimé closed the door and said, in somewhat creaky French: Send the inspector up the moment he arrives. There's no need to ring, I'll be waiting.

The room was luxurious. Drapes hung from golden triangles above the windows, the mantle was adorned with curios. The room was warm and softly lit, and it put him at ease despite the hint of wind that never stopped blowing outside. Aimé waited patiently for his contact to arrive, studying one of the two vases symmetrically arranged on a coffee table. He poured a drink, to pass the time and feel the liquor on his gums. The crystal bottles were intricately carved. From the high south-facing window slowly being covered over by frost he could picture, above the skyline, the dark, flowing St. Lawrence which refused to freeze, and the black silhouette of Victoria Bridge, which he had just crossed.

There was a knock on the door and Aimé, throat burning from the inferior rye, jumped up to answer it. Before him stood a giant man, as tall as he was, in an overcoat covered in snow on the left side. Aimé beckoned him in, helped him take off his coat, and hung it next to his own. The man took a cigarette case out of an inside pocket of his jacket, and offered it to Aimé. He was clearly happy to meet at last.

"No thanks, I never smoke cigarettes. But do sit down. Can I offer you a drink?"

"A whiskey would warm me up nicely, thanks."

"'Whiskey' is a bit of a stretch for what we have here, but it's the best I can do."

Aimé proceeded:

"I haven't been in Montreal for a long time. It's true what they say, it's impressive!"

"I don't know about 'impressive.' Cold, mostly. And it'll take them two weeks to clear the streets. Fingers crossed this snow will stop falling one of these days. It's been coming down sideways like this since Monday!"

Aimé lit his guest's smoke with a silver lighter and tried to convey understanding with a smile, to show that he too knew what it was like to get through a harsh winter. He passed a well-deserved whiskey to the inspector, who slowly moved to take it and got down to business.

"But I imagine you didn't summon me urgently to discuss the Canadian weather. Last time we spoke, it was important business, and you didn't even come in person."

Aimé sat down in the armchair facing him. He undid the buttons on his shirt and his watch chain reappeared. He listened to himself speak. His French was lifeless, mechanical almost, like a rusty machine in need of oiling, one he'd think twice about using. It made him want to pull his jaw muscles taut and spit, to wash his mouth of those English-inflected 'r's he couldn't seem to shake. How could he speak so poorly when he still thought and dreamed in French? He imagined the word *"effectivement,"* and in his mind pronounced it perfectly—but that wasn't how it came out, instead it was squeezed through his tongue and teeth and his lips in a strange, foreign way he could not control.

"Effectivement, but this time it's a private matter. Nothing to do with business. That's why I'm here. This is not a matter that could be handled by telegram. I'm looking for someone. I need your help finding her."

"A woman."

"That's right. I'm almost sure she still lives here, some-where in the city. I need your help. It's an urgent matter for me."

"How much time do I have?"

Without waiting for Aimé to answer, the inspector continued:

"What's her name?"

"Langlois. Jeanne Langlois."

"Langlois? As in Langlois the judge?"

"I've never heard of any judge named Langlois. Is he an acquaintance of yours?"

"Yes and no. Everyone in town knows who he is. The youngest judge ever appointed to the Supreme Court. He left for Ottawa, no more than a month or two ago. He's not even forty. It's been all over the papers."

"I don't know. Could be."

Aimé seemed worried suddenly, and stared into space. The inspector continued:

"Langlois is a common name, might be nothing. I was just thinking out loud."

"No, it's a good lead. Langlois the judge. Start there, it's a good lead."

THE INSPECTOR PHONED the hotel a few hours later, at dawn, to let him know where the woman could be found. He understood the urgency now: Jeanne Langlois, mother of Justice Pierre Langlois, recent Supreme Court of Canada appointee, was in Notre-Dame Hospital. She was dying of cancer. Terminal phase, they said, barely able to recognize her loved ones, children, husband. Aimé thanked the inspector and hung up. His ankles hurt, as if he had aggravated an old injury, as if a metal plaque were slowly rusting away under his skin. He had to sit down. Along his legs he felt a very old pain, which reminded him of his childhood, one no one could hope to understand anymore, least of all him, who had been dragged through the mud and thrust into the arms of well-meaning nuns with rotting teeth and putrid breath.

Aimé had been through two *fins de siècle* and had seen two new centuries dawn. They were always moments of turmoil: everything was dying and brimming with life, the number came up for some, while others lived in an optimistic swirl of new beginnings. He'd seen the grand celebrations that ushered in the nineteenth century when the excitement was at its apex. He was young then, hesitating between becoming an explorer and embarking on a life of crime. In December 1799, he remembered, people were equally scared

and excited, anything seemed possible, both heaven on earth
and the apocalypse seemed to loom just around the corner.
It was possible to believe the white race was fundamentally
superior to all others, that white men could own men of
other races; books and convincing learned treatises were
written on the subject. Aimé had been through that century and was amazed at the great changes in the world and
people's minds, the sudden arrival of automation, the work-
ers' revolution and the explosion of industry, the way these
upheavals were at once so violent and so gradual. He'd settled on the life of a criminal explorer in which every friend-
ship, whether with man or woman, dog or other animal,
was fleeting. He had allowed himself to become attached
to few things, and always tough ones, only things tougher
than himself, things that gave him perspective on his own
very long journey.

His legs gave out on him when he hung up the phone,
and he was sitting in the armchair, thinking of the possibility of his own death, of what it could mean. The people
he'd known who were dead numbered in the hundreds, all
had died of different causes, some understood and others
not. When he saw how some of them died, shrunken and
defeated by time, he was left speechless as a child, despite
his venerable brain.

He'd started thinking about Jeanne for reasons obscure
and impossible to pin down, though he wasn't afraid to
explore them. His intuition had brought him back. And
now here he was, a couple miles away from the body poised
to give up the fight and relinquish her soul, or whatever
you wanted to call that unnameable thing inside her. He

got up, opened the door, and hurtled down the stairs. He
climbed back up to get his coat and hat and, after closing
the door, hurtled back down the stairs and set out into the
blizzard. He came back inside, his moustache all messed
up by the wind, and asked the young man at the front desk
the way to Notre-Dame Hospital. It had been so long since
he'd lived here, he didn't know where anything was. The
hospital hadn't even existed back then. Easy, just take Rue
Saint-Jacques east toward the port, then head south, you'll
find the hospital right by the big market, you can't miss it,
even in the snow and gusts of wind that strip the world of
its colour. A big white building facing the port. He couldn't
miss it. It was barely a mile, but he might have a hard time
finding a carriage willing to take him there in this weather.
The front-desk man drawled on, politely talking to himself.
Aimé was already gone.

The whirlwinds of snowflakes formed a vortex in the
street and Aimé leaned too far forward, his body bent at
an incongruous angle so he wouldn't be blown over. He
was walking against the wind, and suddenly the wind was
pushing him in the back, or spinning all around him in a
spiral. Aimé held his hat in his left hand, which was getting
chapped. The hair in his nose and his moustache had frozen
in seconds. Day was breaking, the first bundled-up work-
ers were showing up at the port and greeting each other
in between the banks that might or might not open today.
On the corner of McGill St. a group of young men waited
for a coach to stop and pick them up, but there was at least
eight inches of snow in the middle of the street. Without
proper boots it was hard for Aimé to move forward. He

pulled himself along by walls and lampposts. His cheeks and nose hurt.

Each step only seemed to take him backwards. No building, no matter how high, afforded protection from the wind, which actually seemed to be gathering momentum in the spaces between buildings, rushing into the alleyways and climbing the facades of the tall banks, like an eagle determined to perform the role nature has assigned it. Several times during a trip that seemed to get longer as he went, Aimé was forced to leave the sidewalk and walk in the street. Faint desire paths were being traced in the snow, but were visible only with psychic powers or from a perch high above in a church steeple. Would the city wake up once the wind died down, or spend the day in contagious torpor? The last few storms Aimé had witnessed had been sand, not snow. He wondered which was worse. At least he could open his mouth to breathe deeply without choking on the mortal grains. Again and again he reached a street corner; it was never the one he was looking for. Though he had lived there for more than fifty years, nothing was familiar anymore. Everything was completely different; he couldn't recognize a thing, not even the old signs at the port. The St. Pierre River had been filled in and paved over. The St. Lawrence had retreated noticeably, its presence receded into the distance as industry encroached.

As a final trial before reaching his destination, a snowbank had been plowed in the night to clear a path for emergency vehicles. It was an immense mountain of hardpack and ice, built up and then abandoned, as if in a panic, obstructing the one-way street on the north side. It must have taken a large team to clear the path. Once he reached the top of this miniature mountain, Aimé was level with the second-floor windows. If they hadn't been thoroughly frosted over he could almost have seen the bedridden patients inside, warm and sheltered from the storm but not from death.

He would return to Phoenix with plugged sinuses and a runny nose, like a careless boy. The air popped his blood vessels. His coat was ruined. He put his hand in his pocket to check that his compass was still there. The metal was so cold it stuck to his fingers. His ears were burning and growing red in the grey light of day when he triumphantly threw open the door and entered the hospital lobby.

He was breathing heavily and a nurse came up to ask if everything was okay. Was he in pain? Hurt? Injured? Had he slipped on the ice? She was practically holding him up with a hand on his shoulder and another on his flank. Her cap fell off and she made no move to pick it up off the ground. A lock of blonde hair slipped out over her face. Aimé stood up straight. He was fine, just a bit out of breath on account of the cold. His ears started twitching in time with his pulse. There was nothing wrong, he wasn't here for medical care. He was here to visit a patient. It was urgent. He was here to see Jeanne Langlois, née Beaudry. Could they point him in the right direction?

The nurse guided him toward a hardwood counter sculpted with religious carvings, and opened a register.

"Madame Langlois is in the recovery room, access is restricted. Are you family?"

"No, I'm an old acquaintance of Madame Langlois's. I absolutely have to see her. I recently learned of her illness, and travelled from the United States to see her. I arrived yesterday. I only just learned she's in the terminal phase. I'm an old acquaintance. Tell her I'm here, she'll agree to see me."

"I understand, sir, but Madame Langlois's health requires that we—"

"No, you don't understand. I've known Jeanne Langlois for a very long time. It's imperative that I see her before she dies. We haven't spoken for years. I've come from Arizona. I left last Tuesday. I'm sorry, I—I don't mean to be impolite."

Aimé had placed his hands on the counter in front of the young nurse. His fingers were clenched over the edge. She gave him an empathetic look, visibly seeking a solution. She felt for him. No matter how hard he pressed, the wood refused to break into pieces.

"Yes, I see now, I understand your situation. Wait a moment, I'm going to speak to my superior. What did you say your name was?"

"Aimé. I'm Aimé Bolduc. Tell her Aimé is here."

She disappeared down a dark hallway and Aimé heard a door open. The lobby had electric lighting, completely electric, the lights never flickered. He could see the black wires running along the stone walls, and now noticed other people, sitting and waiting. Nurses in uniform, just like the one who had dealt with him, walked around the large room with a vaulted ceiling, talking quietly and calmly. No one raised their voices, only the wind could be heard when a gust worked its way inside. Aimé's body was slowly returning to normal temperature. His throat was scratchy and he massaged his Adam's apple as he looked around. When she knew he was here she would ask him to come to her.

A quarter of an hour later, when it seemed the sun was breaking through the layer of cloud spread over the city, Aimé heard the already familiar footsteps of the young woman, a typical sound of shoes on granite. The nurse came back, with a Grey Nun whose skin bore the marks of scarlet fever. She came up to Aimé and held out her hand in a way that was at once professional and welcoming.

"I'm Sister Élodie Mailloux. Follow me, Madame Langlois will see you. She's waiting."

AS THEY WALKED down the straight, rectangular hallways of the west wing toward the cancer ward, Sister Mailloux told Aimé that, while Jeanne no longer reacted to the presence of visitors, she had said his name more than once. Neither she nor the doctors had realized it was a name, not the infinitive "to love," until Sister Valois came in to tell them there was a man in the waiting room demanding to see her.

"She's very weak. Don't be alarmed. She doesn't have much time left, I'm afraid. We stopped treatment last week. But when I went to see her just now, to tell her you were here, her eyes lit up."

Their footsteps echoed off the walls and ceilings, and they conversed in polite whispers. Sister Mailloux kept her hands in her uniform's front pockets. She stared at her toes as she walked, giving directions as they went. She told Aimé that Jeanne had been admitted for breast cancer, and the cancer had spread. Experimental treatments using electricity had been tried without success. She wanted to be clear, even stopped for a moment as she said the words; this was no longer the woman Aimé had known. Her face was swollen and radically transformed. He might even have trouble recognizing her, both her face and her voice. She wanted to be crystal clear: Jeanne was nearing the end of the line, his visit was one final favour they were granting her, before she passed on. Aimé listened, and was grateful, a gratefulness the sister surely felt. Sister Mailloux nodded her assent. When she smiled, her scars pulled tight. She moved sideways and, behind her, a door appeared. Yes, he could go in now. She was waiting. Her bed was at the end, to the right. She was waiting for him.

Aimé turned the knob and pushed the metal door. It squeaked on its hinges. He had to lean a little to avoid knocking his head on the doorframe. He was standing in an immense room, as big as a gymnasium, with dozens of beds. A heavy silence accompanied every sound, every complaint. Patients lay under white or pale green sheets. Aimé surveyed the room and then walked toward the beds at the end. He was anxious to see Jeanne again, talk to her one last time, but he suddenly felt bad for giving in to this impulse. It might have been a mistake. She wouldn't have forgotten him, but that didn't mean she'd forgiven him for running away. He trod carefully so as not to bother the patients, his presence felt only in a gentle dragging of his heels. His throat was scratchy, he could feel his sweat and his sticky clothing.

And there she was. Lying on an uncomfortable-looking mattress with her arms hanging out of the sheets and a bracelet on her wrist, lips parched, a shadow of her former self. Her white hair was cut short, still curly but now scrubbed of all its colour. Aimé had the hair of a thirty-five-year-old, still dark as a tree branch full of life. Her eyes were closed. Countless finely etched wrinkles traversed her face in every direction. Her mouth was open, to breathe through, as her nasal passages no longer worked.

"Jeanne."

"Aimé."

"I'm here."

"You haven't changed."

"You neither."

The groaning of the patients lying all around, some vying for a nurse's attention while others simply bemoaned their fate, filled the ears of Aimé, who leaned over a little further to hear what Jeanne was saying.

"My God, you're so handsome."

"You're beautiful too."

"I'm going to die."

"Don't say that."

Jeanne looked him right in the pupils, and hers immediately contracted, as if a bright light had approached.

"Not you, Aimé. My Aimé. I think you're immortal."

It was the thinnest trickle of a voice, the merest whisper. The wind was blowing outside, savage and indifferent. Aimé told himself that he had heard correctly. He put his hand on hers, on her stretchy, soft, still-warm skin.

CHAPTER FIFTEEN

APRIL 1865
THE MISSISSIPPI FORESTS

YEARS LATER THERE was one episode he wouldn't share with Crane, though the bourbon loosed his tongue and the cocaine brought vivid memories coursing back. The fighting was in its final weeks. In the generals' tents, plans were being laid for the Battle of Appomattox, while Sherman's March had left a trail of smoking ruins in its wake. In faraway ancestral lands off in the horizon, the cotton fields were aflame, every day new towns were pillaged and granaries and guns requisitioned in the name of the Union and President Lincoln. Criers proclaimed that the rebels would be defeated any day. Men and women who surrendered could expect favourable treatment. No one doubted how this war would end. Their one concern was burying their jewels in the clay under the floorboards, in the hope the foundations would be spared by the blazes and they might go back home one day.

Aimé's battalion was posted not far from Jackson, where a final offensive to wipe out the last pockets of resistance was being planned. A lot was happening at once, orders were contradictory, manoeuvres often far from clear. One day the men were told the enemy was on its last legs, the next they were ordered to move quickly, as if making ready to attack. The bulk of the Union forces was posted further east, close to Atlanta, where the real decisions were made. They said Lincoln himself might be there. They said Grant had managed to break through the front lines. It was a matter of weeks.

In the field the old soldiers complained of a lack of co-ordination and apparent absence of logic. A feeling that the whole thing was absurd was setting in among the rank and file. Constant movements were taking their toll. People were getting angry. Aimé had noticed this feeling boiling up in him, just as it was in all the others. Boredom made people irascible, nothing was happening, they were keeping busy washing and mending their stockings and gaiters, and then out of nowhere a lieutenant would ride up and bark orders in a barrage of threats and insults.

No matter where you looked the sky was dark blue and orange, as if the garish northern lights had travelled south to the plains and Mississippi forests, starting fires and razing crops. The trees were budding, the morning dew sweet. A few weeks earlier Aimé had been among the troops who'd taken the town of Meridian. A filthy sergeant, second-class, in a torn uniform, had freed a group of slaves, maybe ten, mere youths or even kids wandering down the main street with terror in their eyes and no idea where to go. He'd climbed onto a milk crate and, with his hand on his heart, officially proclaimed them free men. Aimé was exhausted like the others, his chin propped up on his rifle, which was dug into the sandy ground. He watched the sergeant make his declaration. And then: nothing. Go forth, he entreated, and live free. All these men died for you, for your freedom. They fought for your dignity, now they're dead. He pointed at his brothers-in-arms as he spoke these words. The black children disappeared between two houses, afraid, but the soldier had not been rebuffed by an angry officer or a passing authority figure.

Aimé had barely woken up when a lieutenant came galloping, dodging low branches as best he could. A plan for the coming days was taking shape. Patrols would be sent out along the Mississippi, where the Confederate regiments lay in hiding, waiting to take detours along the river and rejoin the troops positioned further north. Aimé and the fifteen remaining soldiers in his platoon were chosen to head off in the early morning. They were pointed out, all the soldiers standing closest to the commanding officer. Their emaciated faces and torn clothing earned them no pity. The man standing next to Aimé, a big fellow from Boston named Conklin, had lost a chunk of ear and the wound hadn't scarred right. Rancid pus was oozing out, which he wiped with a bent index finger that he could not refrain from holding to his nose and smelling. These men could still stand on their own two feet, but it took some doing. One had taken a bullet on the barrel of his rifle right as he readied to shoot, and this coincidence had made him superstitious. He didn't talk about it anymore, preferred to keep it to himself, but in his mind there was no longer any doubt: God had chosen to save him. God was on his side. He must stop shooting at his fellow men. The humming sound you could hear in the night was him, praying in pseudo-silence; he was a very pious man. Aimé respected his devotion, but also sometimes felt the need to grab his comrade by the shoulder and give him a shake, rattle his cage, set his brains in motion, maybe knock them against his skull a bit.

They were told, over and again, that it would be risky. The front and ultimate victory lay far off to the east; their mission was to take to the forest in the opposite direction and head backwards, back into land where martial law no longer held. Ambushes were a real danger, not to mention Indians.

Off to the side, slurping a cold bland broth of rutabaga and chicken carcass, Aimé figured that, though not far from a suicide mission, this would at least be a break from the routine. If they came upon enemy units they were to surround them, halt their progress, and face them. At the slightest sign of hostility they were authorized to engage in combat. No one would be coming back. Aimé stared at the outer limits of the Yankee camp. Beyond the clearing the land stretched on forever. He'd never seen the Mississippi River, let alone the other side. He knew the great river had at least four thousand tributaries, and a delta somewhere, far to the south, where it flowed into the ocean.

The sun was rising slowly over tall pines when the sixteen soldiers assembled in front of the officers' tents. In a three-minute ceremony, the lieutenant made Aimé a corporal, and the new unit set off with their guns and canteens, their boots full of holes. They didn't come back to say goodbye to the others, as they crossed the line of trees into a forest unbroken by road or path. Aimé quickly found traces of age-old Indian trails, their sole chance of survival in such small company, and they placed their fate in the hands of the gods, who each man pictured differently. After a few hours' walk the vegetation grew so dense they had to clear their path with bayonets. Branches whipped their legs and eyes. Unfamiliar sounds were all around. Their packs lay heavy on their shoulders. It was absurd. They were at once predator and prey, with no way of knowing which. They held their weapons tight and closed ranks.

Each man carried something of importance to him, in a pocket or around his neck, to mark him as an individual in the giant indivisible mass of the army. A saint, a letter, an ivory comb. Aimé had fled Montreal empty-handed, and Van Ness had given him nothing but promises and money in a bank account. He wore a blue and yellow armband, a patchwork of cloth scraps, as temporary insignia of his new rank. When he made it back to army headquarters they would sew him a felt badge. If he made it back. He hadn't shaved since the last snow. His left hand was down to two fingernails, pinky and ring, he'd lost the three others during a skirmish, trying to hold onto a wet stone on the edge of a cliff. The enemy bullets had burst out overhead and he had finally let go, and ended up at the bottom of a ravine, fifteen feet down, surrounded by roots and brambles.

When night fell they got to talking for the first time in hours, with pasty mouths and rotten breath. Aimé was pretty happy with the distance they'd covered. They'd set up a rough camp on the banks of a roaring river none of them could name. The rush of water somehow made them feel they could speak more freely, and they got to telling stories. Aimé realized that, aside from Jim Conklin, he didn't know his men's names. They were the sons of farmers or shopkeepers, they had come from Rhode Island or Maine or New York. One, whose flattened nose had suffered more than one break, told them he had a girl waiting, with sweetness in his voice; they all did, came his answer. As they built a fire and as they ate they told stories of normal life, talked about livestock and pets, dogs and cows and even cats. One described a three-legged cat, on a dairy farm in Pennsylvania, who'd seen enough in her life to rival all General Lee's attacks. They should have seen that damn cat! Everyone started laughing, and the fire crackled louder. The sound of the current in the river bend was reassuring. In a way they understood that all stories were means of recovering their own memories, and losing themselves in a camaraderie that knit them tight and even had the power to allay their fears and calm their trembling; they were all the same when you got right down to it, united by that one shared notion.

At dawn they set off westward along the path of the winding river. Aimé was a good guide, no one questioned his directions. They'd been issued an impressive store of ammunition, and divvied it up equally, and it weighed heavy on their backs and kidneys. They didn't all carry knives, some had lost their blades long ago in a battlefield, a chest, a throat. Aimé moved silently, avoiding the branches strewn across the forest floor.

The echo of a crack could be heard to the south. It sounded like a tree being chopped down, but was surely something else. Aimé signalled to the others to stop. Still and silent, they listened, trying to concentrate to isolate the sounds of the river from the rest. Aimé's neck muscles tightened. His skin was deeply tanned by winter sun, and dirty, his muscles taut and well defined. It was getting closer, coming at them. It was very close. By gently placing the palm of his hand on a tree trunk, as if to hold himself up and feel the bark at the same time, he ordered the others to camouflage themselves as best they could in the ferns and prepare for action. A laugh rang out through the wall of trees.

Aimé waited for a clear view of the grey uniform emerging from the dense field of vegetation, a man on the move with his comrades, advancing with difficulty, beckoning to them from behind his back, a sign the others understood immediately. A tight clutch of Confederate soldiers was crossing a small clearing. Some looked scared, others carefree, whistling while they marched. No one thought to surround them, or take them prisoner, it hadn't occurred to any of the young soldiers in blue, who came out of hiding without yelling, without savage war cries, but with weapons drawn and pointed at the enemy. They all fired at once, Aimé first, or second, with a focus and strength in his forearms he hadn't known for months. Sixteen shots rang out at once, followed by a weak, disorganized, shapeless counterstrike. Tucked behind a stump, Aimé reloaded and then shot again. His aim was true. A redhead was hit in the face, and before falling backwards he leaped up in the air, as if he'd seen a monster.

A few seconds of silence, then the birds started chirping again. Aimé watched the gun smoke dissipate behind the trees and called out to his men. All seemed to be alive. Conklin had caught a piece of shrapnel in the shoulder, near the collarbone, and was in a lot of pain. Five others had been injured, including the youngest, who'd tripped in the moss and thought he had a twisted ankle. A stupid injury, he felt bad. They all agreed the fall may well have saved his life. He rubbed his shin, sitting on an empty tree trunk, staring out at the meadow in front of him, supine bodies spread out in the tall grass where they'd fallen in the April sun.

On their own they had killed fifteen enemy soldiers, traitors to the nation, barely pubescent kids in stockings knit by their mothers. They started checking the bodies, running their hands over them, searching them. Not one had regulation kit, their grey vests and caps were collections of patches, some wore crudely stitched breeches clearly stripped from Union dead. Aimé pulled at a boot that looked to be his size, but when it came off the stench was so horrific he jumped up and away. The foot was sliced from toe to heel, with bunions growing between the veins in three different spots, and the ankle bone stuck out of the skin through a pustulent wound that was black and white around the edges. As he backed up, he accidentally trod on the face of one of the dead, whose brains lay splattered on the ground. He was startled, then black spots appeared in his field of vision. The body moved and he shot it, making a large hole in the ribcage. The others raised their heads for a fraction of a second. They looked like vultures going about the business of survival.

Aimé instructed his men to gather what food and ammo they could. Rifles too, they'd find a way to carry them. Already they'd been there too long, the clearing was a bad

position, they shouldn't stay any longer than they had to. He
was battling the stubborn leather strap of a canteen with his
knife when he heard sounds coming from the forest nearby.
He figured it might be a sixteenth man and raised his gun,
but there were whispers in his ear that a whole section was
arriving. Had he heard? More men were on the way, over
twenty for sure, on their way to a massacre. They had to take
the enemy by surprise, it was their only chance. In under
a minute Aimé's men disappeared under the trees, further
north, where they had come from. It wouldn't work, there
was no way to surprise them this time. They'd have to fight.

The black spots weren't going away. Aimé's peripheral
vision wasn't right, when he shifted his focus to the left his
vision fogged over almost completely. He no longer knew
where the others were, and tried hard to penetrate the blur
of colour all around. The sunny clearing was the one place
he could look without feeling like he was going to faint.
He was still holding his knife when he saw a human figure
emerge from the clearing, far away, facing him, dispro-
portionately large. It was coming toward him, silently and
without hesitation, confident yet cautious, arm held behind
the head to signal to the still-invisible others whether to
follow or stay put. Aimé saw an old uniform yellowed by
sun and rain, a large upside-down knife, and long hair
reaching down to the creature's chin, as dark as the hair
of the Montagnais he'd once known. The figure was moving very fast with a controlled nervousness, and remained
out of focus. It stopped a few steps into the clearing, above
the bodies, towering over the bodies. A dozen rebel soldiers emerged from the woods and took in the scene of

the massacre. Several immediately pointed guns at the surrounding trees. Others got down on their knees, as if felled by exhaustion or kneeling to pray. This single tall, thick person, clearly the party's leader, who Aimé couldn't take his eyes off and who scared him as he'd never been scared before, started stripping bodies of whatever the soldiers in blue had left behind. The large knife severed the leather thong Aimé had fought with a few minutes earlier. Objects taken from the bodies were packed in pockets, a saddlebag, and a sort of quiver worn behind the back.

Aimé stayed focused on the moving form, unable to identify it or understand why exactly he was so afraid. It was both anchored in the moment, in every act and movement, and totally detached, as if elsewhere, in another dimension or another life. It looked like man and woman simultaneously, from a distance its traits seemed almost soft, an illusion compounded by the lack of beard. When you looked closely the jawline was rough, with strong lines, and the dark skin was creased like an Indian chief's, but this person was white, you could tell by the shape of the eyes.

Aimé inadvertently stepped in a pile of dead leaves, and the sound travelled to the group gathered around the bodies. The figure lifted its head and its pant legs dropped down over its calves. Upright, it stood as tall as the sun it blocked out. Aimé, squatting behind a trunk, unable to look it in the face, imagined this creature could see him through the bark, and that nothing could save him now. He felt naked and weak, as if neither knife nor rifle could protect him.

Aimé heard the figure addressing the soldiers:

"What are you waiting for? Take what you can, we're next."

The voice belonged to neither man nor woman, and the foreign accent took Aimé back in time and far from here, far from Mississippi, to the banks of another river. His nausea wasn't going away, and he couldn't seem to regain the strength in his muscles. Hunched up in the bush, he felt his Adam's apple moving around his neck and his uvula swelling. Silence returned and Aimé could sense the group advancing toward him in tight single file. He didn't know what he could do to avoid dying here, shot full of lead or disembowelled with a dagger, and started tearing out strips of fern as camouflage to cover himself. His limbs were unresponsive, his movements choppy, he was trembling incessantly. He closed his mouth and took a deep breath.

There were footsteps right next to him. He could see men through the foliage, men as leery and fearful as he was. The forest was dense, almost unpassable. The leader was making signs and sending men off in specific directions: go that way, step here, move forward. Aimé could feel fear rising up all around him, not only in his body but in theirs as well. He could feel their conjoined contempt and admiration for this person leading them straight into an ambush they probably wouldn't survive. Once he was certain everyone had passed, and they were disappearing from view through the trees and the rays of sunlight piercing the gaps in the branches, Aimé forced himself to follow them. He went from trunk to trunk, slowly, breathing deeply and attracting no attention. He didn't know where he was anymore, had lost all trace of Conklin and the others. In the distance he could hear the burbling river. He could see which direction they had come from, but was still disoriented. From his position he could make out the back of the leader's neck. He had to take his gun and aim, he was a good marksman, several officers had told him so. It helped that he'd learned to shoot with such inferior weapons, guns that exploded in your hand and burned your cheeks; next to these, the Union Army standard-issue rifles were technological marvels. He'd never been so afraid of dying, despite his invisibility. In front of him, sticking out like a target, was the back of the creature's neck, and he could barely move a muscle.

As the spaces between trees grew larger, the leader stopped and signalled to the men to take aim, the enemy was near. This battle was going to happen. Behind the giant's head, a fist unclenched one finger at a time. At the end of the countdown, shots rang out, loud and crisp, in the air, in the middle of nowhere, powder exploded into a thousand sparks and a cloud of smoke formed, strafed by rays of sunlight. Then Aimé saw men emerge from every direction to attack, desperate and completely disorganized, running and hollering; men with wounds and broken rifles set upon the rebels and Aimé saw six of them fall as one, as if yanked from behind by giant hands.

Then it began.

Before the men in blue could fire a single shot the leader grabbed Conklin by the hair and dug his eye out. Conklin screamed in pain. Then the enemy thrust the dagger into his throat, and sliced his neck from side to side. The rest of Conklin's body fell limp, and rocked from left to right, still held in place by vertebrae and tendons. The leader held it up by the hair, dead and jiggling, and the others stood still for a moment, as if to take measure of what had just occurred.

Two soldiers in grey were felled by bullets and Aimé saw two or three rebels hit the ground to reload. He started breathing faster and faster. His hands were no longer co-operating. He had to grab a weapon and join his comrades. Behind him cries rang out from every direction, increasingly violent, decreasingly human. It was all around, closing in on him, the only way out was to remain unseen. Whichever way he turned he saw a spray of blood and smoke darkening the atmosphere.

In the thick of the fighting, the rebels had taken control. Awestruck at first, the men grew bold immediately after Conklin's decapitation. Shots came from every direction. Aimé saw the leader signal to two soldiers, who leaped on an enemy tangled up in his own gear. As the man struggled to pull out his knife, one of the men in grey thrust his own blade into his chest, then came in close to look him in the eye as he sliced upward with great force. Aimé could see the effort in the man's clenched teeth. To the left, in between two dead stumps that had lain there thousands of years, a man had shoved his bayonet up the anus of one of Aimé's young soldiers, the first to hit the ground. A Confederate soldier's sharp, powerful cry rang out and the others joined him, slapping their mouths like the Indians of legend.

Paralyzed and on the verge of losing consciousness, Aimé watched the scene unfolding in front and behind and around him. He was both part of it and in the background, unable to bring himself to act, unable to summon the absurd courage he would need to die alongside his comrades. But who were these young men, when you got right down to it? He didn't move, didn't stir, let himself completely disappear while the leader applied boot spurs to a soldier's face. The blows followed one after the other, he didn't stop kicking until the soldier's face was little more than a squashed-in black and purple lump.

The outcome of the skirmish was soon beyond doubt. Every man in blue lay on the ground in unfortunate positions. Of the fifteen Aimé had left Jackson with two days earlier, only five or six were still alive. They were trying their best to get away or take refuge in a thicket to reload or throw random projectiles. Aimé, eyes wide open, unable to question the evidence his senses presented, saw the leader lean over one of the dying men and slice open his chest to then pull out his heart. Instead of biting into it like a piranha, the giant gave it a good toss.

The still-smoking heart fell at Aimé's feet. He clenched his teeth so as not to throw up. Years later, he wouldn't share this episode with Crane, the young man with the kind eyes and good manners who had never fought in a war and yet wanted so badly to describe it, realistically and without artifice. He talked about plenty of other horrible things, and Crane listened attentively, ready for whatever would come his way.

They yanked the weapons from the hands of those still putting up a semblance of resistance, hit them on the neck and shoulder blades, breaking bone and tearing muscle. They sliced Achilles tendons, pulled them taut for no other reason than to watch them snap back. Though their enemies were already dead they pissed on them, as if to warm their final dying thoughts. The leader ripped off their genitals and the others followed suit, with a shower of insults. The faces of the living were red, those of the dead almost black. The leader took one of the northerners' guns and opened the man's chest with the bayonet, to pull his guts out into the light of day, and kept pulling until all the intestines were fully removed, and the others kept pummelling the dead, blows raining down until a sort of palpable exhaustion set in. They seemed to be in the process of making up their minds whether to go to sleep then and there, or keep on beating these inert things that had once been men.

The sun started going down and one of the soldiers spat on the ground and, as if they were drunk, as if they were disoriented, with jackets unbuttoned and haggard eyes, they got back into formation and disappeared into the woods, toward the river.

CHAPTER SIXTEEN

MARCH 1960
PITTSBURG, KS

HE WENT BY Kenneth Simons now. No one knew exactly where he came from. In town, people thought he was a crackpot and scarcely acknowledged his existence. A few brave souls had visited his house for the 1959 census. They'd knocked on the large oak door that was painted white like the six columns on his porch, grabbed the wrought-iron knocker and knocked, and the sound resonated over the surrounding prairies. That's one big house, maybe a haunted house, they thought as they headed back to town without looking back.

People knew that the weekly paper they picked up from its box every Monday was printed somewhere in that giant house, but didn't talk about it. The *Headlight Sun* ran articles on all kinds of social issues, retellings of historical events, and editorials under different bylines every week. Whether these articles were tragic or funny, no one could really say.

There were stories about alien abductions and Pawnee kidnappings, expert advice on local flora and fauna, stories about the coming climate changes, sun spots, the ozone layer, the acid rain that was going to shower the earth. The paper was tolerated, in its boxes all along Broadway, why not? Who would want to stand in its way, and why? There were recipes no one would ever try because the ingredients weren't available in local grocery stores. In Pittsburg, Kansas, no one stocked black salsify or manioc root.

Once, in August '54, something like collective hysteria erupted when townsfolk found copies of the previous week's *Headlight Sun* with an article about the coming tornado, strewn out on the street amid the wreckage of a storm. People demanded explanations, there was even talk of rounding up a mob to go to his house. But a few days later people were too busy cleaning their streets and homes and schoolyards, getting the traffic lights working and the power back on, and everyone forgot all about it.

Every Sunday night the newspaper boxes were emptied and then refilled. The kids would read the comics, never sure whether they should laugh or cry. Then, although it was free, they'd put the paper back in the box.

Though he was never seen around town, everyone knew influential people called on Mr. Simons. Sometimes people claimed to have heard someone, at City Hall or at the bank, talking to him on the phone, completing a transaction or doing some business, making deals to do with infrastructure projects on the outskirts of Pittsburg. Some said Belmont Street, overlooking the lake, was named after him, but it had never been confirmed. He lived far from downtown, near the county and state borders his property line ran along the border between Kansas to the west and Missouri to the east. To the north was the Shawnee Reservation where the Indians had been resettled during the great deportations in the nineteenth century. They said his ancestors were the men and women who'd starved and frozen to death on that interminable Trail of Tears, or Scottish immigrants in the fur trade in New England and Canada. He might be descended from a bootlegger as well, someone who'd seen Prohibition's silver lining and made a fortune before retiring in a sumptuous house, a mansion in an elegant yet vernacular style, built of European marble on ground scorched by the War of Secession. They said he'd been a friend of Bernard and Morrie Gursky. They said he'd spent time in jail.

In town, people didn't talk about him much, but when they did everyone put their two cents in. If you struck up a conversation with the barber on Locust and 6th, he'd tell you he cut everyone's hair in this town — everyone but Kenneth B. Simons, the man was a ghost, his hair and beard must drag behind him like a train, dirty and full of insects and unknown microbes. If you talked to the mayor he'd tell you that the man's taxes were paid, beyond that it was none of his business. Simons was an ordinary citizen, entitled to his privacy like everyone else. At night you'd hear strange noises coming from over there, but even the teenagers with greased hair and leather jackets didn't dare go out to see what was going on.

IT WAS THE beginning of March and the sky was wild, shot through with lightning and ridged with whirlwinds that tore young buds right from the branches. The day before, he had celebrated his fiftieth birthday with a Richebourg Pinot Noir. The wine had aged and taken on depth, its taste had developed over years spent lying on its side on a shelf in the dark, oxidizing and oxygenating at the ideal temperature, forgotten by the world, biding its time. Aimé uncorked the bottle without ceremony, but there was solemnity in his movements. His hands shook when he tried to hold them flat in front of his eyes.

The night had passed in silent nostalgia, overlain with regret and even doubt. It had been so long. Images of the past came flooding back, now that he too could feel his body ageing, like everyone else's, could feel it losing elasticity and vigour. He'd seen himself in situations he claimed to have invented to make himself interesting — but interesting to whom? He had no one to share his life with, no one to dissuade him or encourage him in his phobias and obsessions. He felt bitter, as if he'd spent his life lying and had only himself to blame. He had his gun collection, his stuffed trophies. An impressive library, if anyone would take the time to have a look and decipher the gothic script on the spines. There were reference books, treatises on sorcery and the occult sciences, two-hundred-year-old almanacs in French detailing the allotment of *seigneuries* along the banks of the St. Lawrence River. He had aged slowly, it was true, but he was an old man now, he could feel it. So this was what it meant to be old. Thoughts of his eventual death kept him company as he gazed into the flames.

A fire burned in the hearth as night gave way incremen-
tally to day and thunder rang out, shaking the windows.
He fed the fire with documents that might have hinted at
his true identity. A daguerreotype of Aimé at twenty-eight,
somewhere in the Wyoming plains, in the audience for one
of Bill Cody and Jack Omohundro's very first travelling cir-
cus shows, and dated in black ink, on the back: June 23, 1873.
A contract with the city of Syracuse, signed by himself and
the city manager, from the end of the Great War, concerning the provision of rum for clinics treating the Spanish Flu.
Dozens of pages from his personal journals, which he had
begun while he was a prisoner in Quebec. One by one he
tore the pages out, reread them, and threw them into the fire
as he sipped his wine. There was something in the atmosphere that lent itself to this, it was the fiftieth leap year he
had known, the rotations of the earth, its irregular shape,
were in agreement, and his personal story was taking on
the appearance of a grotesque farce that he no longer felt
like believing in. He doubted the words he had spoken to
men whose biographies graced his shelves, bound in leather
according to the strictures of a dying art.

Thinking about it made him laugh, at himself and at the
thousand episodes of despair and exaltation that stretched
out like the life of one of those giant turtles on the world's
untouched islands you could read about in Darwin. They were
the only living creatures that had walked with Napoleon, aside
from the trees, those ever faithful, almost immortal beings
whose company he never tired of. He fell asleep with a thousand projects for the future spinning around in his head, the
one thing in his existence he could be certain of.

THAT MORNING HE again noticed a slight trembling he was struggling to control. When he shaved he had to pay particular attention to his double chin, touching it and pressing it between his fingers and moving it from side to side. His teeth, which had been straight and solid, now seemed to be planted in soft, blood red flesh that was malleable and fragile. When he touched his gums he felt their incipient decay.

Spread out on the table in front of him were drafts of plans for an organization he'd dreamed up yesterday between two moments of introspection. It would be a federation, an association, both a bit of a joke and the one serious thing he'd ever attempted. An opportunity to find other people like himself and let them know they weren't alone, not at all: there must be thousands, in the United States alone, maybe even just in Kansas and neighbouring states. It would be a closed and exclusive society, a refuge for kids who were sick of being made fun of at school, tired of being constantly teased and told they were only two years old when they were in Grade Four. It would be a secret fraternity of sorts, with lifetime membership. Every member would be, by definition, special. He thought back to what it was like to be young and afraid, with no idea of what tomorrow might bring. It would be an order: the Order of Leapers, a.k.a. Twentyniners, those born in that strange vortex in time, who were special by definition, who time did not consume in the same way as everyone else. At once a brotherhood and a temple where they could meet. A place where, like gold miners, their search might be rewarded, where they would find other men and women who recognized their shared qualities and the mysterious signs that hinted at so much more than faulty calendars and celestial pathways.

Aimé took an open notebook off the table and read what he had written on one of the pages. It was good: it captured the thrust, the tone was right. "You are hereby enrolled in the elite fraternity whose membership is limited to those who have birthdays only every four years. There are no initiation fees, no membership dues . . ." The March sky was clear and cold, after the storms, and Aimé could feel a sense of serenity, a sort of communion taking shape, in his chest, with these children who, he imagined, must feel as alone as he had.

There would be no meetings, only a single grand conclave, a spiritual coming-together once every four years when thousands of Twentyniners like himself would communicate telepathically, connecting with each other at the same moment, for the simple joy of knowing that the others were there, elsewhere, spread over the continent but special as well, each with eyes closed and membership certificate in hand: born together on the twenty-ninth day of the second month of the year, a day that exists only one year out of every four. What could be more special, more magical than that?

Aimé smiled; it was the first concrete initiative he had taken since founding the newspaper. He hadn't created a single thing since the machine that measured the radioactivity of the powerful winds that blew in from the west, where the government was conducting atomic testing. He couldn't remember being a child, but he'd been young once, he'd been young for a long time, he knew the value of adventure and the pure pleasure of keeping a secret.

He smiled. A new era had begun.

CHAPTER SEVENTEEN

NOVEMBER 1864
SAINT-HENRI-DES-TANNERIES, QC

THE RAIN DRIPPING in through the barn roof formed streaks along the boards and sheets of tin, and you could hear it beating on the roof like a drum. Aimé and Jeanne were lying on their backs, naked, their clothes hastily spread out over the straw and moist dirt. Their chests rose and fell in time and they were breathing deeply, Aimé consciously matching his to hers. I'm happy, she thought to herself. She wasn't looking at anything, save the insides of her closed eyelids, a thousand white and yellow spots as illuminated by electrical currents. Her hand had slid into Aimé's, palm backward. Their eyes were closed, they breathed as one.

Minutes earlier, Jeanne had told Aimé she was almost sure she was pregnant. This was a matter of speaking. She was sure, and he hadn't known what to do, how to react. They kissed, like the first time, it came as a surprise and she wasn't yet fully ready. Her arms fell down beside her body, which seemed to melt under Aimé's embrace, she was enamoured, she was in love, she didn't know what to do either, she let herself go. He unpinned her corsage, tore a stitch in her blouse. He kissed her at the point where her neck met her clavicle, and then higher up, near her earlobe. It was very dark in the barn, the lantern was out. Jeanne's wet hair covered her shoulders.

They'd known each other, and had been meeting in secret, for over a year. Jeanne was nervous every time, so the first thing Aimé had to do was calm her down and make her comfortable. He'd appear when she was least expecting it and whisper a quick word before disappearing. A few hours later they would be together, Jeanne's neck sore from turning around so many times to make sure they weren't being followed. She was increasingly worried by her younger brother's temper. Jean had finally taken his place as the family patriarch, refused to listen to others, and was dangerously obsessed with the idea of his father's murder. The investigation was progressing, they couldn't keep him in the dark forever: soon he would find the perpetrator and exact his revenge. He was constantly on the lookout, searching for clues, everyone around him was a suspect. It was hard for Jeanne to get away, to find excuses, and especially to lie, to be constantly lying, lying even to her younger sisters who never let her leave without asking where she was going, and if she had a secret lover. They did it jokingly, but deep down Jeanne knew they knew something was going on.

She opened her eyes in the middle of this night of love and revelations. She was afraid. It was November, a cold rain was falling and clouds hid the moon. For weeks she'd been suffering from nausea. Her breasts hurt, nothing tasted as it should. Her period hadn't come and didn't seem to be coming anytime soon. She had to face facts. She turned to the side, and suddenly felt cold. Her skin was pale and rough from the goosebumps that never seemed to go away. They were starting to see in the dark, the eyes can adjust to nearly anything. She wanted to talk to him, but Aimé wasn't saying a thing. He was there, right next to her, this handsome young man who had appeared in her life without warning, who'd one day helped her board the tram, who'd posted himself in front of her door so discreetly no one noticed except her, as if he appeared solely in her personal field of vision. He was breathing less quickly and seemed to be at peace. She was in love. As a child she'd sworn it would never happen to her, yet here it was, and as she lay on her side she seemed to dream more than experience this moment of irresistible distress.

On rainy nights like these the crickets stayed their song, huddled in the tall grass or burrowing for winter, and fat raindrops pounded the barn roof in slow waves. Without changing position, without even opening his eyes, in a confident, loyal movement full of unspoken tenderness Aimé picked up his coat and placed it over Jeanne, who was starting to shiver. She began to detail Aimé's profile in the darkness that was just starting to lift from the planks of the back wall, tracing the curve of his forehead and nose, nostrils swollen with air, up to his closed lips and the beard making incursions onto the soft slope of the chin. Aimé lay silent, lost in thought, and she spoke, it came out as no more than a whisper in their moment of intimacy. At the edge of her

reach she could caress his hairless chest, feel the ribs protruding from his skin, count them by running her index
finger along the interstices, like tiny mountains linked into
a chain; she could feel and touch the physical manifestation
of his being, his undeniable presence at her side, the flagrant
impossibility of his disappearing. She moved to speak and
saw him literally prick up his ears, his ears moved, and his
eyelids too, alert to the possibility of a truth or a mystery to
be plucked from the air above him, but maybe these were
one and the same thing, she wasn't sure.

"Aimé."

"Yes."

Jeanne was biting her lower lip, pushing hard on Aimé's
throat, her fingernails digging into the skin. He was distant,
there in body yet somehow evanescent, sitting at once right
next to her and somewhere very far away.

"You're not going to disappear?"

"No."

"You won't abandon me."

"Never."

"I need you."

"Me too."

"You aren't going to die."

"That's impossible."

He said this last word with a slight smile and a hint of
irony that she liked a lot in him, a blend of rebelliousness and
pride that made it seem as if he wasn't afraid of anyone or
anything. He started turning his head toward her, to further
reassure her, hold her tight in his arms, symbolically marry
her, why not? A marriage of mind and spirit, with only the

two of them as bride and groom and celebrants. But at that moment they heard cries and the sounds of footsteps fast approaching, and a second later a dozen lanterns lit them up, faces appeared in the dripping windows, and Jeanne's brother yelled louder than the others, filling the barn with cursing, a confused stream of orders to his accomplices, and death threats, and he kicked the old door, which splintered and broke. His silhouette stood in contrast with the black sky behind him. A group of men stood around him, with lanterns and pitchforks. He held a rifle in his right hand, and in his left a large white sheet he immediately threw over Jeanne, as if he'd known in advance he would have to cover her nudity and protect her innocence in the sight of these men. He threw the sheet, revealing a large red brick held underneath. He threw the sheet at Jeanne and, in the same movement, raised his rifle, his dishevelled red hair shining in a circle of light, as if aflame. A million particles of dust and hay floated around his head. As she started yelling as well, overcome by panic, Jeanne wrapped herself in the sheet and reflexively drew herself close to Aimé, who immediately grabbed her by the hips and neck. He was hurting her. She didn't understand. He shoved her in front of him, to protect himself from the bullet that was sure to come. She closed her eyes, then opened them again on a scene that was totally transformed. She said, No, Jean, no, wait, you don't understand. Pointing the rifle at her, her brother yelled at Aimé to let her go, now, give yourself up. Aimé, with Jeanne in his large hands that seemed to encase her, backed up toward the other end of the barn, on nervous tiptoes, naked.

The whole thing was over in a few seconds, the time it

took the lightning to strike outside, as long as the thunder-clap that struck right near them, uprooting a tree or reducing a clock tower to rubble. Jean broke the barn door and threw the sheet over Jeanne, and Aimé grabbed her as a human shield. Jean yelled to let her go and the others pointed their guns at the couple. There were at least eight of them, men they knew by sight, from a distance, shopkeepers and work-ers her brother sometimes talked to, had quiet talks with in their home, she'd seen them gather in a second-floor room that she was forbidden to enter.

Aimé held her tightly, with one arm around her neck and the other on her waist and hips. He didn't say a word. There was a low window with broken panes, he backed up to the edge and easily pushed a leg through it. Jean yelled to let her go, now. He raised his gun to his eye to take better aim and yelled at Aimé, Give up, let her go, give up, don't even try to resist, bastard, rapist. Aimé easily threw his other leg over the sill and, in a series of perfectly executed movements, was outside in a fraction of a second. Jeanne barely had time to notice what was happening, the word "impossible" still res-onating in her ears. She collapsed to the ground, her naked body inadequately covered by the sheet. With no one there to hold her up she fell, her ankles gave out, and she ended up sitting awkwardly on the hay in the barn while the men all around yelled and sprang into action. Jean screamed at the others to catch him, not to let him get away. He ran past her and stood by the window and aimed his rifle into the night, toward the surrounding woods where Aimé had already disappeared. He swore a few times as he looked for his mark in the dark, pivoting left and right. Jeanne was sure he was going to shoot, but then he too straddled the windowsill and jumped out of the barn. The sound of the rain changed, for a second, and Jeanne started breathing very quickly, she had a hard time catching her breath and her lungs refused to fill with air.

The sheet was on her, on her shoulders, but didn't cover her at all, she could see her naked body from above, her breasts and her sex and her stomach, which hadn't yet started to swell. In Brody's field and throughout the district and beyond, the manhunt had begun, she heard men shouting directions and her brother promising someone, promising God, that he would catch Aimé and get revenge. Not a single shot rang out, but you could see lamps being lit in the bourgeois houses further south. The firehouse bells clanged.

She could see herself from above, her bent neck and still-wet hair that parted at the nape and fell over her shoulders. Her breathing was fast, the words rang out with a strange metallic sound at once piercing and unpleasant. She could see herself naked and alone, the straw hurt her backside and thighs, sitting there like a doleful Madonna, hurt without understanding why or from where. This pain came from a place she didn't know. She looked like someone trying to find an arrow lodged in some inaccessible region of her body. Aimé had squeezed her hard and sworn he loved her and would stay with her, and smiled with so much confidence she found herself unable to erase the image. He had set off barefoot into the woods. Jeanne could already see the first traces of bruising in the spots on her body where he had pressed too hard.

CHAPTER EIGHTEEN

FEBRUARY 1987
PITTSBURG, KS

THE YEAR BEFORE he'd seen the comet for the third time. It seemed somehow serene, at once highly dangerous and at peace as it ran its course to the outer reaches of the solar system and back, completing its ellipse. The sight of it had made him think, as did so many other things he interpreted as portents of his absurd, uncertain longevity. Several countries had sent satellites into orbit, or probes equipped with sophisticated instruments to photograph the comet's nucleus and gather data on the composition of the stardust disintegrating in its wake. In today's world it was possible, conceivable, to send a probe into space and measure, in real time, the slow decomposition of a stellar object travelling thousands of miles per second. You could send messages over the waves, analyze and graph their content, this was the universe we lived in and the space shuttle sent up to explore its outer reaches had blown up on live TV, in curls of grey smoke in the blue sky, shapes like letters, you could read signs in them like clouds. No one was left indifferent, schoolchildren cried, what did it mean, even here in our faraway homes, what did it say about us, the explosion of this shuttle and the astronauts it carried, their honest smiles immortalized on camera a few minutes prior to takeoff. It set Aimé thinking.

The comet was back from a long voyage to the outer confines of the galaxy, would be back to light up our nights after seventy-six years of absence, that was how they put it, one of those phrases you heard everywhere. Aimé had observed it with naked eyes, fascinated, a tail of white and pink powder crossing the southern sky, sometimes slowly and sometimes swiftly, in a straight, hypnotic line. In his yard, amid piles of scrap metal he no longer knew what to do with, he'd set up a powerful homemade telescope. The conditions were far from ideal, but he'd managed to glimpse the small, white, triangular shape between two constellations.

He wasn't even twenty the first time the comet passed over his head, over the island of Montreal and the entire continent at one and the same time, and had only a confused notion of how this moving light could be at once present here and falling, in one and the same way, over Illinois, and still further away, over Mexico, where farmers in their fields expressed amazement in Spanish, with unfamiliar intonation, holding their hats as they stared at the sky and crossed themselves. The experience was magical, there was no other word for it, and he had resigned himself, had started calculating: the comet had also appeared in the year of his birth, if he wasn't mistaken, or maybe just before.

With eyes full of wonder, like everyone else, he'd

watched it trace an arc across the sky, along the path pre-
dicted by astronomers. The newspapers had been covering it for months, publishing stories about the comet and
retailing old legends and learned opinions from academies
in London and Washington. A respectful silence descended
on the town, people held their breath, Aimé could remember the atmosphere, the clear sky, the absence of smoke, and
then the arrival of the light, which someone had been the
first to point toward. It might have been him. City Hall had
organized an intergalactic dinner event where merchants,
performers, and politicians came dressed as moons and
planets, came with star-shaped masks over their eyes and
Saturnine hats on their heads. On the night of November
16, 1835, in accordance with the astronomers' predictions,
the street lamps were left off and the curfew was lifted, for
this special occasion. Aimé broke into one of the large buildings being built for McGill College, and took up a position,
alone, in one of the tower's dormer windows, eye trained
heavenward, legs dangling over the ledge. He wasn't scared
of heights.

In the last year Sir Halley's comet had returned to its
perihelion and Aimé greeted it like an old acquaintance,
something that made him think incessantly and revealed
something of his true nature. But it had long ago ceased
to be a revelation. He thought about it more at night than
during the day, it was only natural. He would wake in the
morning from messianic, nihilistic dreams where he played
the role assigned him in the outer reaches of space and time,
in private salons where they studied serious matters destined to forever alter how men thought. He wasn't hearing

voices but did fear he'd one day start to. His tinnitus would become syllabic and he'd be visited by messages, words, and cryptic phrases. He was an aberration, an incongruity, but very real at the same time; something to be both endured and imposed on human life and on history, traced out in a long, straight line that was neither circular nor elliptical, and these very concepts he once believed he understood were now beyond his grasp. His thought and his intellect were powerless against the reality he represented, and it was getting hard for him to live with himself. In his dreams he was important.

It was all food for thought: this comet's great beauty and meticulous course, how it never strayed from its path, whereas his life was a collection of digressions and truncated episodes that were almost impossible to fit together into meaning, trajectory, or even significance. Aimé told himself, he asked himself: Was it really possible to be conscious of everything, to witness every event in all these lives, without having a role to play in their coming into being? While he pursued this line of thinking he also tried to cleave to reason, not to give in to the magical thinking that would make him an extraordinary being. Aside from longevity there was nothing extraordinary about him. He never wanted to forget that.

Aimé gazed at the sky and felt something akin to love, love for the elegance of gravity as destiny. But what did it imply? It implied nothing. He wasn't the son of a comet. Comets didn't have sons. He was just a man who didn't exist three years out of four. He became transparent, a miscalculation only later corrected, a clause hotly disputed behind closed doors at Royal Society meetings centuries earlier. In a way, in a certain way, for life to go on, terrestrial life, equinoxes, and solstices, for the days and nights to follow one upon the other, allowing others to exist, and not to be put out of phase until the inevitable correction, he would have to sacrifice himself. That was how he saw the past, and the future as well, waiting for him again and again.

It's not like he went crazy standing there surrounded by piles of useless hunks of scrap metal and concrete that were no longer of any use to anyone, except as grotesque sculptures in a hinterland. It was just that he lost his sense of time, surrounded by fields, standing there looking at the stars and watching the universe reaching out and cracking, expanding and staying still.

Aimé was humble, you could see it in the way he walked around his house and the great care and patience with which he handled small objects. But it was hard not to think of himself as important, more important than everyone else, he felt bad but who could hold it against him? Not us, not this man who had taken part in the war that ended slavery, met presidents and suffragettes and aviatrixes and clergymen, saved animals from certain death, traversed wide-open landscapes on horse, on foot, and in a Boeing 747.

The previous year he'd seen the comet when it turned up faithfully at the appointed time, and he'd been thinking about it and about himself and what they had in common ever since. And today it was on the front page of the papers, in the news, and people were talking about it: they had just seen a supernova well outside the Milky Way. Somewhere in Chile an astronomer had pointed his telescope toward

the edge of the universe and found an anomaly in the shape
of a star. He'd notified the authorities. It was all unfolding
live and people were amazed. You could observe the beginnings of an explosion, atomized, full of colour, silent, like
ten thousand suns, a hundred thousand suns, light years
after the initial detonation.

He was having trouble sleeping.

AIMÉ DIDN'T GET a lot of mail. He almost never checked
his mailbox, but that morning, through the second-floor
window, he saw a man in a dark blue uniform get into his
truck and drive off. He almost felt like opening the window
to ask what it was, to yell it out. A day-old newspaper lay on
the bedside table. He knew the mailman had no desire to be
there and his one wish was to get back to town. The tires
might even have squealed, but he didn't hear them. He felt
like yelling out but he stayed there, unable to comprehend
his own frustration, silent and bitter. Was he becoming a
misanthrope on top of everything else? The sounds in his
head were loud, they blocked out the constant burbling
of the world. The engine noise was too far away to reach
him. He went out quietly, one step at a time, stopping to
pick up a jacket hanging on the wall in the stairwell and
went to see.

The air was cold and dry. Aimé crossed his property with
his hands in his pockets, his breath visible in front of him.
His dented metal mailbox stood on the side of the road.
Sometimes wild teenagers, their hair dyed every colour of
the rainbow, drove by and pounded it with a baseball bat. He

never heard a thing, just figured it out a few days later and
came out with his toolbox to put everything back in place.

The envelope wasn't standard size, the mailman had had
to bend it to squeeze it into the box: a thick, heavy envelope, as if full of documents painstakingly collected over several years. It was addressed to his old *Headlight Sun* PO box,
which hadn't been current for a long time. If it weren't for
the postman it would never have made its way out here.
Aimé turned it over to read the return address. Looking at
his house in front of him, in a woolen jacket with his mail
in hand, he looked like a strong, solitary man, the last of a
long line of landlords, a patriarch who no one talked to anymore because he'd committed a sordid crime. That's how
he looked as he surveyed the immense house that had once
belonged to a rich farmer, a man who owned other human
beings, a house with beautiful green blinds fronted by an
arch that opened onto the porch, supported by two columns
and the silent baying of two mythical alabaster beasts. From
here, he looked like one of those beasts, or a crazy old her-
mit you'd cross the road to avoid meeting, just waiting to
accost you to reveal the Masonic secrets of the universe and
predict your future. The trembling in his hands kept getting
worse, but he hadn't gone to see anyone, not a single doctor.

He turned the envelope over again and walked toward
the house, which seemed to recede as he advanced. His knee
joints were giving him trouble, and he grimaced. He was
letting himself go, it wasn't worth it anymore. His land was
desolate. For years the gravel path had been poorly main-
tained, the grass was growing tall, came up to his knees,
and the frost made it all look even dirtier, covering the

countryside and robbing it of colour. What had he accomplished? Sold some bootlegged liquor, built a few useless inventions. He hadn't saved anyone. He didn't matter. But he might still be a patriarch. He might have had children with dozens of different women, all the women he'd met since the end of the eighteenth century.

I was born in 1760, or so I've been told, and my memories confirm it. He blushed at the thought.

He thought of secret dynasties unknown to him, his blood living on in frail mortal bodies and ending up in shallow graves, while he lived on eternally. A long and winding path led to his house, stretching as far as the eye could see. Aimé thought of his descendants in various cities and towns, illegitimate children who had themselves tried to understand their obscure origins, hair that didn't match their brothers' and sisters'. He thought of these children, poor or powerful, all carrying his genes; he only knew of one for certain, the one he'd had with Jeanne, who'd been called to the bench before turning forty. He thought about Jeanne too. And his own disinterest, selfish and total, in what had become of her after their short time together. Since their last meeting, more than eight decades ago, Aimé had made no attempt to find out anything about the child. He'd gone back to Phoenix, where he tended his dusty bottles and his flourishing business. But he imagined his son, imagined the child and later the adult this person had become, a man long dead and himself the founder of a new line. He was more of a founding father than Aimé. How could Aimé give himself that title? By what right? Because he was still here to bear witness. If he didn't, no one would. He tried to remember

the name of Jeanne's first son, who had been recognized as
a Langlois—she'd told him, someone had told him—the
family of the man she'd married after he ran off into the
night in Saint-Henri. Langlois took the adopted boy as his
own son, he became the Langlois's eldest child, a respected
man, first a lawyer and then a judge, a man responsible for
laying down the law, establishing truth, and meting out justice. Aimé was rifling through his memories, mail in hand,
as he walked back home.

Justice Pierre Langlois, Supreme Court of Canada. Victor
Langlois's son. Now he remembered. The air was cold, even
for a February morning on the Kansas–Missouri border.
Later, a little snow would fall and the wind would kick up.
A supernova had exploded several million years before at
the edges of the visible universe, and yesterday they'd been
treated to a glimpse of the luminous echo of its death. Aimé
remembered his son's name: Pierre, born in 1865, while he
was deep in the Appalachian forest armed with a knife and
worn-out rifle, a new name, and a blue uniform. He didn't
turn around to see the path he'd followed, just climbed the
steps to his porch.

As he went through his front door, Aimé already knew
what was in the envelope.

Chattanooga, October 13, 1986

Dear Mr. Simons,
I hope you won't find me presumptuous for writing this letter in French, a language I have not had
much occasion to use in recent years but one which, I

believe, will enable us to understand each other fully. If you are still reading after these first few lines, my choice must have been a good one. I'm aware that I'm taking a risk, and am happy to do so: I haven't come this far only to settle for the path of least resistance. That this letter has made its way into your hands is already a great victory for me, achieved after many years of searching for you; for you to read it in its entirety would be more than enough to confirm my intuitions and deductions. Time will tell whether I was right or wrong. I dare not venture a guess on that question myself. This letter, then, represents both the end of a long and painstaking search, and the beginning of a new phase during which my fantasies will confront reality head-on. I cannot say whether this encounter will be a fruitful one, but there is no reason to wait any longer. You are within reach, the window is open. I cannot be certain of anything, but have no choice but to act as if everything were now clear. There's no time for any other course of action.

We've never met, but I feel I know you well. I know who you are, where you come from, what you've done with your life. I also know that we're connected in the most astonishing manner. In spite of your best intentions and legendary discretion, you've left more traces on this earth than you imagine. Don't be afraid, I'm not crazy, and I bear you no ill will—quite the contrary. Think of me as a simple researcher, a humble archeologist of continental shifts and the movements of the moon, a man whose vocation is panning for

gold, knee-deep in rivers of tattered old documents.
No, I'm not crazy, though I'm certainly obsessed, and
determined as well. It's my sincere belief that our des-
tinies are inextricably intertwined. Only you can confirm it.

Aimé's damp hands left marks on the letter that disappeared
seconds after they appeared. He shook the papers, and
quickly slid his finger between the pages to grasp the last
ones, his eye drawn instinctively to the name smack dab in
the middle of the paragraph. He skimmed what was written, apprehending its full meaning, and though he was rusty
he was not tripped up by any of these words in his native
tongue, they were snapping into place in his head.

But if it was Schoedler who triggered this passion of
mine, one that has always stood me in good stead,
the true beginning of my quest was something else,
deep in my family history, which you were no longer
part of. Not long after I discovered the *Book of Nature,* I
found, quite by accident while searching through my
grandfather's things, Jeanne Beaudry's journal covering the years from when she met you until her death
in December 1900.

Aimé breathed deeply. He didn't know what else to do,
beyond going back to the beginning and rereading the intro-
ductory paragraphs, which quickly strayed into digression.
On the third page, though, the tone changed slightly.

...allow me to briefly introduce myself, and in that way explain my purpose in writing you today, which I seem to have forgotten already. My name is Albert Langlois, and I was born in 1959 in the small town of Sainte-Anne-des-Monts, between the St. Lawrence River and the Chic-Choc Mountains. When I turned nineteen, I left my country to pursue the genealogical research that had become important to me. My investigations led me here, far south, to Chattanooga, where I met my wife, an American. We had a child, Thomas, who was born on February 29, 1980, as you may be able to guess. The feeling I've had since becoming a father is indescribable because this fundamental, deep joy available to all was compounded in my case by the certitude—perhaps noble, perhaps unhealthy—that destiny was being fulfilled. My son would be a leaper.

A leaper. The Order of Twentyniners. It came back to him, he remembered it all: inventing the federation, the love that had driven him to make it work. At one time the Order had saved his life, he was sure of it. He remembered corresponding with children all over the country. He'd provided certificates of authenticity, membership cards, buttons, and pennants. Aimé still had boxes of little collector's items he had designed himself in his basement. It had been an accomplishment, and he had souvenirs to remind him. What had Albert accomplished?

I, Albert Langlois, through sheer force of will and good faith in my intellectual enterprise, had given birth to a leaper, one who would not only survive me, but also be privileged to know the shape of human civilization in the centuries to come. My son, Thomas Langlois, would be your direct descendent, and also your second coming, produced by the happy congruence of the earth's revolution and pure math. But wait, I'm getting carried away again.

He was getting carried away indeed, Aimé thought. The handwriting looked dashed off, as if it had been set down on the page by an improperly calibrated mechanical wrist. There were more and more errors. Aimé noticed them even though many years had passed since he'd used French. Albert had crossed out certain passages, written with a sense of urgency; his tale skipped around all over the place before ending up in dead ends of conjecture and excuses.

. . . as Executive Secretary of the Order of Twenty-niners. Please rest assured it's not that. My aim in writing you is different: I'm not looking for advice or assistance, I just need you to listen, to be there. But you must also know that this position with the Order, one you likely no longer hold, was the spark in my mind. Yes: thanks to your letter, I understood. Suddenly it made sense. All the pieces in my personal puzzle slid into place, and I knew you were the one I was searching for. It was you. You were he. Kenneth B. Simons was you, and you were he.

But let me explain myself. Last year, as a treat for my son, to help him be patient as he waited for his second birthday, and demonstrate just how different he was from the others, just how special he really was, I took out an old letter I'd kept, and showed him. We sat down together, his tearful face straight across from mine, and I read it to him. I'd found this letter long ago, at one of many visits to local flea markets. It caught my attention because it seemed to conceal some hidden truth, another connection to you. Or, more accurately, to Aimé.

The letter didn't say much, but everything of importance was there: a new leaper was welcomed, membership into the Order of Twentyniners confirmed, and a small donation requested. Nothing out of the ordinary, really, except perhaps for a careful observer such as myself. The paper, from the 1960s, impressed Thomas deeply, and the letter (signed by your hand) quickly became our most prized shared possession and a touchstone of our relationship. Thomas and I had a secret to share and to cherish: his membership in a secret fraternity open only to the most special children of all. My son (like myself) quickly became convinced that the letter was meant for him, and we read it together, over and over again, enthralled by this new bond that his mother, my wife, could never understand. But that's another story . . .

He skipped a few lines, and reached for a pitcher of warm water on the other side of the table. It was a strange day, the light was barely sneaking through the windows. Aimé calmly continued reading, at once interested and skeptical.

Somewhere in Tennessee someone had been trying to find out about him for years, had carried out research, connected his various identities, had — was it possible? — tried to a make his own son in the image of his forefather. Somewhere in Tennessee, Chattanooga to be exact, where Aimé had not set foot since the previous century, was a family that was, in the deepest possible sense of the word, his. The man who wrote this letter was a direct descendent of Jeanne Beaudry.

Though I was enthusiastic, and Thomas seemed receptive, I didn't make the connection. A whole year went by before the evidence jumped out at me. I pursued my research, all alone, and started gathering the information I'd need to reconstruct, piece by piece, the story of this elusive ancestor, the original leaper, the one whose life contained the entire puzzle. I was reading your letter from the Order for the twentieth or thirtieth time when the solution finally hit me on the head. In recent months I'd managed to trace Aimé to his home in Pittsburgh, in the early 1960s, but I got the place name wrong. A single letter had thrown me. Of course, there was another Pittsburg, without an "h," in addition to its much better-known namesake in western Pennsylvania, at the foot of the Appalachians. Aimé was in Kansas.

After days spent reviewing notebooks and notes and piles of documents, and reorganizing my synchronous piles, I went into my office to write this letter. There was no longer any room for doubt. We were ready to make contact and...

And nothing. The sentence hung there, unfinished. Albert had crossed out the words that came after, and begun writing again an inch below, with what was obviously a different pen. Aimé imagined the child Thomas had been and still was. He saw a seven-year-old, maybe wearing glasses, already a normal kid, sitting on his controlling, authoritarian father's knee, the child fully absorbed by the father's intensity.

There was no doubt about it: he idolized his father.

So here you are, witness to my confusion and excitement, all that remains for you is to decide how to respond. Let me lay my cards on the table.

Kenneth. William. Aimé.

My ancestor, my contemporary.

I feel you so near to me. I know you so well.

According to my calculations, you are fifty-five today, if we skip the non-leap year of 1900. That makes you twenty years younger than my own father, Jean Langlois, your grandson, who was born on July 20, 1910. I am his last child, born late in his life. This means that you are also, according to the chronological time of ordinary men, 226 years old. Forgive me if my hands aren't shaking with wonder as I write this figure, it's just that I've been obsessed with it for such a long time that I've gotten used to it. "Such a long time"—what does that even mean, to a man such as yourself?

Aimé looked at the page, one of dozens in his hand, all filled with this handwriting that grew indecipherable in stretches.

Appended to the letter was a thick stack of photocopied documents. He was exhausted. "Such a long time": it was the phrase that had dogged him, like a faithful companion or a nemesis, as long as he had lived; four words crushed into two, *suchalong time*, a nasal dactyl brought to a close with a thud. Albert was presumptuous, his writing convoluted, almost a provocation, but his purely rhetorical questions gave Aimé pause. He read between the lines. The big house was empty, and he was all alone with Albert's words and a few primitive, rusty automatons to do the housework.

When I try to see the world through your eyes, my heart starts pounding, vertigo overtakes me, and I'm left speechless, at a loss for words that could calm me and restore some order to my thoughts. It was through words that I came to know of your existence; it is through words that I can still today conceive the inconceivable. Writing has always been a great help to me. It has always provided a way to organize the flow of information, synthesize it, keep it from descending into chaos.

It surely won't escape you that my entire theory is based on science, not idle speculation. Obviously, you are the empirical proof of the validity of my original hypothesis (which is not mine alone, far from it) — that a human baby, born at a precise moment in the lunar cycle and planetary revolution, will be affected in its cells, just like the earth's tides and currents. Writers since antiquity have discussed this phenomenon, you can find it in Archimedes and Thucydides, whose esoteric enthusiasm is not incompatible with scientific facts and verifiable data. Out of interest's sake, I should say that my own obsession with this strangest of dates stems from the now sadly forgotten Dr. Frédéric Schoedler, whose great opus, *Le livre de la nature, ou leçons élémentaires de physique, d'astronomie, de chimie, de minéralogie, de géologie, de botanique, de physiologie et de zoologie*, was published in 1865. This was a respected scientific treatise in its time, and its theoretical framework is still current, no matter what a few cynical MIT astrophysicists have to say about it. Schoedler makes a fine teacher, and even a youth of twelve, as I was when I first laid hands on his book, could find something of value in it. I was immediately drawn to the description of the mathematical and astronomical history of the Gregorian calendar, in which he explains how leap years play a vital role in human affairs, and much more. According to Schoedler, the fact that the leap year can only be expressed in fractions (the famous ¼ added to the 365 days in the year) does not mean it does not exist, in the economy of the universe. This 29th day existed before we took notice of it. But have you read Schoedler, Kenneth? As I write, I ask myself the question and suddenly the answer seems obvious. One thing is certain, however, and I don't think I'm overstepping the bounds of politeness to point it out: If you have read him, you couldn't help but notice his mention of "leap-year babies," as I did, which he notes with a list of a number of cases recorded since the Council of Trent, of children whose "abnormal" lifespan caused them to be deemed to be "heretics" by the Christian authorities.

Aimé hadn't just read Schoedler, he'd attended the man's lecture, on the meaning of what he called the "days forgotten by history and time," at the 1893 Chicago World's Fair. Of course, the eminent physicist had discussed leap years and the Gregorian calendar, as well as the famous ten years excised from the history books in October 1582. Impressed by the panel of historians and scientists, including Frederick Jackson Turner and Henri Bergson, Aimé had taken copious notes. He looked back on this lecture as one of the best moments of his life. Images of the magnificent fair grounds leaped into his mind. A new dynamo was on show, along with the latest internal combustion engine. Flying machines, both hot-air balloons and dirigibles, glided overhead. An enormous blimp, aptly named the *Inconvenience*, narrowly avoided a collision with the clock tower, but successfully crash-landed outside the fairgrounds. The ambulance, Aimé remembered, was electrically powered. His memories were indescribable, the omnipresent smell of gas and noise of telegraph waves and ringing telephones, and the joy of outpacing a bicycle-racer by walking on a rubber conveyor.

At the very end of the lecture he'd managed to slip himself into the crowd and shake hands with Schoedler, a giant of a man. He was getting on in years but still sharp, with a cigarette hanging from his mouth. Aimé's signed *Livre de la nature* was still in his library.

. . . and at twelve, still fascinated by my readings in science and history, another matter captured my attention: the story of Adolphe Scheler, executed by the Helvetian government in 1608 for "refusing to age according to God's natural order." This was huge for me. And there were others. Men and women burned at the stake by the Portuguese Inquisition; those who committed suicide after decades of unending youth grew too heavy to bear. Men and women with smooth features and smooth skin after living one hundred and even one hundred fifty years. All this is to say that you are probably not the only true leaper the world has known. There may have been dozens, if we are to believe the writings I've studied. According to the theory put forward by Schoedler and his disciples, no one leap year is particularly fertile: a genuine lunar child, whose longevity stretches the bounds of the possible, may be born every four years, as long as the small temporal breach opened by the rotation of a satellite has a direct effect on the mother's pregnancy . . .

Aimé felt the urge to contradict his correspondent. He had misunderstood Schoedler, that much was clear. And who were these "disciples" Albert was invoking to justify not only the conduct of his inquiry but also experiments carried out on the bodies of his wife and son?

I can admit, in all humility (and this may be my greatest regret at this point in my life, as the breakup of my marriage is irreparable, and I made the error of

believing that something of your immortality flowed
in the veins of your descendant, me, to be passed on to
my offspring): I tried to put my theories into practice,
but I believe I have failed. My son Thomas is an ordinary child, who will die just like myself, like everyone,
long before you, despite his date of birth.

Had this date of birth been deliberately chosen, then? That's
what Aimé most wanted to know, as he read and reread
these few lines. Had Albert induced his own pregnant wife,
to make sure his son would be born at a predetermined time,
to coincide with this "temporal breach"? He seemed to be
implying as much, without coming out and saying it.

Aimé got up. He was thirsty and needed sugar. He
returned to the passage about Jeanne, which he had merely
skimmed earlier. He was old, and could feel his high blood
pressure somewhere in his wrist. His joints were losing elasticity; he was far from immortal. Jeanne had been wrong
about him.

... she never let go of you. From both a "factual" and
a "psychic" point of view, she always remained close.
Can't you feel it? Your name comes up everywhere, in
the most unexpected places. For example, on January
12, 1896, Jeanne writes in her journal: "A book has been
published that deeply affected me. Mathilde brought
it back from Boston as a gift for me, she knows of
my interest in veteran's stories. The author — a young
American, not a day over twenty-one, with no actual
combat experience, tells an unvarnished, deeply

touching story of two days in the life of a Union soldier in that Civil War that ravaged the United States
three decades ago. Few books have affected me so
deeply with such a mix of pain and joy. I don't know
why, but I feel as if I recognized my Aimé in Henry
Fleming, that handsome young soldier, unable to
decide whether his destiny was to be a coward or
a hero. Sometimes Pierre reminds me of him too,
and then it all comes back to me. He's still with me."
This is but one reference of many. Her journal quickly
became, for me, an inexhaustible treasure trove of
information and an object of fascination: Who was
this mysterious Aimé, who had haunted her all her
life? Two years later, in May 1898, she traced you to
Arizona, thanks to a photo in *Harper's Weekly* out of
New York, which her husband received every week.
She describes the photograph: "Under the article, a
caption states that the photo was taken by a certain
Mathew Brady. I'll copy it out here, there's something
pretty and mysterious about it: *Man Standing in Front
of City Hall, Phoenix, AZ, 1895. Last Known Photograph by
Famous War Photo-Journalist Mathew Brady*. He's standing very straight and his silhouette is like a cutout
against the white wall of the City Hall. I recognize
his features, no one will believe me, but what does it
matter, since I'm not addressing anyone here? Who
would believe me? Who can I talk about him with?
He's there, staring at me, a prisoner, his soul offered
up to me. He hasn't changed. He's so handsome. I
recognize the lips and the eyes. He hasn't changed,

and never will. I'm not at all surprised to see that he's so far away: my Aimé never thought about anything except travelling, setting off to conquer mountains, forests, an entire continent. Phoenix. What a beautiful name for a city! I'm sure no one ever dies there, people are just reborn, constantly reinvented, that's what he wanted...I told Victor I wanted to keep the article. As always, he didn't ask why." A few days later, she first makes reference to a persistent pain in her left breast.

He thought some more about their last meeting and pictured Jeanne's scarred, swollen face as she lay dying. She had recognized him so quickly, so easily, as if she had been waiting for it. Their conversation had been too short, brought to an end when she lost consciousness and the nurses arrived. Aimé had slipped away, as he did so well. He kept the taste of her words in his mouth and the impress of her voice, the memory of their secret nights together in the Brody barn.

His head was clear of all thoughts soon, and he started reading again. The daylight no longer worked its way into the house, it was blocked by some sentiment perhaps, or just tired of always being there, faithfully in position, where we all expected it to be. He needed to get up once more and turn on a lamp, a single bulb with no shade, or a crystal chandelier hanging from the dining room ceiling.

...other document, which would complete my trajectory and reveal the path I'm meant to follow. It was a narrative I found in the special collection at the public library, in Sainte-Anne-des-Monts, a tiny room I knew like the back of my hand, and where I was given free rein. It was an old, tattered volume, you had to handle it with care or it would fall to pieces: a first edition of *L'influence d'un livre*, by Philippe Aubert de Gaspé, *fils*, from a small edition printed privately by the author, containing retellings of several legends and stories. In subsequent editions these were bowdlerized, probably under pressure from the publisher. One of these was titled "The Leap-Year-Man, an Appalachian Legend." To give you the thrust of the story I'll include an excerpt here, as my own copy is too fragile to reproduce. The long passage below is the part that is of interest to us:

Among the many figures gathered around the massive chimney's blazing hearth was an old man who appeared to be crushed under the weight of the years. He sat on a very low bench, holding his stick in two hands, one of which supported his bald head. Even without catching sight of his satchel, it was apparent that he was a wandering man, a beggar. Yet it was just as clear that, within this fraternity, he held the highest rank. The master of the house implored him to take a seat among his guests, in vain; he answered these hearty entreaties with a bitter smile and a finger pointed at his bundle. A deeply penitent figure, he'd told the host that he'd return to sup in his room. Though he had been kindly offered much more, his wish was to eat bread alone. It was thus with a certain respect that they beheld this old man, who seemed lost in his thoughts. A conversation did ensue, nevertheless, and Jim O'Bailey lost no time in steering it toward his favourite subject. "Yes, gentlemen," said he, "not in vain have genius and books been given to mankind! With books we can summon forth spirits from the Other World, even the Devil himself." A few doubters shook their heads, and the old man leaned his own forcefully against his stick.

"Even I," Jim said, "six months ago, I saw the Devil in the form of a pig."

"A pig it surely was," cried out the young notary's clerk, the local wit.

The old man sat up straight on his bench, with the sternest look of indignation on his face.

"So, Mr. O'Bailey," said the young clerk, "one must truly be ignorant of science to not know that all these ghost stories are no more than old wives' tales, dreamed up to put the grandchildren to sleep."

Here the wanderer could no longer contain himself.

"Let me assure you, good sir, that there is indeed such a thing as ghosts, ghosts most terrible, and I have good reason to believe it," he added.

"At your age, old man, the nerves grow weak, the faculties are enfeebled, and as for a lack of education, I wouldn't dare venture a guess," replied the learned one.

"At your age! At your age!" the beggar repeated. "That's all they know how to say, it seems. But you listen to me, Mr. Notary: At your age, I was a man. That's right, a man. Look!" he said, painfully standing up with the aid of his stick. "Look, look with disdain if it brings you pleasure, at this hollowed-out face, these dim eyes, these scrawny arms, this whole emaciated body. Yea, when I was your age I had muscles of steel to move the body you see standing before you now, little better than a walking ghost. What man would then have dared," the old man went on, filled with vim and vigour, "what man would have dared take on Lewis, nicknamed 'iron-arms.' Education? Perhaps I have not had my nose ever thrust deep in the books of science, not as often as yourself, but I've learned enough to exercise an honourable profession — had not my passions blinded me. Yes, sir, at age fifty I had a terrible vision, and that was twenty-five years ago now. That was the beginning of the downward spiral I find myself in today. But, my God," the old man yelled, raising his two bony hands heavenward: "If You have let my life draw out so, it must be that Your justice has yet to be fully done. I've yet to atone for my horrible crimes. May they be finally erased, and I shall believe my penitence too short!"

Exhausted by the effort these pronouncements demanded of him, the old man fell back onto his chair, tears streaming down his hollowed-out face.

"Listen, Old Man," said the host, "I'm sure this fellow meant no harm."

"Certainly not," said the young clerk, extending his hand to the old man. "Forgive me. It was all in jest."

"How could I not forgive you," said the beggar, "when I myself am so often at the mercy of others?"

"And as a token of our reconciliation," said the young man, "won't you tell us your story?"

"Very well," the old man agreed, "as it's one whose moral could be of great use to you."

And so he began:

"It was a winter night, the year of our Lord 17—, the twenty-ninth of February, which, you may know, is a momentary breach in the flow of time and the alignment of the stars. The old stories tell of this 'extra' day that returns once every four years, coveted by men but rejected by God; a portal to another world. At twenty I was a cocky young guttersnipe, well acquainted with every vice known to man. A quarreller, a brawler, a drunken debaucher, a swearer, and notorious blasphemer — that was me. My father, after trying everything in his power to correct the errors of my ways, cursed me and then died of sorrow. I wasted no time in squandering my inheritance, and soon found myself with no means of sustenance, so I was only too happy to find employ as a common soldier in Captain Boone's militia, charged with protecting small Virginia towns from Indian attack. The Choctaw and Cherokee chiefs had sworn to destroy the White Man's villages, and the atmosphere when I took up my post that cold winter was tense. The memory of King Philip's War was still fresh in people's minds.

"The villagers posted us in drafty barns, with only our daily pittance and makeshift sheets and blankets for warmth. The battle was coming the next day, and my fellow militiamen were nervous. I quickly fell into comradeship with one fellow stretched out nearby, a man of barely twenty who claimed he hailed from the faraway colony of Canada, a place I had never had the pleasure of visiting. We talked all night and, at the stroke of midnight, he let me know it was his birthday. I laughed deeply, out of sympathy, instantly grasping that this was a birthday celebrated but once every four years, on the return of each new leap year. I asked whether that was for him a source of discontent. He answered, mysteriously, that that was not for him to say, over the course of his life he'd seen every idea he held sacred turned on its head, and could no longer be certain of anything at all. I didn't understand a word of what he was telling me, but I felt for him, each of us had our problems: me, my squandered inheritance and vices; and he, but one birthday every four years.

"In the distance the village clock rang once. It was then I witnessed a horrifying physical occurrence that confounded those laws of nature you seem to hold so dear, Mr. Notary. Before my very eyes the young man I had been talking to suddenly transformed into a grizzled old man: his ears grew

in a single bound to rest on cheeks ravaged by another time,
one out of joint and beyond comprehension. He looked me
in the eyes and I saw the suffering slumbering inside him,
mixed with the fearsome rage of a diabolical creature born
of incomprehensible circumstance. The callow youth who
just a few seconds earlier claimed to have given up on judg-
ing the length of his life, was suddenly a foul-smelling old
wretch, at death's door, ready to crumble to dust at any
moment. His mouth seemed pasty; his teeth were turning
brown before my eyes. I had never seen anything like it. I
tried to convince myself it was a hallucination, or maybe
a bad dream, but he was really and truly there, a terrify-
ing, grotesque figure doubled over upon himself, like the
prisoner of a wrinkle in time cracked open by the new day
and the ringing bells of the town's most Christian clocks.
He was sinking, all alone, there was no helping him, no
way to catch him in this fall, I was so terrified I closed my
eyes and pushed this creature of filth with my two hands
blindly out-thrust. When I again opened my eyes, he was
nowhere to be seen.

"He had disappeared into the woods with an infernal
cry. The Choctaws, armed with tomahawks and poison
arrows, attacked at dawn and we held them off with great
difficulty and heavy losses. I was the sole witness of his
transformation. We counted our dead and never spoke of
it again.

"I never recovered from this dreadful experience. For
long years, nightmares haunted my sleep. I kept believing
it was a matter of letting time do its work, that one day the
sun would rise and my fears and trepidation would be things
of the past. But I was asking the impossible, my friends:
never would the demon I had seen that night leave me in
peace, far from it; he came calling again, decades later, when
my body was no longer what it had once been. Sure, they

still called me Lewis Iron-Arms, but I was already the bent-backed wandering man you see before you today. I had a job with the Hudson River Company. It was a fine spring day around noon, and we were making our way up the river in the George Washington, a two-masted schooner. A pleasant breeze pushed us along. I was sitting on the rail of the poop deck when the captain summoned the crew and said, 'Listen, boys, in four hours we'll be at the Devil's Post. Which of you will man it?' All eyes turned to me, and everyone piped up at once: 'Old Lewis Iron-Arms, that's who.' I could see it was unanimous, so I clenched my teeth together so hard they sliced clean through the metal stem of my pipe, pounded the rail I was sitting on, and gave vent to my rage: 'Thundering typhoons, yes, it would be me; I'm not afraid of God or of the Devil, and when the Fiend comes I'll not be afraid.' 'Bravo!' they cried out. 'Hooray for Lewis!' This compliment made me want to laugh, but my laughter was frozen in a horrible grimace, and my teeth chattered as if I were in the throes of a terrible fever. All hands gave me a drink, and we spent the afternoon in our cups. It was a post of no account, always held by a single man for three months at a time. He would hunt and fish, do a little trading with the savages. Every one of us lived in fear of this lonely posting—that's why we called it the Devil's Post—so we'd agreed, for years, to draw straws for it. But the other traders knew I was a proud man, and understood that if they named me, all together, I'd be too proud to refuse, and they'd all be spared this infamous posting. And, two birds with one stone: they'd also be rid of the toughest man among them, feared by one and all.

"It was going on four in the afternoon when we sailed up to the post, whose very name still gives me the shivers fifteen years later. When I heard the captain give the order it stirred up a well of emotion within me. Four of my companions set me down on land with my chest, provisions, and some baubles to trade with the savages, and then put distance between themselves and this cursed place. 'Good luck!' 'Farewell!' And I answered, 'The Devil take you all, you gang of—.' (The curse that followed was so vile I won't repeat it here.) 'Well,' cried Andrew Connely, who'd suffered two broken ribs from old Iron-Arms, 'your friend the Devil will be seeing you before us, I reckon.' 'Keep laughing, Connely,' I cried, 'but take my advice: Let the Indians tan your hide, because if you see my fist again in three months, I swear by—here I inserted another unrepeatable curse—I swear your carcass will be picked so clean there won't be sinew enough left to mend my boots.' And Connely replied, 'As for you, the Devil won't leave enough to make a single leather thong.' Now I was mad! I seized a stone and hurled it with all my strength. My aim was true: the stone struck Connely and knocked him out cold on the deck of the schooner.

"'He killed him!' his three comrades cried out. Only one man came to his aid, the others were busy rowing, trying hard to right the boat. And I believed I had indeed ended his life, so I ran off and hid in the woods, in case the boat landed here, but after half an hour, which felt more like a century, I saw it raising sail and disappear in the distance. Connely didn't die on the spot; it took three years. He forgave his killer with his dying breath. I hope God too will grant me His pardon, come Judgment Day, just as this good man did. Seeing the boat set sail set my mind at ease a little, after this brutal act, and while I was still thinking that if I had killed Connely outright, or even just mortally wounded him, they would be coming for me, I was also making my way to my new home. It was a cabin, twenty feet by twenty, with no light save a tiny glass-paned window facing south-west. There were two little sheds built right onto the cabin, so you went through three doors in a row, one at a time. There were fifteen beds, bunks really, built along the walls of the main room. I'll spare you the rest of the description because it has nothing to do with the story. I had drunk plenty of brandy that day, and kept right on drinking to distract myself from this woeful state of affairs: Here I was, alone on a beach, far from any human habitation. All alone, just me and my conscience. And my Lord, a heavy conscience it was! I could feel the powerful arms of this very God, who I had spited and blasphemed so many times, bearing down on me like a heavy weight on my chest. The only living creatures here to share my solitude were two enormous Newfoundland hounds. In fierceness, they were their master's match.

"These dogs had been left for me so I could go hunt the red bears which were plentiful in those parts. I'd eaten dinner and was smoking my pipe, right next to the fire, my two hounds sleeping at my side; the night was dark and silent when, out of nowhere, I heard a scream so bitter, so piercing, that my hair stood on end. It couldn't be the bark of a dog, not even a great wild wolf. In that great shriek I clearly heard the voice of Satan himself. My two dogs answered with howls of pain, as if their bones were breaking. I took my time. My pride got the best of me, and I set off with three bullets in my gun. My two dogs followed me, trembling with fear. Silence had fallen again, and I was getting ready to come home when I saw a man coming out of the woods with an enormous black dog; he was taller than most men, and wore a giant hat as wide as a millstone that left no part of his face visible. I called out to him, yelled at him to stop, but he walked right by, and he and his dog disappeared into the river. My dogs were quaking with fear, pressed up against me with every limb, begging for my protection. I went back to my cabin, overtaken by the fear of death. I closed and barricaded all three doors with whatever furniture I could find, and then my first movement was to cry out to the God I had so offended and beg forgiveness for my crimes—but my pride got the better of me, and I put off this moment of Grace, and lay down, fully dressed, on the twelfth bunk with my two dogs by my side.

"I'd been there around half an hour when I heard a scratching on my cabin, as if a thousand cats, or some other creature, were clinging to the walls with their claws. What I saw, though, was countless tiny men, all around two feet tall, climbing up and down my chimney at an astonishing speed. After watching me for a moment with an evil expression they climbed back up the chimney in a flash, to the sound of diabolical peals of laughter. My soul was so hardened that this fearsome spectacle didn't make me want to retreat, far from it—it sent me into such a rage that I bit my dogs to give them a jump, then grabbed my gun and hit the trigger hard. It didn't fire the first time. I made unfruitful attempts to get up, grab a harpoon, and attack these diabolical little men, when a new shriek even more piercing than the last nailed me to my spot. The little creatures were gone, a deep silence fell, and I heard two knocks on the first of the cabin's doors. There was a third knock and then, despite all my precautions, the door opened with a horrible racket. My arms and legs were covered in a cold sweat, and for the first time in ten years I prayed. I beseeched God to take pity on me. A second scream made it clear that my enemy was making ready to break through the second door, and on the third knock, it opened like the first one. 'My God, oh my God,' I yelled. 'Save me!' And the voice of God rose up like thunder and answered: 'No, miserable creature, you shall perish.' Then the third scream rang out and a silence descended that lasted around ten minutes.

"My heart was beating double-speed; it seemed my head

was opening and my brains leaking out, drop by drop, my limbs growing stiff, when, at the third blow, the door splintered to pieces. I stood still, as if defeated. Then, the fantastical being I had seen walk by came into my cabin, with his dog, and took up a position facing the chimney. The last dying ember was snuffed out, leaving us in total darkness.

"I began to pray, desperately, and swore to good Saint Anne that, should she deliver me, I'd spend the rest of my days wandering from door to door, begging for my daily bread. I was distracted from my prayer by a sudden flash of light: the ghost had turned toward me and lifted his enormous hat, and his two giant eyes shone like flames in the night, lighting up the horrific scene. Then I recognized this henchman of the Fiend: it was the young man I'd known thirty years before, under the leap-year moon, the mere youth who had transformed into a grotesque werewolf before my very eyes. He looked exactly the same, with the same skin, smooth as the finest ivory, that had led me to believe we were the same age. The face of an angel fallen from heaven it was, a face that had inspired affection and trust while we lay in wait for the Indian attack and while we lay in panic in our sketchy shelter. Now he stared at me from above. He stood above me, his face towered over me with a beauty as awful as the night was dark. He was still twenty years old, whereas I was fifty with deep wrinkles carved under my eyes and forehead.

"At the same time, like a flickering flame shining in the darkness, giving no heed to the unspoken laws governing mankind since time immemorial, or the latest scientific treatises, he took on the look of a demon straight from Hell: his nose covered his upper lip, his giant mouth spread from ear to ear, and his ears drooped down to his shoulders, like a jackrabbit. He was two creatures in one, Angel and Beast. And I was trespassing on his territory, here in this Alleghenie

Mountain valley, homeland of his secret immortality—that was the message he was sending me. He looked furiously all around and ran his clawed hand the length of the first bunk, and then the second, and so on and so forth, until he came to the eleventh bunk, where he took a short break. And poor, miserable me: I was counting bunks all this time, figuring how many lay between me and his infernal claw. I had stopped praying, was out of strength, my parched tongue was glued to the roof of my mouth and my heart's beating, which fear could not stop, was the only sound breaking the silence that reigned all around me in the fearful night.

"I saw him reach out toward me; then, summoning up all the strength I possessed, with a jerky movement, I found myself standing upright, face-to-face with this ghost whose flaming breath burnt my face. 'Ghost!' I cried out to him: 'If you be a Creature of God, stay; but if you be an envoy of the Devil I beseech you, in the name of the Father, the Son, and the Holy Ghost: Leave this place at once.' Now Satan—make no mistake, gentlemen, this was the Fiend incarnate—let out a piercing shriek that shook the whole cabin like an earthquake. Everything disappeared at once, and the three doors closed with an abominable racket. I fell back on my pallet, my two dogs close to me, barking through much of the night, unable to resist so much cruel emotion, and I lost consciousness. I don't know how long I lay unconscious, but when I returned to my senses I was stretched out on the floor, dying of hunger and thirst. My two dogs had also suffered terribly; they had scarfed down my boots, my snowshoes, and every other scrap of leather in the cabin. It took a herculean effort to summon the strength to get over this terrible shock and leave the cabin, and when my companions returned, three months later, they scarcely recognized me. I'd become a walking ghost. I had seen The Aberration."

This text was where I first encountered you —
not once but twice. The impetus behind my research
started between the lines of this ghost story. Because
the villain of this story is you, is it not? Are you, Aimé
Bolduc, not this fallen angel? This "flame" described
by the beggar, altered by the light, and obscured by
orbiting stars? Or are you no more than a man, no different from the narrator, imprisoned in a particular,
fatal conjecture of time, looking at yourself through
the mirror of your own obsessions and vices? That
man that my great-grandmother loved more than anything in the world seems far from diabolical. It's up
to you to show me who he really is. Now that I've
found you.

The Aberration. Yes, he was the man in the story, of course
he was. But at the same time, he remembered — or did he? —
being the *teller* of that story, that exact story, so very long ago.
Everyone had leaned in and listened, spellbound, even the
fiddlers stopped playing to give his words space to ring out.
He, the man who never spoke, the one everyone was wary of
because they knew nothing about him, had taken the floor.
The music stopped, the fire was stoked again, and he started
spinning his yarn like an expert storyteller, a wise old man,
or maybe a crazy old man, or some combination of the two
working together to convince every listener present. And
then he'd disappeared. No one on the worksite ever heard
from him again. No one came forward to claim his pay.

As he read the legend of the leap-year man, Aimé was
haunted by this memory and by the strange impression

that he was at once the story's protagonist and author. The images were mixed up in his mind: a man taking the floor to tell a story, making it up as he went along, clearly inspired, and the memory of reading an old story, a story as old as his own reminiscence. Albert seemed to be saying that his version dated from the 1830s, long before the miner's life Aimé knew only later.

After the transcribed story, Albert's writing grew erratic. Visibly, he could no longer control his own wrist, which was giving him a throbbing pain. Aimé struggled to decipher the jumpy handwriting. The lines no longer ran straight but instead angled down toward the bottom-right corner of the page, one after the other, like a flock of desperate animals.

> ... my one request is that you never stop being the person I know you are. Be true to yourself, you who, for so long, have dreamt only of being uncovered and unmasked. I know it. I feel it. But now it's up to you to stop letting the secret of your very being crush you and carve those pointless wrinkles in your immortal face; it's up to you to come and join me. I don't know exactly where you are, but I know you will listen to my story right to the end, and I know you won't be able to ignore my call.

Even before opening the envelope Aimé had known what he would find inside: the urgent, ambiguous words of the person who had been tracking him all these years, crouching in the shadows, waiting to spring up as soon as the opportunity arose. Someone had been searching for him, someone had wanted to find him enough to dedicate his life to it. In the end, he'd succeeded.

Aimé felt admiration, disgust, and pride that he had been the subject of such a fervent obsession, combined with despair that rendered his existence even more futile, despite what Albert might have thought at every thrilling step in his great search.

He read the closing lines of the letter at the same time we did, but understood them differently, and tried to imagine what he would do next.

... conceals a profound nervousness. Yet I have no choice but to go for it. So here's my proposition. I'll be waiting for you on the corner of Broadway and 4th, on Sunday, March 13, from 10 a.m to 1 p.m. After that I'll go back to my home in the province of Quebec, where I'll build a new life far from my friends and family, whom I have hurt irreparably by pursuing this obsession of mine for so many years.

That's all. If I don't mail this right away, I never will. You have six months to make your decision.

Warmest regards,
Your descendant and contemporary,
Albert Langlois

p.s. I have enclosed photocopied excerpts of some of my notebooks, along with various documents illustrating my research. The timeline you will find on page 54 of Notebook c was developed in early 1977, when the information I had concerning Aimé was more fragmentary; it should be taken as a rough guide only. However, I like to think of it as the true starting point of my investigation, and return to it often when I am assailed by doubts as to the accuracy of so much contradictory information. Notwithstanding any factual errors it may contain, the linear beauty of the path it traces gives me a sense of my ancestor's life, and illustrates both the folly of my project and its fundamental truth: everything may be wrong but the actual Aimé, forever on the run, can already be seen there, in the half-light, painted in halftones. Do you recognize him?

The timeline was preposterous: among the locations it placed Aimé were the Bay of Ungava in 1855, where a certain Aimé Bilodeau set down an account of a legendary beast living beneath the eternal ice cap, who returned every nineteenth lunar cycle. The points and arrows scattered everywhere plotted out the rough outline of a ghostly existence, a life examined to reveal not only eternal youth but also geographical ubiquity. Albert must have realized early on, despite the excitement that took hold of him as he unearthed new sources and brought new information to light, that there was no way for Aimé to be simultaneously in Georgia enlisted in the militia walking alongside the Indians down the Trail of Tears and on Quebec's North Shore piloting a ferry toward Newfoundland. Yes, Albert must have realized and resigned himself to the contradiction. Certain notations had been crossed out, places where Aimé could not possibly have been present, either on the ground or as the crow flies. There were a hundred printed pages in manuscript, cross-referenced in the most convoluted manner.

He saw himself in the enlarged detail of a photo from the end of the nineteenth century, the one in which Jeanne had recognized his likeness. The dark cheeks, red from lack of sleep. The empty, distant stare. His poorly fitted cap and long greasy hair. The fragile shoulders. He looked himself in the eye for a moment, as the distance expanded, then he spread the pile of supporting documents over the table, to go through them systematically before the last stars stopped shining.

CHAPTER NINETEEN

MARCH 1994
JOHN F. KENNEDY INTERNATIONAL AIRPORT, NEW YORK, NY

A FEW YARDS ahead in the zigzagging lineup he noticed a pretty, thin young woman with a ponytail, and without getting his hopes up wondered whether he might be lucky enough to sit beside her. She wore faded jeans and a white T-shirt, held a U.S. passport in her right hand, and was tapping out a rhythm on her thigh. From a distance Aimé couldn't tell whether it was the air conditioning that was giving her goosebumps, but he was looking at her naked arms. She broke into a fit of shivering and leaned over and opened her suitcase. There were hundreds of people around Aimé, hurriedly making their way to other terminals. She took out a white wool sweater and put it on, pulling out her ponytail and checking the tag to make sure it wasn't inside out in a single, fluid movement. She was shorter than the man behind her who never stopped clearing his throat.

Every time the line inched forward, Aimé picked up his

own suitcase and then set it down again, safe and sound between his knees.

The loudspeakers never stopped broadcasting important information, a rotating cast of voices and languages, beautiful voices speaking English and Arabic and German. They were calling passengers, pronouncing names as best they could, reminding the public of upcoming departures and preboarding, repeating flight and gate numbers. Everything was white, from the floors to the walls to the very high ceilings where giant circular incandescent light-fixtures hung. Aimé was concentrating on the racket of footsteps, clacking high heels, and suitcase casters on the floor, and also the sound of people speaking among themselves, kissing and saying goodbye. On the other side of the large open area where he found himself, a nervous crowd was gathered, waiting for loved ones to arrive via the corridor across from them.

He saw her moving forward to check in, wheeling her suitcase behind her. It lasted a few seconds, maybe a minute. She placed her bags on the conveyor, and they disappeared. Aimé moved forward a step or two. She put her passport and ticket in her handbag and left without turning around. The line didn't move for a few minutes. An airline employee took over from a colleague. There were only three open counters. Aimé heard an exasperated sigh, even felt the hot air on his neck. He could be easily mistaken for a man of sixty, a man who was still in good shape but had been through his share of ups and downs, with a sadness deep in his eyes that came from somewhere faraway, no one knew quite where, mixed with an inborn curiosity undampened by time. One of his greatest regrets, he had realized with the passing years, was not showing up to meet Albert. It wasn't always on his mind exactly, he didn't even think about it a lot, it was more a thought that cropped up from time to time, an ill-defined regret impressed on his psyche, overlaying the blurry, monumental panorama of his memories. Maybe he'd write Albert once he got to Europe.

She disappeared into the labyrinthine airport.

He thought she was pretty, and would love to spend the flight beside her, talking to her about what he was planning to do and the radical changes he wanted to make in his life. He had sold his house at a loss and transferred his assets. She would understand and listen attentively, enraptured by his cultivated manner and speech. He'd tell her about the Jura, where he owned a sizable property with a house even older than he was and a vineyard. He started imagining the sound of her voice, like a song, the tonic accents of the South mixed with a Californian lilt. In Paris they would become friends, he'd show her how to pronounce a few words with his old nineteenth-century French. Time passed as he told himself stories, like everyone else in the line, and then it was his turn. An American Airlines agent hollered "Next!" and Aimé approached, his lips dry.

After check-in he had more than three hours to kill. He didn't look for her too hard in the terminal, just took a stroll through international departures, where the giant windows overlooked the aircraft parked on the tarmac and others arriving in the distance, tiny points that moved and took shape in the cold midday light. He wandered around without a clear aim, not straying too far from his gate. The terminal was crowded, all business. Sunlight reflected off the pink granite floor, flight attendants' heels clacked. Feeling thirsty and somehow bereft of purpose, without a clear idea why, he ordered a scotch on ice, his first alcoholic drink in nearly five years.

WITH HIS TICKET and passport in hand, he examined seat numbers and did his best not to bump the other passengers with the coat he'd thrown over his forearm. His beard was grey and neatly trimmed. He was careful about his appearance. These last years had been trying ones. His self-esteem was slumping, he'd been told in private sessions in the offices of professionals who charged dearly for their expertise, serious men and women who probed his state of mind based on the things he told them and those he tried to conceal. They hadn't prescribed him drugs, yet, but he figured they'd get around to it one of these days. Sometimes he described his dreams, as accurately as he could and in response they would repeat, like a mantra, that change was good.

She was looking out the window, and he immediately recognized her ponytail. His eyes scanned his ticket, and then the number written on the overhead compartment, her neck to her shoulders and her wool fisherman's sweater. She turned her head and smiled a nervous smile, barely noticeable, her nervousness under control and concealed behind the need to be polite and friendly. Aimé stared at her for a fraction of a second, as if he recognized her, as if he was trying to recognize something in her. This lasted a few moments, deeply charged yet barely perceptible, and he slid his carry-on into the compartment. He was thinking about her when he sat down in his seat, right beside hers, thinking about what they would say, in a few moments. The passengers were all chatting, a hum of voices both joyous and solemn. He fastened his seatbelt, automatically, didn't think about it. When she saw him do it she imitated him, like someone who follows the rules and, for that reason, shows that they deserve to be spared, in the event of a mechanical failure, or human error.

She kept smiling though, and said, in a burst of laughter, as if trying to poke gentle fun at herself and include him in her mild anxiety:

"God I hate planes."

And she breathed through her nose, scrunching up her eyebrows a bit. Aimé nodded in understanding. He also smiled to himself, reassured and full of authority. He had worn glasses for a few years now, his eyesight had suddenly deteriorated. He wore them on a cord around his neck, so they hung on his chest when he took them off. He looked like an internationally respected university professor, one of those people who, in certain circles, are even more famous than the movie stars they sometimes hang out with and marry. His beard was neatly trimmed, mostly grey with patches of white near the ears. It had been a long time since he'd opened his mouth to say something important to anyone, something beyond the niceties of social intercourse and polite conversation. He felt oxidized from the inside, but she trusted him, already, you could see it in her posture. She was tense, but let herself be slowly won over by his calm.

"Think of it as a big bird," he said. "A really big bird."

Her face looked pensive, but her smile was still there, present. He took it as encouragement.

"Go on."

"Well, when you see a bird flying, from the ground, are you afraid it'll fall?"

"No, I'm not."

"Even if it's real high up in the sky?"

"Yes."

"Do you ever think about the possibility of one of its wings being broken, or its navigation system malfunctioning?"

"No, you're right, in fact, I'm in complete awe watching it and trusting it to, well, just be itself. To fly wherever it's flying to."

"Just try to remember that feeling and the way you feel when you watch that bird, and everything's going to be all right."

She didn't answer, but watched him as if he were an old sage she wouldn't dare to contradict, out of deference, but didn't totally believe either. Was he just talking shit? He had to wonder himself. She seemed deep inside herself, looking to recover a feeling, a mood, not just to make him happy. She breathed deeply and seemed to hear the song of a cardinal, maybe a jay, or the scream of an eagle crossing the mountains, gliding serene and majestic.

"I'm Laura, by the way."

"It's a pleasure to meet you, Laura. I'm Kenneth."

"I like the sound of your voice, Kenneth, it reminds me of someone."

"It's a very old voice."

They heard the engines starting and the substance of the

air changed in the cabin and the lights blinked along the aisles. A flight attendant with a serious expression sat down on a folding seat in front of them and fastened her seatbelt. The plane started backing up and the grim landscape around the airport paraded by the window. You couldn't see New York, neither its skyscrapers nor its streets, all you could see were the metal and concrete hangers and electricity pylons, tiny men in hard hats and safety glasses. Aimé smiled at Laura, who seemed more tense suddenly. She leaned back in her seat, clearing her throat, with a very straight back and her eyes open wide. He placed his arm on the armrest between their seats and she put her moist, warm hand on his, which was only beginning to display the elasticity of old age.

He lowered his eyes and turned his hand over to take Laura's, so she could squeeze it, interlace her fingers with his, and feel reassured. He smiled again, for himself and for her, for this irrational fear that took hold of her, and which she communicated to him. He whispered that everything was going to be okay. That she could trust him. That she was safe.

PART THREE

CHIC-CHOCS

CHAPTER TWENTY

AUGUST 1998
CHATTANOOGA, TN—SAINTE-ANNE-DES-MONTS, QC

WE'D LIKE TO be able to paint a clear picture. Thomas is dirty, exhausted, and out of breath. He shows up on his father's doorstep one afternoon at the end of August and finally sets down his dusty backpack on the wooden balcony and knocks on the door. We can almost see him weaving back and forth as he emerges from the mountains under storm clouds, heading down clearly marked paths in the eroded foothills, steering clear of Highway 299 where the tourists speed along, and then walking, and walking some more, toward his father's village, through fallow fields, with a firm grip on a pilgrim's stick he'd picked up by the wayside. In our imaginings he would have crossed the Appalachian Trail from end to end, camped in the White Mountains and the Green Mountains and the blue ridges of the Alleghenies, alone with only basic gear and a bottle of water and a notion of redemption that involved making up for past wrongdoings.

He'd have slept in uninsulated shelters, rough wood cabins with gaps that let in sun, rain, and mosquitoes without discrimination, and rolled up in a ball when other hikers came to share these spaces that belonged to one and all and were there for whoever might need them. He might have come across a bear or other wild animal, like a deer with magnificent antlers who turned toward him in a sudden, clean movement full of fear and confidence. And he'd have correctly identified their species, thanks to the images remembered from his childhood picture books.

That was how he imagined it as well, his trip up North, that's how he thought it would go in his dreams about the legendary hiking trail and the personal fiction about the path his life was taking and what this reunion would mean. When he rang the doorbell of the pretty home that belonged to his father as it had belonged to his father's deceased parents before him, a pretty house with painted shutters and bay windows, he imagined walking down mountains so old they had no summit, disappearing in the distance behind the fog and the drizzle. He saw himself crossing a creek, walking along the bank, scrambling up a rock so massive and imposing that it was itself a sort of volcanic hill.

His right cheek was still scarred. He'd had seven teeth replaced and had needed an operation to reattach his lower jaw.

TRUTH BE TOLD, he'd taken a Greyhound to Atlanta, then another to New York a few hours later, and after two days on the bus he had gotten off in Montreal. He'd heard good things about the city. Completely out of it from lack of sleep and lulled by the rhythmic pulsing of the heartbeat he could feel in his swollen lip, he boarded another bus for Quebec City, then another that did the milk run around the Gaspé Peninsula, hitting the thousand little towns that lined the St. Lawrence as it broadened into the sea.

Earlier, between Charlotte, North Carolina, and Richmond, Virginia, where the driver stopped for a break in the middle of the night, he'd found himself trapped in conversation with a young pregnant woman who rubbed her belly in a circular motion while sharing her thoughts on the magnificent North Carolina landscape. Thomas was in the window seat, so she kept leaning over him to point things out: a flock of ducks in the sky, a lonely willow in the middle of a wheat field against the dark red dusk. The details flew by through the window, the bus made its way along the highway in gentle curves, but she didn't miss a thing, and was more than happy to discuss all the sights with Thomas. He always agreed—it was true, it was pretty, she was right—but really he would much rather have been sleeping. He didn't dare look closely, her stomach was so big even the most basic, ordinary movements were obstructed, even her neck moved along with it, like an outgrowth. A man was waiting for her when she got off in Richmond. He enthusiastically grabbed her suitcase and sports bag. Thomas watched them from his torn plush seat on high as they kissed before disappearing into the white-walled station.

Later, between New York and Albany, they made their way into the mountains, into the Adirondacks, the day fully upon them, the sun breaking through a layer of grey.

The bus hugged the mountainside, overlooking drop-offs where he saw shimmering lakes, lost in primeval forest that reminded him of those old War of Independence battles he'd memorized in school. Ethan Allen and Benedict Arnold crossed these lakes in birchbark canoes, delivering messages to generals who'd spent weeks waiting for the word to leap up and attack the English. He imagined Washington calming his men, telling them one more time that Boston would fall any day now, while a bonfire burned and the well-armed, patient English held their position across the river.

Sitting on a Greyhound bus, fingering a book he hadn't read for hours, Thomas was moving a thousand times faster than the pace of war back in those days, a thousand times at least. And he moved without expending effort, carried by eight wheels and an engine over mountains and winding asphalt roads; it made him think about lightning and about light. If he were to compare, it was almost as if he were the light, especially when he imagined covering distances on foot, what it would entail, what it would mean, back then, to tell your wife or father, "I'm going to Quebec," and then set off from Virginia. He thought about excursions, explorers, someone reckless and courageous, maybe just a touch foolhardy, who would be asked to follow the Mississippi to its source and answer, "Sure, why not?"

The bus was hurtling along, eating up the miles, Thomas almost felt sick: there was a rising nausea coupled with dizziness, a feeling that hadn't left him since Chattanooga, layered on top of a nagging pain in his head. Now his legs were tingling from sitting still for too long. When he tried to sleep he grew aware of the driver's jerky movements, his arms stretched out on the wheel, his accumulated fatigue as he tried to keep driving while listening to Haitian music in his headphones. It was to fight off his fatigue that he hummed the Creole words and bobbed his head, Thomas was sure of it. The driver was exhausted, it made it seem as if everyone else was feeling something similar, a heaviness of the eyelids, a loss of vision and depth of field. And he would wake up at the slightest turn, certain for a fraction of a second that the bus was going to roll.

He'd made a point of saying his goodbyes to his grand-parents, to give them the sense of peace Laura had denied them when she ran off with Albert, slipped off into the night with bags so stuffed they barely closed, her clothes spilling out the sides. Now he too was leaving them, to live with the same man who'd taken their daughter from them. He wasn't planning on coming back, but had sat himself down in their living room anyway, right at the top of the hall stairs, to give them a kiss, hold Josephine in his arms, and thank Wright for everything he'd done for him, no matter how bad the last few months had been. He felt responsible, though he couldn't condone what his grandfather had done. He refrained from saying the words, the words that would hurt him, the words that would accurately describe the man in front of him. Words he never thought he'd have to say, but which had crept back into his life these past years, like bombs, or old stories kept secret, tucked away for polite-ness' sake, and out of a certain respect, he had to admit. Wright and his past, Wright and his family, his beliefs, his speeches, Wright and the things he had written in news-papers and small-circulation magazines. Those terrible things his mother had told him about in the evenings, and that he associated with old white-supremacist films that showed men with crosses and flames and masks, swept up in their enthusiasm, screaming on the altars, brandishing their speech and their threats. He'd looked at him one final time, the monumental Wright who was now smaller than Thomas, with his white hair elegantly combed back, and repeated that, though he was grateful, the time had come for him to find his own path.

At this cliché his grandfather batted his eyelids, and in his reaction Thomas saw poorly concealed disdain: disdain for his cowardice in fleeing northward to another country while the battle was just beginning. The disdain of a man who saw himself as abandoned once again, by someone who refused to understand that it was all for his own good, all in the name of Good, the Greater Good. Deep in his grandfather's eyes Thomas could see a form of conviction that scared him. It had sparked up again with the Keysha-Ann affair, which made Wright feel ten years younger, and made him feel like fighting, he said, to restore the balance of a twisted world in deep decline and poised on the brink of collapse. A world devoid of values, a world thrown off-kilter, a world with no tomorrow.

Thomas had shaken his hand. He'd wanted to show his sincere gratitude with a firm handshake, a handshake with conviction. But his grandfather's grip was too much for him, the grasp of conviction itself, the fist of a man who'd never doubted anything, never questioned anything, and Thomas's hand went limp upon contact.

Josephine drove him to the bus station and they had one

final conversation, full of euphemisms and commonplaces about the North, the strength of filial ties, how cold the winter was up there, the possibility he might be disappointed. They didn't mention Albert explicitly but his presence was palpable. As usual she finished his sentences for him, found the right words before they had time to come out of his mouth. He felt a great affection for her, in the old car, his nose full of the smell of old leather. He kept his eyes on the road and so did she, praying silently, and they arrived at their destination. Josephine didn't get out. She turned to him and said:

"You're eighteen now, go ahead and do what you want. We can't make you do anything you don't want to."

It was a strange way to say goodbye, as if the argument they'd never had was now beginning, with Josephine turned toward him, one hand on the wheel, the other on his wrist, while he got ready to open the door and get out of the car. Thomas didn't answer. His grandmother's bracelets tinkled, there were lots of them in different colours. The trunk opened at the push of a button and he was off, with his big backpack on his shoulders. His name was written in permanent marker, Thomas Langlois, two words he'd never pronounced properly.

A few minutes later he was on the bus. No one knew where he was going. It wasn't written on his face alongside the purple and red marks. Even the driver who tore Thomas's ticket had no idea, it was somewhere real far away from here, Sainte-Anne-des-Monts, *Kwee-bec*. Several days away and in another country.

HE DIDN'T WAIT long after knocking. There were footsteps inside, he could see a long hallway through the screen door, and his nervousness ratcheted up a notch when he saw a broad-shouldered silhouette take shape in the half-light and heat. His last memory of this man was from way back in early childhood: he saw his father in the darkness of his bedroom, there was no night light, he was leaving, telling him to go to sleep, as if it were no big deal, just another morning. He was whispering, full of a carefully aimed affection that was comforting. They'd see each other one day, wouldn't they? And his father nodded, yes they would, before he disappeared for good.

The man coming to the door was the same one. The decade between the two memories was a chasm of unfathomable depth, impossible to comprehend yet easily crossed in a single bound. It was up to him to decide, he thought, and he remembered a series of pretty phrases he'd heard when he was young, from Albert, about everything and nothing, in moments of closeness he thought he had forgotten. Sentences spoken in that sophisticated accent of his. When they went to the library together to meet Laura, after saying hi to the security guard, Albert pointed at the stacks. "You see that?" he said, unable to pronounce the "th." "Your mom, she work in the most beautiful place in the world." When they read the letter from Mr. Simons together and Thomas was reassured of his destiy—he who was always in doubt, who wasn't even certain that he existed for real—Albert would rock him on his knee and repeat the mysterious words from far away across the river, explaining their meaning and repeating them so his son would understand they were meant for him. Between two sentences he told him to be quiet and breathe, "Breathe through your nose, Thomas." And, of course, Thomas tried to do just that.

When the door opened, after a moment of stillness, the man who opened it wasn't hunched over or broken by the years and the weight of his own mistakes; his arms were at his sides and he recognized the person in front of him and he recognized himself in the person in front of him, in his posture, neck, and jaw, seen through the screen door in pointillist contrast. Albert smiled, with his lips first and then with his eyes and the rest of his face. Thomas backed up a bit onto the porch, to leave him room to open the creaking door.

The daylight behind him was changing hue. The air smelled like fish and the sea. The houses were white and blue, big and tall, a few had people's names written on wooden plaques out front. He could hear the chirping of grasshoppers in the fields next door, going up and up, and Albert told him to come in, not to just stand there. He laughed, and said it again in English, but Thomas had understood, his father's gestures and the way he moved from place to place and displaced the air around him had always spoken louder than words.

CHAPTER TWENTY-ONE

SEPTEMBER 1998
SAINTE-ANNE-DES-MONTS, QC

IN THE LETTER Albert sent Thomas, care of Mary, he talked about "mending fences" and about "family ties," as if their relationship were a frayed but sturdy length of rope, and all they had to do was tie a few good knots where it had snapped ten years ago, and everything would be made whole again. The tone was that of a changed man, one freed of a weight that had made him a burden to others; if, now, he were given one last chance, everything would be different, you'd see. As Thomas reread his father's words it seemed he was speaking less to his son than to Laura, in a sense; it was as if he'd waited too long, and now there was only Thomas left to accept his remorse. He felt like asking the question, but the opportunity never arose. It would have been awkward to bring up Laura, he thought, in the middle of his father's barely controlled excitement and his sincere, contagious joy at their reunion.

For a month Thomas had been living under Albert's roof, on the edge of the village, next to that boundless body of water covered at dawn by mist that hid the sky through morning. He could see the St. Lawrence from his bay window, and often lost himself in contemplation. The cool smell worked its way into the house and spread from room to room, one at a time, and the old floors creaked wherever he went. The people who had built this house were dead, but life emanated from every hinge and bolt, in the lingering humidity and echoes and incongruous angles where the walls met. The keyholes were like the ones in old movies: you could bend over and look through them.

Albert had welcomed him with enthusiasm tempered by restraint, going toward him and holding back at the same time. He moved to kiss him, then cut it short at the last second when he suddenly understood that it wasn't appropriate at Thomas's age, and settled for an awkward hug that Thomas accepted as naturally as possible. With his arms shyly wrapped around his father's torso, so his hands could touch, he could physically feel the passage of time and every lost opportunity. Despite it all, Albert's smile was beaming, brimming with affection and remembrance. They separated and Thomas went to pick up his bag, but Albert jumped on it in a way that reminded Thomas of the loving, urgent movements of the man he'd seen through the bus window in Richmond, Virginia.

Albert put his son in his childhood bedroom. He thought it was the right thing to do, unaware that Wright and Jo had done the same. Thomas didn't know what to think. It wasn't like it didn't matter, but it wasn't a bad thing either, there was no way he could see it as a bad thing. It was a good idea, in fact, proof that Albert had put some thought into his stay and was taking it seriously. Yet, when he sat on the hard mattress, once he was finally alone with the door shut behind him, he felt like crying for the first time since his mother's death. As if, in this place impregnated with his father's personality, Laura's irremediable absence took on its full meaning.

So Thomas slept in Albert's old room upstairs, the one he had shared with a brother Thomas didn't know. The room was spartan but welcoming, with a sloping floor and inviting symmetry: two beds separated by a nightstand; no football pennants or photos of singers.

They spent entire nights outside enjoying the last of the day's warmth as they talked around the fire. Albert stacked the logs and Thomas watched him, making mental notes. The backyard was big, hundreds of yards, several hectares. You could walk all the way to the road without crossing the property line. The first time he passed under a certain tree planted all alone in the middle of a field, Thomas noticed a treehouse in the branches. Albert told him that he and his brother had built it back in the 1970s, with lumber salvaged from an old shed. They'd done a nice job. Polka-dot curtains still hung from an old window, they'd held on through twenty years of bad weather. Their discussions were friendly, spread out in both space and time; they talked about the area the same way they talked about the past, and the sea, and the salt water that turned fresh, and walks in Chattanooga back when Thomas went to Brainerd High.

Albert liked to make coffee late in the evening, and add

a splash of bourbon. He would put two wooden recliners around the fire, comfortable chairs in which two people could look at each other face to face, and also watch the sky, where burning embers floated through the air along with several thousand visible stars. Thomas understood that from here, even here within it, you could see the Milky Way.

Practical matters had been quickly settled. Thomas would sign up for university next year, there was no rush, they'd look into equivalency rules and straighten up his legal status. He was the son of a Canadian, born outside the country. He was an adult. They'd wait and see. He could spend fall and winter here, resting and building up strength. Albert would support him. Thomas could do whatever he wanted. They had plenty of time: they had so many things to say to each other, so many memories to share and discuss. If he wanted to go walking along the banks of the St. Lawrence, go camping, go climbing in the mountains, or tour around the Gaspé Peninsula, the Baie des Chaleurs, all he had to do was say so. If he didn't feel like doing anything, that was fine too, he just had to say so, Albert would leave him alone.

Thomas would learn French that year—it was one of his priorities. Albert had never taught him anything about the language, except involuntarily, when Thomas heard him talking to Laura, in the kitchen, and they'd switch accents. Then it was Laura's turn to struggle and stumble over strange, complicated words, which Albert sometimes made her repeat because he hadn't understood. This, he often said, was one regret that never left him. His failure to pass on his language to his son, when he'd had the chance, struck Albert as a symbol of the larger failure that was his life. Just

last week he'd talked to a woman in the village, a former
teacher he knew well, who'd known his parents, Mr. and
Mrs. Langlois, and was willing to help Thomas learn. She
was a kind, patient woman. Thomas walked to her house,
stretching his jaw as if to warm up before their elocution
lessons. After a few short months he would speak in full sentences, know enough to get by and ask for what he needed,
enough to explore the village and talk to people. He'd go
fishing for cod at the municipal dock, throw out his line in
his spot between the Ford pickups and the foreign workers.
Everyone he met in town greeted Thomas with a smile.

The first story Albert told him was about the house and
how it came to be his. He'd returned to his hometown in
1987, Thomas remembered, and his parents had died the following year, first one and the other soon after. Albert was
the sole heir, though he wasn't the eldest child. In fact he was
the youngest. Albert was born in 1959, was six years younger
than his brother Charles. But no one else was left to claim
a share. The eldest, his sister Monique, died of leukemia in
1985. Charles, the brother he'd built the treehouse with and
shared a room with, was killed in a car crash not long after
he turned twenty-five in 1978, the year Albert left for the
States. He'd known for a long time that he stood to inherit
everything when his parents died: the estate, the house, the
land, and his father's debts as well. He'd talked about it with
Laura often, in their little apartment, with the newborn in
their arms, he'd told her about Sainte-Anne-des-Monts, the
family property, as if talking about something to be recon-
quered. But that's not why he'd come back. He'd come back
because his marriage had failed, over in Tennessee. That's

what had forced him to leave. To take a step backwards. There was one thing Thomas had to understand: despite everything Laura had told him, they'd never officially separated and, until he learned what happened, about the plane crash, he'd never stopped believing that they might get back together.

He came closer to the dying fire and gave one of the logs a nudge with a metal poker he'd brought outside. Thomas stood up to get a few more logs but Albert told him to leave them beside the fire, he'd take care of it. It had been a strange year, Albert said, as the flames kicked up again. Had Thomas heard about it? In January, southern Quebec had been hit with the worst power outage in history, an ice storm had blown transformers and knocked over pylons and paralyzed Hydro-Québec's entire grid. Had Thomas heard about it? Albert pushed his hands together, forming a circle around an invisible branch:

"The ice was this thick. Everything gave out at the same time. We were lucky up here, but Montreal got hit bad."

As he sat down in the chair he sighed, a sigh of comfort or nostalgia, probably both.

In the weeks after his move back to the village, he'd watched his father Jean die quickly. His mother Lorraine followed not long after. They weren't especially old, but the illness had come for each of them in its own way: Jean silently, Lorraine violently. When he found himself in an empty house after his mother's funeral, Albert had understood just how alone he was in the world, a feeling compounded by the fact that he'd abandoned his wife and son thousands of miles from here. The river wind whistled in the shutters and blew right in through the open door. When he turned to close it, a silence descended. It had lasted for years, until Thomas showed up on his doorstep with a khaki bag and a bruised face.

Then he talked about his parents, his brother and sister, people Thomas had never met but whose pictures adorned the walls of the house. The oldest photos on the staircase showed an eighteen-year-old Lorraine Sénéchal in the arms of Jean Langlois. Behind them, in black-and-white, a gleaming new Packard waited to take them away on their honeymoon somewhere in New York State. There were lots of other portraits, in the staircase and the other rooms, above the mantle, near the clock, and on commodes and sideboards in the room where Albert slept, which had been his parents' room before. Albert described these people to Thomas for the first time, revealing their private lives, hidden secrets, and faults. He wasn't driven by malice, at least as far as Thomas could tell. Albert would smile when he talked about things like the coldness of his father, who'd nonetheless managed to instill certain values — integrity, rectitude, honesty — values that made Thomas think of Wright. Maybe he and Jean would have gotten along. It seemed unlikely. Jean Langlois had been an important union leader in the thirties and forties. He'd helped set up one of the United Steelworkers' first Quebec locals, at the Stelco plant in Montreal. He'd fought against Duplessis and the ultramontanists. While Wright climbed the ranks of the Methodist church in Tennessee, Jean was struggling to chisel away at the power of the Catholic priests in Quebec.

There was also no malice, none Thomas could discern

at least, when Albert talked about his brother Charles, with his innumerable conquests and legendary vanity. Albert remembered the smell of gel and hairspray that permeated their room when he was a kid. He recalled the mirror they'd finally installed behind the door one afternoon in 1965. Charles had managed to convince his mother and was free to admire himself to his heart's content before heading out. Albert could still imagine his young self reflected back as he sat open-mouthed on the bed while his big brother gazed into the mirror, turning in profile and then turning again to make sure the razor line on the back of his neck was perfect.

Charles died doing ninety miles an hour on the 132, outside Rimouski, where he had a girl he went to visit. Around midnight on May 27, 1978, he lost control of his car, which first rolled and then hit a tree a little further down. His death was an indescribable shock for Jean and Lorraine, and for his brother and sister too. Albert told Thomas that Charles was the kind of guy everyone loved, despite his shortcomings. They only made him that much more lovable. He was that guy, a walking cliché but that's the way it was, there was nothing to be done about it. Charles was handsome and generous. He loved a good laugh, but never at others' expense. He stuck up for his little brother, had once gotten into a fight with a much bigger guy to defend Albert. On one of the stairway photos he appeared in all his splendour, leather jacket and pomade in his hair, a sixties teenager leaning on a chromed Chevy with a smoke dangling from his mouth. Looking at the photo, Thomas had no difficulty seeing what Albert meant. Charles emanated confidence. He had that combination of happiness and confidence that had rubbed off on all the family and friends who gravitated around him like satellites and planets. This made him the odd man out in the Langlois family.

Albert had always been more like his sister, Monique, the oldest child. He'd never known her well: she'd left Sainte-Anne-des-Monts to work in a Quebec City department store. A taciturn, solitary girl who kept to herself: that was how he described her, and not like it was a bad thing. In the entire house there was only one photo of Monique. She was laughing with her head thrown back, it was before the first symptoms of leukemia showed up. In summer 1980 she came home to live with her parents. The framed photo on the mantelpiece of the big living room shows her in a blue-and-white striped summer dress, almost from behind, looking a touch mischievous and carefree, a forty-year-old woman with dark curly hair and massive glasses. On closer inspection you could see freckles.

Thomas didn't feel intimidated by these portraits or this family he had never met. Nor did he feel filial attachment. He stopped before the photo of Charles and Albert playing together in front of the house, an old photo whose colours were strangely faded and vivid at once, whose frame was still crooked against the wall, and he contemplated the sheer joy captured on film, without feeling that he was part of it, or belonged to it. No matter how alive these people had once been, they were frozen in the portrait nailed to the wall, prisoners of whatever would be said about them from time to time. When Albert talked about his dead family, whose members had left at various times in his life, punctuating it with deaths and births, he felt no bitterness, but you could tell from listening that he wanted to pass on something that was slipping away from him. Thomas figured his father might be like him, deep down, and could only experience these ties by talking about them, reliving them in his mind, through his memories, putting them back together in order, like a story. He brought these people back to life, blew colour back into them like a bed of coals, for Thomas's sake, but they were growing irrevocably colder, he realized.

One evening, Albert told Thomas that it was strange, or maybe sad, but he was no longer sure what colour his mother's eyes had been. Green? Grey? He stared into the emptiness in front of him, dreaming, and Thomas couldn't help himself from reading between the lines where he heard something like, "I never paid attention."

IN SEPTEMBER THE nights started getting colder and Thomas wanted to know whether Albert had finally found what he'd spent all those years searching for, those years after he'd left Laura and himself. And even before he left, when Thomas was a little kid, when he had been distant and unfathomable, disappearing without warning, or when he would lean over and get down on his knees, to be at Thomas's height (though he never quite was), to try to convince his own son that he was extraordinary, that he wasn't like the others, that he had to cherish this difference. Those years when this endeavour had achieved the opposite of its desired effect, as Thomas felt above all inadequate, sidelined, and rejected. He wasn't criticizing, he wanted to make that clear. He bore no resentment, not really, at least not anymore; he'd managed to find a happy medium between his most private feelings and Laura's stories, his memories and his mother's truncated recollections.

Had he finally found what he was looking for, the thing that had led him to Tennessee, to another country, another culture not his own? In early September Thomas felt ready to ask his father for an explanation. He wanted to know what was behind all the departures, fleeing, research, separations, and midnight farewells in dark rooms. Albert answered that he'd simply wanted to fix his errors, and his errancy, and that meant a clean break and new beginning. When he thought about what he'd put Laura through, it made him shake, he lost his balance. That was why he'd left, that morning. No, he hadn't found anything. There was nothing to find.

He looked at him face to face, and in profile, and from behind, this man who fixed his mistakes in the most cowardly and absurd of all possible ways, by running away and disappearing, and yet could describe the rationale behind his choices so convincingly, with such intensity and undeniable conviction in his eye. Of all Albert's qualities that Thomas couldn't bring himself to hold in contempt or dismiss as mere whims, it was this radical streak that most impressed him. Albert had built his entire adult life around a single obsession, then drawn out his quest over nearly two decades. His obsession forced him to persist, and eventually to self-destruct, like an addict powerless to stop taking a potent, toxic drug. Then all at once, after so much effort, he'd just thrown it all away, taken it upon himself to find forgiveness, far from his loved ones, like an exile.

He didn't tell Thomas that he wouldn't be able to understand, that he was too young, that he could never hope to fully grasp the meaning of his father's actions. He talked to Thomas like an adult, and that impressed Thomas as well, to be treated as an equal, as if he had somehow lost his filial status and become an individual in his own right, a man, in Albert's eyes. He listened to him talk about errors, and redemption, bandying about these esoteric terms, and felt respected by the speaker and transported by this story unfolding one piece at a time. The words floated between them and took on their full meaning, finally spoken directly and out loud.

And in the gaspesian night while these two men renewed acquaintance, in the light of a fire burning in front of them, or will-o'-the-wisps in the distance, to the sounds of crickets singing and firewood crackling and pine needles whistling, Albert talked about Aimé, at length, because the story was worth telling. In his attempt to avoid confusion and not get carried away, no matter how emotional the subject was for him, Albert told his son about the origins of his obsession.

He talked about discovering the journal of Jeanne, née Beaudry, who grew up in Saint-Henri next to the Lachine Canal, and in 1864 got swept up in a mysterious love affair, only to marry Victor Langlois a few months later. The story of his great-grandmother ended with her death, from an aggressive cancer, at the dawn of the twentieth century. He went into detail about the cryptic references he'd discovered in the journal, and the episodic reappearance of this man, in photos described by Jeanne, and in moments of distress and anguish. Thomas was already hooked. He listened patiently, waiting for his own role in this story to become clear. He was aware that he'd been waiting a long time for this moment, this exact moment. Now he was experiencing it. His eyes glued to the orange and yellow flames, he listened to Albert and tried, at all costs, not to be disappointed. Finally his father told him about his research into leap years and the movements of the stars, stellar objects, the Council of Trent. The planets began to align in his mind, and Albert was once again that tall man leaning in front of him, repeating that his birthday was going to have to wait a little longer, for reasons larger than his life and those of his mother and his father. No one could do anything about it: there was a hole in time, so small that only exceptional beings like Thomas could slip through. Suddenly Albert's voice was once again the one he had heard then, with his barely formed ears, his four-year-old's eardrums. The voice was authoritative, competent, undeniably strong, omniscient in scope.

He hadn't thought about February 29 for years, and here was Albert making it the lynchpin of his story. At the very centre of it all, the very centre of the knot itself, was Aimé, his ancestor, the original leaper, the man who hadn't aged like others, the man who had arrived on earth at a specific moment in time, barely bigger than the eye of a needle, shaped by the precise astrological configuration. Albert wasn't afraid of astrology, they were talking about science after all, there was nothing to fear. He looked Thomas in the eye for the first time that night. Aimé was his obsession. If he counted the early months picking through Jeanne's journal entries and putting together the first hazy connections, he had spent exactly twenty-five years, four months, and one hundred and eighty days on his research, with his nose in a book or his feet in the mud, falling asleep in libraries or breathing heavily on mountain paths. At nineteen, he remembered it like yesterday, he'd found his first important clue, involving one William Van Ness who fought in the Union Army before disappearing into the woods somewhere in western Mississippi. On an impulse he'd set off for Chattanooga, where an important new civil war museum had opened. The archives were said to be phenomenal, a boundless trove for anyone interested in the War of Secession and the thousands of anonymous men who'd played a part in it and died on the field of battle, on both sides of the line of fire.

Albert told Thomas about how he walked into the Galaxy diner, in April 1979, and met Laura, and Thomas felt a sort of vertigo, as the two versions of the story butted up against each other, and the moving but still somewhat-static image in his head took on a third dimension.

"Mom always said it was May — May 17, to be precise."

"That's impossible. I remember perfectly, I kept the bus ticket until I left. I'm not saying she lied, just that she got her dates mixed up. I arrived in Chattanooga on April 13, after three days on the road. I met your mother that very morning, at her restaurant. I went to eat there every day for the next two weeks."

From that point, Albert's story subtly shifted, and certain details got mixed up. The family story, his and Laura's love story, was interwoven with this other story of origin and ancestry, the forefather he had pursued in the belief that, with enough effort, he would manage to find and follow his trace. Albert had been driven by his certainty that Aimé was still alive. He talked about it to his young fiancée, talked about it passionately, and when he learned that she was pregnant, at the end of June, they left together, got married, and embarked on family life.

Strangely, Laura's parents had no place in Albert's story. They were totally absent, as if he'd barely gotten to know them or the pernicious attitudes so often described by their daughter. Jo and Wright, their fanaticism, racism, opposition to the marriage—none of it was there.

Thomas didn't stop Albert to ask for more, he let this sudden feeling of simultaneous loss and fulfillment sink in. Albert described the years that followed as a time of both conjugal bliss and slowly eroding self-confidence. He'd found a menial job that left time for research. He could hardly believe his son was born at the right time. He'd been convincing, too, and Laura had agreed to let him do experiments, convinced as she was of the deep love that inspired them. There were birthdays. Thomas was home-schooled. He had a vague recollection, like a burning, of speeches on such subjects as his luck, his exceptionalism, even his destiny. There were years of disappointment and dejection, but also great discoveries: during those years Albert had recovered Aimé's trace, picking up a thread here and another there, in the Appalachian Mountains or a Quebec jail cell. Throughout those years Albert talked of virtually nothing else, unable to see that life went on outside the timeline he never stopped redrawing as it grew ever more complex. He described those years and stressed their capital importance for Thomas to understand his father's personality, frequently repeating that he wasn't proud, no, he'd learned to view this long march toward nothing as a fault line in his life, a failing of sorts, a culpable, almost morbid negligence on his part, a kind of crime.

Today, he said, he realized it had all been for naught. He'd invented every bit of it. Do you understand me, Thomas, I dreamed up this whole thing in a dark corner of my selfish mind. It was easy to say, now that he felt he'd been cured of his obsession: I invented all of it, and forced my family, my wife and my son, to partake of my madness. From the first cold clue to the unshakable conviction of having at last found Aimé, my whole adult life was built on a series of dishonest, factitious connections. He started blushing and almost stuttered when he brought up the interminable letter written in late 1986, in a sort of trance; such a long letter, he had copied out the entire legend, from the first line to the last, imagining his invisible ancestor recognizing himself, believing this man would be so impressed by all the work that had gone into it, so moved by Albert's patience, that he would come running to meet him. He'd written all night. No, it was two whole nights, two days and two nights. Laura and Thomas weren't there, they'd gone off somewhere, he didn't remember anymore, they'd been impossible to find in the house, and he'd written a sort of mad desperate tract stained by wine and tears, all to say one simple thing: I've found you.

The final failure—Aimé's failure to turn up at their rendezvous in downtown Pittsburg, Kansas, on March 13, 1987—changed everything for Albert. He'd waited fourteen hours on the designated park bench, as clouds slowly gathered overhead, forming the embryo of the storm that would finally force him to take shelter along with everyone else in town.

Albert was on the first bus back to Chattanooga the next morning. His marriage had long been over. Laura had made that much clear. In the yard, on his own private property, he burned what little was left of it, burned everything, hundreds of documents, sparing only a single notebook, the one where he had written out his most important discoveries, the one he called his "good copy." If Thomas wanted to see it, he could show him, it was up there, in his parents' room, on a bedside table, in a drawer, in a paper bag. He didn't know why he kept it, it was totally pointless. And Thomas, in the dark of the night, could feel Albert's gaze turn toward him, perhaps unconsciously. It lasted a fraction of a second.

"Did the letter you sent Aimé come back? Return to sender?"

"No, never."

THAT NIGHT THOMAS fell asleep with a feeling of fullness in his chest for the first time, as if an oxygen balloon had inflated between his ribs, expanding to fill all the space where a heavy ball of anguish had been crushing his diaphragm since the accident last April.

Lying on his back, like a man in a coffin, he folded his hands over his heart, that was how he managed to feel good, and thought about his birthday, and about being Albert Langlois's son, and about Aimé, who might still be alive, his ancestor and his contemporary, and the passage of time, which could be measured in such different ways, and what it meant to him, and to his future. He had found his father at last. The wallpaper's golden patterns shone in the moonlight.

CHAPTER TWENTY-TWO

NOVEMBER 2001
MONTREAL, QC

THOMAS'S THOUGHTS TURNED to his mother when he saw the second plane crash into the tower. It was her face that sprung to mind, a young woman's face, she was thirty-four the last time he saw her, the morning she set off for Chattanooga Metropolitan to catch her flight to New York, late as usual, last minute as always. Her suitcase sat on the kitchen floor while she called a taxi and then gave Mary a quick call to say goodbye, the phone wedged between her shoulder and chin, the index finger of her left hand in her shoe, easing it onto her foot, maintaining a precarious balance and already nervous about flying. Thomas had been up for a long time, in his underwear, standing in his bedroom door with eyes wide open. She left and he had to rub off the red mark of lipstick on his forehead. The screen door slammed shut—it was the last sound she would make in his life. No, that's not true, there was the sound of the cab door closing, and the squealing tires as it peeled out and took off at high speed, like a getaway car. She said that by fourteen you didn't need a babysitter, you were old enough to stay by yourself. Mary would come by and make sure everything was okay early in the week. She said, You'll see, I'll be back so fast you'll barely notice I left. Or something like that. She said she'd be back.

It was his mother's face that sprung to mind when Thomas saw the second plane strike the second tower on live TV, while gigantic clusters of black smoke billowed out of the first tower, through windows and pulverized walls, escaping the building, pouring out and dispersing against a bright blue background. Everyone was wondering what was happening, and you could see a triangular point on the right-hand side of the screen, disappearing momentarily behind the flames, then reappearing and causing a spectacular explosion on the other side. There was no sound, the images stood alone, words crawled along the ticker at the bottom of the screen describing what had occurred with a lag. None of the people standing next to Thomas staring at the screen were talking anymore, no one was saying anything, all you could hear was the sound of breath being held, a tiny inhale, a hand held in front of the mouth, and eyes, dozens of pairs of eyes, glued to the screen. As if drawn by instinct, herds of people emerged from classrooms.

He was already at university when the images of the North Tower started playing in a continuous loop on the screens in the student café. A little after eight in the morning the employees changed the station, put on Radio-Canada, and Thomas looked up from his textbook. He saw the World

Trade Center, an image of the World Trade Center as it usually was, two towers he'd never visited. The North Tower was on fire near the top, with a black hole in the upper floors. Helicopters hovered in the sky and cameras zoomed in fast. When the plane appeared onscreen and the other tower began to darken, everyone understood it was an attack, an act of terror, a deliberate act. The first plane hadn't been filmed, there were no pictures to show, but the words crawling along the bottom of the screen told of another hijacked plane that had crashed into the Pentagon. Thomas read the words, let the violence of it all soak in. He'd never been to New York, except to change buses, and had never been to Washington either, he didn't know any more about these cities than the people gathered around him, swearing and repeating again and again how unbelievable it all was, how there was just no way. A journalist with neatly combed hair kept coming back on and people were asking: Why him, didn't he do the arts? Why is he the one talking? People said it must be a coincidence, he must have been in New York when it happened and the station asked him to cover it. He'd been a journalist first, after all, before he got the arts beat. He was a professional, standing on the roof of a building somewhere quite far off, Brooklyn maybe, somewhere safe but still on the front lines, the camera was filming and when he gave specific details he stepped aside and the camera zoomed in on the towers.

Around an hour later, unpredictably, the top of one of the towers collapsed and massive plumes of smoke and dust poured out in every direction. It was incredible, but no one said so this time. Silence had descended on the university hallways again. In the years to come, it was this silence Thomas would remember most: the way they had all watched, from here, hundreds of miles from the action, silent and transfixed, in perfect contrast to the chaos in the streets over there.

The next day and the week that followed, those images cycled in a continuous loop. People waving white clothing in broken windows. Cameramen engulfed in a sea of grey dust. Buildings crumbling like houses of cards. Men and women in black and white and sepia, covered with lunar particles, walking, weaving like zombies through paper-strewn streets.

Thomas didn't know New York, he'd never been outside Tennessee before leaving the States, but he still had a feeling, like a reflex, that this was an attack on him, on both him and his mother, or the memory of his mother and what little she had passed down to him. Could anyone have blamed him?

He hadn't gone to class but it didn't matter, the professor had cancelled it.

TWO WEEKS AFTER what they were now calling 9/11, Thomas started going out and having a social life again. He could look at the unyielding blue of the early fall sky and appreciate its colour and depth. When two planes went by at the same time, so their flight paths appeared to cross, his nerves returned momentarily. There were times, these days, when he wondered how other people managed to keep going about their business, getting into cars, buying stuff on sale. He figured he would never get over it, as everyone else seemed to be doing, but at the same time the world kept turning, even as Ground Zero continued to burn and the water pumps ran twenty-four hours a day. They would never identify all the bodies, all the body parts, just as Laura's body, lost at the bottom of the ocean, had never been officially identified.

At the end of September he was invited to a party at the apartment of some people he didn't know well, and he went, it would be good for him, to see people, talk, be social again. Thomas got ready, got dressed, chose a nice shirt and tucked it in. The address was on the other side of town so he took the Metro, still somewhat amazed at his power to adapt and adjust, how easily he slid his card into the metal slit and pushed the turnstile with his hip, executing the normal, routine movements that made up everyday life in the city. He didn't know anyone who'd been killed in the Twin Towers, not personally. He often had flashbacks of small dots falling from top floors, filmed on the TV cameras by professionals accustomed to zooming in and out, falling points tracked throughout their entire descent, until someone in an editing suite realized these were people, jumping. They weren't things, they were people, in suits and ties and skirts, trying to use their clothing as parachutes. Then the cameras stopped zooming in on the gaping hole and on the windows.

Thomas got to the party early and introduced himself to his hosts, with his unusual accent and friendly smile. Everyone was around his age, he recognized faces from the university, guys and girls from his classes, some of the ones who actually talked in class. He knew a few of the people there, and got along with them; they'd been to his place, he'd told them about his family, how he'd done his schooling in the States before moving up here. When he talked about growing up in Tennessee, people always asked him to talk like a Southerner, stretching out the vowels, making it more nasal, and he'd do it, and they'd laugh. And then they'd ask Thomas all kinds of questions:

"Aren't people racist there?"

"Well . . ."

It stayed hot or at least warm even after the sun went down, and the party spilled out onto the roof. You could see downtown to the north and the mountain behind them with its giant illuminated cross. French- and English-speakers talked and laughed together over cases of beer and bottles of wine. Someone rolled a joint by the fire escape while Thomas's friend strummed a guitar. A girl almost fell off the roof and everyone thought it was hilarious, especially her, leaning forward, her hand over her beating heart, her breath taken away, leaning on someone for support. Thomas was having fun. Soon after arriving he'd untucked his shirt, it was more comfortable. Most of the people were in the same program at the university, but there were also friends of friends and random people who'd showed up with something to drink and been welcomed with open arms. The roof was full of people and a little group had gathered around the guitar player, singing Smiths and Belle and Sebastian songs. The guitar player closed his eyes when he sang, and his nostrils flared, he had a seriousness no one would mock. The others sang along earnestly. It still wasn't very late. The neighbours were far away.

The lights downtown were impressive, you could hear

horns honking and see the searchlights from Place Ville Marie cutting through the low-hanging clouds. A guy Thomas didn't know was laughing. It came out loud and affected, like a demonic cackle, and then he suddenly yelled:

"Anyway, fucking yanks sure got it this time!"

"Finally."

"About time!"

"Motherfuckers had it coming."

"Yeah, Osama!"

Thomas listened, picking up on the nuances, the irony and bravado, the tone and particular features of each person's voice. He backed up to the fringes of the group to watch this scene. Someone was dancing around an imaginary fire with a bottle outstretched like a spear, slapping his own mouth over and over to make a slow, high-pitched sound. Others had joined him in a sort of improvised powwow. The joint had made its way to Thomas, who hesitated a few minutes. He stared at it until he felt the tip burning his finger.

DESPITE ALL THAT had happened, and certain recurring nightmares, he continued to believe that September 11, and its impact on his thoughts and the questions he had around his identity, was little more than a dark episode in a new life he was living, enjoying, with what resembled a long-term plan for the first time, amid this vague pervasive threat. He'd started his second year of university and was living in the student residence, a collection of greyish buildings next to the Metro station. Days went by, each one much like the next. But he was happy. He had friends in different neighbourhoods and was discovering the city's distant, secret corners. When he had free time he'd go for a walk, it gave him time to think. He'd take the major thoroughfares, and head down the Main and along the Lachine Canal into Saint-Henri where, according to Albert, the whole story had begun. He liked to turn around and, with a view of the oratory in the distance, note that he had passed underneath the mountain in tunnels. The campus was enormous. He went to football games and swim meets. Unlike Chattanooga, Montreal felt like living in a big city. It was dirty but resilient, overflowing with echoes and cranes, a city where the sounds never stopped.

At the university library he could access the Internet on shared workstations. He'd check his email during his long breaks between morning and afternoon classes. November was here. It had snowed the night before, but the snowflakes vanished the second they hit the ground.

He talked to his father often, in both English and French. Their relationship wasn't tied to any one language, they'd just find the right words for whatever they had to say at the moment, whatever they were thinking. They weren't afraid of words. Albert had come to visit his miniscule apartment a few times. He said it reminded him of the cadets' barracks, back in the day, something about the strict discipline of the concrete, straight walls firmly cemented into the ground. When he turned up in Chattanooga, Albert had been carrying his old cadet duffle bag, and Laura thought he might be a soldier. But no soldier would show his face in public with a beard like that. Albert visited his son's residence, in that big city he'd never lived in himself, and said something he'd

never said before: he was proud of Thomas. He was proud
to be there, proud of the way things were going, where
they seemed to be headed. When they talked on the phone
he made jokes in English and French and Thomas picked
up the undertones, double-entendres, puns. They talked
about Aimé often, as if he were a fictional character they'd
invented for kicks and given a backstory, invented a life and
enough features to make him real, but not enough to com-
plicate things. Thomas wasn't scared Albert would fall back
into his old obsessive ways. He had successfully detoxed and
was living in the here and now, he said with a laugh; he was
through with the past. He looked after his land, cut trees
all year long, bucked logs to sit on or for firewood. Thomas
had the notebook and kept it like a token of past tribulations,
something salvaged from a great shipwreck.

THERE IS ANOTHER thing we must not leave out of our
account, something that made Thomas's heart swell and ate
away at it at the same time. For months, since he'd received
the first of a series of letters on February 28, he'd been corresponding with Mary. Now it was early November. He hadn't
received any word since the attacks, and he was worried.

It was in his thoughts, burning on his mind. It had happened quite naturally, after two years of silence, without
either of them knowing quite what to expect. In blue ink on
coloured paper, in flowing handwriting with long syllables,
she'd wished him a happy birthday. This year he would turn
twenty-one, and officially become an adult in her country.
It didn't make her feel any younger to think about that, she

wrote, but at the same time, when she did, she didn't exactly feel old either. The letter was short and Thomas replied right away. A few words, quickly scribbled; deeply felt thanks, and a promise to write a longer letter soon to tell her all about the intervening years.

They'd been corresponding for months and, while neither had specifically brought up the idea of leaving, or of coming back, the possibility was hanging there between the lines. Thomas talked about his studies, how much he loved going to class. He'd always been a good student, disciplined and focused. Mary had the handwriting of a librarian, someone used to filling out catalogue cards. Her words were unadorned but clear, gently sloped. Somewhere in the middle of the continent their letters met, wherever it was that letters crossed borders, and the subtle perfume that Mary sprayed on her letters filled up the trucks and mailboxes. She wrote that she had never felt that way. Never, she wrote again, underlined with a single unwavering line. Sometimes Thomas had to stop reading to take a moment to think. To look out the little window and catch his breath, though no one had exactly taken it away from him. A few seconds later, he would plunge back into the world Mary had made for him alone.

They shared secrets. That night, just before the accident, the night they'd spent at her house, he had barely slept. Did she know that? He'd spent hours staring at the white label of her tank top in the dark, a tiny white point sticking out against her skin. Did she know that? He pictured Mary in her Avondale bungalow, stooped over her desk, braids hanging down and a cup of tea at her side. He asked whether

Frederick Douglass and his friends still hung out in front of her house like little sentries. She answered that there were more and more people standing guard as the neighbourhood grew more and more violent. He didn't dare ask for news about Keysha-Ann, but Mary gave it to him anyway. She knew him better than anyone else, after all.

As he read the sentence, Thomas felt love, and understood perfectly well what it was, this thing that held him tightly in its grip and also set him free. He hadn't put it into words right away, but over months, the words grew increasingly clear. He could feel himself growing older, all these experiences pushed back first of all by Laura's death and then by his warm, almost stifling welcome at Wright and Jo's, it was all happening at once. In June 2001 he wrote Mary to wish her a happy birthday, she'd just turned thirty-eight.

He was in love with her, and she was with him. But several weeks had passed without a letter.

ON HIS WAY out he finally found a letter in the numbered cubby he'd been assigned, a little metal cube in the west wall of the hallway. It was the first he'd received since the attacks in New York and Washington, the first in far too long. He snatched the envelope. There was no one around. The scent was faint but still there, definitely. He sat down in one of the armchairs and cut the envelope flap with his pocketknife, a present from Albert that he always carried on his person.

When he'd told his father about the party and the people up on the roof, about their comments and their laughter, their out-of-control euphoria, Albert told him to pay no mind. Those people didn't understand a thing. And Thomas had wanted to believe him, to trust him, even if part of him understood their reaction, or at least couldn't find it in himself to blame them wholeheartedly. That part of him was there, right there, always at the surface, just waiting to take a breath of air before diving back down. A few months before, when he'd talked to his father about Mary, during his summer vacation in Sainte-Anne, he'd looked him in the eyes and said that that was great news, he'd always liked Mary a lot. The two of them wouldn't be there together if it weren't for her. And Thomas wanted to believe it, even if Keysha-Ann's features kept working their way into his mind, behind his closed eyes.

He took the letter out of the envelope. Looked it over first, noting the paper, the colour of the words, the straight lines and margins. In this letter Mary asked him to forgive her for how long it had taken her to write. She had received his letter, and thanked him for it. She then explained, at length, how the September 11 attacks had affected her personally in a multitude of different ways. She'd needed time to think, to step away and catch the breath that had been sucked right out of her. She told Thomas that her uncle, her mother's brother, had been killed in the Pentagon attack, he'd been in the wing of the building the plane crashed into. The family was devastated. Mary had gone to Washington for the funeral, it was family only, the way they wanted it. She'd seen a lot of relatives out there. People she had no memory of had hugged her and cried in her arms. For years Mary's mother had been her one connection to these people. Now Louis's death had brought them together.

He had been killed instantly, Mary wrote, he hadn't suffered as so many others had. Some people were saying that
the building had been hit by a missile, not a plane. People
were talking all kinds of nonsense. After three or four weeks
of respectful silence people were running their mouths
again, saying all kinds of things, questioning what they were
reading in the papers and seeing on TV. In Chattanooga
and all over Tennessee people had theories — about the
war, about high finance, about the Jews — it was getting
hard to take, Mary explained. Was it different up there in
Canada? It seemed like there was no violence at all up there.
People respected their neighbours, people lived in harmony,
guns were illegal, everyone had insurance, everyone got
free healthcare. Down here paranoia was spreading. At the
library she'd been asked, for the first time, to report "suspi-
cious loans." Could Thomas imagine that? Of course, there
was no formal requirement, but she'd been "strongly encour-
aged" to make note on a special form when people borrowed
books about the Arab world, Islam, the history of terror,
etc. For the first time in her career as a librarian, orders
had come down from on high about something other than
encouraging the love of books and reading and culture and
history. She was shaking as she wrote these words, quaking
with anger and fear, it showed through in her handwriting,
Thomas could tell. Her words wore more sharply etched,
less inclined, less generously spaced.

    In her letter she said it was getting impossible to live out
here, people were scared, and disoriented, and so was she.
She laid it all out: She was scared her country would go up
in flames, war on all fronts would be declared, bombs would

start raining down. On the one hand you had Arabs killing innocent people, people who had nothing to do with any of it, and on the other you had the president declaring war on Muslim countries, it didn't really matter which, and borders closing up, maybe even the return of the draft. That day, Thomas, had changed everything. Oh, Thomas, it was the worst day of my life. September 11 had changed everything in her life, she couldn't live there anymore, there was too much she still wanted to accomplish before succumbing to bitterness and fear. There must be libraries in Canada, in Quebec.

At the end of her letter she told him she was coming. If she was welcome she would come. He could hear her voice. She'd written it again, she couldn't live here anymore, she couldn't live without him anymore, she was confused but she'd made up her mind, she'd never been so sure of herself, I could learn French, I'm not too old to start. At the airport, a few days later, Thomas took her in his arms.

CHAPTER TWENTY-THREE

MAY 2014
QUEBEC CITY, QC—SAINTE-ANNE-DES-MONTS, QC

IT WAS STILL chilly, the spring weather had been slow to settle in the city and on the Plains of Abraham, when Thomas went to see his ailing father. The heat was coming in short bursts, in waves like warm currents in a river, gone the moment you felt them. It was mid-May, still below freezing at night, and even the most eager buds weren't in bloom yet. Albert was going to die amid the shreds and patches of a winter that seemed intent on outstaying its welcome.

Thomas and Mary took their car and drove along the north shore of the St. Lawrence River, a road they'd taken dozens of times in recent years. They caught the Saint-Siméon ferry, then took the Gaspésie highway, a long and winding road exposed to the breezes and winds of a spectacular river growing wider and turning into sea before their eyes. A point came where they could no longer see the other bank, and focused on the vistas in front of them. She almost always drove. Thomas, who was so good at everything, had never really learned. Even when she was tired she never made him take his turn. He was a careful navigator, that was enough. When he wasn't there she got lost, though she'd done the drive hundreds of times, thousands of times, there was a fork in the road at Cap-Chat she missed every time. The car was humming along on new tires. They didn't talk much. Mary listened to music on the radio, Thomas stared out the window at the landscape, the trees were almost bare. He thought he glimpsed a deer. It might just have been branches swaying in the wind.

The news had come a few weeks earlier. He got a call from Mary on the way from his lab on Dorchester in the lower town to his house in the upper town, not far from the Badelard stairway. He'd just unbuttoned his collar, to breathe more freely, and was walking fast, the day was cold and grey, and his telephone rang. She said that Albert had just called, the results were in. He had the same blood cancer that had killed his sister in the 1980s. He'd been diagnosed. Yes, of course he was going to die, he'd known it for a long time, deep down. They'd been trying to get him to see a doctor for months, but Albert hadn't set foot in a hospital in over thirty years, not since Thomas was born in fact. Mary told Thomas she was waiting, they'd get ready to go see him, she was sorry. She told him he should call his father as soon as he could, he'd like that.

Albert was going to die, and Thomas ran up the stairs, in his clean shoes and his raincoat, briefcase swinging in his arms. Their house was a little higher up, on Richelieu, he'd be there in a minute.

Mary was waiting for him at the door. They hugged, she lay her hand on the back of his neck, and his hands stroked her spine, and she cried because Albert had finally confirmed what they both knew. It was sad, she was sad for Thomas and for Albert, but his death was bringing something to a close. Thomas held her tight and leaned on her. They remained in a tight embrace for a long time, in the doorway, at the top of the covered outside steps, at once inside and outside this house that belonged to them, in a neighbourhood so different from the one Mary grew up in, so old and lopsided and colourful. They went in and Thomas immediately phoned Albert to tell him that he knew, and to pin down certain details about their arrival.

"I can't leave until the lab tests are finished, they won't let me."

"I know, I understand. I wouldn't want you to leave everything hanging. Come when you can. Maybe I won't die. You never know. With the treatments and stuff. There's new treatments."

"Did they tell you there's a chance?"

"No. No chance."

"What did they say?"

"Six months, tops. That's the best case."

And Thomas started counting the number of days in those six months, without actually doing the math, while Albert tried to be funny, saying as he always did that it was high time he bought a big bed for the guest room, after all these years, so he and Mary could finally sleep together in the same bed, under his roof, at least once before he died. Six months was one hundred and eighty-two days. Thomas told

Albert he'd do his best to get time off as soon as the preliminary results were in, in two weeks, three at the most. His team would get by without him, his colleagues could handle the analysis. He and Mary would leave right after that.

"You gonna drive?"

"Probably not."

He could see his dad's teasing smile.

WHEN THEY GOT there Albert had done it: he'd ordered a big double bed to replace the two singles in his childhood bedroom where Thomas and Mary always stayed. They felt at home at Albert's. For years the three had formed what they called a family. Mary made the best campfires, she'd been a Scout far longer than Albert had been a cadet. She knew tricks to get it going, and quickly took over. She also chopped the best firewood.

Mary and Albert got along well. They had Laura's memory in common, a thing they shared between them, and Mary had decided to stop fighting for a bigger share. It was time to turn the page, there was no other way. She'd told Thomas, on their first trip to the Gaspé Peninsula, at the start of their relationship: You know your father has a lot of things to be forgiven for. And she made herself available, ready to listen and accept his version, and Albert took the next two days to give her just that. He didn't try to charm or convince her, just meet her halfway on a specific patch of neutral ground where they might live together.

No one, least of all us, could hope to know how their lives would have unfolded if Laura hadn't died in that plane crash back in 1994. But there was no point living in that other world, where Laura lived happily ever after, and Albert had done nothing wrong, and Thomas never got to know his grandparents, and he and Mary never met. There was no point, they all agreed. Mary tended the fire, it was something she loved doing, and she and Albert talked about her new job, how easily she learned new languages, the process to become a Canadian citizen. Thomas never thought he'd be able to say it one day, but he felt very close to his father. The thought of it still astonished him sometimes.

That night, for the first time ever at Albert's house, he and Mary slept together under the same sheets and the same blanket. Albert had gone to bed early. He walked slowly now and had lost a lot of weight. Thomas had helped him up the steps, his arm around his father's shoulders. They went to sleep knowing full well that it wouldn't be long now. At dinner Albert had tried to make it sound less serious than it was. It wasn't like it used to be, when his sister Monique died. Cancer had taken both his parents as well. But he thought he might make it. Did he really believe it? You couldn't tell by looking at him in the cold, bright daylight.

He said no to chemotherapy and the doctors prescribed drugs, an end-of-life cocktail of painkillers. He was going to die at home with his son and his daughter-in-law. It was his choice. He wasn't old, barely fifty-five, people lived to a hundred these days, a hundred and ten, even. People pulled through infections and contagious diseases and cancers of the brain. He wasn't old but his body was no longer responding, the blood vessels were compromised, the red blood cells and white blood cells and platelets were all out of order. His skin had changed colour. It was somewhere between grey and yellow.

For the next two weeks, Mary and Thomas took care of him. No one thought it would happen so fast. Forty-five of the promised one hundred and eighty-two days, and it was all pretty much over. Albert went to bed the night they arrived and never really got up again. Mary kept him clean. Thomas oversaw his treatment. He called the hospital and took over the procedures. Albert had made a decision they had to respect. A nurse came on May 20, in the afternoon, to make sure everything was going smoothly, though those weren't the exact words she used. She smiled at Thomas and Mary, on her way in, and went up to the next floor. She talked about the house, couldn't help herself, it was beautiful, she had always dreamed of having a house like this, with a giant yard and a balcony and those little flourishes on the front columns. She was young, with the bloodshot eyes of someone arriving from outside, where it was still chilly along the river. As Mary listened to her she thought about the growing age gap between her and Thomas. Whenever she brought it up he was reassuring, he tried to make it clear that she was still pretty, he still wanted her. Mary didn't talk about it much anymore, refused to let it turn into an obsession. It's true that she was pretty, heads turned when she went to town to buy fruit or meat at the grocery store, she didn't go unnoticed. Her hair hadn't turned grey yet, she had never worn much makeup.

They took care of Albert as best they could, affectionately and patiently. His health started going downhill around the time they arrived. Mary parked the car and he waited, leaning against the doorframe, Thomas could see that he'd lost weight, but then he knew he'd started losing weight the moment the diagnosis came in. Already, the year before, he remembered noticing that Albert had lost his appetite. He got out of the car and his father came toward him. After dinner, he went to bed early. His plate had barely been touched. For two weeks, they took turns sitting beside him, to make sure he had everything he needed.

Before he died, Albert asked Thomas to indulge in one last flight of fancy, one final inside joke between father and son: Tell me the story of Aimé Bolduc, the leap-year man, the one who didn't age like the others because his soul was in phase with different planets, because he'd been forgotten at the Council of Trent. Albert's eyes were glassy, he wanted Thomas to tell him one more time about eminent mathematicians and theologians who had solved the problem of the revolution of the earth back in the sixteenth century. Thomas knew Albert's notebook inside out. He took his father's hand and told him about when Aimé met Jeanne, their clandestine trysts on borrowed time, the years of wealth and wandering, confidential letters delivered to Montreal into the hand of Ben Franklin himself, the time the Devil made an appearance on the banks of the Hudson, at a remote trading post somewhere in the Appalachians, deep in the night; he told the story of the *Headlight Sun* and the Order of Twentyniners, and of Aimé's many and sundry inventions, none of which he'd bothered to patent. Thomas had been talking to himself for several minutes. But that too was a form of listening.

A FEW HOURS after Albert closed his eyes for the last time, on the morning of May 28, Thomas's phone vibrated on the white commode in the hallway. They were sitting at the kitchen table, in silence. Mary was boiling water for coffee. Thomas got up and went to answer. The chair scraped on the floor. Sunlight poured in through every window at once, from both east and west, exposing the ancestral dust dancing throughout this old house. The light was almost liquid, as if you could burn it for fuel.

His father had been dead two hours, his mother for many years, he was thirty-three and everyone said he was ageing well, without even an inkling of what that might mean. He had nice features. A good personality. Intelligence and something else, a certain sensitivity. The lab number was flashing on his phone. His feelings were mixed up with those of Mary, who knew it was an important call. He pushed the button with his thumb to talk. He heard the click of the electric kettle, boiling water, and the voice of Pierre, Dr. Monette, his colleague, skipping the small talk and telling him that the analyses were all complete. Blood, cells, muscles: the results were in. His tone was professional but excited, like a boy who can't wait to tell you about what he found, his treasure, a gold coin found under a tree in the yard, a gold Louis from colonial times, perfectly preserved, impervious to the years.

Pierre spoke quickly. There was no doubt, the curves were clear, the data robust, they'd observed the behaviour of the telomeres.

"They got younger, Thomas. I can confirm it: the cells got younger."

CHAPTER TWENTY-FOUR

MARCH 2020
QUEBEC CITY, QC—WICHITA, KS

IT STARTED WITH an encrypted file in his professional inbox. He thought it might be a prank, but the information was accurate, there were no spelling mistakes, the English was perfect, and there was an office phone number and address in Kansas to confirm that it was a legitimate message. Dr. Thomas Langlois was cordially requested to contact Allan Kreiser, Attorney-at-Law, as soon as possible, regarding the dormant assets of a certain Kenneth Bolduc Simons. A document was attached.

It was the other name that made him react, more than his own: their two names side by side. He leaned into the screen, then backed up, skeptical. The email was barely three lines long. He printed a copy, on which the watermark of Kreiser, Littell & Moore, LLP appeared, and placed it in his personal cubby, in his office at the lab.

Beside his computer screen, at face height, Thomas kept

a plant he watered once a week. Everything was normal, there was nothing especially strange or hard to believe going on around him. His life was structured around a series of self-evident facts that didn't leave him time to think about how the equipment that surrounded him might be interesting in itself. He lived among it, worked in an environment precisely determined by their functions, each was in its place. One morning a week he spoke to his colleagues in Auckland on his retinal screen, to share both surprising and expected results.

He still walked to the lab every day of the week. He and Mary had never moved. They'd bought the building they lived in, and then another, a touch further north on Rue de la Tourelle. Mary drove an electric car, recharged it at night. In the narrow neighbourhood streets you could hear the hum of private charging stations, a sound that helped them sleep, that had been engineered with that in mind. Thomas watered his plant and looked out the window, onto the boulevard, a few floors below. He lived life at a normal pace, it wasn't exhausting or out of control, though his work had changed the shape of history, the nature of things, the course of human life and its meaning and ultimate purpose. He owned several different coloured ties, some by the best brands. He and Mary enjoyed choosing his outfit in the morning, to match the day's weather. She worked at the university campus. They didn't have children, it would have been surprising if they did.

Every day for fifteen years he'd left the upper town and walked down the same staircase. Sometimes he recognized his own footprints on the steps the following day, as if no one else had walked up or down in the last twenty-four hours. When he got to work he slipped on his lab coat, passed through several sterile rooms, opening doors by swiping the touch sensors with his finger. It was a professional but friendly workplace, the kind of place where people would stop and say "Hi" in the hallway. He was well known, the head of a team active on two continents. Leading international scholarly journals cited him. Respectful smiles greeted him wherever he went. He spoke several languages. He was a top authority in his field.

Sometimes, before work, he'd take a walk by the river, a few blocks further north, where it was all winding curves, and then retrace his steps, counting each one as he went. It was an unconscious reflex, a ritual he'd never tried to analyze, and never talked about with Mary. Why would he have? It was something he did for no reason and without a second thought. It wasn't anyone's business but his own. He'd watch the river's current for a moment, no longer, the wind in the reeds, the big willow tree, and then head back downtown. He thought about the names of birds he heard, the names of trees. Sometimes, staring at the water in perpetual movement, it occurred to him that his mother would be proud of him, of what he had accomplished, of what he had done with his life, and he felt an inarticulate despair. But he would smile right after, and the smile and the despair were one and the same, two emotions fused into one in his mind.

Low-altitude drones flew above the surface of the water, transmitting live data on flora and fauna and residual pollution. In winter the wind blew so fiercely it was hard to keep your eyes open, it spiralled all around him, freezing everything in his path. All alone on the river bank, with the bike path behind him, he would spend a moment in silent reflection, appreciating the life he now enjoyed, moved by the past he now missed in ways he couldn't name. And then he'd come back, retrace his footsteps and go back to work. The whole process took just five minutes of his time, barely five minutes.

IN ONE OF the lab's common rooms the wine and beer glasses were still lying out from the previous night's party. After office hours the champagne had started flowing. The federal government grant had been renewed for three more years. They were almost there, that was the talk in the hallways throughout the building. Six years after the recovery of the creature affectionately nicknamed Minnie, and officially designated 34-3B, after successfully regenerating the brain cells and cortex of this first and original subject, several others like her had also responded positively to treatment. Minnie was still alive, in a ventilated glass cage at the opening of the inside laboratory room, in an elegant corner alcove. She had the sharp look of a perfectly healthy adolescent mouse. Regular testing had been carried out on her organs and muscles, to make sure they were still viable and to detect any trace of compromised health, but for the most part she was left alone, no one bothered her. Some of the researchers would stop by for a chat on their way in, it might have been a superstition, they'd stop by her cage, wait for her to appear and press her nose against the glass, and then say a few words, kind words, and sincerely apologize for the pain they'd inflicted on her over the years. They'd thank her for her dedication and place a finger on the cage, which she'd pretend to feel, with alert whiskers and pointed ears.

In the early years they'd injected Minnie with various viruses and bacteria, both common ones and rare specimens procured in Norway and shipped in top secret containers with the convoluted paperwork required under international treaties and scientific protocols. In these early years she had contracted twelve different virulent forms of cancer. They broke her limbs, pierced her eardrum, ripped off her tail. And here she was today, at peace, free of scars and unpleasant memories, alive and well. In the lab she had a reputation, of course, they loved her, there was something special about her, she would be famous one day, even if no information about her had been made public yet.

In a meeting one day, Thomas suggested they build tunnels in the walls, so Minnie could circulate more freely. Everyone agreed. Nothing had been done yet, but it was still on the agenda, an item that came up in meetings now and again. The other mice were all white with red eyes. They lived in a series of numbered cages in another space reserved for growth and observation. This was where the daily experiments were performed.

It was a small team, much smaller than that of their collaborators in New Zealand who had managed to isolate a component that hadn't been rejected by human skin samples in January. Over here they were still testing exclusively on animals, but it didn't make a difference at the end of the day: it was their project, Thomas was lead researcher, everyone reported to him. He'd travelled several times to meet his colleagues in person. He'd loved the plant life in Auckland, the lush smells of greenery on the other side of the world, unknown constellations in an upside-down sky. Over there they were working on human skin cells, and had created the ideal conditions for isolating and eliminating undesirable variables. The climate made a difference, somehow. Over here, Thomas and his team had managed, after years of work, to make six hundred and twenty-two mice grow younger. They had been kept alive, without harm or side effects, in a fixed state where their bodies, membranes, cartilage, and nerves were developmentally frozen and did not age.

Thomas's office was in a restricted area, so there were very few people around to witness his astonishment and excitement. He got up from his chair and headed for the exit, crossed the hallway and got in the elevator, then went through the lobby where the research centre's name was written in large golden letters on the back wall, and where the cell-phone waves wouldn't interfere with scientific research. He dialled the number that had been stored in his head for a long time, and somewhere in the distance a friendly voice informed him that he had reached the right place. This confirmation made him blink. A man walked in front of him and talked to the receptionist. Was Allan Kreiser available? Doctor Langlois. Mr. Kreiser wrote to me and asked me to call him as soon as possible, it's about . . . He was asked to wait a moment, music played. His eyes were dry, he blinked a few times, and focused on various spots around him, the sliding doors, the snowflakes outside, and then he heard the voice that must be Kreiser's, confident and friendly:

"Doctor Langlois, yes, hi! What a relief it is to finally reach you."

"What do you mean, finally?"

"We've been looking for you for weeks. Search is over."

"Yes. It seems so."

"Well, this is your lucky day."

"My lucky day?"

"Sir, we have to talk. When can you come to Kansas?"

A FEW HOURS later, Thomas had intentionally lied to Mary for the first time in his life, for a few different reasons but mostly because it would take far too long to explain, especially in the state he was in. He was more nervous than he'd been since his father's death and the myriad events it set in motion. He could still hear Albert's voice in his head, a tale winding like a river, whose ramifications got lost in the realms of conjecture. He and Albert had spent full nights discussing Aimé and his life. How could he hope to explain all that to Mary before leaving? He had ended his conversation with Kreiser with a promise to be in his Wichita office the next day. He'd be on the next flight out, he promised. They'd pay for it, the lawyer said. Fly first class. They'd meet him with a car at the airport.

He'd explain everything when he got back, of course, he'd have time, later, when he got back, to explain and make everything clear, he might even have some answers for Mary. A few hours after the end of his phone call he'd booked a seat on a flight, with two stopovers. He told Mary something had come up and he had to go to the States, to the

University of Wichita, where a scientific panel was holding an emergency meeting on ethics: they'd reanimated a lemur, seven minutes after death. His presence was required, as an authority on youthing. But his work had nothing to do with resuscitation, Mary said. It was totally different. And he'd said yes, he knew, that was exactly why they needed him, they needed an outside perspective, the point of view of a researcher in a related field.

High above the mountains, so high overhead he was impervious to their influence, Thomas began to imagine what this meeting with Kreiser might entail, what he could expect from this lawyer in charge of the "dormant assets" of Aimé Bolduc, of Kenneth B. Simons, of William Van Ness, his forefather and the founder of his family line. He'd refused to believe the evidence before his eyes, imprinted on his retina when he'd seen the two names written side by side on the computer screen. It wasn't possible. He spent the hours of his flight, his flights, looking out the window, as the continent grew smaller and smaller and at the same time took on its full scope and vertiginous size.

Between New York and Wichita he almost fell asleep, from all the thinking, about the mice and the fabricated lemur and Mary who didn't suspect a thing. He never understood why, but every time the flight attendant came to offer him a glass of wine or rum, she mentioned that it was compliments of Kreiser, Littell & Moore. Thomas thanked her with old, familiar stock phrases and smiled, realizing he was happy to speak English again, he and Mary had stopped doing so a long time ago, by choice. When he got back he'd explain everything to her, and they would simultaneously

understand what he was doing on this plane, today, somewhere over the Great Plains.

As promised, a car was waiting for him at the airport, and
he got in after the chauffeur opened the back door. He didn't
say anything. He put on his sunglasses; the oppressive March
sun provided no heat. The city was frozen, at the mercy of
the cold wind sweeping along the river and gathering force
in the wind tunnels formed by buildings. On the highway
between the airport and downtown, the car drove fast, and
Thomas stared at the chauffeur's hands clenching the wheel,
struggling to stay in his lane. He heard the wind outside, buf-
feting the car windows and metal body, clawing its way into
any conceivable opening. It was as cold as Quebec, maybe
colder. These were the same winds, alternating north and
south, they gathered strength over the Great Lakes before
they unleashed on the Prairies.

He didn't say a word during the drive. He wasn't there
to talk, he understood, but to be driven, transported from
one point in the city to another, to meet people who would
reveal something he had been unwittingly waiting for. He
kept his hands in his coat pockets, unable to fully warm up.
It was four in the afternoon, the sky was clear and full of
colour, dark, even through the windows. Thomas had just
turned forty.

The car stopped in front of a building and he got out on
his own, without waiting. The door shut with a dull, muffled sound. People walked past without noticing him. In
the opulent lobby, a man in uniform indicated the correct
floor. In the elevator another man pushed the corresponding
button. On the sixth floor, the elevator doors opened and

he got out, thanking this other man with a nod of his head. The woman he had spoken to the day before stared at him for a moment, with a welcoming look, she smiled with lips pressed together. Thomas did the same, and started to say his name. He was nervous. When she spoke, each languorous elongated syllable flowed the length of the Mississippi and Missouri rivers. Doctor Langlois! Please take a seat, Mr. Kreiser will see you in a moment.

He sat down on a black leather sofa. He knew why he'd been summoned, what they were going to tell him. Aimé had chosen him, named him. Aimé wanted to make contact with him. The entire enigma was encapsulated in this one idea that was so quick to formulate but slow to penetrate. He pictured his father and felt sick to his stomach, a sort of violent stab of uncontrollable joy and nervous excitement. His father had been gone six years. He'd left it all behind in exchange for a healthy relationship with his son: said goodbye to his obsession, abandoned his quest, moved on to something else. In his jacket pocket, under his winter coat, he'd brought Albert's notebook, not to show Kreiser, but to have with him, like a lucky charm. He always carried it with him, and touched it, like a reflex. It reminded him of his father, of course, that was only natural, but also of longevity, of what people called longevity, life's boundless elasticity, the possibility of stretching life out and regenerating it ad infinitum, it reminded him what he was working for, why he went on with his research. The light was nicely dimmed, the bulbs silent. He heard the receptionist's Nano Pen gliding over a paper. As at the research centre, large golden letters mounted on the back wall displayed the firm's name against a dark wood backdrop.

Allan Kreiser, Attorney-at-Law, came silently out of the hallway. The soles of his shoes glided over noise-dampening carpet. Thomas stood up. Kreiser was a big, clean-shaven man. He was smiling. Thomas could see the skin on his neck pulled tight by his shirt collar. They shook hands and Kreiser asked Thomas to please follow him. The reception- ist nodded her head as they passed by, as if giving her bless- ing. It was much warmer inside Kreiser's spacious office, and Thomas took off his coat and was shown a series of hooks on the wall behind him. Kresier sat down and set his elbows on the armrests of the swivelling office chair, and waited for Thomas to join him. Through a massive window you could see downtown in black-and-white, the winding fro- zen river, the vast blue sky, and the horizon beyond where the sun would soon go down. Only a few moments of day- light remained. Just before Kreiser began speaking, Thomas became aware of two other people in opposite corners of the room. They approached slowly, as if summoned by a signal.

"So. Doctor Langlois. As I've already mentioned, we're here today to discuss the last will and testament of Mr. Kenneth B. Simons. You are his sole beneficiary. Let me first introduce Mr. Goldstein, to my right. He's an intern, and he'll be taking the minutes of our meeting. And this is Ms. Cartwright, the firm's notary, who can answer any specific questions you may have, at any time. We also require legal supervision for the reading of the will and listing of the bequeathed assets."

Thomas got up, holding his tie, to shake hands with these two new, no-nonsense members of their party. Goldstein looked barely twenty-one. Cartwright was sitting on an antique chair, slightly off in the background. Thomas sat back down. Kreiser continued:

"We made an appointment with you today, Dr. Langlois, to inform you that you are, let me say it again, the sole beneficiary of the fortune, property, stocks, and dividends of Mr. Kenneth B. Simons, whose will we recently received by mail. No one else is mentioned in the text, which was signed in December 1987 by Mr. Simons, and certified on the same day by Willmore, a Kansas City law firm. We successfully authenticated the document on March 12. We are now ready to proceed with the official reading of the will, which is why you are here.

"Did Mr. Simons just pass away?"

"No, he didn't *just* pass away, but we only just received the documents."

He gave Ms. Cartwright, the notary, a look from the corner of his eye, and proceeded:

"We don't fully understand *exactly* what transpired, but here we are. The papers arrived at our office in early March, and we immediately took steps to find you."

"Do you know the date of his death?"

"Not for the moment. All we know is that he didn't commit suicide, as the text might lead us to believe, since his body was never found. The documents list an address on the outskirts of Pittsburg—a small town in northeastern Kansas, not the Pittsburgh you're surely thinking of. But this address ceased to exist in the late 1990s."

Now Ms. Cartwright spoke:

"According to the municipal archives, all we've been able to access for the moment, the land was appropriated and dezoned in 1999. In the coming months, as our investigation proceeds, we'll be able to tell you more about several points of legal interest, Dr. Langlois. There's a chance that other assets may be added to the list that will be provided to you shortly. But let's not get ahead of ourselves."

"Exactly," said Kreiser. "For now, our focus is of course on verifying and validating the assets listed in the will, those that are known to us. That's why we insisted that you come as quickly as possible, so we could get the process started without delay."

"So you don't know when he died."

"The fact is, if I may speak frankly, this will is only valid because we have no later document to invalidate it. Given how old it is, and certain irregularities concerning the circumstances of—"

"What irregularities?"

"As I mentioned, in his will, written and signed in 1987, Mr. Simons states that he will end his own life on his sixty-fifth birthday, on February 29, 2020—it's a leap year—which is to say, just two days before the documents arrived here, on March 2. He specifies the means he intended to use to end his life, and the place where the authorities would find his body. We have no idea who sent these documents. Everything concerning the act itself is crystal clear, but, again, neither his body nor the weapon was found in the specified place, and we are looking into the possibility that, in fact, he had been dead for years, through circumstances beyond his control."

"What kind of circumstances?"

"Oh, it could be anything, Dr. Langlois. A car accident, a hunting accident, a fall while hiking in the Jura, where he owned property. He could have been lost at sea, on one of his boats. There's no way to be sure, it's all guesswork. One thing is certain though: the date of transfer of property, when the estate passes from his hands to yours, is of primary importance, and we're still trying to—"

"It's my birthday."

"Excuse me?"

"I was born on February 29, 1980."

Thomas didn't say another word. His mind was made up. Kreiser, Goldstein, and Cartwright didn't need to know anything further, about him or about Aimé, or Albert and his research. He focused on what was coming next, stayed calm and breathed deeply.

"Interesting. Very interesting."

Goldstein was taking notes on a tablet, his hands gently tapping on the screen, using complex stenographic shorthand. His eyes stared intently at Thomas's face, he didn't have to look at the screen to see what he was doing. He wasn't wearing glasses, none of them were. The sun had set, the lighting was gentle and even.

"Happy belated birthday, Dr. Langlois."

"Thank you."

"Before we begin the reading, if I may, do you think you could tell us your connection with the deceased, Dr. Langlois?"

"I don't know him. I've never heard his name. In fact, I have no idea what I'm doing here with you today. What about you? What is your connection with him? How can you be sure he's actually dead?"

Kreiser experienced a moment of distrust and hesitation, before regaining his composure.

"I've made inquiries. Mr. Simons was a client of my grandfather's, who founded the firm in 1975. No one remembers him, but his name appears several times in our files. As for his death, it is confirmed by multiple declarations with financial and fiduciary institutions, and verified, since our agents have made contact with the institutions where Mr. Simon's assets were held. The 2016 federal law stipulates that dormant assets can be liberated to the estate after a period of fourteen years with no contact with the depositor."

"Don't worry, Dr. Langlois. Mr. Simons is absolutely dead," said Ms. Cartwright, placing her hand on her other wrist and playing with it. Her golden bracelet tinkled. Kreiser looked down, following her hands, then looked up again, along her arm, to the shoulder, then her chin. He sighed, confused, and looked calmly at Thomas's inscrutable face. Kreiser's look was piercing, as if he were trying to recognize the man standing before him, trying to remember him. As if, by searching his memory, perhaps he might manage to place him in context, in a family story that went back to his own ancestor. He put the palms of his hands on the sheets in front of him. Thomas stared at him, perfectly still, waiting to get rich.

"Let's begin."

THOMAS SAT BACK in his first-class seat. A flight attendant approached with a glass of champagne. She placed her hand on the back of the seat and leaned toward him. Her skin was like Mary's, the same dark brown, like a young Mary with a New York accent. Thomas took the glass. He was much richer than he'd imagined, than he ever could have imagined in his wildest dreams. After liquidating Aimé's European properties and real estate holdings around the United States, Thomas Langlois's fortune would amount to $50 million. Everything had appreciated, like wine, Kreiser had said, and now he was on his way home to the love of his life, who would listen to his very long story, and if anyone was able to understand the intricate clockwork making this story turn, he thought, it was surely Mary. She would be patient and attentive, as she listened, at the kitchen table, in their little house in Saint-Jean-Baptiste in the centre of Quebec City. He'd show her the notebook, she would get right to the bottom of this story, and they would remember Albert, he'd come back and envelop them in his contagious laughter once again.

He drank his champagne and was asleep a few minutes later, his head full of the laughter of his parents, and his grandparents, and Keysha-Ann, all grown up and happily getting on with her life, and another laugh, Minnie's, with her whiskers, when she put her face up to the glass of the cage to brush against the outstretched finger of a superstitious scientist.

He carried an old compass with wandering hands in his suitcase that had been given to him by the lawyer and notary before he left. It had been part of the package of Mr. Simons's documents they received. It must have belonged to him, this rusted metal object that didn't seem to work, or whose works were jammed, at any rate. When he opened the front cover he couldn't make out north or south, not one of the four cardinal points, just a series of symbols and four unmoving needles, pointing every which way, a sort of buried, secret truth, or perhaps the very last thought that ran through Aimé Bolduc's mind.

CHAPTER TWENTY-FIVE

OCTOBER 2047
QUEBEC CITY, QC

THOMAS CAME IN through the visitors' entrance. They let him come and go as he pleased, he was a regular. He still looked like a forty-year-old. People greeted him like a youthful prodigy, star researcher, a genius. Why not? Wasn't he already running a national research centre? His hair and carefully trimmed beard were blond again, ash blond with red highlights here and there, almost the colour of his childhood hair. Its texture had changed too, his hair was finer, like when he was a kid. He didn't need to comb it, it fell on his temples and neck without a hint of waves or knots. When he looked at himself in the mirror, he noticed certain long-forgotten features coming back, like high cheekbones quick to blush, reminding him how violently embarrassed he would get as a teenager. It resurfaced in waves, flashed back before his eyes, memories written on skin still elastic despite the sixty-seventh birthday he'd celebrated in February.

He walked quickly down a dim hallway, lit sparingly with subtle accent lighting. The guards greeted him with a nod. As always he carried a briefcase with important reports he had no use for. He'd been hired as a consultant. He saw himself reflected in the large panes of glass to his left and right. He thought he looked like his maternal grandfather, Wright Howells. If he looked like anyone, it was Wright. But at the same time that was mere speculation. There was no predicting the very long-term effects.

It wasn't just when he passed a mirror. He didn't have to see himself to experience this feeling, a falling back into his past, now that everyone who had been close to him was dead, he had lost wife and friends and was all alone in a world whose course he had fundamentally altered, among people he had, in a sense, saved. He'd been granted eight honorary doctorates in the last two decades, and been received with great pomp by foreign governments. His name had gone down in the annals of science. A university building was named after him in Chattanooga, his hometown. Sometimes the mere act of closing his eyes for a moment, or focusing on an everyday object, was enough to send him hurtling back in time: there he was on a Tennessee summer day, between his mother and his father, out hiking on Mount Lookout or walking the rails of the old railway, keeping his balance, arms outstretched so he wouldn't tumble and land in the stinging nettles. He'd had freckles then. Now, in the sun, they were coming back. Sometimes he could even see his parents kissing, pictured them together, with himself not very far away: a family. It was rare but it happened.

On the other side of the picture windows, holographic

projections showed static or moving scenes, narrative recon-
structions of the various stages of human evolution. In ultra-
fast forward, an oxygen atom chipped away at iron over
a thousand-year period. Cyanobacteria bored into pyrite,
building up geological strata before your eyes. Trilobites
swam in the Paleozoic ocean, with bronze highlights, full
of mercury. Thomas walked against the current of visitors
wearing immersion devices, slipping between families pointing fingers and holding out hands, as if to catch a modelled
molecule or electron.

One of the first changes he noticed was the size and shape
of his ears. He'd noted this in the encrypted file where he
recorded precise details and developments about the potential for rejection. He'd discovered a softness of the lobe, a
flexibility in the auricle that he'd lost as he neared fifty. His
hearing had improved as well, but that had taken longer,
and he'd noticed the external physical details first. His ears
had grown slightly, but not like an old man's, more like the
kid who gets made fun of in the schoolyard.

His body reacted extremely well, it was almost shocking in the early phases. He'd lost twenty pounds in just a
few months. The age spots on his skin disappeared. His
nostril hair thinned. His appetite was healthy as ever, and
he started eating meat again. In the official reports, where
everything was expressed in curves and in numbers, they
repeatedly mentioned this general and pervasive feeling of
health, from head to toe, as if large amounts of endorphins
were being released continuously. His mind was always
sharp, constantly alert, he was eager to discover new things.

Thomas had injected the serum years earlier, as the

experiment's first human subject. He'd acted out of scientific duty and methodological rigour, with the approval of colleagues all over the world, in a closely supervised operation in the Quebec City laboratory where he'd remained under observation for several weeks. Sometimes they put him to sleep, at other times they woke him up. They'd open his eyelids and ask him to blow into tubes. He felt a little like a lab rat, but also uniquely blessed; that seemed an apt description of his life, up to now and as a whole. As if finding himself there, lying down, held in place by electrodes, nicely summed up something about him, the series of steps that had made him who he was, the people he had loved and who had now left him behind, each and every one.

Minnie had lived with him for years in the house on Île d'Orléans. He'd built the tunnels he'd been dreaming of for so long, so she could be free to move about as she wished, without visible restrictions or the feeling of being shut up in a cage. Days would go by without seeing her, she hid her food in the secret passageways that not even he knew about. And she would come back after long excursions, same as ever, young and good natured. They understood each other.

His skin was healthy, the sun no longer affected it as it had before. Most of the time, always really, he felt himself imbued with a heightened self-confidence. It was as if the strange and heavy sense of guilt that had clung to him since childhood had evaporated, he'd seen it slipping out through his chest, a ball of flesh the size of his skull that exploded before his eyes. Now when he breathed in and out or saw the world around him in all its splendour, the vineyards and strawberry fields and faraway circular mountains, and took a deep breath, his lungs filled up with a renewed ardour.

He walked around the reception desk, where the line of visitors was getting longer. In front of him, behind a series of reinforced windows, was the grand hall's main attraction, a triceratops with blunted horns. He stopped for a few seconds to think about it. The blood flowing through his veins was at once old and new. When they took samples, the results showed that the white blood cells had regenerated, there was no trace of the beginnings of sclerosis detected a decade earlier.

Of course, he had only Minnie by his side to enjoy the island's cool days and colourful sunsets with him. He lived slowly, according to a new rhythm, but was happy all the same. He didn't really talk to anyone anymore, except a few vague acquaintances whose names escaped him.

It almost never rained except when they needed it to.

MARY HAD DIED right before they developed the elixir, as it was informally known at the research centre. She had died just as she began to grow old, from a heart attack in her garden, one morning in July 2042, while Thomas was at work. As she leaned over to pick a vegetable in her garden she fell to her knees and never got up again. The service was at City Hall, with a moving eulogy from the mayor himself, who talked about Mary's contribution to the community. The bells rang and Thomas came back home to put her affairs in order. He saw to certain urgent matters, and then went through her boxes, where he found things he'd forgotten all about. There were boxes of souvenirs, photos from the early 2000s, postcards, old tapes they used to listen to with Thomas's mother, books she'd loved, South American musical instruments, knick-knacks, Aimé's old compass.

He and Mary had travelled all over, seen the far-flung corners of the world. As he sat cross-legged in the basement of the large house on Île d'Orléans he'd bought with his inheritance, he teared up at the fact of his wife's absolute absence, he felt it even in his things. He remembered their trip to Eastern Europe. Dozens of countries, bungled attempts at speaking local languages, friendly people they'd met and never seen again. He remembered how easily Mary made friends, how she could make herself understood with nothing but her hands and a smile. She had died one morning, in the garden, with a weed puller in her barely wrinkled hand, her dark skin scarcely touched by age.

Thomas spent a week settling the inheritance, took time off to sift through the layers of the intimate, private details of their shared past, details known to no one, not even us. He'd loved her his whole life, he thought, yes, even as a child he'd loved her, when she'd come to the door and borrow his mother for a few hours. When he tried to return to that exact location in his memory, that's what came back: Mary's smiling face, as she came in the kitchen, rattling the screen door behind her. He'd be on the living room couch with a picture book, and would hear them laughing. They'd put on music. Mary would sing the words she knew by heart, she knew them all. Through the window, he could see the cars and the pedestrians who never stopped to listen to her.

At that moment, entangled in this skein of memories, he understood.

A few days later, Thomas had brought the compass to the laboratory, placed its face under the microscope, and taken a sample of his ancestor's skin. Between two esoteric symbols etched by patient, expert hands, between the four needles that had stopped working ages ago, a DNA sample was conserved: a trace of Aimé, a residue of his skin. It was the first time Thomas had ever seen or had direct physical contact with him.

There was, they said, no observable difference in the test tube where the final serum was concocted, at least not to the naked eye, but the ingredients were already starting to act.

He had taken measures, his colleagues had been notified, and there was a sense of anticipation in the air.

HE PASSED THROUGH other buildings where other eras of human history had been recreated in painstaking detail, summed up concisely with a touch of humour, for the kids and the parents as well. He went in. There was the new hall that would be home to the new exhibition he was consulting on. He entered the honeycomb-like structure, all onion domes and mezzanines, with a large glass sphere that let the sun through. They were waiting for him to finalize the details and ascertain certain facts. Thomas was not only a great scientist, he was also well known as a popularizer, and they'd brought him in as someone who could handle last-minute adjustments. The room was almost ready, it would open to the public in January 2050. Everything was on schedule.

He came in and shut the heavy temporary doors behind him.

The re-creations were superb, and the interpretive walk had been reviewed by historians, ethicists, and Thomas's fellow scientists from a wide range of disciplines. The expert committee had been approved by all levels of government. He walked in and was taken to his colleagues, other scientists like himself and programmers and modellers who had worked on the project; his role was to check the details and the accuracy of some of the more theoretical assertions. It was one of their final meetings. All that remained was to pull it all together, choreograph the many parts of this virtual ballet and finalize the stunning beauty of the whole. It was one of the last meetings, to discuss an important, surely critical, issue. Their task was to use holographic projections and digital displays to tell, in accessible but not reductionist terms, a story. They had to make it real without sugarcoating or trivializing it. Their job was to encapsulate the glory of human history in all its shapes and forms.

As Thomas often said, with a smile in the corner of his mouth but still as serious as can be, they had to show visitors the meaning of this new phase of human history, now that no one would die anymore.

TLO VA SA

JANUARY 2000
MONTREAL, QC

BUILDINGS REMAINED STANDING, planes flew as before, the electrical grid kept working, and no one's computer blew up. When you got down to it, nothing really happened. Eventually the TV pundits moved on to the next story. It was strange to think they'd experienced something important without noticing, as if this thing they'd all been waiting for with fear and trepidation had happened at a microscopic or even an atomic level, so no one even noticed. No one died in hospital from defibrillator malfunction. No electronic system failed in prison, setting thousands of inmates free. The night had passed without event. In Manhattan, in Times Square, there were even more people than usual, despite the authorities' fears. It was absurd and reassuring at the same time, though no one said as much. The skyscrapers still towered over the city, tall and straight and imposing in their rectitude. It was very cold, but that was normal. Nothing was out of the ordinary.

Thomas was walking along Saint-Laurent with his hands in his pockets. His breath formed an opaque cloud in front of him. A pebble in his left boot was bothering him, but he didn't stop to pull it out. It was one of the ones you found in with the de-icing salt. The street was already full of garbage and decorations for the festivities: empty beer cups, Happy New Year streamers in silver and gold, confetti and water bottles. Everyone had gone home after the party, you could barely see anyone in the streets. The faraway sky was still, as if it too was frozen solid. Thomas stepped over a toppled garbage can. He heard a siren in the distance, it sounded like it was coming from the south somewhere but it was hard to tell, the sound could be bouncing off the front of a nearby building. A taxi went zigzagging by. When he ran into people, couples and groups of friends walking toward him, he tried to imagine their features and body type, hand movements, whether they spoke French or English. Though he was wrong almost every time, he persisted in the belief that it was possible to guess. He tried to define certain criteria—hair, chins, foreheads, hand gestures used to punctuate a point—there must be particular traits, but he couldn't figure them out. Everyone wore thick mittens, but he'd forgotten his, and his hands were freezing, despite the relative warmth of his jean pockets.

The first snow hadn't come yet, they'd had nothing but freezing rain since winter began, nothing but icy raindrops coming down at a slant, whipping cheeks, gathering speed in spiral winds. Drops like thorns, and not a single snowflake. But this morning the air was dry and somehow too pure, as if oxygen levels had been reduced to a strict minimum, at high altitude, for the final part of an ascent. Thomas's cheeks were red and his glasses stuck to his nose. He got to the corner of Sainte-Catherine and stopped a while to wait for the green light, jumping on the spot a bit. To his left was the city's west side, stretching out endlessly; to his right, the east, extending even further. He knew nothing of its far reaches, the riverbanks and hinterlands of this sprawling island with a mountain in the middle. Just up ahead it would start to rise toward a plateau, the gentle slope would get steeper in a couple blocks. He started jogging, as if it might warm him up, maintaining a rhythm somewhere between a run and a walk, taking care not to slip.

On the corner of Ontario, Thomas stopped at another red light. There weren't many cars now, but they were coming fast and appearing out of nowhere, from places he hadn't thought to look. He waited. For a second, a cloud formed in the sky, then immediately disappeared, as if swallowed up by frozen particles. He could see, lower down, clinging to the rooftops, the smoke from the factory chimneys that was also being swallowed up. The cold made every detail sharper and every angle more acute. In front of him, two men came out of a building on the other side of the street, where a couple red flags hung in the dry air, on either side of a glass door. They spoke loudly and made sweeping gestures. They looked piss-drunk, and Thomas started watching from a distance, couldn't help himself. One of the two didn't have a winter coat on, or seem to care. He wasn't frantically rubbing his arms to stay warm, he was happy to keep one hand in his pocket and gesture with the other. His hairless skin was dark and tough as leather, his hair black and long. He was walking backwards. His cheeks were ravaged by permanent acne scars. He stopped in the middle of the street, lit a smoke, and kept yelling. The light turned, a truck honked, and they started heading west, barely moving, giving the driver the finger. The first started yelling again, in English it seemed to Thomas. Something about a cigarette, a pack of smokes, a carton, just a smoke. He was making signs, and having a hard time standing upright. The other guy was making fun of him with a lit cigarette, blowing smoke in his face, in the searing morning cold. He smiled and Thomas could see what was left of the man's teeth from the other side of the road as he crossed.

Then, suddenly and without warning, the first guy, with his T-shirt, jeans, and torn runners, and steam escaping his body in the early morning light, jumped at the other guy and punched him in the face. He fell down to the asphalt but got right back up. When he fell he landed almost right in Thomas's legs, he had to jump to avoid him. He got up suddenly and went after the other man, spitting blood and yelling. His smoke was on the ground, far away, not even broken. He grabbed the first guy in his long arms, and they remained interlaced like that for a few seconds, staggering together in a violent hug, groaning incomprehensible words. The second man held his own until he got kneed, then crumpled over, landing a blow to the other guy's stomach on his way down. He grabbed onto his shoulder, dug his nails into his skin, through the T-shirt, and, with a violent movement, sent him rolling on the ground.

Traffic had stopped at the intersection. You could hear the honking horns and insults flying from every direction. There was blood between the chunks of ice. People came out of another building, a store, but when they saw that the men were Indians, they went back in right away. Someone might have called the police. Thomas looked away, blinked a couple times, as if to erase something, and kept walking.

END

The author thanks Catherine Leroux, Maxime Raymond Bock, and Jean-François Chassay for the permission to give certain of their characters a second life in these pages.

DANIEL GRENIER was born in Brossard, Quebec, in 1980. He is the author of the critically acclaimed short story collection *Malgré tout on rit à Saint-Henri*, and his first novel, *L'année la plus longue*, won the Prix littéraire des collégiens and was a finalist for the Governor General's Literary Award for French Fiction, the Prix des libraires, and the Prix littéraire France-Québec. Grenier has also translated numerous English-language works into French. He lives in Quebec City.

PABLO STRAUSS grew up in Victoria, British Columbia, and has lived in Quebec City for a decade. His translations of Quebec authors have appeared in various online and print publications.